OLIVER ROGERS

THE TRANSFIGURATION OF NO

BOOK ONE
THE SHAPES

STEGOSAURUS BOOKS
iamstegosaurus.com/no

Copyright © Oliver Rogers 2019

The right of Oliver Rogers to be identified as the Author of the Work has been asserted by him in accordance with the Copyright, Designs and Patents Act 1988.

All rights reserved. No part of this publication may be transmitted or reproduced in any form by any means without permission in writing from the author.

All characters in this publication are fictitious, and any resemblance to real persons, living or dead, is purely coincidental.

ISBN: 9781698825854

Cover design and illustration by Oliver Rogers.

Stegosaurus Books
Hastings
UK

www.iamstegosaurus.com/no

For Vic & Jesse Cosmo

ONE
A Shadow Over Iremouth

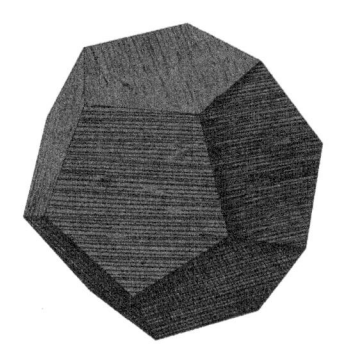

'No! Don't you see!' cried the old man, 'I hadn't any choice!' He scrabbled desperately away from his assailant – only to find himself backed against a wall.

The brute with the remarkable handlebar moustache advanced upon him with the languid movements of one whose conquest is not merely assured, but inevitable. His immaculate brogue shoes crunched through the debris that littered the floor of the tiny cottage until he towered over the cowering fellow. In his vast shadow, the wretch quaked and snorted in fear, eyes rolling and hands clawing across a tattered scalp to which scraps of reddish hair clung like dying weeds. A matted tuft came away in his grip.

'You told him everything?' growled the brute with the moustache, his voice a bass rumble, impossibly deep. He loomed forward with his fist still raised, ready to smash it into the decrepit fellow's bloodied face once more. In his other massive paw, he clutched the handle of a bulging carpet bag.

'For Gods' sake, man!' screamed the wretch, cringing pitifully. 'He had a revolver to my temple! *I had no choice but to tell him!'*

Another punch slammed into his jaw, bursting apart his lip like an overripe fruit and all but knocking the consciousness from him. Tiny fireflies flickered and danced across his dimming vision.

'*What* did you tell him?' demanded the moustachioed brute, drawing back his fist once more.

'I... I t-told him about the experiment!' spluttered the wretch between frantic gulps of blood and air. 'Ab-bout S-Sebastian and the Formulæ! I t-told him that I was s-scared and that I c-couldn't stop him – that he wouldn't *listen* to me!'

'And what else?' The immense fist clenched and unclenched in anticipation.

The wretch uttered a small sound of fear and began to rake at the wall behind him, as though the sheer intensity of his desperation might lend his fingers the ability to pry stone from mortar. 'I t-told him that *he* did it!' he stammered. 'And I told him that... *that I ran away.*' He covered his face with shaking, bleeding hands. 'Oh Gods, I ran away! I left him there to die! And now he's here again, and he's haunting me! He *knows* that I betrayed him! He told me not to tell... *not to tell...*'

The brute lunged forward and grasped the quivering wretch by his collar, pulling that fellow's broken face so close to his own that his moustache brushed its ruined nose. The moustache writhed on the old man's withered skin, seeming to taste the iron tang of his blood as might the twitching antennæ of some hungry insect. Through fading sight, the old man saw that its bristles radiated out from the brute's lip to carpet his gums and his teeth.

'*Did you tell him of the Zhoth?*' the brute roared. The globes of his huge, amber eyes seemed to burn with a feverish light.

'*No!* I swear! I know that they are w-watching me as well!' An admixtured stream of blood and mucus was flowing from the remains of the old man's pulverised nose. He tried vainly to wipe it away. 'Oh Gods!' he sobbed. 'Oh Gods, oh Gods! You don't understand, man! He was my *friend* – I never wanted him to die! *But they said they would take away my face!*'

At this the moustachioed brute smiled beatifically. He crouched down and set the carpet bag on the floor in front of him, aligning it precisely according to some unseen criterion. Its catch came undone with a click. He shook his head, sighed a deep sigh, and looked up at his quivering prey.

'Poor, poor Danforth,' said the man as he opened the bag.

Danforth's eyes widened in horror, and his dripping mouth twisted in a wordless scream. He started to scramble wildly away, but this time there was nowhere to go.

∾

The tiger's eyes were full of stars.

Her face was frozen in a snarl, ivory teeth gleaming dully in the light of the moon, and silken flowers of intricate craftsmanship garlanded her neck. Once, the proud beast had looked upon the teeming life of a lush and nameless jungle. But she had new eyes now, and tonight they stared – glassy, unblinking, and unseeing – into the star-dappled, inky blackness of the night sky high above a windswept island. Atop a sea of canvas, beyond ruffling swathes of golden ribbon and snapping pennants, silver gleams of moonlight winked in other eyes and picked out other teeth.

The animals to whom they belonged ought by rights to have roamed the remotest corners of the globe, but tonight they sailed the night air as one unlikely herd. The ornate balloon to which this taxidermic menagerie was fastened seemed almost too cumbersome to be floating at all.

Yet float it did, drifting ponderously through the night, and in the gondola that hung suspended beneath its imposing canopy were two men. At the fore of the gondola stood Lord Naught, a telescope pressed firmly into the hollow socket of his eye. His knotted twine fingers made minute adjustments to the settings of the device as he stood, apparently transfixed, staring out into the ebon void above him. He murmured something quietly to himself, causing his companion to glance up from his desk.

'Sorry, sir?' enquired Nicholas Flintwick, a fellow who had about him the air of the severest sort of schoolmaster. He was not in fact a schoolmaster of any sort, but neither was he a stranger to the correctional application of the switch. Flintwick was prim to the point of punctiliousness, but somehow gave off the impression that a quantity of dust had settled upon him as it might upon an uncomfortable old chair in a forgotten hallway.

'Eh? Oh, nothing, Nicholas,' replied Naught without turning to face his manservant. 'Nothing at all.'

Flintwick's pen began to scratch again. Then, after a moment, he set the pen down once more. 'A fine display tonight, sir, wouldn't you say?' he ventured.

'I suppose that it is.'

'Isn't that the – ah – Great Cormorant over there?' Flintwick continued, nodding towards a constellation that winked in the eastern sky. 'It looks uncommonly bright this evening.'

'Yes, Nicholas, it is. And over there's the – '

'Narwhal?'

'Quite.' And with that, Naught released the apparatus from his grip, allowing the telescope to bob freely upon its arrangement of springs and pulleys. He turned on his heel to face Flintwick. 'Nicholas?' he asked. 'Nicholas, do you have my monocle there?'

'Why yes, sir. It's here with your maps and your starcharts. Would you like me to pass it to you?'

'Thank you, Nicholas.'

Flintwick's pen resumed its scratching.

Naught grasped the monocle and pressed it to his eye, which was beady, black and small like a currant. Even through the monocle's polished thickness, that eye seemed sunken and tiny; that any man should actually find such an organ sufficient for the act of seeing would surely have proved a marvel to any sensible oculist.

Indeed, Naught's physiology was fit to provoke bemusement and head-scratching in practitioners of the vast majority of the human scientific disciplines. His complexion was of a sort unfamiliar to dermatologists, being approximately the colour of a well-matured shallot and of the texture of tanned leather, but which in places was mottled with lighter shades where it became delicate and brittle-looking, resembling nothing so much as crepe paper. The skull across which it was stretched, however, was more marvellous still. Quite what a learned phrenologist should make of that vast, heavy, hairless head – so much like that of a horse in its largeness – was unclear, and the unlikely angle at which the dome of Naught's cranium swept up from his brow was doubtless as bewildering to the anatomist as it was to the eye. From the centre of Naught's face protruded a cruel, pointed nose, and even the humble dentist would have been hard-pressed to cite a precedent for the small and pointed teeth that lurked behind wet, red-painted lips in the mouth beneath it.

With the monocle installed, Naught's face began to take on a slightly ruminative air.

Flintwick appeared to notice this. 'Is everything well, sir?' he asked, a frown of concern adding further furrows to the network that already lined his face. Lord Naught was uncharacteristically subdued; on a night such as this it was usually all that Flintwick could do to keep pace with his master's relentless effusion.

'Of course,' answered Naught rather tersely. 'Why should it not be?'

'Well, it's just that you seem rather... *distant.*'

Naught sighed deeply, and for a long while it seemed that he would say nothing, but then his brow crinkled in a frown to match Flintwick's, and he spoke again. 'Ah, Nicholas,' he said, squaring his slight shoulders. 'Don't you *see?*'

Flintwick pursed his lips, unsure quite what it was that he was supposed to be seeing. 'See what, sir?'

'Why, the *Kosmos* of course!' Naught flung out his scarecrow arm in an expansive gesture to indicate the presence of the universe around them, knocking a brimful ashtray flying from the gondola's handrail in the process.

Flintwick imagined that this gesture was probably intended for dramatic effect, as the glittering dome of the night sky was already quite evident without such signposting. 'I fear I don't understand, sir,' admitted the old manservant.

Naught sighed again in apparent resignation. 'No, Nicholas,' he said wearily. 'I'm rather afraid you wouldn't.' He shook his head, then stalked once more to his telescope – but it seemed that he no longer wished to gaze starward. Instead, with a beetlish ticking of painted nails upon varnish, he grasped the elaborately carved handrail. He bowed his head, and this time he stared down to where the benighted countryside slid by far below.

The balloon swept over the fields of Cold Ghastia, its monstrous, moon-lent shadow slipping across cottages and barns and the little tracks that meandered through the countryside to merge with the empty highway. It was a broad and evidently well-travelled road, flanked often by clusters of cottages where some lonely lights still burned forlornly in the night. To the æronauts, the silvery ribbon of that road might have recalled a river, were it not for the actual river that snaked through the fields close by. At the mighty river's source, and the road's terminus, was Iremouth. The city lay sprawled across the foothills and the slopes of the mountain range that sprang, incongruous, from the plains: a soaring dune of jagged rock like a crescent wave frozen in the instant before breaking.

Flintwick straightened and set aside his stack of papers then glanced up at the gaunt figure of his master, skeletal and stiff beneath the embroidered crimson velvet of his flying jacket. He drew breath to speak, but something in Lord Naught's manner, still and pensive, made the words die in his throat. Naught did not stir; his massive head was bowed low, apparently watching the forest of towering pines that choked the foothills slide by beneath them.

As the absurd balloon swept nearer to the lower reaches of the mountains, Flintwick cut the puttering engine and adjusted an ornate valve so that a blossoming gout of flame momentarily illuminated its bulk from within. They began a steep ascent over the outlying fringes of the city, where few lights could be seen and a pall of greasy smoke loitered in the air. Flintwick was well aware that his master had no wish to pass one inch closer to this unsightly sprawl than was strictly necessary. Tonight, however, Lord Naught did not raise his head to avert his eyes from the festering slum below.

As they sailed on over the rooftops towards the ancient heart of the city, the streets grew broader and more orderly. Here were wide, cobbled avenues and beautiful squares with playing fountains, all a-glow with gentle, amber gaslight. The imposing crags of the surrounding mountain range shaded this place from the silvery beams of the moon, but even so it remained a sight to charm the æronautical eye.

In this, the most civilised of the city's districts, it was possible still to espy the occasional helmeted and black-caped figure patrolling the streets, lantern in one hand and twirling truncheon in the other. But the vocation of the constable was ever bound to be a lonely one at this hour, for the streets were all but deserted. The denizens of Iremouth – from scullions to physicians – had quit the night air in favour of their beds, and the last of the evening's cabs had long since deposited their weary fares and rattled off into the night. It seemed that the only other waking inhabitants of the city were the cats who manned their own patrols half-a-dozen storeys above those of the constabulary, stalking between thickets of chimneypots and turrets on the rooftops of the tall and closely-pressed houses.

And, from the still greater height at which the balloon drifted, at least, the city seemed quite as silent as it was still. Lord Naught had not uttered so much as a word since his enigmatic pronouncement regarding the Kosmos. Since Flintwick judged it best not to disturb him, the only sounds to reach his ears now were the occasional rustling of the balloon's canopy in the night breeze and the roaring of the river Irem, a sound that grew steadily louder and more insistent as they sailed ever closer to its source in the rocky peaks.

The Irem thundered forth from the mountains in the north of the city to become a mighty waterfall that cascaded down the mountainside in a fashion that was generally held to be quite spectacular – a description which tonight could hardly be disputed. As stony grey as the mountains that birthed it by day, by moonlit night the plunging Irem was a torrent of sapphire and diamond. At the foot of the falls, where the churning wall was transformed into a roiling, white cloud of foam, the waters were constrained by a dam of monstrous proportions. Observed from above, this marvel of architecture appeared slender and graceful with a shape like that of a full sail, and so seemed to rein the raging Irem with deceptive ease. However, from the ground – the vantage point from which it was more commonly observed – its aspect was rather different. Its polypous, black bulk was rooted in the earth as is an ancient tree, and it had about it a disturbing air of impregnability. On nights such as this, nocturnal travellers shivered and hurried out of the shadow of the dam – for it was said in the city that when the moonlight fell upon its black expanse it looked for all the world like the shoulders of some great beast straining to hold back the waters, or a pair of vast and leathery wings.

Beyond the dam, the river flowed unmolested down through the steep slopes upon which Iremouth nestled, carving its path straight through the city and dividing it into two parts of near equal proportion. Even at this height, Flintwick often fancied that he could feel the spray from the booming falls upon his face. He wiped his cheek, but it was dry.

Upon the craggy mountainside that overshadowed the city was the House, towards which the balloon and its two passengers were sailing. The House grew out of the precipitous terrain around it like a forest of undersea flora, a fabulous cluster of turrets and spires that were as unlikely as they were peerless. Illumed as they were by the moonlight, those black towers deceived the eye with their queer lines so that they almost seemed to sway languorously like the fronds of seaweed whose semblance they bore. The House, though, was in fact quite as solid in its structure as it was dreamlike in its appearance, and it had inhabited the mountainside for far longer than the grey city that it overlooked.

A pair of servants awaited them on the vertiginous jetty, and one of them caught the rope that Flintwick slung down and tied it fast to a mooring-post. Naught waited until the servants, shivering in the night air, had hauled the balloon onto the deck, then allowed Flintwick to unlatch the gondola's door. He tottered out onto the jetty, his eyes seemingly fixed upon the boards beneath his feet, and disappeared through an archway and into the House.

∼

To the æronauts the highway might well have recalled a river, but to the two passengers of the coach that was bouncing and jarring along that same road at precisely the same time as the balloon breezed overhead, this comparison would have seemed tenuous at best. In point of fact the road had nothing in the least bit silvery or flowing about it; it was deeply rutted and certainly not devoid of its share of wheel-bothering rocks. Indeed, thus far there had been nothing remotely fluid about this particular journey. Even the segment of it that had actually involved a body of water had been turbulent, for the voyage across the channel to the scattered-crumb archipelago of which this island was the largest particle had been dogged by high winds and higher waves. The churning motion of the storm-wracked sea was echoed uncomfortably in the motion of the coach.

It seemed to Edward Stoathill-Warmly that he had not been truly still for quite some time, and that this was a state in which it was far from agreeable to be. He looked and indeed felt even more bedraggled than usual.

His brownish hair of no discernible style had been sculpted into fantastic peaks, gullies and plains by his efforts to eke some small comfort from the journey's succession of erratically shifting environs, and his perennially waxen complexion had taken on a greenish cast, for his stomach had scarcely recovered from the violent sickness that the sea crossing had brought on. He had never been a man of particularly stout constitution (being ever so slight of frame and habitually sickly, a physiology that virtually predestined him to academic pursuits), and now the jouncing coach had added a gnawing headache to his usual catalogue of woes. The clopping of the horses' hooves and the unforgiving grinding of the wheels upon the road was all he could ever recall hearing. He pulled his woollen blanket tightly around his aching frame, elbowed aside a wandering pile of books, and attempted to sink deeper into the seat – which persisted enthusiastically in its pursuit of squeaking piercingly in concert with every movement of the vehicle.

The rigours of international travel were, it seemed, not affecting Doctor Obadiah Carnaby quite so profoundly. He dozed on the seat opposite Edward, displaying every outward symptom of great content. A small, dog-eared book, a journal perhaps, was clutched to his chest; Edward was surprised to find that he did not recognise it. The book rose and fell steadily with the Doctor's breathing, and he grunted occasionally in his sleep, twitching his mobile lips as he did so.

The Doctor was a man of formidable appearance. His brow was stern, his moustache brush-like, his jet-black hair cropped closely at the temples and lacquered neatly to his skull. In repose, though, his visage took on an uncharacteristic air of vulnerability, which Edward attributed to the absence of his penetrating, empirical gaze – a gaze which a lesser pair of eyelids might have been hard-pressed to thwart. No passive globes were those set in the Doctor's head. Edward had often thought it was as though, in seeing, the lenses of Obadiah's eyes projected outward their own withering rays, rather than deigning to confer this responsibility onto the admission of mere reflected light. Edward watched his companion for a while until the rhythmic motion of the book in the slumbering Doctor's arms began to inspire in him an even greater sensation of nausea. With sleep evidently being out of the question, he turned his attention instead to the scenery that was lurching past on the other side of the rattling window pane.

Nausea notwithstanding, Edward was forced to admit that in reality the Cold Ghastian landscape was rather more scenic than the imaginary counterpart that he had concocted for it. Pleasantly undulating fields rolled past on either side of the coach, for now stretching away almost to the horizon, although far ahead he could see that the scattered trees began to press closer to the highway until they resolved themselves into a forest of almost mythic proportions. The night was an unusually bright one, and beyond the distant mountains that lay to the north and east, the stars glittered in what one might even have construed as a friendly fashion. Edward allowed himself a small smile: perhaps their stay in Cold Ghastia would not be quite so horribly unpleasant as he had imagined.

The Cold Ghastia of Edward's mind had been a perennially grim and rainy place. This, he was now forced to admit, had been an altogether irrational presumption, and based upon no real evidence at all - besides perhaps the somewhat grim connotations of its name. Even this was groundless, for he knew full well that its etymology was not even Urish. Indeed, upon hearing that name pronounced by the locals he had discovered that its two constituents were run together in a single guttural sound that recalled the forcible clearing of a throat.

This ignorance was forgivable, though. The island's very existence was known to few more than a handful of lower-caste clerks within the Imperial Department for Fiscal Affairs, and the vagaries of its accent to even fewer. Even Edward – who had for some time been all but obsessed with certain peculiarities of this place obscurer yet than its dialectical eccentricities, its pecuniary administration, or even its location in the Atlas of Verdra – had never once imagined that he would find himself upon these shores. Never once, that is, until the morning that a wild-eyed and triumphant Obadiah had swept back into their workshop and announced that they would be leaving for the far-flung province with all the haste that might possibly be contrived.

Obadiah had been absent for more than a week. He had left in the dead of the night, as was often his fashion, leaving nothing but a hastily-scrawled note. The note indicated that their long months of research had finally borne fruit – that he had happened upon a source of information that had the potential to place Cold Ghastia squarely back upon their map. Edward was not to learn the full implications of this until the day of Obadiah's return, but mere hours later their effects had been stowed and their journey had begun. And, as the innumerous miles between Grand Uria and Cold Ghastia had fallen away behind coaches, steamers and ferries, the Doctor had divulged the story that had occasioned a rare budding of hope in his colleague's breast.

Suddenly an incredible crash jolted Edward back to the present.

Obadiah started from his seat with an inarticulate shout. The coach ground to a halt, hurling Edward and various pieces of paraphernalia into the opposite seat. As they rocked to stillness there was a series of unpleasant sounds of metallic protest from the roof. Something fell onto the road with a thud.

'*Driver!*' The Doctor's roar of rage was almost bestial. 'What in *blazes* is going on?' He flung open the door and leaped out of the coach.

'I don't think – ' Edward began, but Obadiah had already pulled the fellow bodily from his seat and was shaking him wildly as the bemused horses nickered and blinked behind their blinders.

'*What* sort of behaviour d'you call *this*?' Obadiah demanded. 'Do you have *any idea* what your vehicle is carrying, man?' The driver opened his mouth, but the Doctor was not in the least bit interested in his reply. 'No, I'm sure you don't!' he barked. 'Although your ignorance *in no way* excuses your complete disregard for its value! This equipment is irreplaceable – unique! *Unique!*'

Edward stepped gingerly outside, and immediately noticed a piece of the apparatus lying by the roadside; it had been flung from the precarious mound of luggage lashed to the roof beneath a straining tarpaulin. He picked up the metallic canister, dusted it off, and placed it carefully into the pocket of his waistcoat. Then, as Obadiah continued to rage, he hoisted himself onto the footplate, and thence onto the roof of the coach.

The equipment was in a state of serious disarray.

Three tubes and a coil had been thrown out of place by the momentum of their sudden halt, and some of the leads were tangled badly. This he was able to see because the sheet stretched over the equipment had somehow acquired a gaping rent. When Edward thrust his hand into the tear to investigate, it came into contact with a now badly-splintered packing case that was hæmorrhaging scraps of paper – thank Gods he had packaged the devices so securely! – and also something less familiar. Retrieving the object, he was surprised to find that it was a brass gewgaw cast in the form of a pair of manatees disporting themselves around an ornate basin. Crusting this basin's interior was an amount of ground-in cigar ash, and clinging to it were odd wisps of tobacco. The mysterious invader appeared to be an ash-tray. Edward raised an eyebrow. It looked for all the world as though the thing had fallen out of the sky.

He craned his neck to scan the heavens for a potential source for the brassy missile. At first he saw nothing – but then, blotting out a patch of stars, his eyes alit upon something huge and ungainly hovering in the air high above them. He squinted.

It was a *balloon*! How thoroughly eccentric! Why in the world would anyone possibly choose to be abroad at this hour in such a contraption as that? Edward shook his head. How queer these locals were!

He shouted down to the Doctor, who seemed to have quietened down somewhat. 'Obadiah! The equipment's mostly undamaged, and I'm sure I can make short work of repairing the rest. I think this is the culprit – why, it must have fallen from that balloon!' He gestured skyward, and waved the offending ash-tray at the frowning Doctor.

'Well I can tell you it bloody well better be undamaged or there will be repercussions!' growled Obadiah in the general direction of the driver. *'Repercussions!'* The fellow flinched visibly with the impact of each spittle-flecked syllable upon his eardrums. Then, appearing suddenly to lose interest in his tirade, the Doctor turned and mounted the footplate. 'Well then, let's be off, Edward!' he said with a grin. 'This good man tells me there's still a good way to go before we reach Iremouth!'

Flintwick allowed his master to lean upon his shoulder as they walked. Lord Naught was not a heavy burden for even a man of Flintwick's years to bear; his frame was not much brawnier than that of a child. Indeed, although in Flintwick's estimation childhood was a generally unbecoming state of existence, he at times entertained the fancy that his master was possessed of some of its more endearing qualities. Feeling the weight of Naught's great head nodding against his own, Flintwick permitted himself a small, private smile. Just as an infant's does, that head seemed too large by far to belong atop his master's neck.

The hour was late. The evening of ballooning, stargazing and conversation that they had shared had evidently tired Lord Naught, for he shuffled his feet sleepily as they trailed through the House. Even so, Flintwick made haste through these low, dark halls. The corridors here were oppressive; their walls and ceilings were lined with panels of aged, blackened oak, and this coupled with their stifling narrowness had the effect of aggravating his already claustrophobic nature. He took especial care not to tarry as he hurried Lord Naught past the various shadowy alcoves, in which groups of peculiar little statuettes and busts could be seen huddling furtively together as though plotting some midnight alabaster conspiracy. This, of course, was for his own sake – for although their carven faces were in all probability no stranger than that of his master, he found that in the sparse lamplight they had about them something that was vaguely disquieting. Naught considered them to be homely.

The door to Naught's private apartments was opened for them by a maid who was already within, and the slightly acrid smell that emanated from the tank inside wafted past her upon a breath of humid air. The maid curtsied nervously out of the way and proffered a plump armchair, into which Naught sank gratefully. The interior of the room was, like the hallways, lined with fine, dark oak panels, but it was also hung with tapestries. Naught had selected these for their pleasing depictions of mythical scenes.

The tapestries had been purchased from a travelling vendor of rarities and antiques – a fellow who apparently had been at great pains to impress upon Lord Naught the fact that these particular pieces were the epitome of both rareness *and* antiquity, and that their price was therefore an exceedingly reasonable one. Having examined the hangings upon his master's return, Flintwick had found cause to doubt that they possessed any of these virtues in great abundance (especially reasonableness of price), and had wholeheartedly rued his decision not to accompany his master to the auction house that day. He had elected not to voice these concerns, though; Lord Naught was not a man of any small means, and an ill-considered purchase or two was unlikely to alter this dramatically. Besides, his master was inordinately fond of them.

Naïvely rendered depictions of scenes from Cold Ghastia's mythic past held no particular appeal for Flintwick (whose preference was for instructional manuals, encyclopædias and almanacs) but for Naught they were a source of vicarious joy. Feats of derring-do, wild romance and epic battles: these were the things that seemed to transport his mind and lift his spirits to a place more colourful than the Iremouth he inhabited at present. Quite why anyone should be desirous of such a thing was beyond Flintwick, to whom the pleasing palette of greys, greens and greys that comprised Iremouth's æsthetic had ever been quite sufficiently stimulating; but as such fancies tended not to impinge upon the practicalities of his master's life, he did not allow it to trouble him overly.

Flintwick studied the hangings as the maid helped Lord Naught to disrobe for his retiring. The manservant was busily scrutinising a particularly fanciful hunt scene wherein riders chased down a herd of fallow deer amongst the colossal trunks of the forest, when Naught, who had not uttered so much as a word since they had returned to the House, broke the silence.

'Nicholas, I...' he began, wringing his twig-bundle hands a little. 'That is, I... Would you mind very much staying awhile – perhaps until I get off to sleep?'

The maid instantly became as engrossed in the *décor* as Flintwick had been.

Flintwick, seeing again that thing in his master's manner that spoke of discomposure, nodded his affirmation.

The maid, dismissed, hurried from the room. Thanks to her efforts, though, Naught was now dressed in his sleeping apparel: a fitted suit of rubberised fabric with a dark, parti-coloured sheen upon it like that of oil upon water. Together with the impossible thinness and angularity of his body, it lent him the appearance of a monstrous insect. The illusion was spoiled, of course, by the incongruous size of his bulbous, leathery head. Flintwick, though he had seen them a thousand times and more, still could not help but marvel at his master's comparatively miniscular feet. He watched with vague embarrassment as Lord Naught climbed the stepladder that led to the top of his tank.

The vinegary-coloured liquid within the tank bubbled a soft welcome to its nocturnal tenant. Naught perched on the little platform at the top of the ladder and gingerly tested it with his big toe, rather as one might as he made ready to enter a hot bath. The soup was not steaming hot though, but kept at a constant temperature somewhere on the tepid side of lukewarm by means of an elaborate network of heating pipes, a tangled choir whose secondary task it was to sing to Naught his nightly lullaby of gulps, clanks and thumps. As the fluid washed between his waggling digits, a rearrangement of facial topography which may have corresponded to an appreciative smile spread across Naught's visage, creasing his skin in a variety of unflattering ways and exposing his little teeth.

He turned to Flintwick, fixing him with his beetle-black eyes, to which the smile-thing seemed not to have spread. Flintwick thought those eyes looked a little watery.

'You *will* stay until I have crossed to the other side?' Naught asked in a voice that was soft, like mould.

'Rest well, sir,' nodded Flintwick. He would remain awhile, of course, but both knew there was no way for him to judge the point at which his master had drifted away. In sleep, Lord Naught's eyes would remain unclosed.

Naught seemed satisfied enough though, and slithered into the tenebrous depths.

The amber gruel slapped softly against the sides of the tank before calming once more. Flintwick narrowed his eyes to focus on his master, an emaciated foetus bobbing in a seething glass womb. A stream of bubbles belched from Naught's mouth and streamed from his nose as the last of the air left his lungs.

Flintwick too breathed out. He realised then that he had been holding his breath, and that he felt strangely tense. He shook his head and blew out another long sigh, this time one of conscious disrelish. Whether he liked it or not it was time, at last, to admit the problem.

Lord Naught was unwell.

Even a stranger could see that the man was at a low ebb, but Flintwick had served his master for the greater part of both of their lives – and even he had never before borne witness to such a display of ill-ease from Lord Naught as that which had transpired that evening. This was no mere bout of melancholy. No, this disarrangement of his master's spirits was something far more serious than a doleful mood. This was something *deeper*.

But when had this all begun? Flintwick chewed at the inside of his lip. How long was it now since Lord Naught had been enlivened by a philosophical discussion? How long since he had *laughed*? How long, indeed, since he had shown the slightest whisper of interest in the elaborate follies in which he had heretofore positively delighted? Though he was loath to admit it, for it showed him for the lackadaisical fool he was, Flintwick found that he could not say. The old manservant shook his weary head, and ran a hand through his bone-white hair, inflicting upon it a rare moment of dishevelment. What could be done this night? Nothing useful, surely. But tomorrow was another day, and it would be the first of his master's recovery.

Whisking his notebook from its home in his breast pocket, Flintwick began to write. An itinerary was in order, and the first item on his list was its creation. He scored three lines under the words "Create Itinerary", and moved onto the second item: he would have the kitchens prepare a delicious haddock's liver omelette upon which Lord Naught might break his fast, in order to ensure the best possible commencement to the first day of healing. Something in the oils was good for the temper, was it not? Flintwick added another item: "Check medical texts &c".

THE SHAPES

And what next? Flintwick thought for a moment, and then snapped his fingers. *The zoological gardens,* of course. Since he had insisted upon their assembly, Lord Naught had barely set foot within their walls. But that had been before the itinerary. Surely the bewildering variety of creatures ensnared in the wild and hidden places of the world would serve to arouse at least a *little* of his master's usual avidity for life's curios. Yes, this was excellent stuff! Flintwick sprang up from the chair and began to pace the room, his pencil darting back and forth across the page.

Naught had not truly expected to sleep at all – so many nights of late had passed in an unbearable, insomniacal sludge – but something about Flintwick's silly, seagull strut was oddly comforting, and a drowsiness began to settle over him. Soon enough it overcame him, and as the amber liquid swirled about him like an old, familiar eiderdown, he began to slip away. Waves of russet ebbed into the delicious, disorientating places through which he drifted on the way to dreaming, and the slow hum began to build in the roots of his teeth. Then, as the surges of vibration spreading through his body made him arch his back like a cat and stretch out his limbs in delight, he widened his eyes in the soup to find that he was once more atop the cliff.

He had been here before; he was sure of it.

But the memory of that place was uncertain, sliding infuriatingly away from the corners of his mind. It was red and cold at the top of the cliff, and he began to cry.

∼

It soon became plain that, despite every ounce of encouragement that the driver could muster by means of his whip, the straining horses would not haul the coach much closer to Iremouth that night. The fellow was of the opinion that one of his sweating nags had sprained a fetlock in their earlier incident, and gingerly suggested that it would therefore benefit from a period of recuperation. In any case, it was now well into the small hours according to Edward's pocket-watch, and the blunt teeth that had been worrying at the inside of his skull remained as gnawingly persistent as ever. Obadiah seemed at best unmoved by his partner's ailments but did not relish the imminent prospect of another potentially costly mishap, and it was therefore agreed that they should seek lodgings for the night.

Out in the open countryside there had been houses scattered sporadically along the roadside. However, some time ago now they had entered the forest proper, and here traces of civilisation were scant indeed. Even the highway itself – if such the convoluted, needle-strewn smear of dirt could now be called – was permitted to negotiate only such a seemingly arbitrary path as the colossal, tower-like pines deigned to concede to it. Now and then they reached a crossroads of sorts where rutted tracks branched away to ramble off into swaying blackness, and it was down one of these that the driver reined his beasts, shouting back to his passengers in his queer Ghastian accent that a friendly homestead was to be found some short way off.

Edward discovered that there was strikingly little correlation between his and their driver's concepts of 'a short way'. Had he remained beguiled by the evening's charms as before then this disparity might never have presented itself, but things were no longer as they had been. From the vantage point of the country road he had judged the forest rather picturesque – indeed, he had even remarked to Obadiah how amusing it was that the towering mountain range before them appeared from that distance to be packed with heads of broccoli. However, he was now discovering that from this altered perspective it was in fact a fairly unnerving place in which to find oneself. This was due partly to the precarious way in which the coach teetered down the little track, the ground on either side of which often fell away without warning in a sheer drop of unknown proportions, and partly due to the fact that he was quite terrified of the dark.

Bright though it doubtless was, the moonlight seemed unable to penetrate through the heavy boughs to the forest floor, and so the coach's lamps alone were left to offer up their comparatively feeble glow into the tangle of knotted trunks around them. In their sparse guttering, the majestic, ancient pines were transformed into leering fiends. Edward shivered and pressed himself back into his seat. Despite his aversion to the gloom, he felt that sometimes a little light could be worse than none at all - for that which one could barely distinguish often seemed imbued with a greater potency of malevolence than that which was out of mind due to its being entirely out of sight. He shrank further into the corner of the cabin, attempting to avoid the sight of skeletal limbs looming out of the night, scratching at the glass with their twiggy fingers as the trees pressed ever closer to the road.

Obadiah gave a small snort and a roll of his eyes as he apprehended the anxious expression upon his companion's face. The Doctor was a man well acquainted with the circumstances in which one should be disquieted by the dark, and evidently did not consider this situation to warrant the least concern. In his corner, Edward turned his gaze on his fidgeting fingertips.

To Edward's very great relief, they reached their destination at last as the tortuous track disgorged the coach into a little glade lit wanly and almost apologetically by the moon. The driver reined up his beasts and leaped down from his perch, making for a tumbledown cottage on the clearing's far side. An inviting amber glow leaked from between the cracks in the dwelling's closed shutters.

Edward surveyed the clearing warily.

The hoary pines, which seemed to soak up and retain the darkness like great sponges of night, still closely surrounded them. His pulse quickened, and he swallowed down a rising bubble of panic as a suggestion of sinuous movement flitted between the branches. With practiced effort he diverted his attention, turning it once more to the cottage. Determined but evidently underfunded renovation allowed it to exist, for the moment at least, on the quainter side of true dilapidation; it looked an agreeable enough place to spend the night. He was not left to consider its merits for long, though, as moments later the driver was jogging back towards them, beckoning for them to join him.

'Come along, old boy,' grinned Obadiah, grasping Edward's arm and shaking it with what Edward considered to be unnecessary vigour. 'Let's make our way inside, eh? Don't want to be out here in this chilly night air any longer than strictly necessary, hmm?'

'Certainly not,' replied Edward, pretending not to have noticed the sardonic tone in the Doctor's voice. 'I'm very much in need of somewhere to lay my bones. This journey has entirely worn me out, Obadiah.'

'Not built for travel, were you?' chuckled his friend. 'Always had your curious nose stuck in a *book*, eh?' He punctuated this latter comment by slamming shut the shabby volume in his hands.

Edward said nothing, but shot Obadiah a resentful glance. Then he snatched up his scattered effects and, as hastily as the appearance of rationality would permit, he scurried towards the light and safety – and, he hoped, the still and horizontal resting-places – of the cottage. The truth was that he was feeling a fatigue far deeper than even that which a week of long-distance travel could instil.

Obadiah raised his formidable eyebrows for a moment then, hugging the book closely to his broad chest, he followed Edward inside.

TWO
How Things Can Seem Different in the Morning

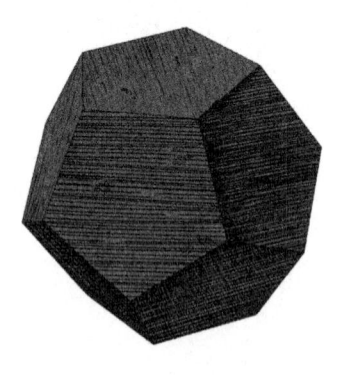

Flintwick strode purposefully through the hall with something of a spring in his usually measured step. He had descended the eighty-four steps from his office with a strenuosity that defied his years, and had barrelled through the entire of the east wing at such a brisk pace that more than one of the staff had been obliged to leap out of his path in order to avoid injury. And now as he marched along this, his regular course, he could not help but admire the pleasing fashion in which the sun's rays slanted through the high windows of the House, brushing his face with warmth as he passed each of the irregularly-spaced openings. Flintwick had oftentimes pondered upon the practicality of the windows, which were unlikely ever to afford a view to any person not possessed of a ladder, and which were singularly ineffectual in terms of supplying illumination; even this morning they provided no real light beyond the few lancing shafts that danced with lucent dust-motes.

As ever, a gloom redolent of rainy autumn evenings still prevailed in the long stretches between them.

This morning, though, Flintwick hardly registered the dark.

This morning he was filled with a sense of promise so overwhelming that even the sombre surroundings of the House could not quash it. Something was to be *achieved* to-day, he could feel it. Smiling, Flintwick thought of a fitting analogy he had once heard: this morning, his glass was most assuredly half *full*.

The productive use of time was important to Nicholas Flintwick, and to this end he rose at just after dawn each morning so as to not waste too many of the day's valuable hours in a state of insensibility. Flintwick did not begrudge having to sleep – it was after all necessary in maintaining a healthy level of vim – but indulging oneself too deeply in dreams and other such intangible fancies was at best counter-productive.

It had been suggested by some of the less respectful members of the household that Flintwick's incessant activity was a symptom of his advancing years, and the awareness that his remaining days in useful service were likely numbered few. However, since none would dare voice such an opinion within the old manservant's earshot, he remained largely ignorant of such churlish words. Although Flintwick's face was lined and careworn, and although the time when his hair had been anything other than a dusty white was a distant memory to all, he remained a vigorous man – and on mornings such as this he was a force with which to be reckoned.

Flintwick burst through the double doors at the end of the corridor and emerged into the full daylight of one of the upper courtyards.

Although it was still enclosed by the dark, undulating stuff of its walls, this area was quite a contrast to the drab interior of the House. It was a breezy, landscaped garden of lawns and mosaics of ingenious pattern, with little manicured shrubs and trees planted all about. However, if when ascending the endless flight of stairs that spiralled up the inside of the black tower that overlooked this place an ambitious and sturdy-legged climber should pause for breath in a little alcove and take in the view from the window, something strange would quickly become apparent to them. For despite its bright and pleasant aspect, the garden lay uncomfortably in the grasp of the courtyard. The plants and trees seemed to shrink away from the House as though recoiling from something unpleasant, turning themselves away from its walls as others might bend towards the sunlight. No climbing plants scaled the masonry here.

The garden had been laid in the time when people had first come to this place and discovered the great House on the mountainside, hollow and vacant, its black walls bare, and its wide expanses echoing and empty. The Naughts of centuries past had caused the clever gardens to be made in the courtyards, and they had brought artisans to line the labyrinthine halls with carven oak in order to impress their mark upon it, and so claim it for their own.

But what they had also sought was to correct the strange, disorientating proportions of the place; its angles and lines were perplexing to the unsuspecting eye, and were wont to confuse the wanderer within. Equally perplexing to those early tenants had been the fact that no evidence could be found of a single door ever having been hung in the place, nor indeed of so much as a shutter or a pane of glass having been installed in its windows. Now of course its cavernous halls and claustrophobic oubliettes alike were hung with wooden panels and stopped by iron-studded doors that were blackened and wormy and ancient (though in the main part its windows remained resolutely devoid of casements), but even these things had about them a sense of frailty and impermanence. It was as though the ancient House might at any time shirk them off like a parasite-infested skin. Nothing in the garden would grow in the shadow of the tower, and so the gardeners had eventually resigned their futile watering of the plants that always came up twisted and withered and brown.

Flintwick, though, who passed through this garden on a basis of at least twice per day, was not paying particular attention to his surroundings.

His mind was swirling with thoughts, strategies with which to combat the malaise into which his master had fallen. Flintwick's realisation – or rather his admission – that there was indeed a serious issue to be addressed had already been of enormous benefit to him. He now supposed that, prior to this point, his mind had intercepted and banished to its most distant recess the awful thought that Lord Naught was ailing. Perhaps there was some merit in all this fashionable talk of a 'sub-conscious' after all.

Rather than plunging him into despair – as well might have been expected – acknowledging the truth had filled Flintwick with optimism. He had been in the service of Lord Naught for many years, and this vocation had brought him into contact with a singular variety of unusual experiences. Whilst it was true that Lord Naught's current condition was unprecedented in even this unique repository of experience, Flintwick was of the opinion that such knowledge rendered him uniquely qualified to resolve it.

Indeed, he was now sure that his master's state was probably nothing more than the result of glandular stress. Flintwick was no physician, but his parlour knowledge of the mechanics of the human mind and body lent him a certain understanding beyond the layman's. Thus he was in a position to hypothesise that Lord Naught's elevated standing in society was taxing his nervous brain-glands beyond their allotted capacity. Flintwick had learned of such conditions in a most enlightening medical paper recently; the author of this seminal study was a quite brilliant man whose reputation had originally been garnered in a little-known field related to the correction of bowel torpidity. Prior to reading his work the operation and purpose of the glandular system had been hazy at best in Flintwick's understanding (as indeed had its existence), but apparently it could be affected by such divers factors as the quality of local gravity, excessive richness of diet, improperness of climatic humidity, and the perpetration of that most immoral of vices, self-abuse. The latter could of course be ruled out in Lord Naught's case.

The demands of formal dinners, excursions, and other such engagements all took their heavy toll. Considering these constant pressures and the crushing weight of expectation upon the powerful and wise, eventual brain fatigue seemed almost inevitable. This morning Flintwick would suggest to his master that they should have a professional physician call and confirm his diagnosis, and would also present him with the itinerary of self-improving, constitutional activities that he had drawn up. Lord Naught would be restored to his habitual state in no time whatsoever.

Distracted though he was with these matters, Flintwick could not help pausing to take in the view from the terrace. This was a place in which he and his master often lingered of an evening to appreciate the unparalleled vistas of the city of Iremouth as it spread out below them. Steep, rocky slopes cascaded giddily away for seeming miles from below this perch, sweeping gracefully downwards to join the distant forest and the green and rolling countryside beyond it that stretched off to the far horizon. Huddles of little grey houses could be seen clinging to the upper hillside like hardy mountain goats, and the wisps of smoke from their chimneys mingled with the early morning haze that, despite the bright sunshine, still hung over the city.

Flintwick was sure that he could hear tiny, distant voices above the washing of the Irem, carrying up to him through the clear, still air: the bustle and clamour of a waking city. Already people were moving about the broad, terraced streets of the city's beautiful, higher region, stepping out of the tall townhouses that lined the banks of the Irem or driving animals loaded with wares up from the lower city and the highway. Even the labours of the ordinary seemed picturesque from here.

He left the garden and trotted down a flight of steps, then re-entered the House by means of another door. Lord Naught would be inside, hopefully enjoying his breakfast or a morning aperitif at this very moment. Flintwick was sure that his master would already have risen; he required very little sleep, and of late had been sleeping even less than was his habit. This assumption was proved correct when he heard the unmistakeable sound of Lord Naught's raven-croaking laughter echoing down the corridor from the door to the breakfast room, which had been left ajar. Perhaps the tincture of this pleasant spring day had already begun to raise his spirits! Smiling, Flintwick gathered his itinerary and his other papers under one arm and pushed open the door.

'Good morning, sir!' he declared, in as close an approximation of cheer as he had ever felt moved to muster.

The laughter died.

'Eh?' grunted Naught, a crumb of meat falling from his mouth. 'Ah. Nicholas.' His gaze flicked suddenly to the opposite end of the breakfast table.

Flintwick's head turned instinctively, following his master's glance to its destination.

'Flintwick!' exclaimed the woman in the metal hat through a mouthful of haddock's liver omelette. 'How pleasant of you to join us!'

'You!' spat Flintwick, simultaneously launching all of his carefully ordered papers into the air as though the force of his sudden vexation had blown them from his hands. 'What – '

Half a moment later he had snatched back his composure, along with pages two and six of the itinerary as they flapped in panic in the air before him. His face, however, had become as hard and cold as winter stone.

The breakfasters watched as the rest of the papers settled onto the floor.

'I was not expecting to see you here, Viscountess Aspic,' Flintwick intoned with slow venom as the rustling of stationery finally ceased. He glared pointedly at the omelette on her fork. 'Especially at so early an hour.'

Viscountess Aspic laid down the fork next to her empty plate, still greasy with fish oil, and dabbed at the corners of her thin, tight-lipped mouth with the corner of a folded napkin. The face into which that mouth was set was sallow and of indiscernible age; the sneer that perpetually adorned it was perhaps a result of her singularly immobile features. Her overly-long neck, which was encased in a starched, grey collar and tied about with a black ribbon, also had about it an air of inflexibility – rather as though it too had been starched. This was probably just as well as far as her upper vertebrae were concerned, as her huge hat looked to be exceedingly heavy.

She wore the hat fitted closely to her head, so that only a wispy frill of hair, the colour of rusty steel wool though characterised by a lankness not shared by that material, escaped its rim. The hat itself was of unique design: a tall, ugly thing of dull metal, intricately filigreed on both of its curved planes and having about it more than a little of the high-priest's headdress. It was secured to her head by means of two cruel spikes which were thrust through apertures in its base, presumably into her tightly-pulled hair. Flintwick was not given to the entertaining of fantasies, but he could not deny the enjoyment he gleaned from imagining that one day she might accidentally transfix her scheming brain instead. However, the diminutive nature of the target meant that this hope remained similarly small.

'Evidently,' the Viscountess replied, one rusted-steel eyebrow raised. 'And, in answer to the question that you so nearly asked me, I have arrived at this hour so that your master and I might make the most of the day we have planned together.'

'Planned?' shot back Flintwick in a voice like sharpened lead.

'Why, yes!' ejaculated Naught. 'Caviglia and I are going on an excursion! Oh, I must admit that I was feeling somewhat under the weather, but the prospect of a day spent in the company of our old friend here has quite cheered me up.' He beamed across the table at Caviglia and began to pull excitedly at the brocade cuffs of his flounced jacket of puce satin.

Flintwick noticed that there was no omelette on his plate. 'But sir, I believe you will find this is most inadvisable,' he growled. 'You see, I have been organising – '

'Well, Nicholas,' said Naught, cutting short Flintwick's protestation and rolling his beetlish eyes. 'I'm sure that we will have time for your outing another day! Caviglia has, after all, gone to the not inconsiderable effort of the journey up here to see us this morning.' He turned once more to the Viscountess, who smiled as a wasp might and almost imperceptibly batted her eyelids.

Flintwick's face solidified into polar granite as he glared at the Viscountess, whose eyes returned the ferocity of the ocular assault with the implacability of a mirror. In the space where their gazes met a repulsive force wavered and shuddered, friction transmuting the chill into a furnace blast. Just as this seething energy threatened to ignite the very atoms of the air between them and send them all somersaulting skyward in a cataclysm of flame, Flintwick gave a sudden snort and bent to snatch up his scattered papers.

Naught, oblivious to his good fortune, sprang to his feet. 'Come along, Caviglia!' he cried in his queerly burbling voice. 'The zoological gardens await us!' He rounded the table, grasped the handles that protruded from the rear of her chair, and heaved. Begrudgingly, the chair rolled backwards, its iron-studded wheels grinding out a highly unpleasant sound upon the flagstones as it did so.

'The... zoological gardens?' repeated Flintwick in hoarse incredulity.

'Yes, indeed!' the Viscountess grinned. 'I have managed to procure the most fascinating new exhibit!' She tightened the broad leather belt which bound her to the chair, and settled her pointed elbows upon the inlaid ivory of its armrests. 'Oh, I do so love the little creatures, don't you? Those poor, dumb things – sometimes I think they don't realise how fortunate they are, safe in those little houses of theirs. Indeed, one wonders how the lower orders would cope at all without their betters to... watch over them. To provide for them. To decide their proper places, you understand?' She offered Flintwick a smile that had evolved from wasp's to hornet's.

With his stick-like body straining visibly with the effort, Naught manoeuvred the chair in the direction of the door. The image of an industrious dung beetle rolling his filthy bounty sprang, unbidden, to Flintwick's mind, but he quashed the beetle part of the thought immediately. The dung, however, remained.

∽

It was strange, thought Edward, considering the long days that they had spent travelling, and the vehemence with which he had detested the most part of this experience, that he should now be perambulating the streets of this city entirely of his own accord, especially so soon after their arrival. He was alone, and wandering along a narrow, cobbled street that was overlooked on both sides by tall, grey houses. Every street in this city, it seemed, was overlooked on both sides by tall, grey houses.

Edward had left Obadiah cursing at a group of unkempt boys whom he had employed for the task of unloading their equipment. Obadiah, he reasoned, was quite capable of carrying out acts of gratuitous rage without assistance, and besides, the stream of loud profanities issuing forth from the Doctor's whiskered mouth was causing Edward to wince rather more than it usually might. He still felt bruised inside as well as out, and he was weary to his very bones despite a night spent in a relatively normal (though, he suspected, flea-ridden) bed. So, having made his excuses and thus his escape, Edward had wandered off into Iremouth in order to explore what this quaint place had to offer.

The steeply-sloping street in which Edward now found himself was shaded from much of the mid-morning sun by the houses that loomed overhead. They were built of sharply-chiselled blocks of dour, grey stone, no doubt cut from somewhere on this very mountain, and their construction, he noted, was very fine. It had surprised Edward somewhat when their coach had finally rolled into the city earlier that morning (over large cobbles, to his great dismay) that its architecture was so agreeably accomplished. He had expected Iremouth to have consisted of little more than a huddle of dilapidated shacks: a crumbling town on a mountain in the middle of nowhere. Just as most of his assumptions concerning Cold Ghastia were proving to be, though, this was quite incorrect – the buildings did not even have the tendency to lean crazily against one another as did the ageing piles back in Hingham.

However, Edward was aware that other parts of the city were not so pleasingly presented. Upon passing out of the forest's fringe their coach had passed through a den of awful squalor before coming upon the area in which they had found their lodgings. Thankfully, the considerate driver had cracked his whip as they traversed this unwholesome place, speeding his beasts onwards down the pitted dirt road. Obadiah and Edward had averted their eyes, each – after his own fashion – appalled. Some of the habitations had been little more than hovels, with grimy faces peering from their glassless windows.

There was really no excuse for poverty and destitution in this age, or so at least Obadiah had declared as he had whisked the curtain closed. Edward had been inclined neither to agree, nor at that moment to argue, for to engage in debate with the Doctor was not to a thing to be done lightly, especially when one had reasonable cause to doubt the robustness of one's eardrums. And besides, in some ways one might have supposed him to be right – for it was true that, with the exception of a few minor skirmishes, War had not troubled Grand Uria or its Empire's territories for a generation or two, and that times were tentatively prosperous if not precisely utopian. What's more, thanks to the efforts of the Abatirian Church and its Holy Mission of Benignity and Eternal Mercy, the indentured labour procurement industry continued to provide the chance of at least temporary work for menial types such as these. And then of course there were the boundless opportunities presented by the 'factories. No, these were evidently characters of inherently flaccid morals, the Doctor had concluded, predestined by the slackness of such fibre to lifelong careers in rascality. Such indolent vermin would crawl over each other in this scabrous nest for what would doubtless be the brief duration of their lives, contributing nothing to the world but their countless, mewling young.

Indeed, Obadiah had ventured to wager the unseasoned consumption of his hat that there was not a one among them that was not a pie-eyed gin swiller; his nostrils purportedly detected its filthy reek even through the tightly-closed windows of the coach. These rapscallions were pickling their brains, he had stated with an illustrative tap to the temple, but for the life of him Edward could not see why he should find this so singularly hilarious.

However, at that moment in time Edward had much besides the socioeconomic shortcomings of the Empire to dwell upon, and so, frankly, he did not.

As Edward walked, he observed. Of course, that a person should choose to look around him as he trod the streets of a city was by no means unusual (were this not the case then pedestrian collisions and acute disorientation would surely proliferate wherever buildings do) but true *observation* Edward judged to be an altogether rarer enterprise. To suggest that city dwellers are unobservant on the whole would have been equally imprudent – but the fact remained that once a person attained a certain level of acquaintance with a place they simply ceased to *observe* it. For this reason it never failed to amuse Edward should he chance to overhear passersby remarking upon the sudden, unfathomable disappearance of *this* milliners shop or *that* charcuterie, or the apparently overnight arrival of such-and-such memorial drinking fountain, when it was perfectly plain that the closure or erection in question had taken place a number of months beforehand. For if Edward Stoathill-Warmly could be said to be anything then it was observant, and if he could be said to be any other thing then it was curious. And when Edward was going about the business of observing a new place it was his preference to do so by looking *upwards*.

This, he found, was a further contrast to the habits of even lifelong city-dwellers, whose self-blinkered eyes stare always straight ahead, seeing for the most part the things that do not exceed their height, and exclusively the things that it is necessary for them to see. To Edward's mind, there was much to be missed if one persisted in taking such a pedestrian view of a place; it was a question of perspective and perception. The things that the common person of conventional persuasion *needs* to see are rarely indeed the most interesting things that exist to be seen.

Thinking thusly, Edward thrust his chin into the air as he strolled so that he might direct his gaze above the level of the pine-shuttered windows and the weighty, carven doors that predominated here. At first his neck protested somewhat (it, along with the rest of his long-suffering spine, was still rather more than sore from the journey), but he soon forgot this minor inconvenience. There was, after all, a good deal to see.

THE SHAPES

High above him stretched row upon row of ornate balconies; indeed, it seemed to Edward that every apartment in every one of these towering, grey buildings was possessed of its own little platform bounded in wrought-iron, and that each of these had been designed with the express intention of outdoing its neighbour in terms of intricacy. To begin with it struck him as peculiar that such elaborate creations should adorn edifices built with such strict economy of imagination and cheer, but soon he began to warm to what he felt sure any travel itinerary would refer to as a 'charming idiosyncrasy'. The swirling, black lattices of branches and antlers and ivy contributed as much to the agreeable character of the place as did the quaintly cobbled lanes or the fresh mountain air.

The air, besides being uncommonly clear by Edward's estimation, was infused with the aroma of baking things and the scents of herbs and flowers drying in the morning sun. There were other things besides such bushels twisting in the breeze that morning, though, things that happened to be especially noteworthy to a person of Edward's vocation. Of course, without closer examination he could not be absolutely certain, but it certainly appeared as though there were traditionally crafted apotropaic devices of the domestic-talismanic genus - possibly of continental pagan extraction - strung from a goodly number of the balconies. Being well aware of the interconnexion of such things with his present field of study, he made mental note of the most common configurations.

But there would be time enough for work in the days ahead, and having committed these things to memory Edward resolved that - for this morning at least - he would explore with no agenda but that dictated by his own leisure.

Ambling onwards up the hill (every street in this city, it seemed, involved a hill in one capacity or another),

Edward paused awhile to admire a particularly well-established growth of algæ, vivid green and slick, that stained the frontage of an otherwise pristine building. The proportion of sightseers who would appreciate the beauty in such a thing was surely a small one, but Edward's æsthetic preferences had ever been far from conventional. More pleasing yet was the sapling he espied moments later, a perfect miniature oak that sprouted from a rent in the masonry many storeys above. A smile touched his pale face as he pictured its foraging roots sipping at unsuspecting tenants' cocoa in the dead of night, or caressing whichsoever of their extremities were not afforded the protection of their blankets.

Here and there fluttering clotheslines were strung like ships' rigging between the great stone hulls of the buildings, each proudly flying the city's traditional colours of slate, fog and storm cloud. Their presence had the unfortunate effect of obscuring Edward's view so that he was forced to turn his head this way and that as he walked in order that his observation might continue without interruption, albeit of the freshly-laundered kind. Despite his efforts, the spirited flapping of a voluminous pair of breeches very nearly cost him the sight of a curious little sundial positioned in a plainly lightless nook. What time did such a clock indicate when the whole of its dial was forever in shadow, he wondered? Was it all time at once, or no time at all? Or could it be some altogether weirder hour?

Pondering happily upon this pleasant little conundrum, Edward pushed ever onwards, ever uphill. As his gradual climb continued, he found that the breadth of the streets and the grandeur of the houses that lined them seemed to increase relative to their altitude, and that they were now interspersed with commercial and civic buildings. Rounding a corner by a delightful though decidedly over-patronised little baker's shop (only the rambunctiousness within prevented its delectable aroma from waylaying him) he chose the quieter of the streets with which he was faced, and proceeded along it.

It transpired that this was something of a backstreet, overlooked by a good many barred and ivy-grown windows and bordered on both sides by low stone walls, upon one of which sat a group of men in dusty workers' apparel. The men were smoking cigarettes and conversing loudly, evidently enjoying a well-deserved rest from the first portion of the morning's manual labour. One of their number shouted something vulgar in Edward's general direction as he passed, precipitating an eruption of coarse laughter from his fellows. Edward suspected this rudeness was prompted by his being a well-to-do and scholarly-looking foreigner, or perhaps by the fact that he was walking with his chin thrust into the air. In reality, it was both of these.

Edward was as fond of labouring types as they seemed to be of him (which was not in the least bit), but even had this not been the case he would still have ignored them. Unlike Obadiah, he had never been one for unnecessary confrontation, and besides, he was still thoroughly engaged in sating his curiosity. Even in such an alley there was much to pique it; indeed, Edward considered that the places one was not strictly *supposed* to see were often the most intriguing of all.

The workers, Edward ascertained with a sidelong glance, were gathered about a wooden palette bearing a miscellany of boxed items. This was attached by means of a lengthy rope and pulley to a gantry jutting from the uppermost storey of the overshadowing building, just below its sagging, nest-barnacled gable. Beneath this gantry was one of the most intriguing attic windows that Edward had ever laid eyes upon. He fought the impulse – the uncouth bunch, he could tell, were eyeing him with amused disdain – but it was no use. He could not wrench his gaze away from it.

Edward was inordinately fond of attics (so long as there happened to be lamp to hand), and he delighted in the thought of the hidden things that might be found inside them. Splintery tea chests and battered old trunks filled with maps and medals and foreign coins, locked tin boxes and hoards of dusty old books: this was the bounty that filled his mind as he stared up at that dark, shuttered portal. Indeed, places such as this one were often the terminus of the trails he and Obadiah followed, places where things had been put in order that they might be *forgotten* – sometimes with the aid of steel chains and padlocks whose proportions recalled fists, or of sturdy planks nailed across hatches.

Guarded upon either side by a rain-weathered gargoyle, the aperture spoke of mystery so profound that it almost seemed to exhale a dark breath into the morning air. Its ancient shutters creaked open a fraction as though beckoning to Edward, and a shiver ran down his spine. However, a moment later it was the base of Edward's spine that was tingling – and not in such a pleasant fashion.

His behind hit the cobbles with some force, and before he knew why he was falling, or indeed that he was falling at all. The labourers roared with laughter. Scrambling to his feet, his face burning with the embarrassment of it and his posterior throbbing with pain, he realised that he had fallen foul of lax paving standards. An un-mortared cobblestone had skidded from beneath his foot; the reprobates must have been waiting for him to tread on it. He stumbled out of the alley with hoots of mocking laughter echoing behind him.

It had ever been this way with Edward. He had always been curious, he had always been awkward, and he had always been something of a figure of fun to those who did not understand him. It was perhaps unfortunate for him that there were so few who troubled to do so.

As a child, Edward had been the very epitome of precociousness. No sooner had he mastered the art of reading (which, to the very great surprise of his first tutor, the boy had done well before chalk had ever been set to board) he had set about systematically filling his mind with every shred of knowledge that was available to him. Admittedly this meant that for much of his early life his learning had been restricted to whatever happened to be contained within the dusty pages of his father's books, but the library at Fivesides Grange was by no means inconsiderable. Indeed, it contained roughly thrice the number of tomes as did the public library at Eggerton Hopes, and was in itself more capacious than a good many of the houses that had the displeasure of comprising that remote village.

Edward had always been a pale child, maledicted with the appearance of perennial ill-health, and hidden in the friendly shadows of the library he had grown into a positively wan young man. Those who knew of him said (and quite rightly) that barely a moment passed when he was not bent over the reading desk or burning lamp oil in his room, feeding his ravenous craving for knowledge. Never was the young Edward Stoathill-Warmly known to climb a tree or throw a ball. Edward had been unconcerned by the boisterous life his peers were leading outside, though. He had known that his own life was immeasurably richer.

There was not a one in Edward's village so erudite as he; he positively consumed literature, both contemporary and classical, and within him burned a great passion for the chronicles of the rich, bloody history of Verdra, though in the perusal of those annals he had learned to despise the Empire that had tamed her. When he was older (though not so old as one might imagine) he had read existential and metaphysical philosophy, and so he had begun to ponder his place in the Kosmos – but it was only when he discovered the Sciences that he found he could begin to conceive of this place. He had delighted in the kosmic secrets that the Sciences had begun to reveal, and against his father's advice he had even gone so far as to dabble in the nascent chymical and elyctrical arts.

Soon enough the library at Fivesides Grange had been quite drained of material, and Edward had come to epitomise autodidacticism too. He was by no means a master of every discipline (for his knowledge was as yet of the abstract sort), but his eager mind forged unconventional connexions between the fields that he surveyed. Indeed, his intellectual imagination was such that when by the time he had escaped the confines of his father's sprawling country pile for the University town of Hingham, he had already taken irreversible steps towards forming what his schoolmasters would come to call 'infelicitous habits' and, on occasion, 'an unfortunate liberalness of thinking'.

On Edward's first day as a student of the Imperator's University of Hingham's School of Modern Theoretical Sciences he had all but danced through the courtyard stippled with leafy sunlight and into his seat in the lecture theatre, eyes shining in the galleried gloom and pencil sharp. But it had not taken long for him to be disabused of what he came to learn had been his naïveté. Higher learning, he had discovered, was by no means learning of a freer sort.

Edward's wont had been to follow ideas, chasing flitting evanescences across the landscape of knowledge from one field to the next like a child with a butterfly net. But the masters, Edward found, liked nothing more than to draw borders. They were strict and immutable, these borders in their thoughts, and it was mandatory that they be observed at all times. He who chanced to stumble across one was woebegotten indeed – and most especially if that stumbler happened to be a self-taught recluse from a boggy province of the North whose father had purchased his studentship.

It was as though the masters feared that without their perimeter boundaries one type of knowledge might bleed through and contaminate another with incongruous ideas, and a terrible thing *that* would be. To Edward, though, this was very much the point; where they saw miscegenation, he saw interrelation. To Edward the boundaries swam and blurred, like faces in a dream, only to coalesce once more in strange, new forms. The masters ruled that his mind was clearly unfocused: that he must apply his intelligence to a conventional field of study in which he might excel. Edward had remained unconvinced.

Still, though the masters' atrophic ignorance and their blind adherence to convention had first disappointed and then deeply frustrated him, it was something else that had truly perturbed Edward – something that was both the epitome and the unification of these concerns, and yet something more besides. For if the Modern Theoretical Sciences were riven by borders, then around their territory reared a fortress wall – and beyond it, like an encampment of leprous and malnourished barbarians forever forbidden from entering, lay the lore of the Lesser World.

Much of the material gathered from the far corners of the globe by the Imperial Department for the Archiving of Lesser Cultural Affairs disappeared into the vaults of the Abatirian Church before ever it could reach the vicinity of the academy, of course, or else perished in the cleansing fires of the Holy Mission of Benignity and Eternal Mercy. That which was left might just as well have done the same.

The papyri and the tablets deemed appropriate for academic consideration were catalogued and transliterations of their contents prepared, and the likenesses of savage idols and carven snuff trays were rendered in crisp strokes of ink before finding their homes behind glass screens or stacked in packing cases. Thence pronouncements regarding the stilted sociocultural evolution of the Lesser World were dispensed. The term that the masters had concocted for this occupation was 'Anthropology', and it was one of their favourite conceits, a confection of their hubris. Speaking mountains and feathered gods were all very fascinating, indeed very entertaining, to the anthropologists – for were such novel notions not welcome reminders of how far the Empire had progressed since the benighted days of animism and mythologizing? To see such primitive evolutionary episodes preserved between the pages of journals like pressed flowers, exotic yet desiccated, was proper, but their practices could hardly be allowed to continue in the world at large. How was the better part of mankind to advance with Lesser ideologies retarding its development?

The tale that the masters told themselves regarding this process of betterment they had dubbed 'History', and they were surpassingly fond of it – primarily because it placed them at its apogee, Edward suspected. However, it was as much Science as had been the fables dispensed by Edward's father regarding his heroic work with the Mission, and Edward had quite lost his affection for it since he had become witness to the vagaries of its authorship. Conversely, his hunger for knowledge of the cultures of the past themselves, the raw materials from which History was fabricated, had only grown. But for a Modern Theoretical Scientist, a rational and empirically-minded man of the Empire, to allow his gaze to stray over these works for any other purpose than that of mere diversion, or with anything more in his mind than amused disdain, was tantamount to sacrilege.

In these matters the Church, the Mission, and the academy agreed entirely.

Naturally they would never admit it, for it was not the fashion to admit the influence of the spiritual over the intellectual – indeed, atheism was avowed by the Masters almost to a man, even amongst the theologians – but Edward felt the insidious influence of the Abatirians in all he saw. Just as the shadows of the cathedral's five iron spires fell over the softly dreaming lanes of Hingham like the fingers of a grasping hand, the shadow of the Church fell over the Empire itself. The Interlocutors of the Abatirian Church did not precisely forbid contemplation of the materials that they deigned to release, but the University's coffers would have resounded more hollowly than the inside of a ransacked temple-tomb in the absence of Abatirian coin. Still, that the Church – an institution whose genealogy could be traced to the rabid cults of a distant tropic archipelago and whose every function was to this day encrusted with accreted layers of arcane ritual – should be the one to control the process of *Scientific* censorship was felt by Edward as a burning irony. The whole thing was a collusion between myopia, wilful blindness, and the putting-out of eyes.

For these were the writings of other peoples with other ways than those of the Urish, and to view them through an Urish lens was to diminish them, to reduce them unjustifiedly to a failed attempt at Urishness. Besides, Edward felt that within these records there resided something that was entirely absent from the Science of the pompous old men in their dismal halls, and yet which could not sanely be excluded from any complete theory of existence be it Imperial *or* Lesser. It was the thing that Edward sought to know above all others, the thing which thanks to the efforts of his father had become the *raison d'être* of his intellectual life since long before he had fled Fivesides Grange. It was a ghostly thing, and it haunted the academy unacknowledged as did the spectre of the Church. That thing that Edward sought was the source of the mind that was doing the seeking, the consciousness that dwelt within the seeker, and the thing which to his mind lay at the very heart of its mystery: dreams.

In none of the conversations which had so obviously rankled them had any alienist had been able to provide Edward with a satisfactory explanation as to whence dreams came, and he had been forcibly ejected from lecture theatres for the crime of insinuating that the neurologists and neuroanatomists who held forth within them could not account for whence the dreaming consciousness itself originated to begin with. The evolutionists, ever collegiate with the historians, held that consciousness was an incidental by-product of the body's development, and dreams its effluvia. Some license could be granted to a fledgling Science such as Evolution, but this assertion of the immaterial arising from the material was patently absurd for a slew of reasons, even allowing for the series of grievous oversights and sets of false assumptions that had led to it.

Dreams, Edward had discovered to his dismay, were not the preserve of Scientists.

Dreams were the preserve of shamans, of warlocks, of cunning-women, of soothsayers, thaumaturges and most of all the witch-folk. These were the ones who had walked the shifting paths between here and the Beyond, and had set down their experiences in sculpture and in song long before the Mission had decimated their wisdom and sneered at its remains, had eviscerated once-noble beasts and stuffed their empty hides with crumpled journal pages. And so in the absence of the voices themselves it was to their echoes that Edward had turned. He had done so covertly, of course, for he knew from experience that the Masters would never have admitted the seepage of the arcane into Science. In the minutes and hours shaved deftly from his time amongst the buzzing generators and belching vats of the University laboratories, Edward became a frequenter of museums, a peruser of anthropological collections, and a lingerer in the less-trodden aisles of libraries. Secreted amongst those shelves and cabinets, he had read that which he was permitted to read, yet was forbidden from understanding – and soon enough Edward had become an incognito esotericist.

Despite himself, Edward had not been able to contain his fledgling passion altogether, and during his fourth year in the School of Modern Theoretical Sciences he had made his mistake, in the form of a particularly contentious paper. Although his interest in the subject had been aroused by his occult delving he had thought it hardly beyond the pale considering the evidence that he had amassed. He had known, of course, that the masters of his School would not be kindly disposed towards matters of Astrology – but where did Astronomy end and Astrology begin? Edward's thoughts, it seemed, had already strayed too far from the consecrated grounds of Modern Theoretical Science for such a backwards glance to reveal where its territories lay.

It had all appeared rather self-evident to him. It was after all indisputable that the sun and moon held sway over various terrestrial processes – was it so absurd to propose that other heavenly bodies might do the same, especially something so significant as that great superexcrescence of energy that the astronomers had identified at the galaxy's heart? And who knew what other energies might be at play in the wider Kosmos, as yet undetected by the star-masters' instruments? Why might the tides of human consciousness not ebb and flow under their influence as did the waters of the oceans at the beck and call of gravity? Why might seasons of mind not cycle one into the next as did terrestrial seasons under the sun? What's more, the historical works that Edward had used to chart the rise and fall of Verdra's ages of civilisation had been authored largely within the University's walls. It was all there, in the records. All one had to do was look. The astronomers and the historians agreed, whether they were able to apprehend it not. Edward had felt a rare pride in his work, and more than that had felt its rightness, a resonance somewhere within him that convinced him of its veracity.

The masters had felt none of these things. The boy had breached borders with a flagrancy verging on insolence, and with his suggestion that *dreams* might somehow be related to the nonsensical things he proposed – well, he had annihilated any chance of a pardon for his crime. The paper had attracted comments that were pitying at best, and in some cases it had precipitated laughter which forever afterwards Edward would recall whenever he chanced to hear the term 'derisory'. Edward was humiliated. It was a shaming of such magnitude that it might well have spelled the end of his career in academia – had it not been for a timely intervention. For there was one who had been watching the development of Edward's work very closely indeed; one who did not view such subjects with disdain; one who shared not only his passions for both Science and for esoteric lore, but who also harboured a passion for the mysteries of metaphysics that all but surpassed Edward's own.

Doctor Obadiah Carnaby was a man not so readily disdained as was the pale and nervous young Edward. Indeed, with the weight of the academy against him he had succeeded in establishing the Imperator's University of Hingham's Institute of Arcanology, and he had done so single-handedly. Whether it was genuine academic prowess, the improbably large donation made to the University by the Foreign Secretary, Sir Bastable Carnaby, or sheer mortal fear of his only son that had allowed for the Institute's creation was debatable – but as far as Edward had been concerned this was wholly immaterial. The Institute of Arcanology seemed the realisation of his most fervent wishes, and when on that most dismal of days when Edward had been packing his bags for he-knew-not-where the Doctor had approached the punctured young academic with his proposition of collaboration, he had not waited for the next beat of his heart before accepting.

That had been a little over three years ago, and during that time much had been accomplished. It had not taken long for a symbiosis of sorts to grow between Edward's unconventional ideas and Obadiah's rigorous, uncompromising methods, nor indeed for a close camaraderie to bind them together. If they were not united by a common goal then at least they were united by a common philosophy: there was only so much to be learned from the dreary, mundane academy, only so much to be learned if one persisted in seeing the world through their half-closed eyes. Doctor Obadiah Carnaby and Mr Edward Stoathill-Warmly would channel their intellects into constructing a *new* perspective – and perhaps into using that perspective to peer into *other* worlds.

Dusting down the seat of his trousers, Edward attempted to regain his composure as he exited the alley, whereupon he stood for a moment and looked around. Besides the depth of his festering shame, it was pure curiosity, he reasoned, that was responsible for his general situation, in the respect that it had led him to become a researcher of the occult and the esoteric, and so to Cold Ghastia and grey Iremouth on the mountain. It was also *directly* responsible for his present situation, in the respect that it was the reason for his exhaustion-defying bout of wanderlust – and therefore the reason for his now being completely lost.

He realised that, in his reverie, he had been observing everything except for the direction in which he had been walking.

Edward found that he was standing on the corner of a little paved square with a decorative fountain of leaping stone deer babbling away at its centre, and was forced to ponder the merits of turning immediately right into a narrow street lined with interesting covered stalls or continuing along his present course, which would take him directly across the square, under a stone arch and out into what appeared to be some kind of plaza beyond. As he imagined the long, footsore trawl back to the hotel, he suddenly felt the old tiredness creeping back into his bones. He let out a lengthy sigh and bent to rest a moment with his hands upon his knees. This he instantly regretted; blood rushed to his head, causing it to swim in a most unpleasant fashion. Woozily, he straightened up – and in doing so he noticed something that he had not noticed before. Puzzled, he squinted at it. It was the tip of what might have been some kind of building, now just visible above the level of the rooftops.

It shuddered like a reflexion in water, drawing his gaze to it. He rubbed his eyes, which were – as ever – sore, seemingly endowed with a goodly portion of grit, and at this moment obviously deceiving him.

Edward trotted under the arch and into the plaza the better to see the thing, barely aware that he was doing so, and all the time wondering how it was that he had not caught sight of it before now. He could only imagine that the height of the buildings coupled with the steep incline of the mountain slope must have served to obscure his view of the actual skyline. Now that he stood with it in full view though, Edward stopped dead in his tracks.

The sight of it moved him strangely. Set high upon a massive, beetling crag that rose to yet loftier heights than the mountainside upon which he stood was a castle, of sorts: a colossal thing of fluted towers, domed turrets and vaulted carapaces with ramparts so high and so sheer that it stole his breath to look upon them. Thundering down into the city like a torrent of grey jewels from a place somewhere just beyond it was a mighty waterfall. Perhaps it was some hoax perpetrated by the unusual perspective and scale of the scene, or perhaps it was some refractive property taken on by the mountain air at such an altitude – but although his eyes reported every detail of the castle with the sharpness of a pin, Edward received the distinct impression that it was fluttering ever-so-slightly, like a banner in the breeze. Whatever it was, the feeling that the sight inspired in him was not unlike that which one might experience upon waking from a particularly profound and vivid dream.

The longer Edward stood and gaped in wonder, the more baffling it became to him that the castle – if indeed a castle it was, for the longer he gazed upon it less apposite the appellation seemed to become – had contrived to escape his attention so completely and for so long. It was by no means an exaggeration to say that it utterly dominated the city. Prior to this moment, Edward had felt modestly impressed by Iremouth. Now he felt almost as though he were standing in the midst of some dolls' town or children's playhouse. Despite its dreamlike appearance, the thing had an air of absolute *reality* about it, a sense that all else was rendered counterfeit by its very existence. It was a feeling that Edward had experienced but once before, in a place very far indeed from this one. The thing upon which he gazed was no castle. It could only be the House.

Edward shook his head, a smile spreading across his pale face. 'Obadiah,' he whispered. 'My friend, we have surely come to the right place!'

THREE
Cold Comfort in Cold Ghastia

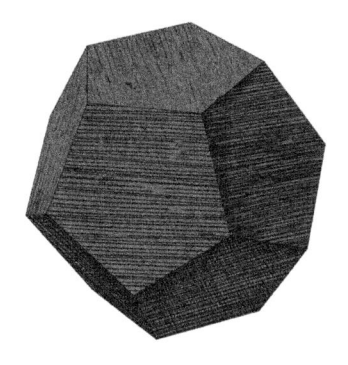

'**D**o come in, Doctor Carnaby,' said the Minister warmly. 'It is a pleasure to meet you.'

'Un*doubt*edly,' boomed Obadiah, springing up from the sagging couch upon which he had been sitting impatiently for the past half-of-an-hour and striding across the dimly-lit reception room. He grasped the Minister's dainty paw and crushed it in his own iron grip, shaking it fit to dislocate the fellow's arm from his sloping shoulder.

The Minister was an unimposing and vaguely ratlike man – though if it were indeed a rat's face that his own recalled it was not that of a lean and feral sewer-haunter, but instead that of a cosseted cage-lounger. 'I am Minister Dirth,' he said.

'Yes,' Obadiah agreed.

'Ah,' said Dirth as he retrieved his slightly mashed appendage. 'Visitors from the mainland are rare in Cold Ghastia.'

'So I understand,' said Obadiah, glancing around disinterestedly. 'I cannot imagine why.'

Just then an uncommonly sizeable gentleman with piercingly blue eyes and a strikingly well-established moustache emerged from the Minister's office and brushed past Obadiah as he made for the lobby. The Minister nodded with familiar deference to the gentleman, and ushered Obadiah inside.

Obadiah surveyed the room, a drab little enclave of bureaucracy crammed with all manner of overstuffed files on shelves and in tottering towers about the floor. The only thing vaguely worthy of attention was a glass cabinet containing a few dozen pinioned and disintegrating winged insects, none of which had been particularly impressive in life.

'Oh, just a little hobby of mine,' said Dirth as he followed Obadiah's gaze. 'Lepidopterism is – '

'Best pursued in an environment more conducive to the expression of its subjects' optimal morphology, it would seem,' finished Obadiah. 'This *Acherontia atropos* is little more than a runt.'

'Oh,' said Dirth, somewhat deflated by the Doctor's failure to be impressed by what he heretofore had modestly considered to be a more than passable collection of moths. He then brightened somewhat as he apprehended the arrival of his tea-tray. 'Ah, a cup for you?' he ventured as the maid left, waggling the steaming pot.

'No,' said Obadiah, settling himself into the Minister's chair. 'I would prefer it if we could simply discuss the matter at hand.'

'Of course,' said the Minister, setting down the pot with a clink of porcelain. Tea was an expensive commodity in Cold Ghastia, imported infrequently and at exorbitant cost, and thus rarely refused. 'I, ah, understand that you and your colleague – Mr Stoathill-Warmly, isn't it?'

Obadiah, who was twisting at the end of one of his moustaches, nodded.

'I understand that you are from the Imperator's University of Hingham?'

Obadiah inclined his head in a nod again, sunlight from the window rippling across the surface his lacquered hair. 'This I see you have quite accurately gleaned from our correspondence.'

Already Dirth was beginning to feel somewhat exasperated. No one besides himself had ever sat in his chair during a meeting before. Further to this, he had not actually bothered to read a single one of the letters forwarded to him by the envoy in Hingham – a fact he felt quite sure would in no way endear him to the somewhat daunting character who was currently reclining in favourite item of office furniture. The chair was not even *supposed* to recline, and was likely in grave danger of a fatal fracture, but Dirth elected not to mention this fact either. Instead, he struggled to remember the little that his assistant had told him regarding Carnaby. 'And your business in Iremouth is... is... scientific research?' he ventured.

'Exactly. Mr Stoathill-Warmly and I shall be engaged in research, as you say. But, more importantly, we are keen to arrange a meeting with an eminent Scientist whom we have traced to this place.'

Dirth nodded as though this information correlated with his understanding. 'Might I enquire as to what manner of research you are referring to?'

Obadiah grinned broadly, exposing his array of large teeth. It was not a friendly grin. 'The field of our study is broad and eclectic, Minister Dirth, and I doubt that its substance could comfortably or accurately be likened to any discipline with which a fellow such as *yourself* would be familiar – our interests encompass both the empirical and the esoteric, you see. Suffice it to say that that the ignorant might refer to the business as *occult*. Myself, I see this as a crude and ill-fitting term. I far prefer *arcane*. Hence *Arcanology*, of course.'

'Arca- ' Dirth began, in that moment recalling the term and his bafflement as his assistant had made mention of it. 'Oh, yes, *Arcanology*. Naturally. Well, Doctor Carnaby, I am a diplomat and not a Scientist, but even so I'll not pretend that I understand much of what you have told me.'

Obadiah stared, unblinking and evidently unmoved.

Dirth fidgeted. 'I, ah, well, I wish you every success in... ah, your *endeavours*, regardless. And who exactly is this fellow that you mention?'

'His name is Sebastian Bellhouse. We understand that he presently resides with one Lord Naught.'

Dirth thought for a moment or two, stroking his overbitten chin as he did so. Whether this was to illustrate the process of thought or to aid it was unclear. 'I don't recall hearing anything of this *Bellhouse* chap,' he said at length. 'Although I'm sure that such a man could not *entirely* elude polite society in our city. How, ah, long did you say he has been resident in Iremouth?'

'I did not. But the answer is nineteen years, give or take.'

'Nineteen *years!*' the Minister spluttered. 'Well then I can say with certainty that you are mistaken! I am rather well connected within society, you see,' he said, puffing up slightly, 'and I am acquainted with every person of repute, from merchants to lawyers to hoteliers and *including* Scientists.'

Obadiah leaned forward, planting his elbows upon the Minister's desk and creasing the upper strata of its residual blanket of papers in what looked to be an irretrievable fashion. He fixed the man with a glare to rival the pins transfixing the hairy bodies in the cabinet. 'I have researched this matter *quite* thoroughly, having spoken to several reliable sources including his relatives and his colleagues, and we have it on good authority that Mr

Bellhouse *is indeed* in Iremouth. Of this we are entirely certain.' He reinforced each syllable of this last phrase with a resounding and document-unsettling slap to the desk.

'Very well. Then I am sure you are correct,' stammered Dirth, loosening his collar with a finger and glancing woefully at the letters settling onto the carpet. 'Lord Naught is, after all, considered throughout Cold Ghastia and the surrounding islands to be something of a patron of learning, a-and what's more an enthusiast of the arts.'

'Intriguing,' replied Obadiah flatly. 'Well, do you think that some time with Lord Naught might be arranged? Myself and my associate have, as I am sure you are aware, travelled a quite considerable distance in order to conduct this meeting.'

'Why then, might I ask,' asked Dirth, 'did you not arrange such a meeting with this Bellhouse in advance?'

Obadiah sighed expansively. '*As* your envoy has previously explained to you *at length* in your correspondence,' he said, 'Mr Bellhouse's *condition* is such that a regular conversation will be a more than challenging endeavour, and written communication is, and has been, entirely out of the question. He is, you might say, currently unable to wield a pen.'

'Oh, I am *sorry*,' replied Dirth with a genuine inflection of sympathy. This unusual story was beginning to make more sense by the moment. 'I did not realise that the gentleman was an invalid. This explains much. Well, I will certainly put this to Lord Naught's aide when I lunch with him later in the day. He is a man by the name of Flintwick. He takes care of the greater part of his master's affairs, as the man himself cares very little to leave the House of late.'

Obadiah stood up and tossed a folded piece of paper onto the desk. 'For that I would be eternally grateful, Minister. This is the address of our apartments. Please send word of any developments in these matters as soon as it can be arranged.'

'Oh, certainly,' said Dirth, scurrying after Obadiah. 'But might I ask, as a matter of interest, from what manner of affliction does this Bellhouse suffer that has kept him invalided for all of nineteen years?'

Obadiah pondered for a moment. 'You might say that he has entirely lost the use of his body,' he replied as he donned his hat. Then, as he was crossing the room, he turned and with a mysterious smile he added, 'Although, I sincerely hope that he is still sound of mind.'

And with that he swept out of the office, the tails of his black coat swirling behind him.

∼

Lord Naught rapped a funereal beat with his lengthy nails of kingfisher-blue upon the window of the carriage.

'Don't you agree, Naught?' repeated Viscountess Aspic, rousing him from his thoughts.

'Eh? I beg your pardon?' Naught blinked, turning his huge head to peer over the voluminous bear's pelt that draped his shoulders. The black beast's frame had evidently been orders of magnitude larger than his own.

'I was just saying that the season's operatic recitals have been somewhat lacking in credibility,' she said again. 'Don't you agree?'

'Yes, undoubtedly, Caviglia,' he replied without even feigned interest. 'Here, take a candied violet.'

Caviglia dipped her hand into the box, rustling the pinstriped tissue paper for an unnecessarily long time, and retrieved one of the fancies. She popped it into her thin-lipped mouth, first biting off a corner of the petal in what might have been construed as a suggestive manner. Naught did what he supposed to be an adequate job of pretending that he had not noticed this.

Initially, he had been quite excited by the prospect of spending a day in Caviglia's company. In seasons past, Caviglia and Dietrich Aspic had been vital accomplices in the uproarious decadence and perversity of the House of Naught, but since the tragic death of her loyal husband, Caviglia had seldom strayed from her home in the neighbouring Viscounty of Spittle. Now that the official period of mourning was over though, she was beginning to make iron-shod forays into the outside world once more. But something seemed to have changed inside Naught, and he knew that he could no longer glean the same satisfaction from their deviant japery as once he had. It seemed that it simply could no longer *be* the way that it had *been*. So, as the morning had progressed, the sombre mood, which had of late surrounded him like a grey cloud, had begun to drift back to envelop him once more.

The zoological gardens had, for a while, proved an amusing enough diversion. In essence, though, the place had been much the same as it had been on his last visit, and he was not able to muster a great deal of genuine enthusiasm for the exhibits. The Viscountess had been wheeled around the grounds by one of her entourage, an exceedingly tall and well-put-together fellow with a fine handlebar moustache and green eyes of impressive lustrousness. He had remained enigmatically silent throughout the day, handling Caviglia's iron chair with effortless ease, and with no apparent instruction from the Viscountess. Naught had found the chap to be far more intriguing than Caviglia, and more than once he had caught his gaze straying dreamily up and down his powerful arms as she had chattered incessantly about the animals, and which members of Iremouth's high society they most resembled.

It transpired that the mystery animal that Caviglia had procured for the collection, a Gigantic Butuuan Ape, had died inexplicably. They had been scrutinising the apparently empty enclosure for some minutes before Naught had noticed the motionless legs of the creature protruding from one end of its hide.

They stayed to watch the keepers remove the body.

The gangly, hairy limbs were locked stiff with rigor mortis, just as Dietrich's body had been when the servants had found him spread-eagled upon the cold, tiled floor of the bathroom in the east wing, his toothbrush still clenched in his fist and a pool of bloody foam issuing from his mouth. Later, the fidgeting family physician had declared to the court that the Viscount's untimely demise, though undoubtedly tragic, had been an entirely natural consequence of an enervated heart.

After the dead thing was dragged off, but not before Naught had given his whispered instructions to the keeper to have its head delivered to the House, they had spent a great deal of time in the humid reptile-house, with which Caviglia seemed utterly fascinated. She had her man wheel her right up to the glass – so close that Naught feared that any sudden inclination of her metal hat would shatter the flimsy barrier and release the deadly, scaly things inside the terrarium. He received the distinct impression that Caviglia could have stayed indefinitely in the company of the flickering-tongued and venomous creatures, but the pungent smell in the reptile-house was too much for his own delicate senses to bear for long.

Naught loved more than anything to see the manatees. He had personally commissioned a crew of whalers who hunted the treacherous Ghastian Sea to bring the huge, sad creatures to the park alive. How well he remembered the arrival of the stinking crates from which they had released the vast, blubbery beasts. Oh, how he had waited for that day! A deep, steep-sided pit had been dug to house them, with an artificial lagoon within in which they might dive. Naught had stood by, open-mouthed with wonder, as they had been winched into the hole, and he had stared, unblinking, into those black, sorrowful eyes that were so much like his own.

After that he had often come just to close his eyes and listen to the manatees' low, mournful howls and the weird, otherworldly barking they made as it echoed up out of the depths of the shadowy pit. It sounded so delightfully human sometimes that it made his spine tingle pleasantly, and in a quiet voice he would say his special words to himself, again and again. His mind would drift to ancient tales of the sea, where mariners would peer from their vessels and behold, through the salty spray and foam, beings waving to them from atop desolate, wave-lashed and weed-strewn rocks. Caviglia seemed quite incapable of appreciating the romance in this, however, and Naught had not been inclined to further explain the feeling that his treasured sea-beasts evoked in him.

So it was that Naught had soon grown weary of the zoological gardens, and thus had found himself back in Caviglia's carriage. And now, as the carriage rattled back into the centre of Iremouth, he gazed from the window at the too-familiar scenery and wondered glumly what was to become of him. For years longer than he cared to remember he had spent his days in sating his lusts by whatever means might be contrived, zoological or otherwise. His every whim and fancy was catered for. But – oh! – how these follies had grown wearisome.

He snorted with amusement as he recalled Flintwick's anxious expression the evening before, making Caviglia start. He could certainly understand why it was that his old manservant would be unable to fathom his deep unrest. Oh, he knew what Flintwick would say: how ever could one harbour such despondency when at his disposal was every last species of life's luxurious pleasures? And Flintwick would be right; he did indeed dine nightly upon the finest of cuisines, and his apparel was indeed selected from the most opulent of fashions. But what good was clothing and feeding oneself in such a manner when, in essence, one led the same, prosaic life as every other on this island? Was it not the same, prosaic life that every other in this *world* endured? Only the appreciation of art, Naught felt, elevated him above the level of an animal. However, as Caviglia had quite rightly observed, even that solace was sorely lacking in recent times, and despite his efforts Naught had found that he was quite incapable of creating such things himself.

Naught had tasted the subtlest of wines, and imbibed the strangest and most ingenious of narcotics from every corner of the globe, and true, they had brought him euphoria, for a while. But each time his head had cleared of honeyed delusion and the wild visions had melted away, he had still been in Cold Ghastia and the world had still been much the same as it had been before the vapours and the powders and the pills had taken hold. Neither had carnal activities assuaged the hunger within him. He had consorted with the costliest, the craftiest and most pliant of whores – but despite the efforts of those beautiful boys and girls, he had discovered at length that the mechanical satisfaction of his body had not the slightest thing to do with the satiation of his soul. And the same was true – to a greater extent or lesser – of every folly and fancy that he had perforce entertained.

Was this to be his life? Was there truly *nothing* more than this?

Naught turned wearily to face Caviglia, who was regarding him coyly from beneath the brim of her metal hat.

~

'Obadiah!' called Edward as he jogged up the steep staircase, raising his voice over the shrieking that the steps still managed to emit despite their shroud of moth-eaten carpet. 'Obadiah, are you here?'

No answer was forthcoming, but the loud thud and accompanying bark of annoyance that resounded down the corridor told Edward that his friend was indeed inside their newly-rented chambers.

Edward arrived, panting, at their doorway and clumped wearily into the drab little foyer. Inside, Obadiah was wrestling with a battered tea chest, which he unhanded with a resigned grunt as Edward entered.

'Have you seen it?' blurted Edward, his eyes shining in their bruise-coloured pits.

'Seen *what*, young Edward?' asked Obadiah, glancing up. He was in his shirtsleeves, and all over dust, although his black slick of hair remained perfectly lacquered in place as though it were a thing of moulded vinyl.

'Why the *structure*, of course! It must be what drew Bellhouse here!'

Obadiah stretched out his fingers and picked at a splinter in his palm. 'Well yes,' he replied, frowning at the little wooden intruder. 'Directly or indirectly I assume that it was. You know his work as well as I. The man was perfectly obsessed with their handiwork.'

With that he turned, gripped the heavy crate once more, and continued in his efforts of heaving it laboriously across the floor. The already threadbare rug appeared to be gleaning as great a measure of enjoyment from this as was the crate; a trail of pulled threads and splinters evidenced its path across the floor.

The Riverside Hotel and Gentlemen's Club had about it a somewhat faded air quite at odds with the cost of letting a room within it. Indeed, were it not for the fact that its dreary interior was almost entirely untroubled by the sun's advances, it might have seemed that daylight had leeched the vibrancy from its dismal and queasily-patterned interiors. As it was, it seemed more likely that if colour there once had been, then it must gradually have expired of *ennui*. In comparison to the brim-full chaos of the Institute back in Hingham, their rented rooms were the very soul of austerity: the only thing to line the walls here was paper that was engaged in descending floorwards in slow curls, not overstuffed racks and specimen cases. And, rather than benches and desks cluttered with instruments and samples in a state of semi-dissection, there was little more to the apartment's furnishing than a few cup-stained occasional tables and a divan that appeared to have relinquished whatever ambition it might once have harboured for the endeavour of supporting of posteriors. This sparseness of furnishing was perhaps just as well, though, for in Edward's absence Obadiah had evidently been quite busy.

What furniture there was had been shoved as far as possible up against the walls to create an open space in the room's centre. Precarious stacks of books and papers already littered the tables, and packing crates stood in huddles all around, their jumbled contents spilling forth. Boxes of phials and powders and bottled liquids littered the floor, along with some mysterious cloth-bound packages sprouting glass tubes and wires, and twine-bound bundles of yet more books. In the far corner loomed an object possessed of proportions not dissimilar to those of a large wardrobe, but whose true identity was concealed by a dustsheet that had been draped over it.

'But have you *seen* the thing?' Edward asked again, irritated by his friend's apparent indifference.

Obadiah gave the stubborn crate one last shove, and straightened up. By way of an answer, he raised his stern eyebrows and jerked his head in the direction of the dirt-caked window, through which a modicum of gravy-coloured light was filtering.

Edward leaned to peer out, and his eyes met instantly with the sight of the distant black spires of the structure jutting into the sky from behind a row of slate roofs. 'Well!' he said, feeling a little foolish. 'I might've known, I suppose!'

'Indeed you might!' laughed Obadiah, leaning back upon the crate. 'For one possessed of such a sharp intellect, you are quite astonishing in your lack of common sense at times!'

It then occurred to Edward that his friend had been even more particular than usual – if such a thing was indeed possible – when deciding upon the guesthouse in which they would be lodging. Much to the private exasperation of their long-suffering driver, Obadiah had outright refused the first three establishments, despite their relatively scenic and seemingly convenient locations. At the time, Edward had assumed that the Doctor was merely ensuring that their usual criteria were fulfilled – for when conducting work such as theirs, several important factors were to be considered. These included a correlation in certain astronomical formations relevant to the site's geographical alignment, and a list of other, less straightforward, variables. It had soon become apparent, however, after several false starts (including the complete unloading and subsequent reloading of the coach outside an establishment entirely lacking in salubriousness), that Obadiah was concerned with something else entirely on this occasion.

Eventually they had parted with what Edward considered to be an overly-large proportion of their University grant in return for the use of three sizeable rooms in this crumbling townhouse, and the hotelier's promise of utter privacy and confidentiality. This, Obadiah had impressed upon the sweating gentleman, was a condition to be held to *no matter what he was to see or hear* over the following weeks from the quarters of his two foreign guests.

It was now apparent to Edward that although he had made no direct mention of it, the proximity of the structure had been the deciding factor in Obadiah's selection of this place.

'Surely you must have had *some* idea that it was here?' continued Obadiah, as though to confirm Edward's theory.

'Now that you mention it, I suppose you're right. That is, you did mention that there was some unusual architecture to be found here. But you didn't mention of the *nature* of the thing! I can hardly believe that you kept this from me! Or that their mark is so blatant here! And yet the town sits so innocently alongside it...'

Obadiah grinned broadly. 'A little surprise for you, my boy!' he said with a conspiratorial wink. 'And I think that *ignorantly* would perhaps be more accurate.'

'*Nesciently*, even,' added Edward, still transfixed by the black edifice that towered beyond the rooftops. 'They do not know what it is that they do not know. Perhaps it's better that way.' He shook his head wonderingly. 'Can it be true that the chap who's holding Bellhouse actually lives *inside* it?'

'Oh yes, Edward, yes indeed he does. His name is Naught.'

'*Naught*, indeed!' laughed Edward. 'Why, he sounds a pleasant chap!'

'In that respect I fear that you may be much mistaken, my boy!' said Obadiah bluntly, cutting short Edward's mirth. 'He is by all accounts a most strange and capricious man. A creature of weird habit, lavish taste and fickle temper, as the errant Bellhouse no doubt discovered. Our time here should prove to be nothing if not interesting! But we are far from home now, my boy, and already we are quite at the mercy of strange forces. This fact did not escape my attention when first I wrote to the envoy – my letter made it quite clear that a political *situation* may well arise in the event of our non-return!'

'Non-return?' cried Edward. 'Well I say! That's a cold comfort if ever I heard one!'

'Edward, you know as well as I that ours shall never be the innoxious of vocations!' boomed the Doctor. 'If you had wished to stay snug, smug, and mollycoddled, you could have remained back at Hingham with those dusty old fools and practised your abstract theories in splendid, pointless isolation!' He captured Edward's gaze in his own smouldering glare. 'But we are the ones who shall truly *apply* our Science. Put aside your fear, my boy! We are on the very brink of the very greatest of discoveries, and few have been as bold or as ingenious in such enterprises as Doctor Carnaby and Mr Stoathill-Warmly, eh?' He laughed good-naturedly and slapped the crate with his palm. 'And an encounter with a faded aristocrat, weird though he may well be, shall be quite the least perilous of our endeavours, no doubt!'

Edward sighed. 'I suppose you're right, as usual, Obadiah. Besides, I was only half serious!' He lowered himself onto the only chair whose seat was not already heaped in piles of equipment. His legs were aching terribly from the morning's lengthy wandering, and now, as he relaxed, he felt the old tiredness creeping back into his bones. He rubbed his eyes. 'D'you truly think we'll find him there?'

Obadiah grinned once more. 'Oh, almost certainly,' he said. 'I'm sure he won't have strayed *too* far.'

'So, how are we to,' - Edward twirled a finger in the air - '*invite ourselves* in? Did you speak to that Dirth man?'

'Naturally! I had the displeasure of visiting his offices this morning. He will do as he says, if he knows what's good for him.'

'And will this Naught allow us to speak with Bellhouse, d'you think?' Edward asked, a little wearily. 'It seems to me that if he refuses to let us see him then there is not a great deal to be done. I fear that our trip will have been a wasted one.'

'Come, now!' chided the Doctor. 'Do you *really* believe that this little excursion will constitute a waste of our time? We have been in Cold Ghastia for less than one day and already you have witnessed something quite unique!' He nodded once more towards the open window. 'Oh, there is much we can learn here, mark my words!'

FOUR
Altitude & Sickness

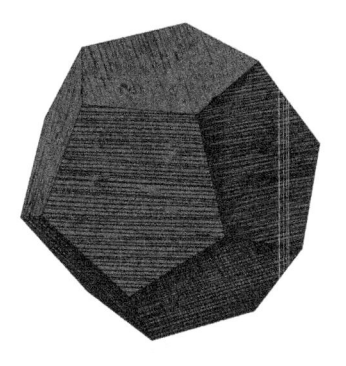

The cab deposited Obadiah and Edward at the end of the precipitous mountain road before an imposing pair of wrought-iron gates. A wind carrying the scent of damp pine drove gusts of drizzle into the faces of the pair as they exchanged a glance with eyebrows raised; those gates were queer things indeed. The bizarre agglomeration of metalwork must have constituted a lifetime's labour for a team of gifted yet quite obviously demented smiths. It was as though some vast, iron spider had crawled between the gateposts spurting strands and gobbets of molten metal behind it, thus ensnaring a cavorting menagerie of mythic Ghastian beasts within its pitch-black web. Wings, beaks, limbs and horns all protruded from within a mesh of crazily twining strands. At either side of the monstrous works of iron, the portal was guarded by ancient pines of spectacular stature, in whose gargantuan trunks might feasibly have been carved out a pair of generously-proportioned houses. The ivy-shrouded wall which the gates served to breach was built of massive slabs of the cloud-hued stone of the mountain, and it bristled with cruel spikes that drooled rusty trails down its surface. Upon each of the gateposts squatted a lichen-encrusted statue which might in some earlier, less weatherworn age, have depicted the offspring of the union of sloth and toad.

The cab rattled off and left the arcanologists staring up at the looming expanse of the House beyond those unlikely gates. Never, even following their harrowing expedition to the shores of Cold Ghastia, had Edward felt so elated to feel solid ground beneath his feet. It was utterly baffling, he thought, that the coachman should seem quite so keen to rejoin that twisting, perilous track, or indeed that his horses could be so easily induced to do the same. For a moment, thoughts of their own return journey found him pondering the practicality of harnessing a team of the huge and shaggy goats that tenanted the mountainside. The straggling herds that he had espied during the rare moments in which he had peeped through the window of the cab had hopped across yawning chasms with every appearance of carefree abandon, and ambled up near-vertical faces of rock as though it were nothing more than an afternoon stroll. One of the snaggle-bearded chaps had wandered onto the drive where they stood, and was gazing at the pair blankly with its weird keyhole eyes whilst its jaw worked away at a mouthful of decorative shrub. The foliate lion-thing upon whose hind leg the matted fellow was lunching looked down in apparent disdain at this reversal of fortunes. This mountain was altogether a place for goats, thought Edward, not one for civilised people.

The journey to the top of the mountain had been a perfectly frightful one, as far he was concerned, and he had been dreading it ever since the arrival of the letter.

He had been awoken by the loud rapping that announced its arrival some three days beforehand and, sitting bolt upright, had realised that he had fallen asleep at his desk, again. Wiping away a string of drool from his cheek, he had opened the door to find a boy hovering in the hallway. He was dressed in funny little suit that resembled that of the Stoancastlian bellhop with its epaulettes and rows of winking brass buttons, although rather than the fetching maroon invariably favoured by the capital's village-sized establishments it was the drab blue of an inclement sky. This, it transpired, was House uniform. After giving the child the smallest of the Ghastian coins in his pocket, he had returned once more to his desk, and examined the envelope. His and Obadiah's names were written in a crabbed, archaic scrawl on the front of it, and rather quaintly it was sealed with a large blob of red sealing wax. The wax was stamped with an elaborate coat of arms which, so far as Edward was able to discern, was comprised of stylised pine trees and something that might have been a fish. He had broken open the seal immediately, and pulled out the letter.

Dear Dr. Carnaby and Mr. Stoathill Warmly, it read in the same spidery script, *may I take this opportunity to welcome you to Cold Ghastia and to the city of Iremouth. I trust that your stay in our city has thus far been a pleasant one.*

There were several more lines of formal pleasantries, which Edward had scanned without interest, then:

It has been brought to my attention that you are under the impression that a gentleman by the name of Bellhouse is in residence here at the House of Naught.

I regret to inform you that in this matter you are unfortunately mistaken; Bellhouse and his assistant did indeed take advantage of Lord Naught's hospitality for a short while, but this visit transpired some two decades ago.

Lord Naught nevertheless extends his kind invitation to you, and asks that you may pay visit to the House of Naught at your earliest convenience. As a generous patron of the Sciences he is, as ever, keen to learn of any developments in such matters, especially from representatives of such an esteemed academy as the Imperator's University of Hingham.

It was signed in the name of Nicholas Flintwick.

Edward had stifled a yawn and nodded to himself: this was exactly what they required. Never mind this Flintwick's obfuscation over the matter of Bellhouse – it was no more than what was to be expected, given the circumstances. Still, invitation or no, there was much to be done before this meeting and whatever fruits it might bear would be of any great benefit to them. Edward had been collating data for the best part of three weeks, but the picture that he had assembled was by no means complete. So much rested on accurate measurement and calculation, the precise calibration of their devices, and the careful plotting of their designs.

Edward's efforts, though, had for some time been somewhat hampered.

Edward knew exactly where the root of the problem lay. Simply put, he was tired. This fatigue, though, was something far beyond everyday weariness. The wincing pains and nagging aches inflicted upon him by their long days of travel should surely have dissipated by now, and whilst the work that they had undertaken in Iremouth had been a strain on his mental faculties, he was well used to studying into the small hours, poring nightly over worm-riddled books somewhere within in the University's winding, labyrinthine archives. A dearth of slumber had posed no great problem to him in the past.

This is where the unfathomable paradox lay. Edward was not suffering from a lack of sleep.

Each night over the recent months, Edward would drag himself wearily into his bed as usual. Each night he would find that as soon as his eyelids met he would descend almost instantaneously into a black and dreamless chasm – from which, invariably, he would not return until the light of dawn sent prying fingers through the chinks in his curtains. But when awaken he did, he felt not in the slightest bit rested. In no way did he feel as though he had passed the hours of the night in a deep and recuperative slumber – he felt drained and bruised and exhausted, just as he had done when he had crawled beneath the sheets the night before.

Edward's once-bright eyes now peered, slitted and red-rimmed, from the depths of sunken, black craters ringed about with creases. His perennially white face was drawn and hollow of cheek, and his hair, which even under normal circumstances could not by any means be induced out of its state of dishevelment, was lank and seemed at all times to contain a dusting of biscuit-crumbs.

It had been around the time of the beginnings of Edward's hypersomnia that his sudden, irrational fear of the dark had manifested itself. He had never been prone to such fads before the onset of the malady, but now the very existence of darkness induced in him an anxiety of a truly phobic quality. He had begun to refuse to extinguish his lamp at night until he had conducted a candle-lit surveillance of every last corner of his chambers – what he expected to find, he was ever unsure. At times he would even sleep with the dim, orange glow of a low-burning lamp at his bedside, as might a child afeared of the gooneymen's black embrace. Edward knew that Obadiah was cognisant of the changes in him; the Doctor's scorn at his associate's unkempt appearance and jittery, agitated manner when faced with even the most mundane of situations following nightfall was quite obvious.

Edward had visited his physician, who had been visibly shocked at the sudden decline in his health, but the man had been quite at a loss to match the symptoms to any ailment in his experience. He had prescribed liberal doses of a health tonic rich in invigorating coca, but Edward had already imbibed every stimulant of nerve, gland and brain that could be procured from pharmacies and from back alleys – and all to no avail. And besides, might one reasonably expect to fight fire with fire?

Yet it was not the fear or the fatigue that concerned Edward most. It was the dreamless quality of his slumber.

Edward was a dreamer. Or rather, he had been one. It had ever been his way; even from infancy, Edward's bed had been a stable, of sorts, a place from which no sooner would he pull about him his riding cloak of eiderdown than his mind would bolt for destinations unknown and unimagined. And once the time of infancy had passed, there had come a time in which Edward had depended upon this freedom, had depended upon this *sanctuary* – and in those blessed twin realms that lay between the pages of books and behind the shutters of his eyelids, he had sought it and he had found it, and he had treasured it.

And yet, Edward's had not always been pleasant dreams. The nights when he drifted queasily for seeming eternities over grey and undulating moonscapes where below him things crawled and screamed were as common as those during which he walked shining, ancient paths through lands of wonder and æthereal beauty. Yet still to dream even such dreams was as dear to him as it was to hold in his hands the pages wherein another's dreams were inscribed, for the relentless pounding of Father's fists had beaten out of him all of those hopeful things which the waking hold dear, and refer to by that absurd misnomer, 'dreams'. Father liked neither Edward's books nor the dreams of his days or of his nights. It was those books that filled his head with bilge and fancy, Father said, and perhaps he had even been correct, to a degree. But Edward knew now that there were other things besides books that were capable of disordering a man's brain.

He knew now of the Flesh of the Spirits.

Edward had never set out to consume the Flesh. No, the thing that Edward had sought had been the *dote*. Ah the *dote*, the storied *dote*! *Dote*, the enigma, the substance of miracles, the soul-stuff whose identity the world had forgotten! Without it, the project was less than nothing. Without it, there would be no conversation with Bellhouse; without it, it would be quite impossible for the interview which they had sought so long and for which they had travelled so far to even begin. Indeed, without it they would not have sought out that fellow to begin with. But finding the *dote* had borne a cost of its own, and that cost had been the toll of the Flesh.

But then, perhaps it had been the hours spent squinting in guttering candlelight, bent over a reading desk like some penitent monk that had seen to his back and his eyes? His ink-blackened hands with their arthritic cracking and the fleshy lump upon his pen-rubbed forefinger attested to the sheaves of notes that the he had generated in the quest for the *dote*. Enough material to concoct his own thesis on the sacramental practices of pagan religious groups, undoubtedly – and neither had the *dote* been the first he had sought. The Ciall held that distinction. But Edward sought the Ciall no longer, and in the quest for the *dote* he could not fail as he had done with that other mythic stuff.

And regardless, Edward had not in truth put stock in this, an idle thought. For even those nights spent crouched in freezing mausolea and draughty museums, mouldering libraries and echoing vestries, poring over papyri and choking on rot-rank dust from decaying tomes could not have done this. Even the days spent stumbling up hills to collapse in the shadow of rune-graven megaliths, or tramping down trails into sucking bogs whose stinking depths wished to claim his boots for their own could not have broken his constitution so, nor for that matter could they have stolen away his dreams. Still, how many forest paths had Edward trudged, through how many grasping hedgerows had he battled, how many thorns had he pried from the flesh of his palms as the ravens cawed and circled above him, mocking him and his fool's errand in their croaking voices?

Could a man fill his head with too much knowledge? Were the ancient tongues in which Edward had granted himself fluency, were the endless archives of scripture and folklore that he had crammed into his memory, to blame for filling the final recesses of the library within his skull, leaving no space for the shelving of new volumes of dream? Of course, they were not. That most dubious of honours belonged to the Flesh of the Spirits. And besides, the brain, as Edward had argued with the neuroanatomists, had never been the manufactory of *his* dreams. Perhaps, *perhaps*, there were some whose nocturnal visions were constituted of regurgitated morsels of their recollections in some turgid soup of sexual metaphor as those fashionable fools, the alienists, were so fond of claiming in their papers *du jour*. But not Edward's dreams. No, Edward's dreams came from somewhere else. Somewhere *Beyond.*

And besides, how else might he have found the *dote*? How else was a man to seek out a substance so long neglected, so long vanished from the memory of the common man? Of course, the Mission had seen to the obliteration of Grand Uria's own pagan knowledge alongside that of the Lesser World. Indeed, that he had managed to find the hag at all had been nothing short of miraculous – and until the day that he had crossed the threshold of that tumbledown crofter's cottage on the moor, he would hardly have believed that a living soul could truly have been possessed of that knowing. And yet he had dared to hope. Theirs were the two remaining strands of a flimsy skein that tethered past knowledge to future: his, the shell of an idea; hers, the knowing itself. She, that tiny, wizened thing in the cottage; she, avatar of ancient cunning, was all that had kept the quest, and Edward, alive.

How terribly weary had he grown before that day? How many times had stinking, gluey berries crusted his fingers with their slime, how many bundles of stinging weeds and toadstools and muddy roots had he emptied from his pouches onto that muck-bespattered bench of his? Until that day, those sodden little bags had contained the last vestiges of hope. And all because it had to be there, *somewhere.* Within crumbling pages or fading into silence within the skulls of the keepers of folklore, or in the papers that the anthropologists had filed before the abject destruction of the very cultures that they documented, it was there. These were the last, dying echoes of the elder ways. And now that the last thread of the skein that tethered man to that knowing had snapped, it was truly no more. Well, besides that precious hoard within the canister in the locked chest beneath his bed, it was no more. He chuckled dryly to himself as he remembered: before that meeting upon the moor, how many nights had he spent stooped over simmering cauldrons as they exhaled their noxious breath into his face and burned his eyes with their foulness? How many times had he watched, his hands balled into ivory-knuckled fists, as oily juices drip-drip-dripped through the still and into the waiting beaker?

Ah, and who else but Edward would have been fool enough to ingest those candidate substances, those pretenders to the *dote*'s identity? What man in his right mind would cram so eagerly into his mouth, his nose, his lungs, his very veins, such a gross panoply of obscure narcotics? But then, Edward had not been a man in his right mind – neither by his own standards nor by any other's – and despite being possessed of a constitution fit to inspire jealousy in the hardiest of oxen, Doctor Carnaby had certainly not been forthcoming in volunteering his own services. Edward had been forced to assume the mantle of his very own laboratory rodent.

In the early days, purely ineffectual had been almost the most desirable outcome for which to hope: *all* was the desire, but *nothing* was its close second. To strike a line through another potion on the dwindling list without belching gouts of foam or simultaneously evacuating both stomach and bowels with a violence and propulsiveness that seemed to increase with each new pair of britches had seemed an almost immeasurable boon. The last of these fæcal incidents had left him bedridden for a fortnight and more, and had very nearly proved to be the limit. Obadiah had been forced to perform vital labour on the machine without Edward's assistance during those weeks, a fact that had upset the Doctor to such a profound degree that he had even spoken of severing Edward's tenure. Would that he had taken up that offer! Ah, for to soil one's britches in place of one's bedpan, that was a sweet thing indeed when compared to the death of one's very dreams. But this was a thing that he had not known before he had devoured the Flesh of the Spirits.

Yes, it was the Flesh that had done it; he knew it now, beyond doubt. Why had he believed that nasty, slippery priest of the Abatirim, that wheedling, swindling Interlocutor who had assured him in such earnest tones that the fungus that blistered the abbey's cellar walls was the sacrament that he sought? His furtive manner, the exorbitant sum of money that he had demanded – nay, extorted! – surely these should have been warning enough that the man's crimes were likely to exceed the breaching of the edicts of Father Church. It was desperation that had clouded Edward's mind – and yet, it was a desperation that had shrivelled into nothingness at the lick of the flames of searing need that had consumed his innards ever since he had feasted upon that awful Flesh.

Yes, he had gobbled the stuff with the heedless greed of a child turned loose in a chocolate shop, one who has not yet learned that his forbidden treats will up-end his belly and make his face turn green and waxy as unripened gooseberries. Except instead of sugary smears of fruit crèmes, it was the fungal gravy of the leathery, desiccated things steeped in the best port to be found in Obadiah's cabinet that had stained Edward's gluttonous face. Marinating those scabrous chunks in costly fortified wine had been a necessity rather than a nicety: they were noisome things indeed, and even the unctuous beverage could not mask their overpowering taste, which was ancient earth and indescribable putrescence in equal measure.

And chewing was vital, the Interlocutor had said; they were to be masticated until they were the consistency of gruel. So he had knocked back that reeking draft, and he had chewed, and he had gagged, and retching he had swallowed the gritty paste all down, and the guinea's worth of port had been the very least of the prices paid that night. And still, even now as then, was it yet too much to hope that that most precarious of gambles might indeed pay off?

What fragmentary visions remained with him of that night of the Flesh, a night drenched in freezing perspiration and wracked by bodily tremors, were dominated by the face of that damnable Interlocutor, gazing out at him from beyond ghostly vistas of impossible, boiling architecture like the ceilings of oriental temples all built of living crystal. Even in that delirium, he had managed to think: how strange, that the vision-priest did not inhabit his own, dreary chamber, the thresh-strewn monastic cell in which their deal had been struck. What significance these shades of architecture sacred to *other* holy men? Still, confounding, infuriating, though these apparitions may have been, Edward held their memory dear, for they had been the very last that he had perceived with the eye of his mind. Since that night, his had been visions only of the mortal flesh, and of mortal eyes.

Of course, when the dream-bereft Edward had stormed back into the abbey, he had found the cell deserted; the execrable little man had gone – traceless, and never to be seen again. Had he not been a stranger, an individual to whom the arcanologist had been brought independently by means of his esoteric delving, then Edward might have suspected a deliberate act of sabotage. But as it was, the Interlocutor (if Interlocutor he had been) was merely a greedy little shit with a cellar full of fungus to sell to a wan young academic with a purse that bulged with University coin. He could have known nothing of the project.

Edward had dared not partake of the Flesh again – who knew what other fell work it might wreak upon him, what other faculty it might steal away? And so, when many months of searching later the hag's birdlike claw had pressed into his hand the little sack that had contained the *dote*, the true *dote*, it had taken all of Edward's failing strength not to fall to his knees in the muck of the cottage floor.

He had known, then and there – *known* that it was right. Some terrible calibration of the Kosmos had occurred then; something vast and dark had fallen into place with an almost audible *click* that had twanged his very being as though it were the bass string of some sonorous instrument. He had known before even he had lit up the pipe and sucked back the first, choking lungful that the quest – this part of it, at least – was at an end. There had come at once the whine, the crinkle, the assault of pure geometry. There had been the hope – however faint – that he would be able to navigate the trance unaided. But without the guidance of the Shapes it had been brief, and directionless: little more than a delirious vision. He might, he supposed, have taken more – but without the Shapes, what would have been the use? Without them, the *dote* was all but useless – worse, it was perilous in ways disturbing to consider. But the *dote* had never been for him, not truly. It was those silent volunteers of theirs for whom the *dote* had been intended – and with its aid, they had indeed spoken again. And now, at last – at long last – might come the machine. Then would come the Shapes.

Edward closed his eyes, sucked in a shuddering breath, and attempted to steady himself upon his feet, blinking himself back into alertness, and the present.

Observing the greenish tinge in his associate's face, Obadiah gave one of his customary snorts, yanked the collar of his greatcoat up around his ears, and marched off in the direction of the one of the massive trees, his boots crunching through the gravel of the drive. It took Edward a bemused moment to realise that his fancy had, in fact, been fact - incredibly, the ancient guardian trees before them had been fashioned into gatehouses. As Obadiah set about giving the bell-pull a piece of his mind, Edward wandered the few steps to the edge of the drive, where a somewhat rickety wooden rail formed a border between the expanse of wheel-rutted gravel and the steep, rocky slope beyond it.

He gazed out over the city that lay sprawled across the hillside far below; now, more than ever, it resembled nothing so much as a model of itself: a toy city. It was as though, thought Edward, this was how the House preferred to perceive it. The sky above the whole of Iremouth - indeed above the whole of Cold Ghastia, for all but the most distant shore of the island could be seen from here - was grey as rain-wet slate, and felt as though it might crush the land beneath its sodden weight. Indeed, Edward did not think that he had ever seen quite such a vast tract of land entirely shrouded in rainclouds. He wondered what had become of the pleasant spring weather that had greeted their arrival.

A shout from Obadiah brought Edward jogging over to where the Doctor stood. Obadiah had produced Flintwick's letter and brandished it in the face of the uniformed fellow in the little window of the gatehouse. The gatekeeper bobbed out of view for a moment before reappearing on the other side of the gate which barred the mouth of the tunnel hewn through the trunk. He removed the weighty-looking chain and let them pass, and then the gate clanged shut behind them.

Edward wondered if the man's wordless surliness was anything to do with the little fez he was made to wear.

Inside the dripping tree-tunnel, which was quite wide enough for a pony and trap, it was almost entirely dark; the gatekeeper had returned to his nook without deigning to light the lamps, and had already buried his face in a magazine. The air in the passageway was heavy with the smell of earth and sap, and more than a hint of fungal decay. Edward was pleased about neither the darkness nor the mushroomy stench, and hurried along with his eyes fixed on the patch of cloudy grey that indicated sky on the other side. It was like walking through arboreal time, he mused: centuries passed beneath his every hasty footstep.

Another driveway, lengthy and lined with smaller cousins of the sentinel firs, awaited them on the other side. As they stamped up the path, with the roar of the Irem seemingly all around them, Edward found his eyes drawn again to the great House. Of course, it filled the sky ahead of them in an almost impossible fashion, but more than this, it was as though it attracted his senses with some peculiar species of magnetism. It was not altogether a comfortable thing. More peculiar still was how *different* the House appeared at close range. In fact, had logic not dictated that the two were the same, he might have fancied it a different structure entirely to the castle on the crag upon whose towers he had gazed these last few weeks from the window of his apartment. Now that he thought of it, no two of his sketches of the thing were quite alike.

Yet more peculiar than even this uncanny effect of perspective was that the House of Naught was evidently not a 'house' by the edicts of any orthodox school of architecture. Whilst from a distance one ignorant to its true nature might reasonably have supposed it to be a work of masonry, observation at close range revealed that it was in fact but one megalithic mass. Incredibly, it appeared to be carved from a single, gigantic block. No, not carved, thought Edward as his eyes slipped over its surfaces, feeling almost that his vision had been oiled: moulded, as though it had once been molten.

But even moulded did not quite convey the queerness of it. In fact, the dully gleaming black curves of the thing – here hypnotically graceful where a gallery with columns like pulled toffee emerged from a sweeping, swan's-neck tower, there nauseatingly tumescent where an incomprehensible wart-like bulge warped the surface of one of its walls – looked almost to have been somehow extruded. The whole assembly, thought Edward, might have been squirted out of the mountaintop as though the whole of that massive pinnacle of rock were a pâtissier's icing bag.

Turning to take in the vista of the grounds, Edward was able to see that the surrounding lawns swept up to meet the structure's base with no apparent delineation between the two at all. The fact that the mountain's stone was greyer than gravestones and looked as though a mason could not polish it if the lives of his extended family depended upon it, was just another oddness to add to this melange. Altogether, it put Edward in mind now, more than anything, of a sort of giant anthill that he had seen illustrated in a gazetteer concerning Verdra's more arid regions. The two shared the same quality of graceful yet unhuman beauty: a dream realised by a mindless sculptor.

Oh, he knew something of their work, of course, but the jumble of contradictory metaphors that assailed Edward's mind in its presence was testament to the fact no mere words could have prepared him for its staggering strangeness.

A long, damp walk along the drive, through landscaped gardens, past ornamental ponds, statues, and the occasional lamp post glowing with effervescent haze in the murk and misty rain, brought them to a paved courtyard that lay directly in the shadow of the House. Its centrepiece was a fountain quite as absurdly ornate as the gate had been. Twin flights of steps arced up from either side of the gushing monument to meet before a massive oaken door; as they approached, Edward saw that despite the admittedly cunning efforts of the stairways' architects to disguise the fact, the doorway that they served to access was oddly off-centre. Neither was the gaping arch of the entranceway itself, a thing ridged and curved as though smeared by the very Gods' butter knife, of anything approaching regular proportions.

Obadiah grasped the knocker and applied it vigorously to the door then, brushing jewels of drizzle from his greatcoat, turned to face Edward.

'*Remember*,' he warned from behind his upturned collar, 'you must not mention Bellhouse until I have broached the subject. I am far better equipped to turn this situation to our advantage.'

For an answer, Edward rolled his eyes.

'Also, Edward, remember that we are to divulge *the absolute minimum* of information regarding our work. And *nothing* of them. For all that this Naught may believe that he is interested in our Science, I doubt that he will be at all capable of comprehending the magnitude of what we intend to achieve. To him it will all probably amount to nothing more than an – ' he waved his hand in a circle, '*amusing diversion* – a whimsical jape about which to brag over dinner. And it will be best for us, *and* for him, if this is *all* he perceives it to be.'

'Yes, we have been over this, Obadiah,' sighed Edward. 'I've no intention of jeopardising the project.'

Just then, the door before them was yanked open. A stern-looking, white-haired man who resembled an aged and angry seagull stood within. He was exceptionally prim – the parting of his hair looked as though it had been achieved with the assistance of some manner of geometrical instrument – but the cut of his suit was woefully outdated. Without making any attempt to disguise his actions, he looked them both up and down with a thoroughness verging on the offensive.

'You are the men from Hingham, I suppose?' he shot, without the slightest hint of courtesy or warmth in his voice. His eyes, Edward saw, were hard like Obadiah's, but cold and sharp as midwinter icicles, not lit by the fire that animated the Doctor's.

'We are,' replied Obadiah, still whisking raindrops from his coat. 'I am Doctor Carnaby, and this is my associate Mr Stoathill-Warmly. Am I to assume that you are Nicholas Flintwick?'

'Indeed,' sneered Flintwick. 'Though I had thought that men such as yourselves are ill-advised to trade in such currency.'

Obadiah frowned, and began to open his mouth, but Flintwick held up his hand. '*Assumptions*,' he spat. 'Men of *Science*, Doctor Carnaby, should never *assume*.'

And without a further word, he turned upon his heel, beckoning over his shoulder for them to step inside.

FIVE
An Audience with Lord Naught,
or The Undesirable Host

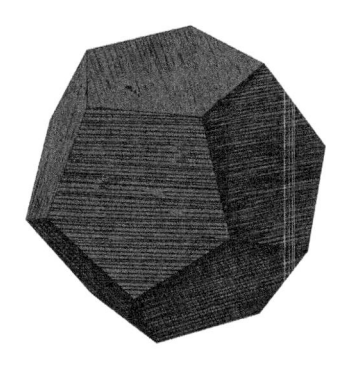

Inside the House, it was only scarcely less gloomy than its rain-lashed exterior, albeit a good deal drier. Lamps burned at intervals down the windowless entrance hall along which they were led by Flintwick's rapidly retreating back, but rather than flooding the place with light, their effect was to emphasise the stagnant darkness pooling in the hollows where their glow did not reach. With such darksome lakelets merging often into seas that lapped distressingly at the peripheries of his vision, Edward found that he was forced to distract himself by engaging in a survey of the hall's decor.

The walls were hung with a strangely eclectic variety of fixtures. Here and there were pedestals bearing what looked to be hunting trophies (or at least, parts of animals), and unusual sculptures of modern design, but gilt-framed oil paintings of conspicuous antiquity predominated. Edward found his gaze drawn to these latter works – though his inclination was born more of his loathing of crass modern art (especially *this* abstract nonsense) than any particular appreciation of painterly technique. The Lords and Ladies of Iremouth's past glared disdainfully back at him from behind their veils of cracked glaze; they were a mirthless and haughty-looking lot, rendered in the pompous yet dismal fashion invariably favoured by aristocracy. Edward shook his head. Æsthetic counterparts of these works graced the walls of his own family home.

The oily members of the Cold Ghastian elite, however, seemed possessed of a quality that was not shared by those of Fivesides Grange. It was not evident in every painting – indeed, the Naughts occupying the foyer had been supernally handsome beasts – but as they made their way along the hall Edward noticed something decidedly *odd* in the set of a face every now and then. Increasingly he felt that there was something queer lurking behind those conceited masks, a disconcerting trait that he found himself quite at a loss to identify.

It might have been something in the proportions of a face, three-chinned yet pinched, the glittering caviar eyes offset. Or in the unusual constitution of a physique whose lumpen contours were not-quite-concealed by the ruffles of artfully-tailored attire. Perhaps it was in the unhealthy tone of their skin. How could one look at once as though one needed *more* and *less* sun?

However, Edward reminded himself, these were merely paintings and not living people; it was entirely possible that the weird quality he detected was nothing but an idiosyncrasy of Iremouth's portrait painters. It was hardly likely they'd trained under the masters in the fine schools of Julais, after all. And well, even *those* fellows were painting like jungle savages these days, as Obadiah was so fond of saying. He found that he had been lagging behind somewhat, and quickened his pace to close the gap between himself and the striding Doctor. The hall was a good deal lengthier than it had first appeared from the doorway.

Flintwick, who had not once looked back or even uttered a further word since their meeting, continued to lead them deeper into the House. They passed several doors of inexplicably varying sizes, all of them closed but some leaking sounds of music and laughter, before he stopped abruptly and yanked one of them open. He disappeared into the room, closing the door behind him. A moment later a pair of young people, each wearing nothing more than lipstick smears, a stained silk bathrobe and a hollow-eyed look, emerged from the door and made off at a staggering run. As they disappeared from sight, a seemingly further-disgruntled Flintwick peered around the doorframe and gestured for the arcanologists to enter.

To their surprise, the pair stepped into an inviting drawing-room. The windowless walls were cosily oak-panelled, and at the room's far end a fire popped and crackled merrily in the hearth. At first Edward thought that the room was untenanted, but then a movement caught his eye and he saw that somebody was reclining in a high-backed leather wing chair at the fireside. A hand, from whose long fingers dangled an embroidered hand-kerchief, rested upon its arm.

'Gentlemen!' exclaimed a croaking and slightly delirious-sounding voice from the chair. 'Welcome to the House of Naught!'

Then, with a dainty flourish of the hand-kerchief, the chair's occupant stood up.

'*Ugh!*' cried Edward, flinching, then immediately clapped his hand over his mouth. 'What *is* it?' he whispered sideways to Obadiah from behind his fingers as the figure stumbled towards them.

Obadiah, exhibiting a good deal more composure than his companion, spoke under his breath. '*That,*' he said, endeavouring not to move his lips – though the slight jigging of his moustache could not be concealed – '*is Lord Naught.*'

Lord Naught tottered across the room, his gait unlikely and his bony arms spread wide like a scarecrow's to welcome his guests. He had on a rather ostentatious smoking jacket, which mercifully was belted – for what he was *not* wearing was any manner of trousers.

Edward had since removed his hand from his mouth, but it still hung slackly open and his jaw was dropping lower by the moment as though amazement had increased its weight tenfold. Realising this, he clamped it closed immediately, hoping that his eyes would not betray the same degree of horrified amazement.

It was simply the most hideous thing that he had ever seen. Even the most bizarre of the unwholesome portraits could not have prepared him for the awful deformity of Lord Naught. The sickly essence of that weird aristocracy seemed to be distilled and amplified in the figure he saw before him – but this time there could be no recourse to artistic convention to explain it away. Even through the padding of the smoking jacket it was obvious that he was freakishly, skeletally thin, although its fabric bulged queasily in several unexpected places. The naked, hairless legs that protruded from it were bowed as though by rickets. It was Lord Naught's face, though, that instantly filled Edward with uncontrollable loathing. It bore only the most tenuous relation to the human visage – in the midst of a countenance like a mouldering walnut, his eyes were pure black and sticky-looking like the eggs of some heroically-proportioned moth, and his mouth was a red, toothy gash. What workings moved *beneath* the surface of that face, Edward could not even begin to guess.

Naught lurched across the carpet with a withered hand held out to Obadiah. 'Hello, hello!' he cooed, somewhat dreamily. 'I have been so *excited* since I heard that you were here! I *must* meet them, I said to Flintwick, I simply *must!* And now here you are, here you are!'

Naught dropped Obadiah's hand, which he had been waggling excitedly as he spoke. Obadiah's manner disclosed no distaste, but it was evident that he had not exerted anything approaching his usual force in the handshake. Edward reluctantly followed suit, clasping hands with Naught and exchanging greetings. The thing smelled strongly of a combination of expensive perfume and some other familiar substance – pungently chymical, though not wholly unpleasant.

At their host's suggestion they seated themselves in the chairs by the hearth, and Naught asked Flintwick to pour them each a glass of sherry from a cut crystal decanter that glittered in the firelight. This the manservant did, before retreating to the other end of the room to conspicuously rustle a stack of papers. Naught sat forward in his seat, steepling his fingers before the lipstick-blotched leech-slit of his mouth.

'So,' he began in a wavering voice, 'now that you are here you must tell me all about yourselves – and your work, of course! I find such things so *fascinating*, you know! Do tell, do tell!' He leaned further forward in his chair, tip-tapping his painted fingertips together and glancing expectantly from Obadiah to Edward and back again.

Edward, as they had earlier agreed, allowed Obadiah to speak:

'But of course, Lord Naught,' said the Doctor with a small incline of the head. 'We have heard that your interest in Modern Science is quite an avid one.'

'Oh, *yes!'* enthused Naught, making jittery little claps.

'Oh, it excites me so to think of the awesome secrets that our Kosmos holds! There is little, don't you think, that is possessed of that true quality of delicious mystery these days?' He smacked his lips as though savouring mystery itself.

'A sound opinion, Lord Naught,' agreed Obadiah as he sipped the remarkably good sherry. 'And one that I think you'll find we share. Indeed, I have heard it proclaimed that Science is shrinking the world at the exact rate that our understanding of it grows, leaving no room for mysteries to hide.'

At this, Naught jumped to his feet. 'Yes!' he cried, as Edward and Obadiah averted their eyes from his un-trousered half. 'It is as though the shining light of Science banishes the shadows of ignorance!' Naught's awful face glowed at what he supposed to be the ingenuity of his own wordplay.

Edward, still keeping his silence, mentally rolled his eyes at the triteness of the analogy. He noted that Naught, too, looked rather dismayed – not by his own banality, Edward sensed, but rather by the import of the words he had voiced. Naught lowered himself back into his seat and, mercifully, crossed his legs.

Obadiah narrowed his eyes and raised a finger to invite Naught's attention. 'But what if I were to tell you, Lord Naught, that Mr Stoathill-Warmly and I believe the very opposite to be true? And that we conduct our Science accordingly?'

Naught merely pursed his lips in a quizzical fashion.

Obadiah raised the finger a little higher and, like a dog's, Naught's eyes followed it. 'To explore the areas upon which the light of Science chooses *not* to shine is our trade,' the Doctor declared, 'to investigate the uninvestigated and to explain the inexplicable!'

'Ah!' breathed Naught, seeming to brighten a little.

He twirled the hand-kerchief. 'Tell me more!'

'Well,' said Obadiah, settling back in his chair and crossing his arms almost as though proposing a challenge, 'it is our belief that to propel Science into the *future*, we must be mindful of the *past*, must remember that which Science has counselled us to forget – to disregard as *un*scientific.'

Blinking, Naught took a moment to digest this information. 'Please expand, Doctor Carnaby. I... am not entirely sure that I understand you. Do you mean to say that you purposely employ *outdated* methods? Methods that your fellows have discounted?'

Obadiah gave a measured shake of his head. '*Methods*, no. We are rigorous fellows, and we recognise the primacy of the Scientific Method. But *subject matter* – ah, now that is something else. You see, Mr Stoathill-Warmly and I are willing to admit to a thing that many who have the audacity to call themselves *Scientists* dare not.'

'And what, pray tell, is that?'

'*Ideology*, Lord Naught. We admit that Science is riddled with it! Riddled!'

Naught flinched, his eyes widening. 'Heavens! Surely not! A fact is a fact, is it not? That's Science's very game, no?'

'Oh, you may be sure of it, sir!' agreed Obadiah. 'A fact is a fact alright, and an inch is an inch.' He cocked his head and pointed one of his extraordinarily articulate eyebrows in Naught's direction. 'But one had better be careful where one waves one's measure, if you follow.'

'I see,' said Naught, although now he was blinking copiously, and his wormish lower lip had begun to protrude as might a flummoxed child's.

'I believe you *do* see, Lord Naught,' nodded Obadiah. 'I believe that you are a perceptive man indeed!'

Naught's lacquered nails tinkled on his sherry glass. 'Go on.'

'We must ask ourselves, Lord Naught, why we are told to simply *ignore* those things that cannot neatly be accommodated by existing Science. *Why* we are told that such things are nonsense.'

'*Things*? What manner of *things*?'

A small smile lifted the corners of Obadiah's moustache. Slowly, he leaned forward until his face was but a hand's breadth from Naught's. 'I am referring, in a word,' he said, '*to the super-natural.*'

For a moment Naught looked sidelong at the Doctor, as though trying to gauge whether or not his guest were putting him on. Then, he slapped his thigh and threw back his head. '*Spooky ghosties* and... and *gooneymen*, and *magick spells*, and suchlike, Doctor Carnaby?' he cried between the gurgles and screeches that appeared to serve him in place of a laugh. 'Ha! Oh, I am singularly fond of such fancies, but I had not considered them to be the stuff of *scientific* study! Oh, no indeed!' With this he made a protracted honking noise, at which the muscles in Edward's stomach tightened involuntarily.

Obadiah's next words sounded very much like an order. '*You will forgive me*, Lord Naught, if I say that your response is ill-informed. Though sadly it is far from uncommon. Is *magick* not merely a term applied by the ignorant to that which they are incapable of understanding?' The Doctor was becoming more and more animated by the moment, and he had leapt up from his seat, swinging and stabbing his finger in accompaniment to his words as though it were a rapier with which he sought to transfix Naught's intellect. 'But nothing is outside – nothing is *beyond* – the laws of Science, d'you see? Ignorance is a *choice*, Lord Naught. And we have *chosen* knowledge. Need I remind you that our ancestors, both here in the Empire and in the Lesser World, believed very much in the super-natural? That their knowledge of it was so great as to utterly eclipse our own?'

Naught's queer chuckles were subsiding. 'But we have grown out of such things, Doctor Carnaby,' he said. 'More's the pity. Why, we are *enlightened!*'

At this, Obadiah wheeled on their host. 'We have *forgotten*, Lord Naught. Oh, we may *believe* ourselves *enlightened*. What progress we have made, we say! We have civilised the world, caused manufactories to be built in every city! The miracle of elyctricity is set to transform our very civilisation from its roots to its most distant branches. And for how long has the Empire ruled this globe? Five hundred years? So much achieved, in so short a span of time! And yet there are any number of cultures – I need not list them to a knowledgeable man such as your good self, I am sure – who owned this globe before us. And some for ten, *twenty* times the length of our own short reign. The Imperial Archæological Mission has proved it. Beyond doubt. And if the finest minds of a culture *ten thousand years* wise believed in an incorporeal realm – believed that they could *understand* it, *interact* with it, then who are you or I to say otherwise?'

'A lovely idea, Carnaby, sighed Naught, 'but would you then care to explain to me exactly why every one of our learned men carry the exact opposite opinion to your own?'

'Why, they have thrown the baby out with the bathwater, Lord Naught!' cried Obadiah. 'Quite simply that, and nothing more! In the process of becoming *enlightened* we chose empiricism, to the exclusion of all else. We chose to measure, to observe, to test, to prove. We chose to do away with superstition, with all those things which we could not lay into the shallow pans of our scales. No more spirits, no more magick, no more gods – besides the Five Abatirim, of course.'

'And what of it?'

'Well, Lord Naught, consider this: suppose that I wished to measure your height. I could take a stick upon which I had marked out inches, have you stand against it, and – *viola*! – your height is known to me by means of this crudest of devices. But suppose for a moment that I wished to measure the dimensions of, for want of a better word, your soul?'

Naught shrugged.

'Do you suppose that I might require a device of somewhat greater complexity? Something more subtle, more delicate, more cunning than a simple stick? Well, well-intentioned though they may have been, those fellows of our Empire's beginnings were equipped with sticks, and nothing more – and finding themselves unable to measure the soul by means of such an instrument they declared the existence of the soul an impossibility. Freeing themselves from superstition, they enslaved themselves to inferior forms of evidence. Do you *see*, Lord Naught? Do you see what it is that two *modern* Scientists are proposing to you?'

Naught pursed his lips. 'I believe I may be beginning to.'

'Do you see that far from banishing mystery, the Scientists here before you propose to throw wide its doors? And that *you*, Lord Naught, may peer within?'

'Well I must say this does all sound rather intriguing, but why are you *here*? What is it that you want from *me*? Money, is it?'

'Lord *Naught!*' Obadiah's tone was that of one who has taken serious affront. 'We have not travelled halfway across the world to beg for mere *money*! We have come to this place because this is the *only* place in which our experiments can succeed.' He lowered his voice. 'The House of Naught, you see, is a special place.'

Naught grinned. 'It *is* nice!'

'Oh, it is far more than that, Lord Naught. *We must be here.* And what's more, you are the only one who can help us to contact another who came here for the very same reason. We *must* speak to Sebastian – '

A resounding boom turned all heads in the direction of the door. On the far side of the room, Flintwick had slammed shut the massive ledger in which he had been writing, and was glaring venomously at Obadiah. He threw back his chair and in a moment was at the fireside.

'*Carnaby!*' he snarled. 'You have been informed *in no uncertain terms* that there is no such person to be found here. You would be well advised to drop this matter *immediately*, or you may find yourself without these walls in far shorter order than you had imagined!'

Even Naught seemed taken aback by Flintwick's ejaculation. 'Nicholas, please!' he cried. 'Do refrain from such outbursts! These gentlemen are my guests, and they shall be treated as such!'

Never breaking the gaze which he had locked with Obadiah, Flintwick addressed his master from behind gritted teeth. 'But you are hardly in a state of mind to discuss – '

Naught glowered at him and made a peculiar hissing sound like a deflating snake.

'But *sir!*' Flintwick protested. 'What about your *glands?*'

'Eh? What *about* my glans, Nicholas?' Naught looked bemused and a little repulsed. 'You can be a very odd chap at times, do you know that? Now please leave us be, will you?'

'*Yes,* sir,' the manservant grimaced. He shot a furious glance in the direction of the table, then abruptly turned on his heel and swept out of the room.

As the door slammed Naught shook his head wonderingly, then as though Flintwick's glance had recalled it to his attention, he leaned forward and plucked a small bottle from the table. He pulled out its stopper and shook a few drops of the colourless liquid within onto his embroidered hand-kerchief. As he set the bottle back down, Edward saw that it was neatly labelled with the word 'Ether'. Noting his apparent interest, Naught proffered the bottle to Edward.

'Oh no, no thank you,' stuttered Edward – in that moment recognising the aroma that lingered around Naught. The gore-bespattered associations held for him by ether precluded its recreational use.

'Please yourself,' Naught shrugged. 'And do forgive Nicholas. He is so very over-protective sometimes. It is most unnecessary.' He lounged back in his chair and continued to suck listlessly upon the enfragranced cloth. 'Well, gentlemen, where were we?'

'We were speaking of Bellhouse?' Obadiah reminded him.

'Bellhouse? Yes, of course. Silly old Belly! I did so love his pretty snowflakes. See!'

Naught waved a finger in the direction of a frame hung by the fireplace. Even from where he sat, Edward could immediately recognise the thirty-seventh Shape of the Transition. The draftsmanship, as he had come to expect, was flawless. And, facile though Naught's term may have been, it did in fact quite bear quite a strong resemblance to a snowflake – as, to some extent, did all of the Shapes.

'No two alike,' remarked Obadiah.

'So they say, Doctor Carnaby. Although how anyone could ever presume to know such a thing is beyond me. What with them being so small and numerous, I mean. And of course they do have a tendency to melt. But what have Sebastian's little fancies to do with your own hocus-pocus?'

'Well, Lord Naught, do you know what Bellhouse's drawings were *for*?'

'But of course! He was a geometrician, no? Isn't it the job of geometricians to do geometry? To describe the structure of Verdra and the Kosmos and so on and so forth?'

'It is more than that, Lord Naught,' insisted Obadiah. 'The structure of Verdra *is* the structure of the Kosmos. As above, so below, d'you see? And it is the structure of our very selves. The structure repeats, on different scales. The microkosm and the macrokosm. To describe a snowflake *is* to describe the mind of a man.'

Naught snorted, and the hand-kerchief inflated momentarily. 'All very mystical, I must say. You are beginning to sound like old Belly now, Doctor Carnaby! He was always harping on about how he thought they would...' he twirled a finger at his temple, '*do something.* To his mind, that is. Like one of those silly Oriental fellows who walks on hot embers and such.'

'Yes, Lord Naught. The Shapes that Bellhouse drew are indeed the basis of a meditation. Although, a meditation of a different kind to those practiced by the coal-walkers. An older kind. Far, far older. Did he tell you of this? Of the source from which he drew the knowledge of his *little fancies* and their... properties?'

Naught shrugged. 'I had always thought that his ideas were his own. Or his assistant's, maybe. They were clever chaps!'

'They were not *clever*, they were brilliant men, both of them. But neither Bellhouse nor Danforth were the authors of the Formulæ by means of which their Shapes were produced. Have you perchance heard tell of one Sir Wilton Prancefield?'

Naught's eyes flicked upwards momentarily as he searched his memory, but finding it empty of the name he shook his huge head. 'It is not a name with which I am familiar, no.'

'No matter. Allow me to provide an introduction. Prancefield was one of the last century's most gifted archæologists.'

'Or an unscrupulous grave-robber,' added Edward.

Obadiah shot him a withering glare. 'For our purposes let us merely say that he was a tenacious man with an eye for antiquities of the rarest sort and a firm grasp of whom best to, ah, *incentivise* in order to ascertain where they might be unearthed.'

'All very interesting, Doctor Carnaby,' said Naught. 'But I was under the impression that we were discussing old Belly, were we not?'

Obadiah nodded. 'Indeed. I digress – but for good reason, Lord Naught, as you shall see. Might I ask you to humour me awhile if I propose to tell you a tale? A tale of... *mystery?*'

'Well, how could I resist!' Naught peppered the air with more of his excited claps. 'You may have my attention, sir!'

'Then I shall begin,' grinned Obadiah, and he positioned himself before the hearth, clasping his hands behind his back. He had about him every appearance of seasoned relator of anecdotes – which, indeed, he was; the tales with which Doctor Obadiah Carnaby was known to regale audiences of every description, from captivated to captive, were of as great renown as were his advancements in the field of Arcanology.

The Doctor cleared his throat.

'Now, some fifty years ago,' he began, 'almost to the day, in fact, Sir Wilton Prancefield mounted an expedition into the burning wastes of the Lithian desert.

It was not his first foray into the Lithian interior – we have Prancefield to thank for many of the finer Lithian artefacts of the great museums, you understand. It was, however, to be his last.

'Prancefield sought a lost complex of temple-tombs. You will be familiar with the fabled Lithian zikkaruts of course, Lord Naught, but *these* – well, these were another matter entirely. Built by the most ancient dynasty of that realm, they were said to house the remains of its priestly caste. Within these sacred sepulchres, it was said, lay vast storehouses piled with goods intended to accompany the priests into the afterlife – incomparable treasures set to humble the finest yet seen. And, isolated as they were in the midst of the howling sands of the extreme South East, they were also likely to be unmolested by the filthy paws of raiding natives.

'The tombs' existence had been brought to light by a man named Donaldson – the fellow responsible for the original decipherment of the Lithian picture-script – during his translation of a document recently rescued from a heathen temple. Sadly, Donaldson had died in a botched robbery mere hours after declaring his discovery of the tombs' location – but Prancefield, who by fortunate coincidence happened to be rooming in the same hotel, had greatheartedly volunteered to continue the work of his countryman.

'Now as I mentioned, that the monuments existed within a certain region of the deep desert of South Eastern Lithia was assured. But to Prancefield's chagrin, their exact location had been taken with Donaldson to the bottom of his dusty grave. Thus it was that the great man found himself stranded in the remotest settlement imaginable – a desiccated cluster of crumbling mud-dwellings not fit to call themselves hovels – without a way to proceed, and surrounded by cowardly desert-rats who whined that the ocean of sand was too perilous a place into which to stray. It was almost as though the spineless savages did not want the artefacts of their forefathers to be preserved for posterity. Until, that was, a remarkable reversal of fortune occurred.

'The head man of the village, a leathery old fellow whose initial reaction to Prancefield's proposal that they lead his party to the fabled tombs had been a counter-proposal of slow disembowelment, had changed his mind. Not only would he personally accompany the party on their quest, but what's more he would lead them to the very valley of the tombs itself. Prancefield's group could hardly believe their luck, and preparations were made for their immediate departure. Indeed, the chief insisted upon it, for there were angry mutterings among the tribesmen, who believed that their head man had fallen prey to a *sietch*, an evil spirit out of the deep desert night who had come to corrupt the tribe and destroy their ancestral treasures. Had they not decamped that very evening, it is likely that every last one of them would have felt the point of a sand-rat spear in his belly – after they had all inhaled the Breath of Sand, of course. Oh, the Breath of Sand is the traditional Lithian spirit-cleansing, you understand. Evil *sietchin* travel upon the wind, and gain ingress to a man's body by means of his breath. To drive out the spirit, the loyal men of the tribe take up the *yám*, a tube of camel-bone, and each one in turn blows sand into the possessed one's lungs. When there is no more air in him, the spirit is forced out of its host and flees back to the Abyss whence it came.

'So, like a flock of *sietchin*, Prancefield and his men fled the pitiful excuse for a village – all of them, including those few tribesmen who had chosen to follow their disgraced leader, now forever banished to the desert. At their backs, a forest of spears and *yám*, and before them a limitless ocean of starlit dunes. The very survival of the Prancefield expedition now depended upon these traitorous natives. Thankfully, the traitors were as faithful to their head man as the man himself was fickle; though evidently torn between loyalty and mistrust, their loyalty had won out. And this was just as well, for though she may deign to tolerate her own, the Lithian desert is not a mistress known to be forgiving of outsiders foolish enough to stray into her scorching desolation. They moved at night, for the sun was a deadly accomplice of the desert, wicking away at their strength and the scant supply of water they had been able to acquire from the village, and laying a crushing, leaden slab of heat upon their backs. Thus, adrift in the featureless sea of dunes, they had only the stars for their guides.

'At first, their runagate caravan moved with relative swiftness. The camels were hardy, and the barren miles passed beneath their hooves at a pace that promised that the valley and its treasures would soon be within their grasp. However, though their striding ships of the desert carried the Prancefield party ever further from the very edge of civilisation, ever deeper into the desert, no mysterious valley presented itself. As dune after mountainous dune fell away behind them, the chief's promises that the valley of the tombs would soon be theirs began to sound ever hollower to Prancefield's ears. However, with no choice but to trust the man who had forsaken his tribe at their behest, the party pushed on. Until, that was, a whispered warning came.

'Isaksen, the fearless Scornländian steersman to whom for decades Prancefield had entrusted his expeditions' navigation, was afraid. Though of course he knew not where the tombs lay, Isaksen had been assiduously charting the party's course, lest anything *unfortunate* should befall their guides following the liberation of the treasures. Gods forbid they should have to find their way back blind! Like his seafaring forefathers before him, Isaksen was a veritable sage of the stars, and like those ancient longboat-men he could plot a route across the globe by the light of those heavenly guides as easily as a fellow may roam the streets of his own home town by lamplight. And so, when the navigator came to rouse his employer one evening with the news that they were *lost* – well, Prancefield was enraged. It was at once evident to him what had transpired. They had fallen into a trap.

'The wizened old dog, Prancefield realised, had not changed his ways at all. The whole affair was a sham – the threats, the mutiny at the village, the promises of the valley, *all* of it. A trap. And they had been led into the desert to die: a sacrifice to the sands. *This* was why the rats still honoured their allegiance to the treacherous chief. Now that they were countless leagues from any kind of aid, the cowardly fools – no doubt terrified by the prospect of man-to-man combat in which they would surely be bested – had poisoned Prancefield and his men. What other explanation could there be? How else but by the agency of some slow-acting venom might the savages have so disarranged the minds of the archæologist's party? For hallucination it surely was: the stars, as the shaken Isaksen whispered to Prancefield, his sextant barely gripped in his trembling fingers, were the stars. *Always* the stars. And yet no matter how frantically he was to rub his sandy fists into the sockets of his eyes, what he saw remained the same. The stars, you see, were *not* the stars – not the stars of *our* world, at least. No friendly, guiding constellations glittered above them now. Eyes and instruments both reported the same: the malignantly glinting scintillæ of an entirely alien Kosmos. It *could not* be real.

'Prancefield immediately ordered every drop of the water poured away, for it was surely that gift given all-too-freely which the savages had contaminated with their odious drug. Let it poison the sand to which their souls had no doubt been promised! But by then it seemed that it was too late. Isaksen had around him a gaggle of terrified men, and all agreed that what they were seeing was the same: stars unfriendly, stars unknown. Not a one of them had escaped the hallucinatory taint.

'The expedition was doomed. Even should the party, who still carried good, Urish pistols, slay their tormentors to a man, they would still remain horribly lost in this never-ending wasteland. Their withered corpses, like the tombs they sought, would never be found – either they would be consumed by the savages, or by the desert that the savages worshipped. Still, the only thing that remained was to die with honour, and that meant, of course, to die last. From beyond the dune where the traitors had made their own camp to wait out the hours of sunlight, the detestable sound of heathen victory chants could already be heard. The men of the Prancefield party blew the sand from their revolvers' barrels - the civilised man's own *yám*, let them try *lead* in their lungs! – and made ready to put an end to the business once and for all. But as the brave men crept, pistols cocked, towards the place where their tormentors were gathered, something in the moonlit scene beyond the crest of the dune stayed fingers upon triggers.

'For you see, the savages were not capering in a dance of gloating triumph. No forest of jubilantly shaken spear-points rived the night there. No indeed, far from it. The scum were cowering like craven dogs, prostrated pathetically upon the sand before their head man. Every spineless one of them wailed and chanted their ungodly mantras, scratching signs upon the air and beating their breasts as their cowardly tears watered the dust. And behind the silent chief – who stood with head thrown back and arms outstretched like some damnable priest of the desert night – the weird Kosmos wheeled across the sky as though somewhere gods wound the handle of a titanic stellarium. Prancefield and his men stood transfixed with awe, shoving off the rats who dropped to their knees before them to beg their masters for deliverance, as an unearthly glow blossomed in those whirling heavens. Isaksen raised his arm and cried out, pointing out the source of the radiance: a single, red star that was pulsing into being in the very centre of the sky.

'Blood-red light washed over the dunes. Prancefield was forced to put a bullet through the skull of one gibbering fool who tore dementedly at his clothes – spilling a further flood of crimson on the sand – but not before he had heard the man's screams. This was the wrath of *Zahra*, the spirit of the desert herself! They had trespassed against she who guards the secrets of the burning sands, and for that they had been cast into the *nehon*: the endless, lifeless waste that had existed before the world was given form.

'Was there no end to the treachery of the maniacal old dog? Why, in his fevered quest to sacrifice the noble archæologists to his mistress the desert, he had put poison into the mouths of his own men, too! Prancefield knew then that it was no less than his very duty to despatch the fiend. But even as he levelled his pistol, he saw the sands beneath the feet of his nemesis begin to eddy and swirl. As though stirred by the motion of that vortex of the firmament above them, the sands rose, spinning faster and faster about the motionless chief, until he was all but lost within the mælstrom. At the last moment, Prancefield saw the man's arms drop suddenly to his sides and his eyes blink open, as though in that instant he had been wrested from his bloodthirsty reverie. The old dog had time for but a single, strangled cry before the desert's fury consumed him.

'Prancefield knew that he must take up a new position to the rear of his men, the better to assess the situation, and so began to reascend the dune at speed, gallantly dispatching the slavering savages who stood in the path of the mission's success as he went. Even so, he had barely managed to lace shut the opening of his new centre of command before the storm swept out from that place, and all was lost to the full fury of *Zahra*.

'He did not know how long he held his position within the tent. The storm battered and raged without relent, and at times it seemed that its ferocity would uproot his canvas sanctuary and send it hurtling into the void. He had been obliged to forcibly repel several intruders who had sought to invade the headquarters, but after some time the sounds of *Zahra*'s rage and of the screaming of the men died down, and he was able to emerge once more.

'A scene of abject desolation awaited him in that red-litten wasteland. Men were strewn about like dolls, many half-buried in drifts of sand, many not moving. In all, death had claimed six of the Prancefield party. Two of the poor blighters found near the command centre had taken bullets at close range – one of the savages must have purloined a pistol during the chaos. Just as well, then, that a good half of the natives' lives had been taken by their mistress's revenge. The head man, they were not surprised to learn, was nowhere to be found, and the petrified savages fell all too happily back under the direction of their rightful masters.

'As the dust slowly settled, the desert became utterly and eerily still. Not a whisper of wind stirred the sand, and the gyration of the heavens had ceased. The moon hung, massive and full in that alien sky – that, at least, was familiar, though stained blood-red by the interloping star. And in their commingled light, the men beheld a scene the like of which none before them had witnessed. For spread all around them were the ruined remains of a city as black as midnight's blood.

'The night, and the city, were endless. No metropolis in history was ever so vast. Saddling the surviving camels, Prancefield and his men rode for seeming days into the labyrinth of broken walls that had arisen from the sands. And, though the waste could be seen from horizon to horizon, never an end to it came within their sight. Neither came there an end to that unnatural night. At least they were to be spared the spite of the burning sun.

'What power had toppled that city, it was impossible even for an archæologist of Prancefield's stature to say. The black walls, glinting dully in the moonlight, were sunk into the sands as far as the natives could be persuaded to dig, as though their foundations were rooted in Verdra's very bones. That, or these were towers of stupendous height whose tips alone breached the surface of the sand. It was a possibility that none cared to entertain to for too long.

'And yet, the city had fallen. Indeed, every indication suggested the absurd conclusion that some mighty force, emanating from above the very place where they had made their camp, had blown down the walls as though they were naught but a child's building blocks in a gale. But they were to learn that something stranger still had befallen this place. For you see, the stone was not cracked or crumbled as from a blow, but warped and smeared like sealing-wax brushed by a careless hand.

And as to the identity of the stone itself – there was not a guess among their number. Three things, though, were certain: firstly, that this was no Lithian architecture, and secondly that no known Lithian edifice was ever built of such stone. The third seemed almost too bizarre to comprehend. And even Buffet, the esteemed geologist among their number, was sure of it. No such stone was known to men of the modern era.

'This was the discovery of Prancefield's career. No, these were not the treasure-laden tombs that he had been promised – they were something far, far greater! Oh, of course, the tomb-goods of the Lithian priest-kings would have been the most wonderful additions to the great collections, and perhaps even the museums – but *this*, well! Prancefield had discovered an entirely new culture! And what's more, it was a culture that would, at a stroke, re-write the very annals of history – and forever secure Prancefield's place in the canon of archæology. For this – a vast, unknown metropolis, set within the Lithian territory yet mentioned nowhere in its writings, uncovered by a freak sandstorm for the first time in what must surely be millennia – well, it could be nothing other than a *prehistoric* city.

'The implications were vast. For this was not the work of a tribe of mere desert nomads, scratching out a pitiful living in the sands – it was a marvel, a jewel of civilisation. The *sophistication* of the place – the streets broad and orderly, their arrangement surely the work of vast premeditation, and well, not to mention that masonry – they all spoke to the work of an almost unbelievable culture. And yes, those walls – those black and sinuous walls – even in ruin, they were a terrible wonder. For where was the mortar? And, for that matter, where *were* the blocks joined? And how might they ever have been quarried when the archæologist's picks and hammers of good, hard steel could make not the slightest dent upon their surfaces? But these were questions to be answered another time, for time, even in that long night, was surely not their ally.

'Their supply of food was growing scant. Thankfully they had been able to requisition the remaining water from their savage servants, now docile with superstitious fear. Whilst Isaksen remained unconvinced, it had by then become perfectly obvious to Prancefield that the strange skies above them were in fact a mirage, and that they had not, after all, been drugged. Indeed, it seemed quite evident in hindsight that some manner of atmospheric illusion – albeit a singularly impressive one – was responsible for the reconfiguration of the skies, and most probably for the seemingly perpetual night, too. Likely some commixture of the desert heat, their remote positioning upon the globe, and microscopic particles of dust thrown up by the sandstorm had conspired to fabricate the kaleidoscopic display – in his time, Prancefield had borne witness to all manner of such illusions, from phantom oases to fabulous, shimmering cities in the sky. Regardless of the exact mechanism, the water was evidently safe to drink, but it would not last forever. And there was much work to do if they were to uncover the treasures of this place.

'Prancefield set his men to work. Under his expert direction, gangs spread out through the city, scouring the tumbled buildings one by one, and spades turned sand that had lain upon these ruins for time immemorial. But, to the very great dismay of the party, it seemed that there was nothing to be found. Not a plate or a coin, a bone or a statue or a sword lay beneath the surface. Nothing to prove to the academy the existence of that place – and nothing, indeed, to prove that a person had ever lived within its black and blasted walls at all. Had the ruins already been picked clean by the hands of thieves? It seemed unlikely. Were the artefacts of its people sunk so deeply in the ocean of sand that mere shovels could never reach them? Or perhaps, as the savages whispered, had this city of the *nehon* been peopled only by ghosts and *sietchin*?

'The water, and Prancefield's hopes, dwindled by the hour. Several of the less manly savages had already succumbed to thirst, and even Prancefield's personal supply was becoming depleted. A new plan was required. They would retreat, regroup, and return with a larger and more loyal party – better equipped and armed with the knowledge of the city's location. Isaksen felt that he could retrace their route, provided that they could return to the spot where the skies had first changed, and thereby make their way out of the mirage-haunted region. Once they were again in the vicinity of civilisation, they would head for a more northerly, and with any luck more friendly, village than the one from which they had departed. Their beasts were being saddled and their effects stowed when the news came. There had been a discovery. One of the rats came sprinting into the camp, shouting almost incoherently to his masters about what he had found. It was writing, he cried, writing!

'And writing it certainly was. As Prancefield stood over his latest find and brushed the sand from its surface, he drew aside the veil of millennia uncounted – and before the widening eyes of his party emerged a script so strange and so cryptic that it would confound the greatest minds of men for decades to come. In the guttering light of a torch, whorls and blooms of intricate markings could be seen to radiate across the ebon surface of the tablet, spiralling in dizzying trails that seemed to creep and pulse independently of the flickering of the flame. The savages watching over the party's shoulders fell away with frightened cries, and even one of the stalwart Urishmen dropped in a dead swoon, so that a sack had to be cast over the thing in order to deaden its mesmeric effect. A whisper of terrible destiny touched Prancefield's soul then, and he knew that this moment would forever alter the course of his life. Such was the power of the *Tablets of Uush'Ton*.

'In all there were nine of the man-sized slabs, arrayed like the petals of some stupendous flower upon the temple floor. The men worked in shifts to uncover them, for none could bear to look upon them for long without becoming faint and feverish, and several of the tents were sacrificed so that they might be safely swaddled in canvas. The things were of such weight that the camels – even had they not kicked and spat when the Tablets were brought near – would never have had the strength to bear them. Instead, they were bound tightly with ropes so that the beasts might drag them through the sand. Thusly burdened with the weight of ancient mystery, the Prancefield party departed the broken city in the sand, leaving the furrows of their passage behind them.

'It was not difficult to trace their path back to the place where the storm had first struck; although their route through the buckled ruins was curiously difficult to recollect, the preternatural calm that since had reigned in that chill and red-tainted place meant that their tracks were as fresh as though they had just been laid. From there it would simply be a case of returning in the direction from which they had come; once free of the mirage's disorienting spell, they would travel north-west under Isaksen's direction until they reached the settlements at the desert's fringe. However, events were not to transpire exactly as they had hoped.

'For though the weary group soldiered on, slower now for its incredible burden and the flagging strength of the men, the foreign stars above them refused to relinquish their reign of the heavens. The merry twinkle of guiding lights was nothing but a fading memory, and the leering

Kosmos that appeared in its stead seemed to mock the travellers perpetually with its unwholesome light. As what must have been days passed away in a delirium of agonising toil, a number of the savages fell to raving and gibbering, and had to put down lest they further damage the morale of the group. Indeed, the derangement among them was such that none could truly say when it was that the crimson-haunted dome of night gave way to the cloudless azure of Lithian noon.

'As though waking from a dream, the men found themselves once more in the presence of that which they had by turns fled and then desperately sought: the glorious, burning sun. A euphoria took them then, and the ragged troop fell to their knees in the sand, thanking the Gods that they had at last conquered the deadly enchantment of *Zahra*. Of the thirty-five who had fled the village that night so long ago, only eighteen men were to drag themselves on buckling legs into the settlement that – thank the Gods once more! – had not shimmered into nothingness at their approach. For this time there was no mirage, and the Prancefield expedition had returned, victorious.'

The long silence that followed in the wake of Obadiah's words was punctuated only by the pop and crackle of the fire in the hearth. Edward looked to Naught. A faraway expression had descended over their host's features, his eyes misty and his lips parted as he gazed at something far beyond walls of the little parlour in which they sat. It seemed to take him long moments to realise that the Doctor was no longer speaking. As his eyes refocused, he drew in a long, faltering breath, and let out a satisfied sigh such as a diner might sigh upon the completion of a full and hearty meal.

'*Wonderful*,' he breathed, blinking like one awakening from a dream.

Edward and Obadiah exchanged glances.

'Yes, a ripping yarn indeed, Doctor Carnaby. A perfect,' – Naught sighed again, and this time the sound was haunted by a hint of resignation – 'a perfect *fantasy*.'

Obadiah spoke slowly, his voice lowered as though to avoid rousing their host from his reverie. 'It is no fantasy, Lord Naught,' he said.

'Do not *tease* this old fellow, Doctor Carnaby.'

'I would not. In fact, for the three of us gathered here in this room, I cannot conceive of a matter of greater pertinence.'

Naught sniffed. 'Well, I must admit that I am still unclear as to *why*. What has this tall tale to do with me, or Belly? Or with you, for that matter?'

'If you will indulge me but a few minutes longer?'

'Oh, I have a lifetime to while away. What odds can minutes make?'

The Doctor smiled conspiratorially. 'I would venture to suggest that you will find these to be minutes wisely invested, Lord Naught,' he said. 'And, let me assure you, I would not have been so convinced of the tale's veracity myself, had I not heard it from the very lips of its protagonist. Oh, certainly the papers got hold of it, and quite a stir it caused, too. But the journals of the academy – well, they would not have a thing to do with it, nor with anything else tarred with the name of 'Prancefield', ever again. And it was not merely the tale of the Tablets' discovery that ruined the man. No, it was the Tablets themselves. For you see, Prancefield's find fell prey to that great paradox of the archæological establishment: in a Science that progresses by the turn of the shovel, that which is *new*, which challenges the paradigms already so well entrenched – well, it cannot be admitted. If it does not prop up the edifice, it must be disposed of. And so, the Tablets were a hoax. Whether Prancefield was the victim or the perpetrator hardly mattered.

'For where did he *imagine* that these fanciful objects would fit into the narrative already so well established? Where was the precedent, the provenance? A *prehistoric* city, already far more advanced than those that were to come *after* it? And in the heart of a Lesser land, no less? Even had the very idea not been patently preposterous, *surely* there would already have existed some indication of such a civilisation? A relic here, a reference there? But of course, there was no such thing. Never had this place been referred to, even by the records of deepest antiquity. And so, a fabled lost city in the sand, revealed by a magickal sandstorm in a location of convenient obscurity, never again to be witnessed by the eyes of mortal man? Ha! Prancefield might as well have declared that the Tablets were given to him by the færies at the bottom of his garden. For after the very authenticity of Tablets had been rubbished, no man would touch Prancefield's increasingly desperate bids to return to what he claimed was the site of their discovery. For yes, even the artefacts themselves – those nine jet tablets borne out of the wastes – were inadmissible as evidence.

'It did not help that neither an antiquary nor a linguist, a philologist, glottologist or cryptologist in the Empire cared to hazard a guess as to what the things might mean. If they *meant* anything at all, that is. It would have aided his deception, he was told time and again, if he had troubled to base the so-called inscriptions on some pre-existing lexicon. As it was, a nonsensical slew of symbols, arranged with utter arbitrariness and neither a hint of internal consistency nor a relationship borne to any of the myriad scribal permutations of mankind's history – well, it was absurd, and lazy to boot. Prancefield was not even a competent forger. What were these markings even supposed to be, anyway? These ridiculous little notches and wiggles that were so obviously moulded onto the surface of the things? This fact was noted by the keen eyes of one incensed scholar, who with magnifying-glass in hand declared – as a final nail in the Prancefield casket – that not the minutest mark of tool could be detected in the so-called engravings. Like his colleagues before him, the man had been taken somewhat faint after examining the unwholesome forgeries, and would not go near them again. Bad taste was what it was!

'Prancefield had become the laughing stock of the world that he had imagined would place him upon its throne. Penniless and broken, he sold the Tablets to a university for a nominal sum in a bid to purge himself of the whole, nightmarish experience. He was drinking the last dregs of this money when I chanced to meet him, alone and broken in a public house in Broadflight where for the price of a plate of kippers and a plum pudding he told me this tale. Strangely, he was not bitter, merely sad. He would hardly have believed his own tale himself, he said, but he was glad to tell it one last time. The next morning, he was found swinging from the rafters of his boarding-house.

'And so, for twenty years and more, the Tablets languished in seclusion once again, hidden away from the eyes of the world in one of the lesser-travelled parts of the university's basement. Hidden, that was, until a young man – a gifted fellow, but not a man of any great means and hence acting as caretaker in the university's employ – happened across them. His name was Sebastian Bellhouse.'

'Belly!' cried Naught. 'Oh, what fun!'

'*Yes*, Lord Naught,' said Obadiah gravely. 'The very same. Belly – Bellhouse – was instantly fascinated by what he saw. Over the following weeks, he returned time and again to the basement in order to make wax rubbings of the artefacts that he had found. These he pieced together on the walls of his garret room, where night after night by the rude light of a candle he would lose himself in their ancient mysteries.

'Bellhouse, as you know, was a geometrician. But there is more, Lord Naught: Bellhouse was a savant – one of that rare breed of autodidacts seemingly born with his Science entwined with the very fibres of his being. And, for years, as he dusted the shelves of the university's libraries, he had been appropriating books – tomes of the classical philosophers, the geometers whose work was to him a joyous nourishment, a feast of polyhedra, of elements and scales and crystal structures and heavenly symmetries. There was something of their cant in the Tablets – he *sensed* it. Bellhouse, you see, owned a skill unseen since the days of those wise old men, and a formula, to him, was not a thing to be puzzled over – it was an artwork, a sculpture. A snowflake. Bellhouse could *see* the machinations of number. The most complex of problems existed only to be *perceived*, not to be *solved* with crude arithmetic. As he was to record in his *Treatise* years later, "I apply my mind and the way is closed; I disown my mind, I drift in æther, and there the thing awaits me."

'The waxen facsimiles with which Bellhouse had papered the walls of his abode held but a glimmer of the true potency of the Tablets, and yet in their presence he would be transported. Throughout the hours of darkness he would sit, entranced and enraptured, the life beyond the walls of his room fading to grey irrelevance as his consciousness was drawn by some strange, inexorable gravity into a dimension beyond the ken of the common man. Thus the Tablets exposed themselves to him. It did not take long for him to realise the thing to which the learned men of the academy, their heads so full of arrogant presupposition, had been so blind. For the inscriptions that swirled before him were not a mere *language* at all – at least, not a language of the type that might ever be expressed by the small mouth noises of mammals, the primitive slap and drone of flesh. No, these were indicators of the very language by which the Kosmos describes itself. This was *mathematics*.

'And so, in that meanest of cells, so far removed in Time and in Space from the unknowable circumstances of the Tablets' creation, *something* came alive. Something that had slumbered for long ages of the world like the wizened husk of a seed found itself once more in fertile soil, and it blossomed into glorious life within the consciousness of that singular man. Bellhouse sensed innately that he had happened upon something of incalculable worth – and yet, he knew also that the Tablets would not speak to every man. Or rather, that not every man was equipped with the ears to hear their call. To speak *for* the Tablets was an unenviable task. Why, one might experience as much success attempting to convince a jury that his wardrobe had dictated to him the secrets of the transmutation of lead into gold. And so it was that Bellhouse set about the creation of what was to become his masterwork.

'In the introduction to *The Treatise on the Kosmic Significance of the Tablets of Uush'Ton*, Bellhouse describes the endeavour as being "akin to describing one's favourite symphonic movements to a deaf-mute with whom one does not share a common tongue, by means of a system of notation entirely of one's own devising." And, to his very great credit, by Bellhouse's efforts the deaf-mute here before you heard those very strains.

'His achievement was nothing short of monumental. With number, with word and with line he filled volume upon volume with transliterations of the Tablets' arcane numerical systems, converting them into an algebraic form that might be understood by the common practitioner of mathematics. Appended to this were his cunning and exhaustive tables of data, and finally the sheaves of drawings. Bellhouse made his images, his mandalas – his *snowflakes*, Lord Naught – so that by the crude mechanism of the transmission of light to retina others might at last understand those most wondrous things projected into his very consciousness by the Tablets themselves: *the Polyhedra of Uush'Ton*. For this, it seemed, was the message of that voice from Beyond. From out of the black city in the sand had come The Shapes.

'And yet, though he was to generate vast numbers of those intricate things for which he was to become known to researchers of the occult, Bellhouse knew not what he had discovered. That knowledge did not come until later, when a happy accident was to secure the entrance of another player into this most cryptic of games. It had become Bellhouse's habit to carry about with him tables of data, which during the rare idle moments of his day he would work on, much as a man may while away time by the solving of a cross-word puzzle. One day as he swept the refectory, he saw a notebook answering to the description of his own, clutched in the hands of a student. Checking his pockets, he found to his dismay that the thing was indeed his. It might have ended there as a red-faced Bellhouse requested the return of his notes from the man seemingly so absorbed in them – but as he handed back the book, Alan Danforth asked politely how long their caretaker had been interested in the solution of ciphers.

'We need not concern ourselves here with the tale of the men's burgeoning friendship. Suffice it to say that the geometrician and the cryptographer together were able to perform a seemingly magickal feat. For the proud old men of the academy had not merely failed to perceive the meaning of the Tablets, but had failed to perceive a *dual* meaning – for like any of the great occult texts, the Tablets of Uush'Ton contained substances both exoteric *and* esoteric. As the young Danforth had recognised that evening in the refectory, the numbers generated by Bellhouse's algebraic transliteration were, almost unbelievably, the elements of a cipher – and infused into the very stuff of The Shapes, there were words.

'At first, a syntax emerged – a pattern within patterns derived from patterns. An abstract thing with no hint as to the nature of the nodes that comprised it. Phonemes? Ideograms? How could they know? This syntax of theirs was a thing without reference. No reference, that is, but the very artefacts which had birthed it. Bellhouse had long suspected that the Tablets' inscriptions bore some relationship to the Lithian picture-script, and this, finally, was the key. As you know, Lord Naught, the Lithians' characters would render up entirely different readings depending upon their relations in space, and to one another. What's more, the message read by a layman would *not* be the message read by an adept. A hyena is the night, but a hyena close to a vase is the Kosmos, d'you see? Such is the nature of esotericism! How fortunate it was that Danforth studied under Professor Chokeheart, the great cryptanalyst of the Wars, and the man who had broken the back of a brace of ancient languages! But as they were to discover, the thing that they were rebuilding was the monumental edifice of which every other hieroglyphic system was but a pale and fleeting shadow.

'And so the walls of the little room grew vined with crisscrossing tendrils of string as Danforth supplied the indicators, and Bellhouse declared their topographical relations upon the Tablets' surfaces. As glyph was strung to glyph, formula to formula, it did not escape their attention how closely their web of twine grew to reflect the arterial structure of *biological* things. And indeed it did seem alive. But what did it mean? Or were they merely chasing a ghost? Without that singular meeting of minds, it would not have been possible to say. But as the forms supplied by Danforth's deductions were united in a shining fabric within the exceptional mind-space of Sebastian Bellhouse, the words, at last, came forth.

'And what words they were. What fantastical words! The Tablets disgorged a story to make the wildest mythologies of our ancient forefathers seem like the diaries of a council clerk. It was the history of a people – a race of Verdra's deepest primordial past. They were the *Eelen*, and from out of the nib of an ink pen clutched in the hand of a lowly student from the other end of Time, their tale flowed. There, in Danforth's notebooks, there opened up a passage to a lost and unremembered world. Here were accounts of the Eelen's mythic beginnings, there the annals of the æon-straddling reign of their glorious empire, and there at last the records of the building of their final and greatest enclave, *Nhionhi* - the blasted desert ruin from which Prancefield had hauled the nine black Tablets.

'But there was more. The Tablets contained also a Scripture, of sorts. It was a collection of the sacred doctrines of the Eelen – but these were doctrines of a kind unknown to modern man. For does not the Church presume to draw a veil between man and the divine – a veil that none may sunder but the dead?'

'Certainly!' blurted Edward. 'But the *Ciallmhar* made no such – '

'*Enough*, Edward!' Obadiah barked, vaporising the words forming upon Edward's lips with one of his incendiary glares. 'The Ciallmhar are most certainly dead! And Lord Naught does not wish to hear of your little *hobbies* at this juncture. We are speaking of the *Church*, not of your dashed witch-folk!'

Edward shrank back into his chair, cowed and cursing himself for his impetuousness.

Shaking his head, the Doctor turned back to their host. 'Now, where was I? Ah yes – *death*.'

'And the divine?' offered Naught.

'Indeed,' agreed Obadiah. 'My point being that even *in* death, Father Church offers one no guarantee that one will meet one's makers! For what if one has not lived according to the dictates of the Holy Interlocutors? What if one has erred, and eaten a whelk on a full moon or some such, and is cast forthwith into the frozen caverns of the Abyss? And, being dead and buried, how may one return to tell one's friends whether the words of the Interlocutor held so much as a whisper of truth after all? Well, Lord Naught, for the Eelen, it was not so. No such priestly interlopers as our own Abatirians decreed themselves the voice of the Eelen's divine, nor presumed to place themselves as the impassable barrier between man and deity. For you see, to reach beyond the veil of death, to experience the wonder and glory of their loving creators, the Eelen had... a *method*. And thus at last, Bellhouse learned the true meaning of the Polyhedra of Uush'Ton.

'Just as the Formulæ were both the Shapes and their lore, so the Shapes were a key and a gateway. And, for the ones who owned the knowledge of their right configuration and the ability meld them in the crucible of their consciousness, there existed the possibility to unlock, and to pass through that gate. To journey to the

Beyond. To commune with the departed ancestors. *To seek out the very Gods!*

'We do not know for certain if Bellhouse truly believed in the existence of the divine, nor indeed in the soul's survival of bodily death. Indeed, we are inclined to think that he considered the Nhionbian Doctrines as we do - as a conceit, a metaphor. Neither do we know exactly what it is that the Eelen experienced all of those uncounted millennia ago. *But we intend to find out.*'

Once again, Naught was silent. But this time, rather than staring into his own Beyond, his eyes were fixed on the drawing that hung by the hearth. His brow was furrowed and his lips pursed. He pointed a manicured finger at Bellhouse's rendering of the Polyhedron. '*This?*' he said. '*This* thing? A *gateway?* To the *realm of the dead?* To the *realm of the Gods?*'

'Not in the terminology of Science, Lord Naught, no. Let us call it a *Portal of Dimensional Transition*. But, semantics aside, yes. That is precisely what it is.'

'A portal, hey? Yes, and where is the door that will take us to Færie, Doctor? I do quite fancy a frolic in the mushroom glades with some chubby little naked folk!'

'One may well ask,' said Obadiah, pretending not to have grasped Naught's jibe. 'Where indeed *is* Færie?'

'Why, it is in the *imagination*, you silly man!' hooted Naught, flapping his hand-kerchief at Obadiah as though the Doctor had made a particularly naughty innuendo. 'Where else?'

'That is exactly what you and I *must* know!' cried Obadiah. 'Or are you content? Content that *this* is all there is?' He raised both palms as though to encompass the parlour and gave a theatrical shrug.

Naught gave a plaintive sigh and his mouth opened and closed as though he were finding the words to speak, but Obadiah thundered on.

'Of *course* you are not! A man such as yourself? I will not believe it for one moment!' He struck the table with his palm, and the sherry glasses tinkled. '*Mystery*, Lord Naught! These are its last bastions! Join us! Join us, for your own sake!' He clutched a handful of air and squeezed it in a shaking fist. 'If you aid us you will be privy to some of the most incredible experiences that a man may have! I can guarantee you that you will witness things that you would never have *believed* possible, things that some would say men were never *meant* to see!'

'But...'

The Doctor glared at their host and drew a silencing finger to his lips. His moustache twitched. Then he bent, hands clasped behind his back, and peered directly into Naught's eyes. When he spoke, his voice was low, firm and measured: 'We must speak with Bellhouse.'

A bemused frown creased the mottled skin of Naught's brow. 'Impossible!'

'Oh, I rather think *not*, sir!' roared Obadiah.

'And whatever gives you that impression? As I have told you –'

'*I can understand your reticence*,' declared Obadiah, cutting short Naught's protestation. 'And I can assure you that we *are* aware of what transpired all those years ago. However, I should also like you to know that we are not in the least bit disturbed by it, nor do we intend to seek any form of retribution *or* involve any agent of the law.'

Naught grasped the arms of his chair and pushed himself back into the seat. '*Doctor* Carnaby, just exactly what is it that you *think* you know?'

'We know enough – perhaps not all, but enough to have considered that making the journey here was a worthwhile enterprise. I will reiterate: we are most emphatically *not* connected in any way to the law *or* its enforcement. What may or may not have happened to Bellhouse does not trouble us; indeed it does not even so much as vaguely concern us. It is simply not our business. Our only concern is our Science.'

'But, Doctor Carnaby – '

'Do this for your *own* sake, Lord Naught!' Obadiah repeated. 'Do not *while away* your *life!*'

For a moment, Naught's eyes seemed to soften and grow wistful, but then they hardened once more and he firmly shook his head. 'Listen, Carnaby,' he seethed, 'what you ask is made impossible by virtue of the simple fact that Mr Bellhouse is *dead!*' He stopped, panting slightly. After a moment, though, he shook his head once more. 'You *know* this! Although, I must admit, I'm not sure *how* you know it. Now, even presuming that I was willing to help you, how could you possibly propose to –'

'*Lord Naught.*' Obadiah held up a palm. 'We have means of speaking to Bellhouse – *if* you will allow us to make his acquaintance.'

'It's true!' cried Edward, slapping his thigh in an uncharacteristic display of excitability.

'Now you are truly asking me to suspend my disbelief!' sputtered Naught. 'Will you... conduct a *séance*? Draw up his spirit with dark incantations? Bah, preposterous!'

'We have a *device*,' Obadiah intoned.

'*A device?* That can *speak to the dead?*'

Obadiah blew a sharp gust from his flared nostrils. 'No, not exactly. It is a device that utilises the miraculous force of elyectricity to animate the tissues of the human brain. Would I be correct in saying that that *particular* part of Mr Bellhouse, at least, is at your disposal?'

Naught blenched. His fleshy lips quivered. 'Oh, very well then Doctor Carnaby – you have me! I do not know where you come by your information, but I am certainly beginning to believe that you must indeed have some means hob-nobbing with the deceased!'

'So I *am* correct, then?' demanded Obadiah.

Naught said nothing, merely nodded, open-mouthed, fear and wonder spreading over his face like creeping mould.

'Then let us make no further delay,' cried Obadiah triumphantly, leaping up from his chair with the firelight dancing crazily in his eyes. '*Bring me the brain of Sebastian Bellhouse!*'

SIX
A Peculiar Occurrence by the Sea

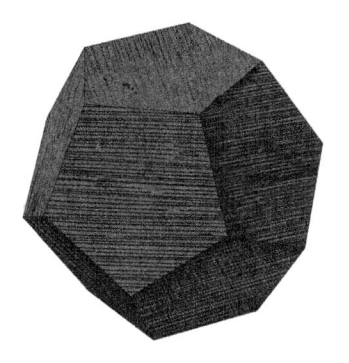

The unexplained disappearance of the Hook's Hill Loon was not greatly lamented in the seaside village of Osbeth. It was not that his disappearance was not remarked upon. Far from it, in fact - the Loon and his ways would doubtless always be remembered, so long as the village had garden fences over which rumours might be traded. It was just that Osbeth was better off without a man like *that*.

Osbeth was a normal place - a wholesome place. The village-folk were normal and wholesome folk. They lived their lives by the measures of the seasons and the tides, just as they had always done. Life was slow, and simple, and good, just as it had always been. And, just as the men wove the nets as their forefathers had done before them, so too the fabric of life was woven as their forefathers had woven it. They lived in the good, stout cottages that their forefathers had built, and they fished the bountiful seas that their forefathers had fished. And so, when the outsider had arrived, with his outside ways, his unwholesome ways - well, it just wasn't *right*.

It did not take long for the Loon to garner his reputation, and it seemed that he did his utmost to uphold it. Tales of his madness were traded by the men across their nets as they saw him scuttle by the harbour, embellished by the wives at their stoves, and guffawed about later in the taverns by both through the foam of a mug of ale. It was rumoured that before he was mad, the Loon had once been a university man – and a noted one at that – but the people of the village saw little evidence to support this, and cared even less. Why in the world would a city man, a man of letters, choose to make his home in such a secluded place as wave-lashed Osbeth anyway? What was there here for such a lofty type? It was a place of sea-spray and crab baskets, not coffee-houses and encyclopædias. Perhaps that was why the Loon had brought his own library with him. The seemingly endless succession of crates that had been unloaded from the cart on the day that that he came must have doubled the number of books not merely in Osbeth, but on the whole of the peninsula.

The redheaded and shifty-looking old wretch had arrived in the village under circumstances only marginally less mysterious than those surrounding his sudden departure nineteen years later – and even from the very beginning of those nineteen years he simply had not *fitted in*. He had made no effort to do so either, that was for sure and certain. From the very day he had arrived, the Loon had not consorted with the village-folk at all. Sheer churlishness, it was. He made use of his reedy stammer only when it could not be avoided (and absolutely never to make conversation, though he was often the subject of it) and it seemed that he made forays into the village only as infrequently as he could possibly contrive. Those forays concluded most often in a hail of pebbles and catcalls flung by the children who would pursue him from the Market Square all the way back up to Hook's Hill, or as far as they could get before they were towed by their ears back to the hearthside. It wasn't right for a child to get too close to a man *like that*. Fortunately for all, he made arrangements with the grocer to have his provisions delivered directly to the door of the tumbledown cottage on the hill, which, like his shutters, remained permanently closed and bolted. It was a strange arrangement, true enough, but he was a paying customer, and he did not have to be liked so long as he paid – which he always did, and he most certainly was not.

His seclusionary nature, though, was not all that had caused the village-folk to decree that he was more than a little touched. He was a strange-looking one, for a start. Those wild eyes in their wet, bruise-coloured pits, and that patchy, red hair, looking like it had never made the acquaintance of a pair of scissors or a comb. What would have been more polite would have been to put on a hat, instead of turning the stomachs of the normal folk with all those blackened, peeling islands on his scalp. Some said he had a scar, too – those who had chanced to see him close up, that is. It ran all the way around his jaw, it was said, and up the sides of his face to disappear into that scabby tangle on top of his head. It was a slim thing, pink and straight. The kind of scar a man might acquire at the hands of surgeon of rare skill. Mayhap he'd been in the Wars. Osbeth was a simple place, an out-of-the-way place, and its folk hadn't had much truck with War business, but them who had knew how War could change a man – steal the light from his eyes and the rose of youth from his cheek, and set a trembling in limbs that before had been sturdy and strong. It was the chymicals in those burning storms they had seeded, it was said, that left the men broken like that. How many years the grey-skinned and craggy-faced Loon might have was anyone's guess, but if he had indeed seen War, then he'd more'n likely been a deserter. He had that fugitive air about him.

After all, the Loon would doubtless lay down his arms if his own shadow were to advance on him too closely. Why, he couldn't even stand to be out-of-doors. When whatever shady business he was about forced him into one of his perambulations of the village, he would scamper about from one nook to the next like a mouse when the pantry door was opened. It might have been funny were it not so pitiful a sight – the wretched wastrel scurrying by the quay, cowering from whatever-it-was that rendered the open skies so fearsome. True enough, the gulls of Osbeth were bold birds not averse to making attempts on a man's lunch, but it was as though the Loon, his mouth agape and his madly staring eyes round with terror, feared not for his sandwiches, but for his mortal soul. What else but insanity could instil such dread in a man? Well, mayhap the remembering of bombs.

And as though all of this were not enough to earn the Loon his name, there was the mischief he wrought from his lair atop Hook's Hill. The ramshackle place with the ever-shuttered windows crouched alone upon the ridge above the village, but the road that rambled by it was used often enough by the village-folk as they travelled to and from the market at Lamprey. Still, the hill was steep and the way twisted like a hooked eel by the cottage (thereby it had earned its name) – and so as a gesture of geniality to their neighbours, the people of Osbeth had by longstanding tradition hung a friendly, amber lamp from a nearby rowan tree. One evening, not long after the Loon had taken up occupancy in his den, the sun was descending on one side of the ridge, and the lamplighter on his rounds was stamping up the other. But when he arrived by the cottage, his tinderbox at the ready, he found that the lantern had been smashed to shards, and lay in bits and pieces at the roadside. But well, the night wind could be sprightly up there betimes as it blew down the hill to the cove, and the lamp was replaced without much further thought. The next night, however, the lamp was again found to be destroyed. This was a spell of bad luck to be sure, but lanterns were not in short supply and a further replacement was fetched. The following night, it had disappeared altogether.

The lamplighter had had enough of this japery. Once was an accident, twice was coincidence, and thrice was surely the work of that interfering Loon. The portly old fellow marched up to the cottage, readying an earful of cross words for the lamp-molester, and forthwith began to hammer upon his door. But as he applied the ball of his cane to the woodwork, the lamplighter saw something that did not belong in a wholesome place like Osbeth. For there, bold as day, was chalked a pagan symbol in the shape of a great, staring eye. Why, this was the stuff of the witch-folk! Disgusted, as any wholesome man would be, he began to wipe off the ugly, ungodly thing with the sleeve of his coat. But when, after the sounds of furniture being dragged aside and the sliding of many bolts, the Loon at last yanked open the door and discovered what the old fellow was about, he delivered such a vitriolic lambasting that the lamplighter was all but blown back down the hill by its force. Something in the lamplighter's face told the village-folk not to ask what exactly it was that the Loon had said, but the little winking lamp was never replaced. It had been hung on private property after all, and if the old fellow's knees had grown too weak to scale that hill every evening then, well, who was to say different?

Even darkened as it had become, the road was still travelled by the village-folk, for they knew it well enough and the carrying of a lamp was no great hardship to most. Some would even pause by the cottage on the hill, and dare one another to peer through the cracks in the shutters nailed fast by the Loon. But none would tarry long. For when the breeze stirred the treetops and the fog crept in from Lamprey Marshes, the noise that issued forth from within that place was fit to chill the soul. They called it the Loon's Curse, and at times when the wind was right it could be heard all throughout the moonlit lanes of Osbeth, and the village-folk would shiver in their beds and pull their eiderdowns tighter around them until the wind had changed or the Loon had ceased his crazy chanting. For those were strange words. Foreign words. *Unwholesome* words, words such as none in a place like Osbeth wished to hear. On stormy evenings, the children of the village would press their blankets to their ears – for when the old lighthouse in the cove cast its warning beam out over the perilous rocks, the Loon's fevered ravings would become maniacal screams, as though the light that swept the churning waves were some harbinger of terror and not salvation. One night, though, was remembered above all others, and even long after the Loon's disappearance its memory still brought sneers and curses to the lips of the few who recalled the goings-on. That night was the night of the sky-lanterns.

The new Town Hall at Lamprey had finally been completed, and it had been decided that in order to commemorate this most momentous of occasions a celebration was to be held. The folk of Osbeth did not as a rule hold with such fancy notions as New Town Halls or sky-lanterns, but as the thing was set to go ahead regardless, it seemed a waste not to see what was to be seen. The paper novelties, a new-fangled fad imported from the continent, were to be released as the climax of that evening's events, following the running of the greased marsh hogs along the High Road. Some of the younger folk had made the journey to Lamprey, while the old ones lined the streets of Osbeth and the children flattened their noses against window-panes streaked purple and red by the sunset. As dusk fell, still others climbed Hook's Hill to ensure their view of the proceedings.

And quite a sight it was. The last of the ember-coloured clouds disappeared from sight as the sun dipped below the horizon and the sky darkened from radiant violet to black, and with a cheer whose echoes could be heard clear across the marshes, the sky-lanterns went up. The village-folk cooed and sighed. Drifting slowly at first and then racing upwards, bobbing and jostling together as they were snatched by the breeze, the rainbow lanterns might have been a troupe of færie folk or will-o'-the-wisps riding abroad on midsummer's æthereal highways. Indeed, as the first cluster of lights broke the tree line, the village-folk pointed and laughed with delight as they saw that their neighbours had decorated the fancies with the wings of butterflies and bees. The lanterns danced on the wind, paper wings fluttered, and a great sigh went up from the crowd gathered there on Hook's Hill. But no sooner had the sky-lanterns begun to dip and glide across the marshes than the gasps of wonder were all but drowned out by another sound.

Such was the frightfulness of that noise that it took the merrymakers stunned moments to realise whence it came: the incredible shrieking and gibbering that tainted the enchanted scene issued of course from the abode of the Loon. It seemed that whatever fragile grip that crackpot had held on his sanity had at last been prised loose by the spectacle of the scintillating lights in the sky. This truly was the limit. Children were herded into the arms of their mothers, and the men fell in together, taking up sticks and whatever else came to hand. The disturbance had gone on quite long enough.

As the men neared the cottage, the way before them painted in pulsing, flickering hues by the luminous flock bobbing over the hilltop, the true nature of the cries was heard. In a wracked and anguished voice, the Loon was screaming forth those foreign words heard so often in the night – and though the summer air was balmy, the men shivered. There was a horrible pang of desperation in the howls loosed from that withered throat, a desolate pleading that clutched at the mens' hearts with chilly fingers. As the justice-dealers gathered in a fearful huddle in the shadow of the cottage, a suggestion surfaced that he be left to his own devices. Whatever anguish the man was suffering already must surely outweigh the flogging that they had been set to administer.

Not all were so taken by the plight of the Loon. Cursing the cowardice of his fellows, the harbourmaster strode up to the door and scoffed at the great eye emblazoned upon it. While the others looked on, their pale faces lit by the gliding flames, he commenced an assault of boot against lock. As blow after blow was landed, the chanting from within continued unchecked and the lock remained steadfastly unbroken. The harbourmaster growled, spat, and readied himself to charge at the door. But that door was barred like a prison cell's, and even so substantial a shoulder as his was not the ram to break it. As the cursing harbourmaster desisted in his siege and rejoined the throng, he brushed away a smear of white chalk dust from his arm. The device that had adorned the door had been all but erased.

Even throughout all the years of debate that were to follow, despite the theories advanced and the arguments tendered, despite the anecdotes regurgitated and the testimonies to which the old boys in the tavern swore upon their mothers' graves – despite it all – still none was able to explain just exactly what it was that transpired over those next few minutes of chaos. The accepted explanation was, as accepted explanations regarding peculiar occurrences most often are, unsatisfying. Was the mooted conglomeration of coincidence itself not as peculiar to contemplate as the supposed occurrence had been? For yes, the winds were known to be capricious up on that hilltop. But was it truly likely that some mischievous zephyr had chosen that very moment to whip across the marshes and loose itself upon Hook's Hill, sweeping up marsh-gas and sky-lanterns alike and sending the whole incendiary concoction spiralling down upon the heads of the vigilantes in an inferno of iridescent flame? But then, what other sane explanation could there be? What else but such a conflagration could ever have produced the coruscating shower that descended upon the hilltop that weird night?

For *something* that plunged out of the sky did indeed send the men fleeing and cowering in terror – a pulsating storm of varicoloured things that swooped and dived and buzzed amongst them. And if dazzled eyes had not been accessories in the bearing of false witness, then in the midst of that burning bedlam, when men were falling and crying at every turn, or writhing upon the ground clutching at scalded flesh, then the door to the cottage may indeed have been flung wide. And there on the threshold, illuminated by the eldritch flickering of the sky-lights, may indeed have stood the wild-eyed figure of the Loon, holding aloft his hand and mouthing strange words into the seething night.

But then the men were tripping and tumbling away back down Hook's Hill, and no one saw what happened next besides Whiskered Sindall, and his story was not much believed. For Sindall swore that he saw the Loon striding forth into the inferno with his shaking arms outstretched and a rage of defiance upon his tear-stained face fit to daunt the very Gods, and that at his roared command a wave broke over the hilltop so that the glowing lights seemed to retreat and rise up in a glittering spiral to disappear back into the blackness of the sky whence they came. But then, Sindall said a lot of foolish things about that night, and like most of what he said, those things were best ignored.

After that some of the men fell sick. The doctor prescribed an ointment to the ones that were burned, but it did not do much for the angry welts, which stayed black-and-red and oozing till winter, and still never did heal quite right. That was down to the chymical fuel in those absurd gimmicks of Lamprey's, the doctor said. *This* was why wholesome folks didn't need such fripperies. Let the city folks keep 'em. Even the men that had not been touched by the lights became nauseated. Some of them were sick all the while so that they could hardly keep a square meal down and could not be allowed to return to the boats. The vomiting grew less frequent after a few days, but the blood that was in it was a worry, and the hair that was lost was lost forever.

When he caught wind of the incident, the Mayor of Lamprey made a special trip to the village in order to deliver a formal apology. The people of Osbeth accepted it, grudgingly. The accident, they learned, was not reported in their neighbouring town. The front page of the Lamprey Herald declared the celebrations an unmitigated success – especially since the Mayor's hog had been victorious in the race – and made no mention of errant sky-lanterns whatsoever.

The village-folk were not much given to enquiry and investigation, and what Osbeth needed most following that most peculiar of occurrences was a return to the rhythms of *normal* life – the crash of the waves and the rising and setting of the sun. And so, for most, the furore died down, though for others the mystery, and still others the resentment, would remain. But as none could say they knew the truth of what had occurred that night – and as, despite a simmering suspicion of the perpetration of dark misdeeds, the best guess did not involve human agency – the Loon could hardly be held accountable. From then on he was seen even more rarely, and so for the most part he faded from the collective consciousness of Osbeth. There were more pressing matters at hand, like the overdue repairs to the quay. The only development, and one that raised a muttering for a time, was that the Loon had made permanent the ugly sigil which previously he had chalked upon his door. The shape of the eye had been hacked and gouged out of the wood, a splintered testament to his stark insanity. Still, forgetting about the Loon and his ways was the way that the people of Osbeth preferred it and so when, many years later, more strangers arrived and started asking after the village pariah, they were not greeted with the village-folk's customary warmth.

The first man was a serious-looking fellow. His hat was black, his cape was black, and his suit was black – and on his lip he wore a fine brush of a moustache that might have been waxed with the same black polish as his boots. He spoke in the fancy tones of a city gentleman, which the men in the tavern supposed that he supposed were cordial as opposed to uppity. The old boys were not keen to speak of the Loon, but the gentleman had a very firm manner, and the severe looks that he dispensed from beneath his black brows might almost have been enough on their own to loosen their tongues even before he had produced his pocketbook. He did not deign to stay a moment longer after fingers were waggled in the direction of Hook's Hill, and shortly afterwards he was spied disappearing into the cottage – for the first time, the Loon had admitted another into his sanctuary. A short while later the fierce, black-clad gentleman swept down the hill and out of town.

The second stranger was possessed of even more substantial moustaches than the first. He came at night, several weeks after the serious gentleman, and he did not ask for directions. His enormous height and build caused quite a stir in the village as he disembarked from his coach with a heavy-looking, patterned carpet-bag in hand. He spoke not a word to anyone, and nobody chose to speak to him; he seemed to know where he was going. That night a storm was gathering out over the ocean and the beam from the lighthouse was playing across the cove, so it came as no surprise when the frenzied cries from the cottage commenced. Little heed was paid to the screams that echoed down the hill.

None of the village-folk saw the second stranger leave. Nobody in Osbeth saw the Loon depart either, for they were all safely huddled by their firesides, braced for the oncoming storm. But in the morning he was gone. The door to his cottage was left swinging open, and he must have left in a great hurry because all of his possessions remained within. The villagers let the place sit empty for a month or two, but when it became clear that the Loon was not going to return, the village council decreed that the cottage be sold, and before long a wholesome young couple moved in. They had to replace the front door, of course, and repaint the walls of every room, over which the Loon had daubed all manner of horrid designs, and not all of them in paint.

They also disposed of the books and the other bric-a-brac that the Loon had left strewn about inside. Some of the things looked very ungodly indeed, and after a brief appraisal the village-folk decided it best that they be burned.

Thus the memory of the Loon was all but erased from the village of Osbeth. Of course, there was some talk of the old days following his disappearance, but memories of those times had become hazy and uncertain over the years. There were practical things to consider, like the scraping of barnacles and the patching of nets. In the end it was only the ageing Whiskered Sindall, once his imagination had been ignited by measure or two of whisky, who persisted in revisiting the night of the sky-lanterns up on Hook's Hill. But then, it was only Whiskered Sindall after all, and no one paid much heed to his nonsense. And whilst none bothered to contest the old man's claim that he alone had seen that Loon screaming his challenge into the boiling night – it *was* the kind of thing that a Loon might do – it seemed a tad beyond the pale when he claimed that Lamprey's sky-lanterns had screamed just as loudly in return.

It was likely the shock of it all, they said as they patted him kindly on the back, that had made him hear such whispers on the wind. Only the breeze as it had rustled at the torn paper. Lanterns didn't have nasty, droning voices, did they now? And nor could they whisper spiteful things into a man's ear. Sindall's audience had usually turned away before he got to saying how there hadn't *been* any wreckage from the lanterns found outside the cottage. And if they had not, then they had always taken their leave by the time he got to the part where the sky was singing.

SEVEN
On the Mechanics of Technologically Facilitated Necromancy

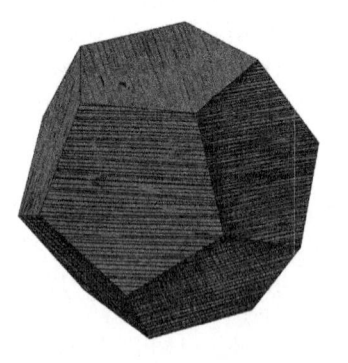

What manner of thoughts are harboured by a mouse? Does he truly dream of cheese? That was what they said. It was probable that a mouse would enjoy cheese – cheese was, after all, delectable. Would a mouse prefer a nice, pungent Uncle's Thumb or a crumbly wedge of Spittlian Blue? A wedge would likely be too much. A crumb, then. Mice ate other things too, though. Chocolates and the like. Cabbage. Naught supposed that as a mouse one had to take what one could get. But there was more, no doubt, in a mouse's mind.

Naught turned the little jar this way and that as he mused. Unlike a man, a mouse did not have to consider where to leave his droppings, so that would not be in there. Where to make his little house, then. Which skirting board should he nibble? Were skirting boards of different consistencies? And with what should he furnish his nest? Scraps of paper and discarded lengths of wool, most likely. And when he had made it nice and cosy, he would think of bringing his mouse wife home to rut. It was all very normal business, really – not so very different to the sort of things that occupied the thoughts of a man.

But when all of this was done with, what came into a mouse's head in the dead of night? Or was it perhaps the dead of day – did they not come out at night? Did he have secret thoughts? Did he ponder his place in his Kosmos of cheese and owls? Did he have forbidden thoughts? Did he dream of defecating upon his rival's corpse, or gobbling up his babies – sinking his sharp, white teeth into the warm translucence, and shaking them until his fur was a matted scab and he had painted the nest with their blood? Someone had once told Naught that if a mouse did not spend his life gnawing away at this and that then his teeth would grow to such a length that they would transfix his own throat. Is this, then, what at last must occupy a mouse's brain? To consume, in perpetuity, or to face slow death? Naught held the jar up to the light. The little thing that bobbed about within it was no bigger than the cyst that Doctor Geist had carved out of his back last autumn. He closed his eyes and pressed the jar to his forehead for a moment before placing it carefully back on the shelf.

Naught rotated the jar so that its label squarely faced the front. 'Mouse'. Well, he hadn't known the creature's name, so it was as good a designation as any. Next to 'Mouse' was 'Otter'. Otter was tiny, too – she would fit in the palm of Naught's hand. Indeed, she had once done so. Still, the rugose, heart-shaped thing was a giant when compared to its neighbour. Did that mean that her thoughts had been more expansive? Had she contemplated more than the sweet flesh of fish and the flashing, icy waters of the Irem? What a thing, to be content. To desire nothing more than what one had. Otters, he felt sure, did not crave that which they did not know. But that meant that they would never see the Beyond. Which was the superior mode of being?

Was she truly still in there, Naught wondered? She had been nice and fresh. Barely an hour from muddy bank to jar. Her body had been blasted to pulp by the pellets, white fragments of rib protruding from the bloody mince, but then Otter had not lived in her lungs, or her intestines, or even her heart. He had seen Flintwick's distaste as he had wrapped her in the oilcloth, seen the sadness in his eyes. Flintwick had not been sad for Otter. But Flintwick did not understand.

Men killed for less, did they not? Men killed for mere food, or for trophies. Why, they did it every year in Iremouth, at the hunt, in their hundreds. But was it the act of killing or the obtaining of antlers that was the aim of the thing? No, despite their beauty, the antlers affixed to the wall above one's fireplace were merely the material proof that one had killed – a memento of murder, a token of man's dominion over beast. It was barbaric, in a sense, this objectless killing and its crude displays. Vulgar. It was not that Naught disliked the hunt *or* its trophies – no indeed, he liked them as well as the next man, and he was by his own admission an aficionado of vulgarity. It was just that his was a nobler pursuit. In a sense, he was a librarian, a keeper of knowledge. A keeper of secret treats. He scanned along the shelf until his eyes alit on 'Ghastian Fallow Deer'. There she was. Hardly larger than Otter.

The jars were arranged in order of size upon their specially-constructed shelves, and each jar was of dimensions appropriate to its contents. It meant that Naught that was obliged to rearrange the vessels each time a specimen of intermediate size was added to the collection, but this he did not mind in the least. It meant that he could take each down in turn, and gaze awhile at the lovely things bobbing within. They were like flowers – so delicate and so beautiful with their folds and ridges and intricate traceries of veins. It was so easy to fall into a timeless reverie of bliss as he wandered amongst the shelves. He was almost fully engorged even now, but it would be all the sweeter to wait. There had been days when he had been disturbed by Flintwick tapping at the door, pestering him with some detail or other about eating or sleeping. But Naught always made sure that the door was safely locked. It was his secret place, his sweet place. No one was allowed in the Pickling Room but him.

He had even given them his special juice. He had known right away that it would keep them safe, just as it kept him safe, and so he had ordered that a tap be diverted from the main plumbing to the basin by the bench where the instruments were laid out. They were happy in the juice, fresh and alive, and it lent them a lovely vinegary colour, especially when he drew back the curtains and the sunlight glinted on the glass. Naught worked his way slowly along the shelf, his nails tinkling on the jars as he went. Here were Dog, Wolf, Bear, Manatee, and here the very freshest of his delicacies – Caviglia's late gift, the Gigantic Butuuan Ape. Somewhere far away within Naught's skull the sound of thunder began to boom and roll, and his teeth prickled delightfully. His breathing quickened and grew shallow.

The largest of the jars was set aside on a shelf all of its own. Naught approached slowly, his vision beginning to flicker spasmodically and the pressure in his loins now almost too much to bear. But he would not say *the words*, not just yet. He reached up and touched the cold glass. There was his treasure, his sweet secret. He had always known that this one was more special than the others. They hadn't even had to tell him that this was the one. He had *known*. They wanted this one – the others were his practice, his test. His treat. But They wanted him to share, too, when the right ones came. He had known that as well. One last time, then.

By now Naught's vision was buzzing with such violence that he could not focus upon the greyish mass in the jar, but its nearness was enough. He unbuttoned his breeches.

'*Hello, Belly*,' he whispered.

∽

'For pity's sake, be *careful* with that, you imbeciles!'

The servants struggling with the packing crate turned their heads at the sound of Obadiah's voice. One end of it had just been spared a potentially damaging impact with the ground by the timely intercession of a cushioning shin. After half-an-hour of Obadiah's firm direction, the fellow had evidently intuited the fact that the bruise would be a lesser injury than its alternative.

'I don't know where he obtains his staff, but I am beginning to suspect that the answer must be a home for the infirm!' the Doctor bawled after the pair as he watched them make their half-limping way into the House.

Edward made a non-committal noise as he looked over the boxes still piled on the gravel by the tracks of the departed coach. He slapped his palm on top of one. 'This one next, please.'

Another man in House livery bent and hefted the box by its rope handles, then staggered off after his colleagues towards the side-entrance through which they had disappeared. Beside the door, his arms tightly folded and a glowering look upon his face, stood Flintwick. He was surrounded by a fizz of drizzle picked out by the baroque iron lamp from beneath which he kept his vigil, but it might just as well have been a visible manifestation of the rancour that was so obviously boiling from his very pores. He was staring at them with undisguised venom.

'Pah!' spat Obadiah.

Edward wondered just how much Naught had told the hoary old goat of what had passed between them two evenings beforehand, and whether he knew just what manner of things his staff were now hauling into the House. His reaction to Obadiah's mention of Bellhouse had been unfavourable, to say the least. And well might it have been.

Of course, Edward had known that the man was dead – why else would they have brought the device? – but somehow to hear from Naught's very lips that he had preserved Bellhouse's remains... Well, it was ghoulish, the behaviour of a dangerous oddball. Still, in some respects Cold Ghastia appeared no different to the rest of the Empire – the aristocracy were not subject to the same law as was the common man, who would by such actions as Naught's have earned a lengthy stay in a lunatics' prison, or a shorter period swinging by his neck from the gallows. At least he knew now why Obadiah had been so certain that Bellhouse would remain 'conversational'. In their experience, nineteen years of interment did not tend to improve the robustness of the organs. It was fortunate also as Edward truly was not given to grave digging – it played merry hell with his back, and the smell was universally intolerable.

'How did you know?' he asked the Doctor as they followed the last of the crates into the House.

'Know what, precisely, young Edward?'

Edward glanced around to ensure that Flintwick had gone. 'About the... preservation?'

Obadiah tapped his finger against his nose. 'Best not to concern yourself with that right now, old chap. Best to keep our minds on the matter at hand, eh?' They paused as the servants ahead of them struggled down a groaning staircase. 'In any case, some questions are best left unanswered when affairs like this are concerned. Is it not enough that tonight we shall be raising the dead?'

Edward sighed. He would get no more from the Doctor.

Eventually, their lengthy stroll through the labyrinthine corridors of the House ended at the door to a basement room. Edward was pleased – he was inordinately fond of basements and cellars, though not nearly to the same degree that he had been before the onset of his condition. He had always found such repositories of the hidden and forgotten just as fascinating as he did attics – and this particular example of the species in no way disappointed him. The space harboured a suggestion of capaciousness, although the lowness of its ceiling and the shadowy horde of dusty boxes and tea-chests heaped all about precluded a clear view of its true extent. Edward allowed the delightful air of mystery to quell his disquiet at the tenebrous nature of their new den. It would do well enough.

At the far side of the space was a row of little windows, through which a suggestion of daylight leaked. Edward picked his way through a landscape of suitcases and rotting books to peer outside. The window – or, more accurately, hole – opened out onto the sheer face of a cliff. Above him the black vastness of the House seemed to rocket upwards into a dizzying skyscape of ash-coloured cloud, and an impossible distance below him was the undulating mosaic of Iremouth's rooftops. He yanked his head back in.

'Edward!' called Obadiah. 'No time for mooning – now let's get to it, eh?'

They assembled the device like a pair of automatons, working swiftly and all but wordlessly in the symbiotic manner to which they had become accustomed. Obadiah hefted the heavier components out of their crates, although Edward had to assist him in the manhandling of the generator. By tossing aside a disintegrating stuffed crocodile and a stack of wicker baskets, a space was cleared for the hulking thing in a corner of the basement where it was least likely to be disturbed – and where it was least likely to disturb them. Taking great care not to come into contact with its more hazardous extremities, the pair sweated and heaved it into position, where it sat looking squat and menacing and stinking dangerously of ozone. The generator – specifically designed by the arcanologists – was to their knowledge the most powerful electrochymical device in existence. For this evening's application, though, it would not be necessary to utilise anything even nearly approaching its full capacity.

Edward freed the sensory components from their wads of protective packing, brushing away shreds of paper, and placed them carefully upon the trolleys that had been set out for them. There were three instruments. The first to emerge was a handsome box of carved and varnished mahogany with fixtures of shining brass, to which was appended a great, flaring horn of polished tortoiseshell. It was a splendid-looking thing and beautifully crafted to its last detail – as were the other instruments of the array. The next of these, a contraption whose defining feature was a shielded drum of fine, waxed paper, Edward placed at a considered distance to the first.

Lastly came the lens, which Edward handled with a caution verging on reverence. The delicate thing was a handspan in diameter; the block of crystal from which it had been cut was among the largest yet mined. Though the stuff was not ordinarily considered to be of any great value – indeed, it was most commonly to be seen adorning mantelpieces in the form of preening swans and other such gaudy trinkets – to the arcanologists its specific refractive properties made it wholly unique. To all intents and purposes, this object was irreplaceable. As Edward slipped off its silken cover it glittered in the lamplight, and for a moment he glimpsed himself in its faultless, obsidian depths. He shivered and quickly pressed it into the mount, where its clasps attached with a well-engineered click. The lens now constituted one end of a long, telescopic barrel that terminated in a swatch of cloth-bound leads. Beneath the barrel, an ingenious system of cogs and gears allowed the assembly to be precisely adjusted in both focus and in angle. Edward inserted a key at various points in the machinery and wound it expertly, aligning the lens so that its gaze fell upon the centre of the room where three chairs had been placed.

Obadiah stalked around the basement, uncoiling lengths of elyctrical cable from a spool and connecting the separate parts of the apparatus in a web of trailing strands. He tightened the screws that affixed the leads to the transformer, and thence to the terminals of the now thrumming generator. The lever that would complete the circuit and activate the array, however, remained to be thrown. Finally, as Edward cleared away the packing crates, the Doctor set the canister upon a low table.

It looked an unremarkable thing. The canister was made of cast resin the colour of mud, and was of comparable size to a human head. With the exception of three small, round apertures at its base and one a few inches above, its dull exterior was entirely featureless. Obadiah unscrewed its lid in a series of purposeful twists and glanced inside to see that its contents were in order.

'Good evening, gentlemen!'

It was Naught, of course. He stood at the door, dressed in a voluminous jacket of fine orang-utan hide and twirling a black cheroot. He was carrying a large hamper.

'Good eve- ' began Edward, but Naught flounced past him in a fug of cheroot smoke and trailing wisps of auburn hair and made straight for the place where Obadiah stood.

'Lord Naught, please!' The cry was as close to panicked as Edward ever hoped to hear from the Doctor's throat. He was prising Naught away from the canister, which had come very close to assuming a second role as an ashtray thanks to their host's incautious curiosity.

Naught shooed Obadiah off and planted his hands on his hips, surveying the basement. 'Heavens!' he cooed, taking in the spectacle of the outlandish machinery. 'Never have I seen such a contraption as this!' He began to strut around the floor, peering intently at the unfamiliar devices. 'So this is it, then? Your necromancing machine?'

The doctor brushed the ash from his hands and jacket. 'I would hesitate to use such an appellation, Lord Naught,' he said. 'It is known as a *cerebral interface array*. And besides, this is Science, you understand – not magick.'

Naught frowned in evident perplexity.

'The suffix "mancy" refers to magickal divination, Lord Naught – not to matters of Science,' explained Obadiah.

'Hmm. Necrology, then?' suggested Naught. '"Ology" is the Science one, is it not?'

'I believe a necrology is something similar to an obituary,' pointed out Edward.

Naught rolled his eyes. 'Oh, you are a pair of pedants,

aren't you?' He stopped before the horn instrument and peered at it suspiciously. 'But this is an audiograph set, is it not? I have several of these! Amusing enough things but they don't hold a candle to real music, eh? Are we to have a little jig?'

Obadiah danced forward to deflect Naught's prodding fingers. 'It is not an audiograph set, no. You will notice that it has no turntable for the disc – but it will reproduce sound. We call it the "vocaliser" This is how Bellhouse will speak to us.'

'Indeed?'

'Indeed.'

Naught was now squinting at the drum. 'Then what, pray tell, is this?'

'An ear, Lord Naught. Of sorts. It receives the tremors of the air, as our ears do.'

'Hmm! And this one, the telescope? An eye, I suppose?'

'Very astute, Lord Naught.'

Naught lowered himself into a chair, shaking his massive head. 'Well, well. Never have I seen the like of it!' He eyed the murmuring generator in the corner. 'Elyctricity? That's what makes it all go?'

'Precisely.'

Naught snorted with apparent disbelief. 'Well I must say, all this really is quite beyond me. Wherever did you get it all from?'

Edward stepped forward and laid his hand on the canister. 'These instruments are of our own design, Lord Naught.'

Naught raised the twin smears of kohl that served him in place of eyebrows. 'Hmm. Impressive. So what's in the tin, then? Biscuits?'

Edward glanced down. 'This is where the, ah, *subject* is placed. The instruments will be connected once the canister is, um, populated.'

The cosmetic arches on Naught's brow remained in their upraised position. 'And then it will extract the thoughts from the brain, somehow? Provided that they're still inside, eh?'

Obadiah spluttered as though he had inhaled one of the spider webs that festooned the ceiling. 'The thoughts are not *in* the brain, Lord Naught!'

'Whatever do you mean?' For a moment Naught grew to resemble some kind of dandy tortoise as his head all but retracted into his ape-fur collar. 'Then how, precisely, do you intend to get them *out*?'

The Doctor held up a hand. 'Apologies, Lord Naught. I forget that you are not familiar with such things.'

'And do you intend to familiarise me?'

Obadiah drew a chair towards him and sat down. 'Certainly. Where to begin...' He drummed his fingers upon his thigh. After a moment, his gaze alit upon the horn of the vocaliser. 'Ah! Perhaps you could consider the matter in terms of the difference between an audiograph machine and a wireless set.'

'But you said that this was *not* an audiograph machine!'

'Indeed it is not. In fact, it is more akin to a wireless.'

Naught gave an exasperated sigh. 'If you are attempting to confuse me, Doctor Carnaby, then – '

'Not in the least. An analogy, Lord Naught, that is all. Now, let us say that, by and large, my learned colleagues of the academy consider the brain to be very much like an audiograph disc. When one converses with a friend, or hears a symphony, or tastes a fine wine, the little needle scratches a groove into one's grey matter, and the thing is recorded, there in the organ.'

Naught shrugged. 'Seems logical enough, no?'

Obadiah grunted. 'On the most basic of levels, perhaps. But in fact it is a specious notion, and almost entirely false. A folly of physicalist Science.'

'Oh. You are proposing an alternative, then?'
'Well - a wireless set possesses no such disc, correct?'
'Correct.'
'And yet at the turn of its dial it can be made to emit music, or voices. How?'
'Ah - ætheric waves, no? The wave carries the voice into the device.'
'Approximately true. Now, do you begin to see what I am saying?'

Naught blew a blast of air through his fleshy lips. 'Not presently, Doctor Carnaby.'

'I am saying that the memory of your words is not being inscribed into the stuff of my brain - it is being transmitted *by* my brain into the æther! Into the Beyond!'

'All very well, but presuming this is true then how do you get it *back* again?'

'Why, by the self-same method of course!' Obadiah pulled at his moustache in what Edward recognised as an indicator of gathering agitation. 'Perhaps I am not being clear. I am speaking here not merely of memory, but of what others may refer to as the soul, or spirit. A non-corporeal thing - an ætheric thing. A ghost, if you will, that is not *contained* or *generated* by the body, but... *received* by it as the wireless receives the ætheric wave.'

Their host sat back in his chair, folding his arms. 'But has it not been proven that the brain *does* make the mind? It's all chymicals and elyctricity and such, no? Why, I have read all about those funny chaps at Broadflight with their needles and wires, and how they made those poor fellows do that merry dance in front of the Society! Hoo! Doop-dee-doo!' Naught waggled his little booted feet about. 'Still, if one is to be a convict then one might as well be useful, eh?'

'Lord Naught, the fact that inserting electrified skewers or needles full of acid solution into a man's cerebellum makes him gasp and flop like a landed fish proves only that one is disrupting the means of *reception*.' He sighed deeply. Edward fidgeted in his seat – a close cousin of the tugging of the moustache, this was a sound heard most often as a precursor to utterances less forgiving of the eardrums. The Doctor scanned the basement again, his eye this time settling upon the glittering lens. 'Take a telescope, for example.'

'Oh! Yes!' Naught clapped. 'Now here is something that I understand!'

'Excellent. Let us say that a man is using it to gaze at a distant star. Now, that star is another sun much like our own – that is, a massive ball of flaming gas, larger by many orders of magnitude than the body upon which the man stands.'

'Yes, yes.'

'And yet, if the telescope is not focused upon it, the man may not perceive it at all. But by adjusting the lens, the star – the sun – comes into view as sharp as a pinpoint, yes?'

'And *your* point is what?'

'My point is that we cannot say that by the adjustment of his lens this fellow has *created* the star. The relative positioning of the components of the device has not ignited a flaming giant in the distant reaches of the void! He has merely made a physical adjustment that allowed him to *perceive* that thing which was already there. The flow of chymicals, the traces of elyctricity that our learned friends observe in their laboratories – these are not the *generation* of consciousness, they are its *symptoms*! Do you see now? That if I smash apart the telescope then the star will not be extinguished?'

'It is rather a lot to take in, Doctor Carnaby, and I am not in the least bit given to the destruction of telescopes.

But I believe I see what you are getting at.' Naught rested his chin upon a ring-encrusted hand, appearing to lose himself for a moment in thought.

Obadiah, who as he had spoken had seemed grow like a lengthening shadow, settled down into his chair once more.

'But who decides whose brain gets whose thoughts?' Naught said. 'What's to stop – say, Flintwick – remembering what I had for breakfast last week instead of who he was going to flog this morning?'

Obadiah drew breath, but Edward placed a hand upon his shoulder and spoke instead. 'There are some who say just such a thing is possible,' he said. 'But these are things that we are only beginning to understand as our forefathers did. There is much that we must learn. That is why we are here. For the moment, we know only that it is something to do with this.' Edward pressed a finger to the centre of his brow.

'Ah! The old spirit eye, eh!' Naught cried. 'I've heard of that!'

Edward inclined his head. 'The very same.'

'I suppose you're going to tell me now that it's not just a tale for old wives?'

'Oh, I would hardly be standing here if that were so. It is every bit as real as your other eyes, Lord Naught. We call it the *pineal gland*.' Edward tapped his head again. 'It is a physical part of the brain – it resembles a pine cone, hence its name.'

'Plenty of those around here!' cooed Naught. 'Pine cones, that is.'

'Ah, yes,' said Edward. 'Anyway, if I may extend Obadiah's metaphor we may say that it is the antenna of the wireless set.'

'But is a gland not an organ of excretion? That's the opposite of reception, no?'

'As I said, we do not know everything yet. But yes, we believe that the gland does excrete something. Something vital to the processes of consciousness itself – the substance which allows our antenna to attract the signal.' Edward and Obadiah exchanged glances. The Doctor gave Edward a single nod of approval. 'We think that thing is something very similar to the *dote*.'

'And what is that, exactly?'

Edward slipped his hand into his waistcoat and drew out the phial. He held it up before Naught's face. The sticky, yellowish crystals inside glinted dully in the lamplight.

'A drug?' asked Naught.

'A substance,' Edward said. 'One might call it a drug. That very much depends upon how it is used.'

Naught stood up and began patting his pockets. 'I have a pipe here somewhere...'

Edward took a step backwards. 'Lord Naught, no!'

'Eh? A syringe, then?'

'This substance is incredibly precious,' Edward was clutching the *dote* closely to his chest. 'If another granule of this substance exists anywhere in the Empire then I would be – well, let us just say that another granule of this substance *does not* exist. I... I went to some lengths to procure it.'

Naught cocked his head to one side. 'Oh, come come now! I have people who can get me anything I – '

'*Not this.* Not this.'

The Doctor turned to their host. 'Lord Naught, to take the *dote* would be a calamitous idea for a variety of reasons. Edward was only able to obtain the stuff after exhaustive researches, and it must only be ingested by those with the requisite mental training. Even *we* do not have that training.'

'Eh? Well, then who does?'

'Bellhouse had,' replied Obadiah. 'The Eelen had. Indeed, we have reason to believe that the *dote* or some form of it was the sacrament of every one of the ancient mystery religions. But to use it rashly would risk becoming... *lost.*'

Naught looked somewhat crestfallen. 'Then what are we going to do with it?'

Edward crossed his arms over his chest. '*We* are going to summon Bellhouse with it.'

'But isn't that what this lot is for?' Naught twirled a gold-encrusted finger at the device.

'Of course.' Edward slipped the phial back into his pocket. 'But it cannot function without the *dote.*'

'Hmm?'

'The brain - indeed, the body - is an electrochymical machine, as we have discussed,' said Edward. 'It is our contention that whilst the body is alive, and the pineal gland is still secreting the sister substance to the *dote*, the brain's bioelectrical charge energises that secretion, thereby activating the antenna and anchoring consciousness to the body.'

Naught nodded. 'I am with you so far.'

'Good. Now, when the body dies and the brain's processes cease, the connection is severed. The consciousness is cut loose, and returns whence it came. Our device,' - he tapped the canister - 'fuelled by the *dote* and activated by elyctricity, mimics the conditions necessary for the living operation of the brain, and thus the return of consciousness.'

'*Resurrection,*' muttered Naught.

A haunted look flitted across Edward's pale face. He swallowed. 'Of a kind.'

'Which brings us squarely to the matter in hand, Lord Naught,' declared Obadiah. 'Have you brought our... guest?'

Naught's painted lips parted, and that same faraway look that the pair had witnessed in the drawing-room misted his eyes. He seemed to be mouthing something.

'Lord Naught?' Obadiah pressed.

'Hmm? Eh?' Naught blinked several times. 'Oh - yes. Yes, of course.'

Their host bent and slid out the hamper from beneath his chair. As Obadiah took the handle, Naught's fingers trailed across the wicker, seeming loath to release it.

The Doctor dropped to one knee, and with trembling hands he reached into the hamper. Then, with a cry of triumph, he swung around to bear the jar aloft, like a man with a coveted trophy. 'Aha! Edward, my boy, here he is! Here he is at last!' He turned his prize back and forth in his hands, the amber light that filtered through it dappling his jubilant face.

Edward said nothing. There within that vessel floated that which they sought. It looked a poor thing, that gob of flesh swimming in its tawny soup, an unremarkable thing. And yet, it was that which would allow them to converse with the greatest mind of their age - and to make real their dreams. As Obadiah continued his gloating examination, Edward averted his gaze.

It was by no means the first brain upon which Edward had laid his eyes. Indeed, during the honing of their device, he and Obadiah had opened countless skulls as though they were bottles of vintage wine to be savoured for their subtleties - although, unlike wines they tended not to improve with age, and some had undoubtedly been fresher than others. And yet, time after time, Edward was struck by the irony of it. Once the shells of bone that had protected them were hinged open, once the arrangements of meat that had carried them were laid to one side, once the clothes that they had drawn around themselves had been burned away to ashes, those things - those lumps of quivering tissue - looked all alike. A vagabond or an Interlocutor or an arcanologist, it mattered not. Grey jelly all.

No, it was not the presence of a naked brain that perturbed Edward. To that he was inured. What perturbed Edward about the organ there before him was that the man who had for two decades preserved it in a pickling jar was the very architect of its owner's destruction.

Obadiah set down the jar beside the waiting canister. 'Come with me, Sebastian,' he said as its lid came unsealed with pop and a hiss of inrushing air. 'We have so much to talk about, you and I!'

∼

Viscountess Aspic reclined in her chair, eyes closed, allowing the soaring voice of the soprano to wash over her in waves. The acoustics of the theatre were by no means perfect, but if there were a spot from which the performance might best be appreciated then this was it. The structural reinforcements to her private box had been of some inconvenience to patrons of the establishment, but it was important that the weight of the chair be borne safely; the auricular recursivity between her hat and the curve of the wall had been an unexpected perquisite. Perhaps her earlier appraisal of the arts that season had been a hasty one after all. Her appreciation of this particular piece was ever bound to be slightly coloured, though; Lambert's *The Chthonian* had long been one of her favourite novels, and so this pioneering operatic production had been virtually predestined to send her into raptures. Indeed, as the hat resonated in sympathy with the solemn voice of the cello, her eyelids flickered and she let out a delighted little gasp – for just for a moment, the gauzy rainbow whisper of a Shape was forming in the cavity above her skull. Oh, what fun! Those ignorant lovelies had struck the right note indeed!

Smiling as the Shape faded like the after-image of a candle-flame, the Viscountess opened her eyes. She gazed down into the auditorium, a dusky landscape of velvet and crinoline peppered by the winking of diamonds, noticing as she did so that some members of the audience seemed somewhat less rapt than herself. One young lady in an elaborately restrictive dress had fainted away altogether, presumably having found the content of the scene too strong. A gaggle of concerned gentlemen were fighting with one another in the aisle in their attempts to revive her with smelling salts and other liniments. The front rows were pinned, rigid and motionless, to their seats, and another smile wrinkled Viscountess Aspic's thin lips as she imagined the stupefaction that was no doubt painted across their faces.

The Chthonian had been roundly condemned by the Church and by several groups of outraged moral campaigners, both for its overt references to violent bestiality and for its graphic representations of dæmon-worship. Under the glare of the spotlights, in a glade of potted tropical ferns, a well-formed young man prostrated himself before a looming, goat-like idol. On the other side of the stage, Hortensia Glitheroe, a promisingly uninhibited girl and the lead in this production, sat astride a stuffed ape with arms outstretched and head thrown back. The Viscountess gripped the arms of her chair and mouthed along with the words of Hortensia's soliloquy – it was the novel's very apex, and she knew it word for word.

Yes, this was proving a pleasant enough diversion, even for a lady forced to keep her own company. Naught had passed up the opportunity to accompany her this evening – apparently he was engaged in entertaining some guests from out of town. The Viscountess found his rebuff to be uncommonly ungallant; quite why it was that she was not permitted to be party to tonight's events remained unclear. Flintwick had seemed rather over-eager to dismiss her, although this was hardly unusual – to detect his abhorrence was not a work of any particularly great magnitude. Still, she was willing to bide her time, and to humour both Naught and his sycophantic old minion awhile longer.

Just as the controversial part with the ape's daughter and the rediscovered grandfather clock was beginning and the music from the pit was swelling towards its apocalyptic crescendo, the curtain behind the Viscountess was whisked aside and a man entered. He stooped to pass through the door (although it was not unusually low), and then crouched by Viscountess Aspic's iron chair and spoke to her in tones that all but matched the thunder of the timpani below. She listened intently for a few moments, gazing into the deep brown pools of his eyes, and then nodded fiercely. The dark-eyed man with the prodigious handlebar moustache grasped the handles of the chair, spun it around on the spot and propelled the Viscountess effortlessly through the archway and off into the night.

∽

'Well? Is it ready yet?' Naught's query emanated from somewhere within the brume of cheroot smoke which during the passing of the last hour he had been densening assiduously.

The Doctor slipped the final needle into its aperture where it was received with a snap of connectors and turned on his heel to face Naught; behind him, the unlikely sprawl of wires and instruments was silhouetted in the murky haze. He nodded. 'It is.'

Edward slipped back through the door. 'All gone,' he announced as he turned the key in the lock.

The Doctor looked to his colleague. 'Flintwick?'

'We are alone,' Edward confirmed as he strode towards the generator.

'Excellent. Then let us begin.'

'How wonderful!' cried Naught. He crushed the remains of the cheroot beneath his pointed boot and looked expectantly from one arcanologist to the other.

The Doctor inclined his head. 'Edward?'

Edward threw the switch.

In an instant, the air in the basement came alive. A low, unpleasant hum filled the room. It was joined a moment later by a keening sound, wavering just at the edge of hearing.

Naught's face wrinkled and he batted at the air as though trying to disperse the sound. 'Are you quite sure this elyctrical business is safe?'

Edward turned to look over his shoulder. 'It's quite safe for the moment.'

'But that sound – '

The young arcanologist had already turned back to his task. 'The sound is quite normal,' he called. 'Remember, we have no mean experience of these matters.' He flicked the switches on the sight and hearing modules, adding yet more whining pitches to the medley.

Obadiah stepped back from adjusting a dial wired to the canister. 'The vocaliser, Edward,' he said.

Edward nodded and twisted a knob on the wooden box, bringing it to life with a grating pop. The horn began to emit a steady fizzing sound, punctuated occasionally by clicks and scratching as though a hive of insects had been stirred up within it.

Obadiah clapped his hands and rubbed them together. 'And now,' he cried, 'to avail our honoured guest of the new faculties that we have prepared for him!'

'Hurrah!' burbled Naught.

With a flick of the Doctor's wrist, the final switch was thrown.

Nothing happened.

The pops and hissing of static continued unabated. As the seconds wore on and the lull continued, Edward and Obadiah glanced at one another. Edward, his brows drawn together, shook his head and offered a shrug.

Obadiah narrowed his eyes, and pursed his lips beneath his great moustache. 'Is the – '

His sentence was never completed – for a moaning, wordless howl burst suddenly from the horn.

Naught shrieked delightedly. 'What *is* it?' he breathed.

Obadiah shot him a black-browed glance, but said nothing. Edward, too, was silent. It was an uncomfortable, insistent sound, undeniably mechanical and yet somehow moronic. Long moments passed, and the weird ululation continued. Finally, the Doctor shook his head. 'I am not sure,' he admitted. He stood up, and reached for the vocaliser's controls.

The sound blared out even louder than before, a horrible cry permeated by ear-splitting crackles and the angry hornet-buzzing of the tortoiseshell on each upsurge. Naught hissed in displeasure and clapped his bony hands to his ears, glowering pointedly at Obadiah.

Oblivious, the Doctor calmly rotated the knob back to its prior position. '*Not the volume*,' he mused. As the lowing sound continued to reverberate around the basement, he strode to the trolley upon which the lens device sat – whereupon he let out an enraged, nasal grunt and turned, glaring, to his companion. 'Edward, you have turned this *off*, you great fool!' he thundered.

Edward winced and bit his lip, silently cursing his idiocy as he did so. This was not the first time his attention had slipped. He rubbed at his stinging, blurry eyes. 'I'm sorry, Obadiah, I don't know what I could have been thinking.'

With an exasperated sigh and a shake of his head, Obadiah snapped the switch.

All three blundered backwards as a cacophonous scream erupted into existence. The deafening blast of animal pain and terror smashed through the room like a wave, sending the men sprawling across the basement in a heap of windmilling arms and upended chairs.

'*Turn it off!*' Edward screamed into chaos.

Naught was still scrambling backwards across the floor. 'Turn the ghastly thing off now!' he shrieked.

Obadiah, his jaw clenched and eyes screwed tight, advanced on the vocaliser step by laboured step, as though battling the fury of some terrible gale. At last, his fingers found the switch.

The scream died with a click.

Echoes of the cry resounded around the chamber before eddying away into nothingness. Edward felt the hairs on his scalp and arms falling flat once more, the adrenalin surge draining from his limbs and chest. He let out a shuddering breath through the fingers of the hand that he found he had clasped to his mouth and dropped into a crouch on the floor. His bones had become gelatinous.

Naught's feet protruded from beneath a toppled pile of knickknacks. He threw off an empty clock case that had found its way onto his head and sat up amidst a small avalanche of assorted items. 'What *in the world* was that detestable sound?' he demanded as the face of the clock rolled off into the shadows.

The Doctor stood with his back to them, hands upon hips, staring intently into the huge, polished lens. He waved his hand slowly back and forth in front of it. Then he shook his head and turned to face the others.

'Gentlemen,' he said, 'Bellhouse's brain has been in a state of preservation for something in excess of nineteen years. And if what we hope to establish is indeed true, then for two decades the essence of its owner has not resided within it. This vessel has lain empty, idle. And now, it may be that it has atrophied beyond hope of recall.'

Naught tutted. 'And? What are you saying, man?'

Obadiah pressed a knuckle to his forehead and blew out a great sigh. 'I had long feared that to be drawn back into a physical shell after such an extended period would prove to be an intolerable shock for the human consciousness – let alone to be drawn into an atrophied brain equipped with mere facsimiles of human senses. It seems that I was correct. I am saying that if indeed we have summoned Bellhouse back from the Beyond, then in the process we may well have driven the man insane.' He stamped. 'Damn it all, I *should* have foreseen this!'

Naught was clambering out of the pile of detritus and brushing something crisp and spidery from his ermine collar. 'Oh! You've broken him, eh?'

'No,' said Edward slowly, and at the sound of his voice both men turned to face the pale young man. 'Perhaps that's not the case at all.' He pushed himself up off the floor, still somewhat unsure whether his legs were up to the task of supporting him. 'You are right, of course, Obadiah – in that Bellhouse has probably experienced mental shocks of incredible severity – but I would imagine that his neural matter is of stronger mettle than you suggest!'

The Doctor sighed. 'What *exactly* are you suggesting, Edward?'

'I think he's surprised,' said Edward. 'And understandably so! He needs time. Time to adjust.'

Obadiah cocked his head to one side, thrusting out his chin and pulling thoughtfully at his moustache. 'It's possible.'

'Then we should allow him to acclimatise.'

'I am by no means an expert, but it seems a sensible proposition to me,' agreed Naught. He had lit another cheroot, and was drawing deeply upon it in a way that suggested that a jangling of his nerves had transpired.

'Very well,' said Obadiah.

'Then let's adjust the array. Dim the lights. Decrease the sensory input so that he's not bombarded with such intensity.'

The Doctor grinned and struck his palm with his fist. 'By Gods, I think you've got it!' He shook Edward by the shoulders – the only thanks he would receive – and immediately spun around to face the array.

The recalibrations were the work of minutes. The dense fug of tobacco smoke that had wreathed the room had dispersed – blown away, it seemed, by the storm of horrid noise – and so Naught applied himself to replenishing the cloud as the arcanologists sat in quiet contemplation. Obadiah lit one of his cigarillos and joined Naught in the endeavour. Nicotine, as he was fond of saying, was an excellent catalyst of neural activity. Edward, who found the habit to be a catalyst of ocular irritation, sought refuge at the windowsill. His eyes were bleary enough as it was. Though the night air was cool and bracing, he refrained this time from extending any part of his anatomy outside of the House, content instead to gaze out into the star-peppered blackness. Unusually, the night was clear as crystal, and he for a time he found himself lost in the machinations of the heavens. Indeed, it seemed that Obadiah had been calling him for some moments before the Doctor's voice filtered through into his consciousness.

'Sorry, Obadiah,' he called as he picked his way back through the dross. 'There's a remarkable amount of meteoric activity this eve– '

'Never mind that, boy. I think we've waited long enough.'

Obadiah, who had positioned himself before the lens, ushered Edward in the direction of the vocaliser. Naught had seated himself at a greater distance from the apparatus than previously, and looked somewhat pensive. The Doctor glanced at his companions, and cleared his throat.

'Bellhouse!' he cried. 'Sebastian Bellhouse! My name is Doctor Obadiah Carnaby. Despite your death, you are now revitalised. What you now see and hear is the material world that you once knew in life!'

Edward found that he was holding his breath as slowly, fraction by fraction, he twisted the vocaliser's control and a whisper of sound began to emerge. Beads of sweat began to prickle on his upper lip. But as the vibrations gathered in the horn and it began to hum with the beginnings of the utterance from Beyond it became plain that, this time, no frightful scream would assault their senses. His hand shaking, Edward released the control and stepped away from the device. Wide-eyed and pale-faced, he turned face to his silent companions.

It was a wholly different sound that now filled the air in that basement room. It was a sound that should have convulsed the body of its maker, had he still been in possession of such a thing. It was a sound of unutterable sadness and indescribable desolation.

It was the sound of a dead man weeping.

EIGHT
Returns

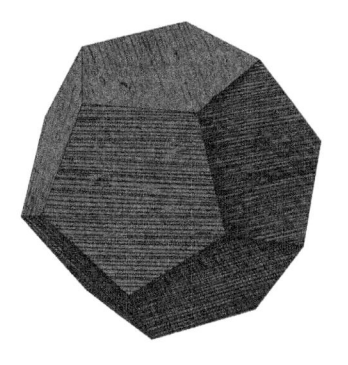

'So, he has arrived at last?'

'Yes, ma'am,' said the unusually tall gentleman with the tremendous moustache. He stood before Viscountess Aspic with his hands clasped behind his back, so that the beautiful brown tweed jacket that he sported stretched tightly across his bear-like chest.

'Excellent!' cried the Viscountess. 'Oh, this is excellent news indeed! In fact, I would go as far as to say its news worth interrupting *The Chthonian* for!'

'We thought so, ma'am,' the gentleman rumbled.

The Viscountess tapped her fingers excitedly upon the inlaid ivory of her chair's arms. 'So *this* is how it begins! I must confess that I was becoming really rather impatient.'

The unusually tall gentleman said nothing. Instead he cast his blue-eyed gaze around the ceiling, appearing to study the plaster mouldings there with some interest. Besides the House, Crag Avenue Apartments was perhaps the most exclusive of Iremouth's dwellings, and throughout its expanse it was decorated in the very height of good taste.

Viscountess Aspic's twelve-room suite was no exception. Flocked wallpaper in a staggering variety of designs enriched its every vertical surface, and the fine bronzewood floor was invisible beneath multihued drifts of rugs and furs. Everywhere gilt-framed mirrors suggested improbable passageways and multiplied patterns and soft-burning lamps. The ceiling of the drawing-room, though, was a minor marvel in plasterwork – a delirium of ornate grottesca that obtruded from above like an accumulation of floral stalactites. Nevertheless, to claim that the ceiling was the room's most interesting feature was to adopt a fairly indefensible position – especially since the capacious cabinet that the room also hosted held such an unfeasibly fine collection of Butuuan anthropological artefacts. What's more, the unusually tall gentleman had already admired that ceiling innumerable times.

'Silas?' said the Viscountess, peering up at him through eyes narrowed by suspicion. 'Is there something you are not telling me?'

Silas cleared his throat more nervously than might be expected of one of such monstrous size. 'Actually ma'am, he arrived in the city some days ago,' he admitted.

Viscountess Aspic gasped and clutched at her grey bosom.

'We have been watching,' he explained hurriedly, holding up his huge hands. 'Observing. We wanted to be absolutely certain that he had secured access to the House before we took further action.'

'Well then?' the Viscountess demanded. 'Has he?'
'Yes.'
'And is he there now?'
'To the best of my knowledge, yes.'
'Alone?'
'No. He has a young assistant with him, ma'am. Ma'am, I am deeply sorry if my actions have displeased you at all.'

All of a sudden the frown that the Viscountess had worn collapsed as might an ageing fruit, and she smiled her thin-lipped smile at him. 'I trust you, Silas,' she said.

'I remain your servant.' He gave a little bow, at which the tweed protested.

The Viscountess sighed and rested her chin upon her knuckles. 'I do hope this all becomes clearer, Silas. At present I am having great difficulty in discerning the meaning in these events.'

Silas smiled, and his unusually large teeth seemed very white against the mahogonal bristling of his moustache. 'I am sure it will, ma'am. After all, we *know* that he will succeed. There has not been another in the history of the Reaping who has come closer. But the means of his success is not our concern. In the meantime we should adhere to our original plan. We must get close. Observe. Become... indispensible.'

'You are right, as ever.' The Viscountess stopped mid-nod and her smile reversed itself once more. 'But what of our little bloodhound?' she said. 'What if he says too much?'

'He will not betray us,' growled Silas. 'You may be assured of that. Oh, I have given him permission to impart the knowledge when he is called. Without it Carnaby cannot succeed. But he knows very well what will happen if he is *disobedient.*'

'Very good,' breathed the Viscountess. 'Take me to the window, won't you, Silas?'

The wheels of Viscountess Aspic's chair hissed through the thick carpet, and she pulled aside the drape of heavy, puce velvet. It was dark as pitch outside, and so the pair's reflexions appeared sharp and clear in the windowpane. The Viscountess's face was pallid and pinched beneath her metal hat, and Silas loomed behind her with his spade-like hands upon her shoulders and his eyes of icy blue shining as though lit from within. She pressed her face closer to the glass, and the scene outside of the window swam into view. The night sky above the rooftops of Iremouth was flecked with stars.

Some of them appeared to be falling.

'They are coming, Silas,' breathed the Viscountess.

'Yes, ma'am,' replied the blue-eyed man.

⁓

The three men looked at one another, each of them struck dumb by the chilling sound that between them they had summoned into being. Edward swallowed, finding that his throat was dry. He was not sure that he could even attempt to imagine the horrors that could wring cries like that from the soul of a man.

He ran his hand through his lank, dishevelled hair, eyeing the canister that sat at the heart of the array, then turned to the Doctor. 'Do you... Do you think he can hear us?' he whispered.

'*I hear you, fiend!*' The ragged voice boomed and rolled around the chamber like thunder, then was silent. The echoes died away, and the hiss of static returned.

'Oh!' This time Edward did not stumble, but stepped backwards nonetheless.

'Your question is answered,' observed Obadiah wryly.

'Fascinating!' exclaimed Naught.

Edward shivered. The voice – Bellhouse – had sounded defiant, imperious almost. But had there been a particle of fear there, too? He wondered for a moment whether their device were truly capable of relaying such nuances of inflection, but then the strangeness of what he had heard filtered into his awareness. '*Fiend?*' he repeated.

Then the voice rang out again, and again Edward shuddered. Though it emanated from an instrument of his own design, that voice sounded as though it carried to him across distant, unspeakable leagues of kosmic emptiness. There was something autumnal about that voice, too – something of the dying, but also of the splendour of that death, and, perhaps, the promise of rebirth. It seemed appropriate, Edward thought.

'*What is this place?*' demanded the voice, a swirl of golden leaves on icy, interstellar wind.

'This is Iremouth,' declared Obadiah, stepping forward to address the lens directly and spreading his arms to indicate the basement. 'On the island of Cold Ghastia.'

It was either a shout of laughter or a violent burst of static that spilled from the horn then; whichever it had been, it stopped abruptly as though a wire had been cut.

As one, the three men leaned forwards.

'*Liar!*' blared the voice, and all three recoiled again. 'There is no Iremouth! There is nothing but dust! This place is nothing but a... a damnable *construction!*'

Now Edward stepped forward. He wrung his hands, uncertain how to address the Bellhouse-machine. 'No,' he said cautiously. 'My friend is telling you the truth. This *is* the real world! This is planet Verdra – the world that you knew when you were alive!'

'*Alive! Alive!*' echoed the distant, crackling voice, as though Bellhouse – if Bellhouse it truly was – were somehow tasting the word. '*I was... alive?*'

Edward breathed deeply, and pressed on. 'Surely you must recall your *life*, Bellhouse!'

'*Bellhouse? Sebastian?*' mused the voice, and then the horn uttered a small, choking sound. 'I was *Bellhouse.*'

Edward nodded to himself. So, at least the owner of this voice seemed content to believe that he was whom they had imagined him to be. Obadiah grasped his shoulder and pulled to one side.

'You *are* Sebastian Bellhouse,' the Doctor said, presenting himself before the lens in Edward's stead. 'And I am Doctor Obadiah Carnaby.'

'You look like... a *man*,' said Bellhouse.

Edward and Obadiah looked at one another.

'Yes,' said Obadiah slowly, 'I am a man. I am a Doctor of Arcanology from the Imperator's University of Hingham. Myself and my colleague,' – he indicated Edward – 'are responsible for your presence here.'

'Impossible! There are no men. All men are dust! Dust and ashes in the wind!' The timbre of the voice altered subtly. '*And yet they wear the faces of men!*'

Once more Edward and Obadiah exchanged wondering glances.

'How have you brought me to this place?' demanded Bellhouse.

'The tissues of your brain are attached to an elyctrical device,' Edward explained. 'We... we wanted to talk to you.'

'*Impossible!* There is no such device! This place is not real. Let me go.'

'We only wish to speak with you, Bellhouse,' Obadiah repeated.

'*Let me be!*' roared the voice from the machine. The shell of a guitar, somewhere off in the gloom, resonated musically for a moment and then was silent again. 'Let me die! Why do you torment me so? You have already taken her... all is gone, and there is nothing left of me! Just let me go – let me die, I say! Give me back to the kind blackness!'

The Doctor looked to his colleague, puzzlement writ large upon his face, then turned back to the lens. 'What do you mean, Bellhouse?'

'*Leave me be!* I beg of you! I have meddled, I know – but you have punished me enough! I will trouble you no longer, I swear it!'

'We do not mean to harm you,' said Obadiah, frowning. 'We are not your enemies.'

'*Leave me be!*' the voice of Bellhouse raged again. 'I will not be gulled by this trickery!'

Edward took Obadiah by the arm and led him to the rear of the array where they could not be perceived by the lens or hearing-drum devices. 'Who does he think we are?' he asked quietly.

Obadiah rubbed at his moustache and shook his head. 'I have no idea. Perhaps he has been driven mad after all.'

'He seems to think that we are impostors of some kind – '

The Doctor waved a hand. 'He is paranoid. Delusional.'

Naught walked over to where they stood. 'What in the world is the old boy ranting about?' he asked shrilly. 'Can he not see us? Is your contraption malfunctioning? Perhaps the lens is smeared or – '

'*That voice!*' came the distorted cry from the horn, at a pitch that made it buzz and crackle with dangerous violence. 'I know it! Show yourself!'

Obadiah's face brightened visibly, and in his excitement he took Naught by the lapels. 'Lord Naught! He recognises your voice! Stand before the lens!' he urged.

'Eh?' said Naught, but then appeared to realise Obadiah's intention, and positioned himself in front of the sight module. He leered into the lens, his black, sunken eyes glistening wetly in the lamplight.

Edward folded his arms and said nothing. Of all the sights with which one could be presented upon one's return from the grave, he thought, what a rum one was this!

'*You!*' spat the disembodied voice, the single word saturated with such venom that even its mechanical reproduction shuddered and dripped with intensity.

'Hello, Belly!' crowed Naught. 'How have you been?' He turned to his companions. 'A somewhat rare opportunity for us to become reacquainted, eh?'

Edward grimaced.

'It *cannot* be you!' blared the voice of Bellhouse.

'Oh, but I assure you that it is!' grinned Naught.

'*Ah! But I am so confused!*'

Something in the cadence of Bellhouse's artificial voice told Edward that those words had not been intended for their ears. Indeed, he had long doubted the capacity of the inferior frontal gyrus to discriminate between thought and utterance, but still it had proved time and again to be the only truly viable location for the insertion of the vocaliser's elyctrode needles. Now, more than ever, he felt that he had been correct: Bellhouse was thinking, not speaking. He continued to mumble and curse, his words swirling in a sea of abstract sound that was by turns burbling, bovine, then strangely musical. This was thought itself made audible, and it was disconcerting.

'*Ah! It is him! No, no, Sebastian... They would not use him – that thing is no bait for me! Perhaps it is true, fool Sebastian! True, after all! To have come all this way... and to find him, at the end of all! At the end of all life, it is him again! No, I will not have it... I must escape! Come to me, my terrible friends! Come to me once again, deliver me from this place! Bear me away to any place but this!*'

'Bellhouse!' barked Obadiah, as though trying to call their guest back to his senses.

'Ah! *They fade... they die!*'

'Bellhouse!' he called again, louder this time. 'Hear me!'

Bellhouse's voice was growing distant and contorted as though it played from a warped audiograph disc. '*No! This cannot be! The black devourer, prison of souls! It holds me fast again! Come, kind Sphere! Let me taste the void!*'

Naught screwed up his face like one who has scented something malodorous. 'What exactly is he gibbering on about now?'

'*The Polyhedra!*' cried Edward, panic sweeping over his features. 'He means to affect the Transition!'

'*Focus! Come, O sweet, awful angles! Focus!*' came the urgent cry from the horn.

'He is going to damage himself, Obadiah!' yelled Edward, grasping the Doctor's coat and shaking him. 'His neural pathways are not indestructible!'

The Doctor's jaw dropped. 'By Gods you are right, boy! Damn it all!'

'The Transition is too much! He will reduce what mind he has left to jelly!' With that, Edward turned and flung himself over the tangle of leads, reaching desperately for the lens module.

'*Edward!*' the Doctor bellowed.

'*Come to me, Sphere, O Sphere of Uush'Ton!*'

Edward's hand slammed onto the switch.

A great roar burst from the horn. '*Ah! Darkness, all! What have you done?*'

The arcanologists exchanged anxious glances.

'I think I have broken his concentration!' Edward called.

Obadiah blew out a sigh of relief. 'Bellhouse, listen to me!' he urged. 'We know that you are trying to affect the Transition of Uush'Ton. If the Formulæ are currently powerless for you, then it is not of our doing. I beg you – do not exert yourself any further. There is little gain to be made, and you must be aware that irreparable damage may be done by excessive visualisation of the Polyhedra!'

'He is telling the truth, Bellhouse!' cried Edward.

'Ah! So I have no choice, fiend!' Bellhouse seethed. 'You have me trapped! Trapped, as I have always been!'

The Doctor shook his head. 'To trap you was not our intention. I say again, we simply wish to speak with you.'

A roar of frustration shook the air. The machine was silent for a while, then Bellhouse spoke again, a shade of resignation now colouring his voice. 'Speak, then, as it seems I have no choice,' he sighed. 'What do you want from me? And why have you brought *him?*'

Obadiah glanced around at their host. 'If you are referring to the presence of Lord Naught, then you should know that it is thanks to him that you are even here at all,' he said.

'*Thanks?*' screamed the voice of Sebastian Bellhouse in a furious surge of elyctrical feedback. '*It is thanks to that creature that I have been to hell!*'

∽

A falling star, thought Flintwick, was really nothing of the sort. Such a term was a nonsense, and might happily be expunged from the lexicon of sensible people. Leave it to those insufferably romantic types who chose to occupy their minds with such frivolities as popular songs. If a star were in reality to fall to Verdra (which from the very outset was an impossible occurrence, for the star's infinitely greater mass would mean that Verdra would be the body to fall) then the planet would be consumed by a raging inferno of flaming gases, and this would hardly be an inspiration for poetry of any kind. Lord Naught's fascination with the heavens was a different matter entirely, of course. Such a man was perfectly entitled to indulge himself in a healthy interest in the Kosmos and its workings. Indeed, there was a pleasing uniformity and predictability to such things, as a rule - until they were disturbed by irregularities. Try as one might, irregularities always seemed always to creep in. Too many irregularities had been creeping in of late. This did not mean, however, that irregularities would be permitted to remain.

Despite his terminological quibbles, Flintwick sat transfixed by the spectacle of the meteorites that flared across the night sky. Having been dismissed, he had occupied himself for most of the evening with a thorough inspection of the west third-floor kitchens, and had already compiled a substantial list of reprimands, hide-tannings and pay-dockings when their glitter had caught his eye. He had closed his notebook and repaired to a seat by the window so that he might observe them awhile. A falling star was really interstellar debris. A simple rock - nothing more or less. Hardly an object of romance. The spectacle of this particular shower of detritus did have something oddly attractive about it though, he was forced to admit.

The meteorites were coming down in great showers of sparks, leaving long, winking trails behind them. Some of the rocks fell in clusters of three, four, five - even half-a-dozen - seeming at times to dance and weave together so that their trails twined briefly into fantastical braids before glittering away into nothingness. An effect of magnetism warring with momentum, no doubt. Meteorites were known to be magnetic.

The shower seemed somehow closer than Flintwick might have expected - for in his admittedly limited experience, such phenomena appeared most often to be taking place upon the far horizon, as though on the very rim of the distant dome of the sky. These particular rocks, however, seemed to be falling so nearby that Flintwick fancied that were he to leave the House then he might run a reasonable risk of being struck down on the spot. He mentally admonished himself for entertaining such a ridiculous idea, but still could not help thinking that at least a handful of them could well have landed somewhere within Cold Ghastia. Indeed, it *appeared* as though a singularly large proportion of them were raining down upon the forest.

It was doubtless a trick of the light. After all, who knew what peculiarities starlight might take on when refracted from objects travelling over such great distances and at such enormous speed? It certainly was a peculiar sight, the apparent changing of course and even the slowing of the flight of the space-rocks as they drew closer to the earth. At times it seemed that they skimmed so languorously over treetops and rooftops that they might just as well drop out of the air.

If not light *per se*, then heat, perhaps, disturbing the light before it reached his eye? He nodded to himself. Yes, that was it. Heat would also explain the vivid colouration of the meteors – for each seemed to wink brightly in all manner of unexpected shades. Over the course of the minutes that he had spent in observing the spectacle, Flintwick had counted every hue in the spectrum, from glowing reds and ambers, to strangely unearthly purples and shining, emerald greens. He had once read in a fascinating tome entitled *The Proposed Behaviour of Celestial Bodies* that meteors were lent their vivid hues by the gaseous auras that they carried, or by chymicals within them that ignited and burned off as they entered the planet's atmosphere. Verdra's atmosphere was now held to be a sort of heavenly furnace, if one could believe such a thing.

Yes, it was quite a sight to behold – but what pleased Flintwick most was that there was always a *sensible* explanation for even such seemingly singular phenomena. He thought of the two troublemaking out-of-towners locked in the basement with his master, and for the first time that evening a smile touched his face. In the wake of irregularity there would always be a return to the natural order of things; once the novelty had burned away, there would be normality once more. Sometimes all that was required was a spark.

Just then, a commotion roused Flintwick from his thoughts. It was a girlish scream attendant upon an adolescent squawk, echoing down the corridor to the kitchen where he sat – and if he was not much mistaken then it emanated from somewhere within the very wing from which he had not two hours beforehand banned the staff. He cocked his ear, and his nostrils flared as he recognised the voices: Laurence, the potboy, and Agetta, one of the less-able serving-girls. Flintwick got up from his windowside perch, cracking his knuckles. There was discipline to be attended to.

∽

'And what, exactly, am *I* supposed to have done?' If Naught was not indeed truly baffled then the counterfeit expression that he wore upon his leathery face was a most convincing one. His lower lip protruded like a shelf of painted meat and his brows were knitted together.

The Bellhouse-machine emitted a blast of laughter-static. 'Ha! Must I really name your crime, Naught?

Did it mean so little to you that you have forgotten already the atrocity that you committed?'

'Now steady on!' Naught objected. 'I know I didn't ask your permission but you were hardly in a state to – '

'By *Gods!*' exclaimed Bellhouse.

Naught's perplexity remained. 'What are you getting at, Belly?'

'You incorrigible brute!' howled the voice from the horn. 'You murdered me, Naught! *You are my murderer!*'

Naught looked as though he had been slapped by an incorporeal hand. 'Well this really is beyond the pale!' He balled his hands into knobbly little fists and turned to address the Doctor. 'If this is your idea of a *joke*, Carnaby, then I fail to see the funny side!'

The Doctor held up his hands. 'Lord Naught, I have told you that I make no judgement of your actions.'

The horn exhaled a sound of rage and pain like a broken church organ whipped by the breath of winter. 'Ah! Held captive by bickering fiends and murderers! Is there to be no end to my torment?'

As Edward looked on at the macabre charade unfolding before him, he felt something rising up from his stomach to his chest. This was not how it was supposed to happen at all. The rising thing burst forth from his mouth. '*Please*, everybody!' he cried, and his companions turned to glower at him. 'Let us speak reasonably!' he implored, and in the intervening silence he flicked the switch to activate Bellhouse's vision once more. 'Bellhouse, let us explain. You deserve to understand!'

The organ rumbled.

'I... it is an honour to meet you, Bellhouse. An honour,' Edward began. 'We are Scientists, too, Obadiah and I. Researchers. My... my name is Edward.

Lord Naught is our host. You died, nineteen years ago, I think, and Naught... he has helped us to contact you. I am sorry if we have hurt you or... if we have hurt you. I... we... we want to know about Uush'Ton. About the Shapes, and the Transition.'

A long moment passed, and then Bellhouse intoned four words. He spoke them slowly, and each one of them was a challenge, a question, a terrible acknowledgement. Those words were the tolling of a bell, the sealing of a tomb, the rearing of a monolith. The irredeemable reordering of something dreadful, somewhere out in the rolling depths of the Kosmos. '*You wish to know.*'

The room pulsed or shimmered, and something in Edward's very core clenched. He stared into the slick, black void of the lens, where for half a heartbeat something glittered darkly. 'Yes.'

When Bellhouse spoke again, there was sadness in his voice. 'You know not what you ask, Little Sorcerer. There are forces at work such as you cannot possibly comprehend. If I were to divulge to you the things that I have learned then... well, it would be as well that I had been captured by Them and not... summoned up by your machine, if that is the truth of it. And I am not convinced that it is. Still, I cannot give you the knowledge you desire. Why, I would sooner hand a loaded blunderbuss to an infant!'

'B-but – ' stuttered Edward.

Obadiah let out a noise of frustration. 'We must know!'

'Oh, you *must?*' boomed Bellhouse. 'You *must?* Tell me, what is that you *must* know?'

The Doctor clenched and unclenched his fists. 'Of the Transition! Of the Beyond! I must know where you have been!'

'*Where I have been,* indeed! I assure you, man, you do not wish to know of the places I have been! Oh, They do not let you alone when you have been to such places – when you have learned such things as I! Such horrid things. Such forbidden things!'

'*Who?* Who does not?' demanded Obadiah, glaring fixedly into the lens.

'When we stumble upon that which we once knew, and the things we will come to know again, They will be waiting for us!' cried Bellhouse. 'They are outside, and They are always looking in! Good Gods, man, are you not *afraid?*'

Into Edward's mind rose the torrent of inhuman shrieking that they had first unleashed from within Bellhouse's consciousness. Shuddering, he pushed it away.

Obadiah seemed not to share this recollection 'I am not,' he said through gritted teeth. 'The man of learning has nothing to fear in this Kosmos. What need have we of a primitive instinct like fear when we have come to know the machinations of existence?'

Bellhouse laughed, long and without mirth, and at such volume that Edward feared the vocaliser's circuitry would be shaken loose. 'Then you are greater fool than even I!' he boomed. 'And I had thought myself the greatest fool who ever lived!'

Obadiah gave an incoherent shout and slammed his hand onto the trolley. 'You will give us what we want!'

'*What you think you want*, foolish man!' snarled Bellhouse. Again the interstellar wind seemed to whip into the room, swirling the geometrician's leaf-crackling words about their ears. The lamps dimmed then flared again. 'I warn you! Continue down this path and you shall glimpse the boiling pits of damnation in which my soul has rotted! Spare yourselves and the luckless people of this sorry rock – destroy this infernal contraption at once! Tear apart its screws and wires!

Crush its every last cursed component to dust! Smash it to atoms! Scatter its pieces in the deepest trenches of the oceans! Break open this unnatural sepulchre and grind the sodden remains of my mind beneath your heels before you condemn yourselves to the very *Abyss!*'

Obadiah drew himself up to his full height, flaring his nostrils like an irate bull. His moustache bristled. 'Tell me what you know,' he thundered, 'and I will release you. Tell me what I came to learn and I will spill the putrid contents of your jar over the side of the mountain upon which we stand and let your brains be dashed to pieces upon the rocks!'

The searing intensity in the one word that Bellhouse uttered in reply raised the hackles on Edward's neck and sent chills chasing over his skin. '*Release!*' The sound terminated suddenly in a sharp, elyctrical buzz.

Images of black eternity filled Edward's mind. He shivered. It was silent then, but for the static hiss from the idle vocaliser, and the sound of the wind-driven rain. As the silence continued, Edward attempted to read his friend's face, but its features had become the characters of a foreign alphabet. The Doctor's visage was lit by an unpleasant passion and his moustache twitched spastically.

Finally, Edward could no longer contain himself. 'What do you mean, Obadiah?' he whispered sharply to the Doctor. 'Do you intend to murder Bellhouse *again*?'

'*Hsst!*' Obadiah silenced him with an upheld palm.

Again the silence was broken as Bellhouse's voice issued from the horn. It sounded weary now, and somehow even further away. 'It is a terrible thing that you offer,' he sighed. 'And yet to me it is also a wonderful thing. Indeed, the most wondrous gift of all.

But you are a cruel man, Carnaby, and I wish that I might have been summoned back to this place by another.'

Edward received a fleeting impression that a refracted light from the lens glimmered in his direction. An illusion, he told himself, shaking his head to clear it. This place seemed at times to make fools of his eyes.

Bellhouse continued. '*However*,' he said, 'I will consider your offer. Please do me the service of turning off this awful contraption until this hour to-morrow, so that I might have the opportunity to use my mind in the fashion to which I have become accustomed – that is, without the interference of human senses.'

'As you wish,' said Obadiah flatly. He unceremoniously yanked the leads from the canister, in an instant sending Bellhouse back to his private darkness. The hissing that had acted as a backdrop to their conversation instantly ceased, and suddenly the rain outside sounded very much louder. It was heavier now, lashing ceaselessly against the walls. With what might almost have been construed as a show of nonchalance, the Doctor began flipping the switches that would deactivate the array.

Edward tapped the Doctor on his shoulder. '*Obadiah!*' he hissed. 'What in the world do you mean to accomplish by this? Will you destroy what is left of Bellhouse? I am not sure that I should allow you! He is... well, he's Bellhouse! It's *Bellhouse*, Obadiah!'

Obadiah spun on his heel, spilling a drop or two of a colourless liquid from a phial in his hand. The dæmonic glow that had lit his face had faded, but his black-browed stare retained its intensity. 'I will personally burst every last lobe of that brain between my bare fingers if it means that I will receive the information I desire,' he said calmly. 'And what's more, I believe that is what Bellhouse wants, too. He may feign concerns, but I am willing to wager that an end to his torments is worth more to him than the fate of,' – he paused – 'is worth more to him than any misgivings he might have about what I intend to do with his knowledge.'

'But what about the... the *dangers* he mentioned?' asked Edward. 'He sounded... Well, you heard what he said, Obadiah! Do you really mean to carry on regardless? We only have our research to guide us, Bellhouse has – '

'Bellhouse was weak and afraid. He had the Formulæ, but precious little else. We approach the situation equipped with superior technology and knowledge. What makes you think that we shall be so luckless as him? And, once we have garnered what we can – well, we will have little further use for him. We shall show him our mercy, and deliver him from whatever it is that he believes is haunting him.'

Naught had been listening to their conversation with an expression something like childish glee on his face. His blackcurrant eyes glinted and twinkled. 'Aha! Aha!' he cried, clapping his hands in delight, and spreading apart his ample, red lips in a parody of a smile. 'This is just beginning to become interesting!'

~

Flintwick hurried away from the basement door, fuming silently. Now he was certain that Carnaby's jib was cut in the most objectionable fashion possible. His suspicion that the Hingham men were not to be trusted had now become a conviction.

He had apprehended Laurence the potboy mid-boast. The lad had been bragging to the serving girl about the about the queer noises that he had overheard as he had been listening outside the basement, and so after boxing the pair of them soundly around the ears for an appropriate length of time he had resolved to do the same.

What he had heard had served to compound his opinion that these men were no Scientists. It had not entirely surprised Flintwick that he was not able to detect any audible evidence of a dæmon orgy from within, or indeed the sound of a troupe of skeletons dancing a waltz, but then he had known that Laurence was a regrettably imaginative boy, and prone to bouts of wild exaggeration if he thought it would impress whichever of the girls he was currently sweet on. No, what he had actually heard was the voice of Sebastian Bellhouse.

At first he had received quite a shock when he realised that the voice belonged to Bellhouse – but this only lasted for a moment before he recognised it as an audiographic recording, and probably a recording of an actor, at that. It was altogether too loud and piercing where by rights it ought to have been quiet and muffled, and it carried strangely. He had shaken his head despairingly. What, he had wondered, could be the purpose of this performance? The recording of Bellhouse had droned on and on, and whilst Flintwick could not catch more than the occasional word or phrase, what he had managed to grasp did not *at all* impress him. Amongst others, he had caught the words 'sorcerers' and 'hell', and more than once the recording had garbled out such guttural tones that it had sounded disturbingly as though the actor were speaking in tongues – or else the machine had needed winding.

This was certainly *not* the kind of thing that Lord Naught would benefit from being subjected to, especially in his current, delicate state. He was doubtless impressionable at present, and might even be fooled by the proceedings – why, Flintwick had even heard him *replying* to the recorded voice, as though he actually believed that a real conversation were taking place! He wondered if the pair had employed the traditional regalia of the spiritual charlatan. Had they hung the room with drapes of purple velvet and dimmed the lights to an eerie glow? Were they passing their hands mysteriously over a glass bauble as the audiograph set crackled forth its counsel of doom from inside a hidden cupboard? Were they hoisting items of cutlery on concealed threads and bumping upon the underside of the table in a ghostly manner?

Flintwick had once accompanied Lord Naught to a show put on by a group of travelling entertainers at one of Iremouth's less reputable theatres. The playbills, which for days had carpeted the pavements of the town, purported that whomsoever dared to witness the performance would be '*Shocked* and *Astounded by the Extremely Super-natural Appearance of A Genuine Phantasm*'. They had filed into the dingy little place, and after much melodrama (supplied primarily by means of a wheezing organ), they had been treated to a timely viewing of the aforementioned Apparition from Beyond the Grave. It had not taken long for Flintwick to spot that the Phantasm was a forgery. Whilst his clanking of chains and ghostly wailing were certainly heartfelt (if not a little over-egged), and whilst nobody could doubt that his descriptions of frozen purgatory were singularly vivid, Flintwick could not bring himself to overlook the fact that he was decidedly two-dimensional in appearance.

This had prompted him into a more detailed examination of the ghostly visitor, upon which he discovered that the Phantasm was in reality not a tortured spirit but a reflexion upon a large sheet of glass, supplied by a greenish lamp and a fellow of limited imagination wrapped in a grubby bed sheet who was standing just off-stage. For some reason the rest of the audience, including Lord Naught, seemed downright unappreciative when Flintwick had pointed out that they had been duped in this way. Surely, he had thought, it was better to be aware of these things? It would have been a whole lot more honest of the bed sheet fellow and his accomplices to bill their act as '*The Appearance of An Imitation Phantasm*' – that way the audience could appreciate the effort that they had put into perfecting the illusion, instead of feeling cheated when they discovered that it was a sham. However, he supposed that a good deal fewer people would be interested in a simulated ghost, and this would surely affect the financial viability of the whole Phantasmal operation. Large sheets of glass and lamp oil were not cheap, after all.

Money was almost always at the heart of charlatanry – it was a profession that preyed upon the gullibility of others – and Flintwick was now convinced that the men from Hingham were in fact charlatans of some kind. Almost as soon as he had heard the recording from behind the door, he had all but abandoned the idea that they were law-men – for whilst he was aware that the practices of the constabulary were often obscure and sometimes highly circuitous, he had never yet heard of them employing methods such as *this*. It would simply not be necessary. Surely they did not intend to trick Lord Naught into some kind of confession? At any rate, an appearance from the deceased would hardly be the ideal means by which to accomplish this. No, in one way or another, they were attempting to dupe his master into parting with money. He had not been able to discern their methods just yet, but he would. Oh, he would.

He would protect Lord Naught from harm, just as he always had.

NINE
Entrance & Egress (I),
or Confessions of a Dead Geometrician

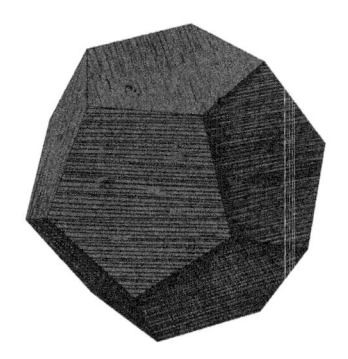

'Come *on*, Tobias!' hissed the young man to his reluctant accomplice.

'Wait up... I'm not so sure about this now! I... I don't know what we were thinking!' Tobias stuttered, lingering several paces back from the broken window by which his companion stood.

'What? You damned coward!'

'But what if he *comes back*, Frederick?' implored Tobias. 'The man's a veritable monster! He'll have our guts for garters and no doubt about it if he catches us in his office!'

Frederick folded his arms, the growing look of anger visible on his face despite the moonless dark of the night. 'I *told* you,' he said, 'he is out of the country doing some research or other – he left weeks ago and he won't be back for weeks either. I checked. Nobody's going to find us, so just stop your childish fretting, will you?'

Tobias looked nervously around him, surveying the darkened courtyard. Despite his fears, it seemed that nobody had heard them break the glass.

'I don't know...' he whined.

'Listen, Tobias, where else d'you think we could possibly lay our hands upon an original edition of the *Vorpish Theories*? Now I'm going in and that's that. Are you coming with me or not?'

Tobias bit the side of his cheek hard and made a small noise of frustration. 'Oh, all right then,' he relented, realising that Frederick was of course quite right, and that there really was not anywhere else that they could possibly hope to come across such a rare and forbidden tome. 'But if *anything* happens then I'm going to blame this whole episode on you somehow,' he added.

Frederick shook his head disdainfully, and put one foot through the empty window frame. Shards of glass still clung to the wood, and he had to twist his body in order to avoid lacerating himself. Once inside, he undid the catch on the window and slid the empty frame upwards so that Tobias could follow him in safety.

Tobias dropped to the floor, splinters of broken glass crunching beneath his shoes. He looked down at the polished wood of the floor.

'Gods, we're making a mess already Frederick!' he whispered hoarsely.

'Of course we are, you idiot! We just broke in through a window! And why are you whispering? There's no one in here. We can talk normally, just try not to be too loud.'

Frederick glanced around. They had entered the building from the rear, and they were now standing in a darkened hallway that stretched off in both directions.

'We need a lamp,' he stated. 'Why did we not bring a lamp?'

'I don't know...'

'Never mind, there's bound to be a lamp or two in here. Let's go this way,' decided Frederick, nodding his head to the left. Tobias gingerly followed him.

At the end of the hallway were two doors. Frederick tried the handle of one and found that it was not locked.

'I'll try in here,' he said, pushing the door open, 'and you look in that one. One of these must lead to his office. The book's bound to be in his office.'

The door swung inwards and Frederick stepped inside. The smell of formaldehyde instantly assaulted his nostrils. It was black as pitch inside the room, much darker than the corridor had been, but there was a lamp on a side table by the door and Frederick wasted no time in lighting it. As the yellow glow flared and the room was illuminated, he saw that this was evidently not the office he sought. It was a storeroom of some kind. The lamplight shone back at Frederick as hundreds of tiny reflections in the rows of glass bottles that lined the walls. Boxes of various sizes, some covered by dustsheets, littered the floor.

Frederick moved closer to a shelf, and held up the lamp so that he could peer at the bottles more closely. Some were filled with powders and pastes, and labelled neatly with their names: camphor, laudanum and the like. One or two had strange fungi stuffed into them. Others contained less readily identifiable things that appeared to be clippings or shavings. These were not labelled. As Frederick moved around the storeroom, he came to a bank of larger jars. The lamplight threw wavering silhouettes of their contents against the wall behind them.

They were internal organs.

Frederick took a step backwards and stumbled into a pile of boxes behind him. The pile collapsed noisily, the boxes spilling their contents onto the floor. What might have been beads rolled off in all directions.

'Damn!' he cursed.

A pile of bric-a-brac lay all around his feet. Rocks and candles had spilled from one crate, oddly-coloured balls of twine from another. One box had contained a collection of bones and teeth – both human and animal, by the looks of them. As he stepped backwards, a jawbone snapped beneath his heel. Shaking his head, Frederick withdrew from the room. There were no books to be seen.

'What are you doing? I thought you said to be quiet!' hissed Tobias as Frederick found him in the next room.

'I tripped. He's got body parts in that room, you know! Jars full of them...'

'Well, he is a doctor, is he not?'

'Not a doctor of medicine, Tobias, no!'

Tobias shrugged. 'Well, I imagine he needs them for one thing or another.'

Frederick shone the lamp around, eliciting a wince from Tobias. Paintings were hung on almost every available space on the walls.

'An appreciator of art, as well as a scientist of repute,' he commented.

The paintings were undoubtedly the work of an artist of no mean talent. Even in the lamplight, the colours seemed to glow with a ghostly radiance. The pictures were mostly landscapes. The luminous skies and mountain ranges were infused with an æthereal light. There was something wistful about those scenes, an essence of something delicate and melancholy like the end of the summer. Such a sentiment was quite at odds with the temperament of the man that Frederick and Tobias knew.

There were also two tall bookcases in the room, stretching from floor to ceiling. A stepladder was set in front of one of them. Hundreds of books, some of them huge and ancient-looking were piled upon the shelves.

Frederick nodded to himself. 'You search these shelves,' he ordered. 'It might well be amongst them. I'll check down the hall in case it's in another room.'

'Fine,' replied Tobias, although he had not heard his friend's words. He was already poring over the spines of the rare volumes with bibliophilic glee.

Frederick extinguished his lamp as he trotted down the hallway so that the light could not be seen through the broken window. When he reached the end of the hall, another door stood in front of him. A brass plate screwed to the wood proclaimed that it was the office of the Doctor. Frederick grinned.

Surprisingly, the door was unlocked.

The interior of the office was lined with almost as many bookshelves as the last room. Several paintings, evidently by the same artist, also adorned the walls. The Doctor was evidently a collector.

In the centre of the room stood a wide desk that was mostly invisible under a layer of papers and books. A reading lamp and a picture frame were the only other objects to protrude from beneath the drift. Frederick stalked slowly around the desk and shone the lamp over the frame. Inside the frame was a photogram of a lady.

She was very beautiful, in a wild kind of way. Her dark hair fell to her shoulders, and her eyes were piercing. Was it his wife? No, the Doctor was not married. Perhaps a lover – but then, Frederick had never seen the Doctor with this particular lady. He peered more closely. The sepia was somewhat blurred and the picture was creased, but now he saw that the lady was in fact quite young. No more than a girl. A daughter, then?

She *did* resemble the Doctor somewhat. What a scandal that would be! Frederick shrugged. It was unimportant.

He scanned the shelves for the *Vorpish Theories*. Many of the books had no titles on their spines, and these he had to remove one by one in order to inspect their covers. Some ominous, blank-covered volumes had to be opened in order to discover their contents. As Frederick tugged at a singularly large, leather-bound tome with a spine inlaid with gold leaf, he heard a click as of a latch coming undone. He pursed his lips, and looked in the direction from which the noise had come.

The edge of the bookcase had come away from the wall, and a black crack now extended from floor to ceiling. He slid his hand down the opening and discovered that there *was* a latch. He slipped it off, and the bookcase swung smoothly open on its hinges. Frederick shook his head in amazement. It was a secret door!

Behind the bookcase was a closet. Frederick was secretly disappointed that it was not some kind of tunnel – it was purported that there were many such places within the old University buildings. The contents of the closet were also quite unremarkable. There was some money in a coffer, which Frederick did not touch. He was no common robber.

Strangely, there was also a rail upon which hung a fine array of beautiful ladies' clothes. There were dresses and petticoats, and even a bonnet. They looked to be old – perhaps twenty years or more. Perhaps the clothes had been in the secret cupboard since before the Doctor had occupied the office, and he was unaware that it even existed. However, a glance revealed that there were also papers undoubtedly belonging to the man right alongside the rail.

'Carnaby, you *are* a strange chap,' Frederick muttered to himself as he swung the bookcase closed once more.

Just then, Tobias appeared at the door with a lamp in one hand, a smug expression on his face and a massive, wormy-looking book under his arm.

'Found it!' he grinned.

~

Several months prior to coming to Cold Ghastia, Edward had chanced to peruse a rather courageous paper wherein a little-known physicist argued that Time and Space themselves – far from being the immutable constants relied upon by every man of Science – were in fact malleable. The contention that these stalwart Forces of Nature could be squeezed, squashed, and pulled about like so much common rubber was naturally much-maligned by the fellow's peers, but Edward, as was his bent, had approached the theory with an open mind. Indeed, in an offhand sort of way he had half-considered that this 'relativity' could go a long way towards explaining certain anomalies in his own work, but the theory, though undeniably interesting, had been somewhat half-baked and so Edward had decided to put it aside until such time as its owner should deign to return it to the oven awhile.

Now, however, he was quite convinced of the theory's validity – for if a day had ever consisted of quite such a considerable number of unendurably long hours as had the one leading up to this moment, then Edward Stoathill-Warmly had not had the misfortune to experience it. Each and every minute that comprised it had been endowed with an unfeasible plasticity, an unbearable elongation of its usual duration that had seen him shaking and tapping at his lethargically malfunctioning pocket-watch in such a way that (had it not appeared broken to begin with) was in all likelihood fit to damage it beyond all hope of repair.

Pacing had been the chief activity of the day. Indeed, to all intents and purposes it had been the *only* activity of the day, for the agony of anticipation had rendered him utterly incapable of anything else. Eating had been an impossibility, for the same force that had acted to warp Time had also had its way with Space, and so had shrivelled his stomach to the approximate dimensions of a walnut.

Concentration had also been entirely out of the question; though a moment was a doubtful measure under even normal circumstances, Edward found that to consider a book or chart for anything in excess of one was quite impossible, for the span of his attention had withered from its usual languid sweep to nothing more than to a brief flicker. Pacing had been the only viable alternative, and so that is exactly what Edward and Obadiah had done, strutting restlessly around the House and its grounds like a pair of concerned crows.

Of course, Edward was well aware of the identity of the thing that had acted to deform Time so, and what's more it seemed that the brave physicist had overestimated the size of the body necessary to achieve the effect. For the glue that had adhered the hands of his watch to its face was not emitted by a planet or even a collapsing star, but by a lump of grey matter barely larger than a grapefruit.

Quite what method Sebastian Bellhouse might employ in determining the hour was beyond Edward. Indeed, it had occurred to him that the geometrician might in fact have no such method, and that his request to be left unmolested for the period of one day to deliberate upon his decision might well have been nothing more than a sort of rhetorical flourish, or else a means of affecting an escape. These thoughts had hardly sped the passage of Time.

THE SHAPES

But – however excruciatingly slowly it had done so – the allotted span had indeed passed, and now Edward paced not the halls of the House but the dim basement chamber beneath it, where the light of a single lamp picked out the shapes of an array of peculiar devices. At the centre of the web of wires and boxes stood Obadiah.

Edward, unable to sit, paced and wrung his hands nervously. Lord Naught, sporting a pajama suit of leopard skin and a baroque pair of curly-toed slippers, busied himself at his own trolley, which rather than elyctrical devices bore a selection of serving domes and bottles.

Obadiah completed his adjustments and, after a final inspection of the canister before him, he turned to his companions. 'All is in readiness,' he proclaimed, then gave a wry smile. 'Now, all that remains is for us to hope that we shall find our friend in a more conversational mood this evening!'

'Oh *yes*,' cooed Naught, dropping a chunk of ice into his tumbler of whisky. 'I for one am simply dying to hear what he has to say!'

At this Edward snorted. 'I believe that Mr Bellhouse is the only one present with any particularly great experience of *dying*,' he said.

Naught, piling a plate with poached crayfish and slices of vinegared peach, turned to the young arcanologist and raised an eyebrow.

'If you are quite finished, Edward?' said Obadiah pointedly.

Edward held up his hands and bowed his head in a gesture of capitulation.

The Doctor pointed to a chair. 'Then stop that damnable pacing and sit down.'

Edward did as he was bid.

Obadiah indicated the array with a dramatic sweep of his arm, as though presenting it to a music hall audience. 'Then let us begin!'

It was then that Time resumed its usual flow for Edward, and it was only a few short moments before the vocaliser crackled into life.

'*Ah!* The darkness fades!' came the faraway voice, spiralling out of the depths of the horn. It sounded, if anything, relieved. It was a stark - and thoroughly welcome - contrast to the cacophony that had characterised their first meeting with the deceased geometrician, Sebastian Bellhouse.

'Bellhouse!' called Obadiah. 'Your faculties are restored once more. Do you hear me?'

'It was so very *dark*,' muttered the Bellhouse-machine. Then, 'I had forgotten quite how disagreeable that experience was.'

Obadiah evidently found little to concern him in this piece of information. 'Have you considered my offer?' he pressed.

'That I have,' replied Bellhouse. 'I have thought long and hard in the terrible quiet of my sensory deprivation.'

Naught turned to Edward. 'He is a melodramatic one, isn't he?' he whispered from behind his hand. A piece of crayfish was lodged between two of his pointed teeth. Edward offered him a brief shrug and turned back to Obadiah.

'And have you come to a decision?' the Doctor continued. 'Will you tell us what you know of the Transition of Uush"Ton?'

'That very much depends on you, Doctor Carnaby,' said Bellhouse wearily. 'Will you swear that you will keep your end of the bargain? I know from my own experience that Naught is hardly a man to be relied upon.'

'Certainly. I am a man of my word, of that you may be assured.'

'You will listen to my tale? And you will heed it?'

'Yes.'

'And you *swear* that when my tale is told you will end my misery? You will do me the kindness of granting me a *true* death? You will destroy what remains of my brain and put an end to the horrible torment that I endure?'

'Without doubt, Bellhouse. I have ever been a believer in the benevolence of euthanasia.'

'Then yes, I will tell you what you wish to know. I will impart to you the tale of my life – and of the life that began *after* my mortal death.'

'Aha!' cried Obadiah, clapping his hands together and rubbing them triumphantly. He turned to Edward with a grin so broad that it set his moustache askew. 'Edward my boy, what did I tell you?' he beamed with a theatrical wink.

Edward grinned back at him, but as the Doctor turned away, his grin faded.

'Outstanding!' exclaimed Naught excitedly.

'Well then,' boomed Obadiah. 'Speak, Bellhouse!'

'I hope that you are prepared for what I have to tell you,' Bellhouse said with a mechanical shadow of a sigh. 'I fear that you are not, but perhaps it is better that you know certain things before – who knows – you may discover them for yourselves. If you are indeed to learn then I must relate *everything* to you – I must begin at the very beginning, at a time long before I had ever so much as heard tell of the *Tablets of Uush'Ton.*'

Now that the geometrician had found his voice restored to him once more, Edward began to suspect that it might well have been one of the faculties of which he was fondest in life. The three men settled themselves.

'I was a simple man,' Bellhouse began. 'Born to simple folks. Manufactory folks. For that was Broadflight, you see – 'factory or university, and 'factory was the lot we'd drawn. Oh, they knew I had the knowing in me, my mother and father – it would not stay hidden. It could not. But learning was not for folks like us. Well, there was schooling, of course – the slate and the cane and the requisite lies. Just enough schooling to serve, you see. So serve is what I did.

'I knew that I would never walk into those lofty halls as one of the favoured few. And so, when my schoolbooks could teach me no more, I crept in like a worm on my belly and they gave me brushes and buckets so that I might scrub away their piss and their shit. So I scoured their shit and I mopped their piss, and felt glad and lucky. For I had seen the 'factories claim eyes, and arms, and smash heads apart. I had seen corrupted lungs coughed out in bloody chunks on mens' overalls. If I was to be broken it would be by sneers and jibes, not by furnaces or hammers or choking dust. And if such was my lot then so be it – for I took from them that which I needed to survive, and they never even knew it.

'It is a boon, to be invisible. To be disregarded. To be an idiot entrusted with a jangling ring of keys to rooms that only the worthy may enter. They never suspected, not for one moment, that the drudge with the broom and bucket might find something of worth in their great cathedrals of knowledge. To begin with I did not take the books – it was enough to bask in their glow. As the last of the scholars and the librarians left, I would busy myself with my polishing and my sweeping, and as the doors were closed and the lights were extinguished, my true work would begin. Ah, I learned so much! And yet there was always so much more to know. So much that these fleeting, nocturnal trysts could no longer satisfy my cravings.

That is when I started to take the books. Oh, I intended to return them – even did return them, to begin with. But it seemed that no one noticed my little borrowings. I think that perhaps my tastes were more obscure even than those of the Broadflight scholars.

'And yet, there was no purpose to my work – no purpose but joy, that is. Would that I had realised that joy was enough. Would that I had held onto it. But I feel now that some dark purpose impelled me then, some strange attractor, some terrible thing that I was powerless to resist. You see, even without searching I had found something. Or rather, I had found nothing. There, in the vista of number that I had painted in my mind, in the infinite panorama of geometry that I knew to be the fabric of our Kosmos, there was a hole – an absence. Little did I realise it then, but I was describing, by the very nature of that which my work could *not* portray, something that the human mind was never supposed to perceive.

'I was not to realise the nature of that thing that harried at the edges of my mind until those primeval tablets of stone came to me. Ha! Or was it I who was drawn to them? It matters not. We came together as fated by that terrible design of which I was so gloriously ignorant, and for a time they were all that I required. They were all that *existed*. I thought of nothing else – neither food, nor sleep. The Tablets were my nourishment, my love, my life, for therein I discovered that which I had not sought. Therein lay the secret of the shadow cast by the very Kosmos itself, the location of the unseen place that outlies the furthest shores of that which we can know. Therein lay the *Formulæ of Uush'Ton* – the gate and the keys to the Beyond.

'Ah, and when Danforth came to me – when poor, dear Danforth came to me, when he too was drawn into the black web that was to enfold us – we felt as though we were kings of the world! To own this knowledge – to know these great and ancient things of which not another on this earth had even the faintest of inklings – ah, it was a drug! And like a drug, it devoured us. Still, intoxicated though we were, we concocted together that work of ours, though we knew that the common man could never wield its power unaided, for the Tablets would expose themselves to me and me alone. And that, I presume, is the reason that you have summoned me here with your blasphemous machine. You seek answers to questions that you know not how to ask. Ask them now, if you can. Ask them now, for no man shall ask of me again.'

The arcanologists were not short of questions.

The Doctor strutted back and forth before the array like a sergeant of the drill, barking out queries and shouts of triumph by turns. The rhythmic pounding of his boots upon the boards became the beating of a shamanic drum, and Edward was swiftly lost in a mathematical delirium. As number consumed him, his pale face glowed in the lamplight, and in their hollow pits his eyes seemed bright. His pen was a blur as it flew across the pages of his notebook, describing in lines of ink that which had evaded his mind for so long. He found that he was laughing, but he did not care. Each new datum was a long-coveted gear in the machine of his knowledge, and he knew then how Bellhouse must have felt as the great libraries of Broadflight were opened up before him. It was joy indeed. As conjectures and solutions flew back and forth between the pair and the singular mind that that they had captured in their device, it seemed almost as though the Polyhedra would shimmer into existence there and then in the elyctrified air of that basement room.

Naught, who at the first hint of arithmetical calculation had begun to yawn expansively, had drawn out a giraffe-shaped pipe of amber and inlaid silver and set to working his way through a slab of hashish. He had demolished all but a crumb of this, then several servings of coddled hare and a goodly proportion of a somewhat violently-hued blancmange by the time the curiosity of his guests had been sated.

Edward looked up from the diagrammatical filigree of his notebook. 'We've got it, Obadiah!' he said, his face luminous with an admixture of disbelief and wonderment. 'I... I think we've really got it!'

'Yes, my boy!' chuckled Obadiah. 'Yes, I rather think we have!'

From the Bellhouse-machine there came a laugh of a dourer kind. 'Ha! Perhaps you have, my foolish sorcerers. Perhaps you have. But do you truly understand what it is that I have given you?'

The Doctor snorted. 'Oh, I rather think I do.'

'You know *nothing*, Carnaby,' spat Bellhouse. 'Just as *I* knew nothing. And your pride, like mine, shall be your undoing. Oh, I *believed* that I knew. For all that I was a scrubber of shit, I was a modern man. The ways of the cowering savage have been swept away by the Empire! No longer do we appease each tremor of the earth with the blood of our daughters, nor do we caper about pyres and totems to call down the rain or swell the harvest. And when the Tablets spoke to me of primal Üo, progenitor of all gods, creator of all thought and matter, the thing who ravens endlessly in the depths of the Uush'Ton? Well, I laughed. How quaint, how delightful! What sublime poetry flowed from the lips of these men of old! What a grand conceit they had concocted, this romantic notion of the First!'

'The first what?' frowned a somewhat red-eyed Naught.

'Merely the *First*, Lord Naught,' said Edward. 'That is how the Eelen referred to their deities. It's a translation of Danforth's, from their term, *On*.' He saw another question forming on Naught's lips. '*Uush'Ton* is the *Beyond*, or near enough.'

'Hmm, I see.' He waved his pipe. 'Do go on, Belly.'

A grumble of displeasure resounded from the vocaliser. 'To describe the forces of the Kosmos thus was a habit of our forefathers,' he continued. 'The mighty sun-god in the sky, his mistress the moon. And so it was with the First, of course. How else might these ancients have spoken of that which awaited them on the other side? How else to conceive of the inconceivable, to communicate the incommunicable? But such pæans were not enough for me. I yearned to know for myself. I needed desperately to see that which they had seen – the hidden structure of the Kosmos whose silhouette haunted the edges of my consciousness – and as Danforth's translation revealed to me the intricacies of the ritual, it seemed that the means was within my grasp. The Tablets had projected the Polyhedra into my mind almost unbidden. All that remained was to step through the gate and into the Beyond.

'But cruelly, that gate was locked. Time and again I found myself standing at the threshold with no way to go on. How it hurt me, to be so denied! But again Danforth came to my aid. It was Danforth who identified the need for the *dote*, who realised that this sacrament was no mere symbolic gesture as those of the hollow rites of our own Church have become. It was Danforth, too, who found the cursed stuff, and I know what a toll that took on him, poor boy. And it was Danforth who brought us here, to this place.

'What a mind that boy had! He saw the thing that had evaded me. Of course, it was he who had first apprehended the cipher, and so it was he who perceived the other vital duality within the Tablets' message. As it transpired, it was the very first Shape of the Transition that was to yield up the secret. As you know, for all its crystalline intricacy that Shape is referred to simply as *The Sphere*. It was only logical, I reasoned, for the first Shape to be named for our planet, for the material plane, for the place whence one's consciousness is to begin its journey into the Uush'Ton. But the Eelen were master esotericists. And as Danforth discerned, The Sphere was both metaphorical and literal. As well as a symbol of it, The Sphere was a map of our own planet Verdra.

'Or rather, it was a chart of points upon that map. A chart of nothing less than dimensional intersections – a chart of every place upon this planet where the way between the worlds grows thin. What a discovery it was! From there it was a simple enough matter to encircle the Eelen's Sphere within our own globe, and thence to determine the locations where that structure's appendages intersected with our planet's surface. As each point was plotted our hopes soared, and then were dashed again. It will not surprise you to learn that fabled Nhionbi in the sands was one such point. Yes, its location is known to me. But countless æons have passed since the time of that place and, as we were to discover, every other point upon that ancient chart lies now beneath fathoms of briny ocean. Every other but one, that is. The very last of those places is the mountain peak upon which you now stand.

'And so we came to Cold Ghastia, Danforth and I. We knew nothing of this place, and we knew not what we would find – only that we had to come. We brought nothing but a few books and charts, the *dote*, and our minds. We took lodgings in a guesthouse. How low I had brought my friend! From his fashionable apartments in the city to this hovel in which we made our home. Still, at least the rats were less bold than those who had menaced my own rude pension.

'We found immediately that things were different here. Here the Shapes were brighter, more real, and the presence of the Uush'Ton seemed tangible, the very fact of its existence somehow urgent. I came to think of this place as the high ground upon which lightning might at any moment strike. But of course, we knew. We knew that even such terrible energies must seek out a conduit. And once we had laid eyes upon the black spires of this place, we knew that our conduit had been found.

'It was surprising how easily it came about. Well, it was easy for a man of means, I suppose. I knew nothing of ways of the moneyed classes, but doors had a habit of opening for Alan Danforth that for me were ever locked and barred. I drew the curtains and meditated upon my transcriptions, whilst he shook the hands and dispensed the compliments that were our keys to this place. We each had been born with our own aptitudes, I suppose. And soon enough I stood by his side in a rented suit of clothes, in a ballroom in this House, while around me the noblesse partook of such incredible decadence that I might already have stumbled into another reality. After that night I wondered often if Naught even so much as recalled his offer of patronage, considering the choking vapours that the apparatus was spewing forth and the tangle of oily limbs from within which he made it. To this day I am not certain what they were doing to him. And yet, the offer was made, and in short order we were quartered here in the House of Naught. Oh, would that there had been some reason to leave this island! A letter to summon me home! Anything to have prevented me from tarrying in this place. But there was not another in this world to whom my whereabouts were of the slightest concern. And so blithely we hauled ourselves up this accursed mountain and began the work that would seal our fates.

'That Naught neither knew nor cared for the details of our labours was of little consequence. We were theoretical physicists, as far as he was concerned, studying the effects of certain geophysical forces unique to Cold Ghastia. If it was a lie, then it was a lie only by omission, and it served us as well as it did him, for it was the cadence of our words that he fancied, never their meaning. And so we endured him. We endured his inanity as he pestered us about our work, and we endured our role as performing monkeys at his endless *soirées*. Never had I seen such conspicuous and flamboyant greed. The amount that *thing* can consume is incredible! Rare birds almost whole, cheeses, wines, cigars, chutneys – ugh! By now my stomach is doubtless no more than a shrivelled scrap of wormy leather and still I feel gorged upon the mere *memory* of those feasts! But how could we protest when that which we sought was so nearly within our grasp?

'For we had not been wrong. Here in this House, the Uush'Ton was close – closer than ever it had been before – and my experiments bore fruits such as I had never believed possible. Something of the Beyond is interwoven with the very fabric of this place, and under its influence the Shapes sprang into being at my merest suggestion, more glorious and radiant with each passing day, and we knew that soon it would be time for me to embark upon my voyage.

'I believe now that Danforth sensed the peril. Somehow he had glimpsed the titanic folly of our endeavour. Somehow he *knew*. Perhaps he imagined that I had not seen how fearful he became, in the end. But it did not escape me. Oh, I saw it – the crease of his brow and the tightness of his lips. The tremor of his hand. I told myself that he was ill, that the climate was to blame – the thin air in this cursed place. But I was obsessed, and I would not be turned aside from my course.

'Even when he came to me and implored me to stop the experiment, I would not relent. And in my anger, I struck the poor boy. Gods, I regretted that! But he was hardly coherent. The way he was gibbering – I could not stand to see it. And his eyes – so wild! We must stop our meddling, he cried, we must stop before it is too late! It was not safe – we would be punished! He seized me then, and when I threw him off he leaped up and like a madman he set to tearing up my papers. That was when I struck him. He went very quiet after that, and he did not mention such things again. But from then on he went about with such a harrowed look that one would think I had died already.

'The very next evening – my last, as it happens, on this plane of existence – I informed my dear, faithful friend that I intended to set forth on the journey into the Uush'Ton. In our little workshop, he helped me to make the final preparations. Together we rehearsed the order of the Polyhedra one last time, and cooked up a batch of the *dotc*, a solution more potent than any we had yet prepared, and with which there would be no negotiation. Then he strapped me fast to a sturdy chair and placed the wad between my teeth. The sadness in that dear boy's eyes as he tightened the tourniquet about my arm is something that has forever haunted me throughout the æons of my miserable existence. Why did he do it, I wonder? In truth I think he knew that none could stop me then. He clasped my hand one last time, and then I saw him close his eyes as he thrust the needle into my engorged and eager vein.

'As the drug surged through my blood, I felt that familiar tightening in my brow, felt the warm vibration begin to pulse beneath the bones of my face and radiate throughout my being. The quivering resonance intensified, its pitch growing higher and higher until it was neither a sensation nor a sound but a thing that seemed to fill existence itself – and suddenly I was on its other side. There was a crackle. A moving-out. An inversion. Colours blared and everything became slow and warm, focused in impossible sharpness, and I knew then that *dote*-trance was fully upon me. I turned my head through the syrup to see a version of Danforth observing me with sorrowful eyes, his face now a radiant, faultless sculpture in geometry, across whose surface chased flickering turquoise sigils. I glanced down at my arms to see the same devices dancing over my own skin. And when I looked up again, Danforth was gone. I called out to him then, but I believe now that he had already been taken.

'I felt the warm melting spreading out from my core. The pulsing, amethyst grid shuddered into being. It was time to begin, but the choice was no longer mine. Here without effort or permission was The Sphere, and I cried out in delight as its ghostly latticework of emerald planes met the *dote*-grid, and aligned. The tessellation sent trails of glassy filigree spiralling into the room and wrung the breath from my body. I willed myself forward, and The Sphere enveloped me. Something insistent pressed at my brow from within. Then came The Hand, that jagged congery of coral fronds, and as it materialised a wave swept towards me, rippling and buckling Space before it and prickling over my being like the breath of a coming storm. I pushed through.

'Again I was enveloped, and now a feeling of pressure began to build around me. Gossamer things drifted just beyond my vision. I pictured the Tablets, and the jet surface upon which the Formula of The New Sun was inscribed. And in a heartbeat, The New Sun filled my vision – a limitless, jewelled cavern, deeper than the sky. So awestruck was I that at first I did not feel the hand that grasped my hair and yanked back my head. But then something serrated was sawing and sawing, and I realised that the sensation of rending meat was somehow related to me. It was my meat, my flesh. My throat.

'I struggled for a while, but my arms were strapped fast to the chair. For a moment I panicked, but by then I was beyond any notion of pain. A sensation of dribbling warmth spread out from my throat, and my head lolled upon my chest. Oh, it is a strange thing indeed to feel one's heart stop, and yet to live! The last thing I beheld of this mortal realm was a fading kaleidoscope of my own gore.

'I realised then that I had never truly given thought as to what the sensation of death might be. I was not a religious man in life, nor a spiritual one. I had seen little in my days to convince me that the Gods were as fond of us as the Interlocutors liked to say, and death would have been a merciful release for many I had known. I suppose that I must have imagined it in an idle fashion, from time to time – a dimming of the light, perhaps, as of the coming of evening. A slow fading into blackness and nothingness. But whatever it is that I had imagined – whatever any soul in this wide world may imagine – I tell you now that it was not so. Nor was there mercy.

THE SHAPES

For I had set the terrible forces of the Kosmos into unstoppable motion, and my body was already far behind me.

'I did not resist it. One after another the Polyhedra unfolded before me, flaring, shimmering, radiating burning streams of geometry into my being. Again and again I was engulfed, twisting, stretching, somersaulting through impossible contortions as I fell or flew or dived into infinite, whirling palaces of glassy pewter and shrieking, shattering galactic chasms of naked existence. I screamed out acid shafts of terror and agony as I was wrenched inside out and sucked into the marrow of my own soul, bombarded, devoured, distended and disgorged by the Shapes that blared faster and faster out of the scorching, limitless void until a flickering succession of pyramids, prisms, blossoms, starfish, snowflakes, crystals, anemones, jewels, thorns, stars and blazing suns seared away all that I was in a scalding sea of blinding, white infinity.'

TEN
The Astral Journey,
Or A Cautionary Tale Begins

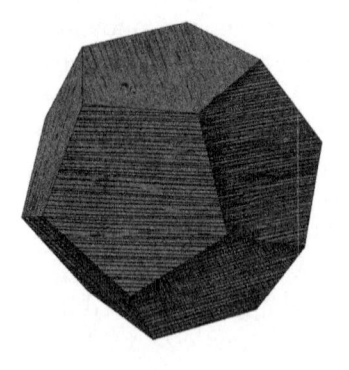

'Æons later, there were stars.

'They were not the jagged, all-consuming portals of the Transition, but the familiar stars of the heavens, or something very like them. For a long time I merely beheld them, those countless suns arrayed about me in the blackness. I was mindless, I think. Without form or will or memory. A scrap of consciousness that was not conscious, a blank thing barely aware of being unaware. I stayed that way forever, or so it seemed.

'But after an endless time, motes of my selfhood began to gather. By the force of some strange gravity, I became a glimmer. A tiny, faltering ember. Over the course of seeming millennia, I found that with the most colossal of efforts I could draw atoms of my substance to me, and somehow in that void I created myself anew.

'It took a far longer time to recall what or who I was – or who I had been. I watched the distant galaxies rolling in infinite slowness, and a germ of understanding came to me. It was the purplish thrumming of the lattice that brought the first flicker of comprehension. I had seen this before at some time, some remote time, some time of supreme importance. Yes, it was unending, timeless, that grid to which the very stars aligned – yet impossibly there had been a time *before* it. A time when Shapes, too, had calibrated themselves to that network of ghostly cables. Burning Shapes. Devouring Shapes. And in a torrent, memory returned. The Tablets. The Formulæ. The *dote*. The Transition. The Uush'Ton.

'Death.

'Utter dread filled me then. I had done this to myself. I had journeyed here to this void alone, and of my own volition. Now my body was dead, yet I was discarnate and undying – and trapped. Forever trapped in dimension of existence beyond even the wildest imaginings of humankind, and without even the vaguest hope of returning to my butchered body. There was no way back. Infinity had no meaning until that awful realisation came.

'I thought then of Danforth. That poor boy, so full of intelligence and passion. That I had led him to his death at the hands of that monster filled me with yet more bitterness and regret. I think that I would have wept – but functions of the body were quite beyond me now. Still, I grieved for a time – for myself, but mostly for him. I hoped that, in some happier place than this, something of him had survived as had I.

'But what now? What possible course of action could there be for this fool who had flung himself headlong into the Beyond? I began once more to look around me, this time with thought behind my gaze. Stars. An ocean of stars, endless and breathtaking. Yes, one's breath may be stolen even in the absence of lungs or air. It is a queer thing indeed, how one's body continues to haunt one's soul as one imagines one's soul might haunt one's body. And now that true consciousness informed my sight, beauty overwhelmed me, choking the throat that somewhere across the Kosmos lay sliced in two. Countless mælstrom galaxies turned, fountaining misty sprays of suns into the void, and milky clouds of star-dusted, varicoloured æther drifted in serenity through the velvet blackness, billows so immense that even the slimmest of their curling tendrils might have swallowed up worlds. It is a majesty and a vastness unguessed by mortal men. Oh, however perfectly you may *believe* that you have beheld the Kosmos as it wheels above you, let me assure you that your experience was nothing but a fraction - a feeble, pathetic, pale imitation - of its true grandeur. The stars burned so brightly and so clearly that I felt I had never truly seen them before that moment. And indeed, I had not.

'For these were not the stars that I had known. I knew this as at last I completed the circle through which I cast my eyeless gaze. For never in life had I looked skyward and seen on one side the glittering of constellations unnumbered and on the other blank, black space. The ocean was not endless after all. Somehow it was the coldest realisation yet: I was truly at the edge of the Kosmos.

'What now, stupid man? What now, now that I was both removed from the physical plane and stranded upon the very brink of the universe itself? This was the Beyond, indeed! That was when it came to me. The Eelen - they had voyaged to this place all those uncounted centuries ago - and they had returned! How else might they have set down their tales to begin with? Those tales, it seemed, were true, for there could be no doubt that it was the Formulæ that had brought me here - yet one thing perplexed me. The purpose of it all had been to look upon the faces of the gods as the ancient ones had done. So why did I find myself alone in the void? The answer came like a thunderbolt. I had not enacted the whole of the rite. Hope flared anew – why, I could follow in the footsteps of the adepts and complete the ritual! Perhaps all that remained was for me to request an audience with divine.

'A *semantic meditation* was the term I decided upon. Even then, as I prepared to speak them, to call them *magick words* seemed absurd. I had never been a believer in conjuring tricks, but neither for the majority of my existence had I believed that I could become a deathless and incorporeal essence wandering the barren places of the void. And so I resolved that if the Eelen's magick had brought me here – why, then what choice did I have but to trust it once more? I would speak the Litany of the Ionuoiu, and summon up the Harbingers of the First. After all, was it so preposterous to imagine that if the visualisation of shapes could so fundamentally alter the state of one's being then the wielding of this other energy within one's consciousness might do the same? Still, though there was not a soul to bear witness, I felt a fool as I began to intone those words. And a fool I surely was, but for reasons at which I could not have begun to guess.

'I had transcribed the words of the Litany out of a sense of completeness. If the primordial scribes had seen fit to encipher them within the Tablets, then for them to be ignored by the one man equipped to read them seemed churlish. Their enunciation had been transmitted to me by the same method as had the Shapes themselves, and like them it still resided within me. They were not words as we know them, and nor did I possess the apparatus by which words might be spoken, but I spoke them regardless. Into the star-dappled void, I gave voice to that which had slumbered in silence.

'After an unknowable time, the chant was done. In the long silence that followed, I waited for a change. But the blackness had swallowed my words without trace, and the Kosmos was unperturbed. Failure! Perhaps I had stuttered, misspoken a vital sound. I cursed bitterly to myself. But what choice had I but this? What choice but to begin again? And so again the Litany welled from within me, and again I spoke those ancient sounds. And again there was nothing but yawning blankness. I chanted on. Syllable mounted on syllable, word upon word, phrase upon phrase. Where one ended and the next began, I soon lost the ability to discern. I became numb, the repetition mindless, all meaning long lost in the endless, senseless drone that tumbled out of me. How long it continued, I knew not. Neither could I tell when exactly the inversion had come. But impossibly, it was so. It was no longer I who chanted the words, but they who chanted me.

'I had brought the words here, and now they were free. And as they spewed themselves forth into the gulfs between the stars, something out in the void began to stir. From the most distant abysses, a whisper came. At first it was but a ghost of an echo, but with each word, each passing moment, it grew. Soon the echo was a resonance, a hum, a buzzing, a trembling. Still that call spewed from me, or I from it, a surging billow of energy that set the very space about me to shuddering. Still the words came. Vision fled in the violence of the tremor. Still the words, forever the words, nothing had existed nor ever could exist but the ringing, roaring tumult of noise that shook moons from their worlds and stars from their axes and convulsed the fabric of Space fit to tear it asunder. The words had struck the very bones of the Kosmos, and now it rang out like a gong.

'And then once more it was silent, and still. The chant was done. The stars around me shone brightly as before, and the planets rolled with infinite slowness and serenity in their orbits just as they had always done. I could not tell how long the silence had reigned; it might have been a minute or an æon. But again, those were moments that I had not the foresight to treasure, those very last moments of tranquillity. For that was when they came.

'Think now, gentlemen, of your great good fortune. Think now of the blessing that is yours – the blessing which you cannot understand. For it is a blessing, though you know it not. Gods, how I have prayed for ignorance as peaceful, as sublime as your own! But once it is gone, it cannot be reclaimed. And yet you seek its annihilation.

'For is that not why you have summoned me here – *because you wish to know*? You cannot possibly conceive what a gift, what a liberty it is to not know of such things as I saw then. Such frightful things! Oh, that their image could only be erased from my poisoned memory – what a mercy that would be! But it is indelible. It is a stain that cannot ever be wiped from the soul. And you – you *desire* to befoul your own, tranquil minds with the unclean image of galactic blasphemy that I witnessed then? Ha! Think yourselves lucky that it is beyond my power to speak of them – that it is beyond the means of mere language to convey even the vaguest impression of those things! Gods, I pray that human speech shall never be required to engender such words as would define their vile and repellent form! There should not *be* words for such awful violations of the sanctity of life. For never in the whole of eternity could an earthly crucible forge such abominations as them.

'And yet they came, screaming out of the void. They came from nowhere; where vacant Space had once existed, there was now a seething miasma, a shrieking, gibbering morass of unspeakable vileness. Revulsion coursed through me, yet the grip of stark terror held me fast as slowly, inexorably, they closed in upon me. And that was when I heard it. The screeching that tore through my paralysed being like waves of burning sickness was no mere animal cry - there were words in that bubbling foulness! Gods, they were the very words that I had chanted! My sanity buckled. Had I done this - had I raised these creatures, these *things?* Could I by my chanting of the Litany have *invited* them here? In a flare of desperation I made one last attempt at flight, but already I knew that it was futile. My being had been caught in a grip of frozen iron, and I had become heavy as stone. All hope and will truly left me then. One thing only I knew with leaden certainty: escape would be impossible.

'I could do nothing as they carried me away, and even had we not embarked from the very brink of the Kosmos I think I would already have known that I was to be borne into darkness. And so into the darkness we went. We left behind the stars, my captors and I, and plunged into the nothingness - the true void - where no light dares to reach and all that exists is frigid blackness. Not even a single filament of the all-pervading grid dared penetrate this place. And once again, there was neither Time nor Space for me - nothing at all by which to measure the unendurable passing of the days or the leagues of emptiness. And for that I was glad, for I knew that once more I alone had done this, and by then I no longer wished to consider how far I had flung my foolish self from all that I had known or could know.

'Was there to be no end to my idiocy? Would I damn myself again and again, until all that was left of me was ashes on the Kosmic breeze? Arrogance, sheer arrogance, had been my downfall. Believing that I knew better.

Believing that a scrubber of shit could know more of the secrets of the Kosmos than had those who had set down those secrets in stone. The words of the Eelen had not been grand conceits masking the reality that my piercing intellect had perceived. Those conceits were my imaginations, my fabrications, my projections. The Eelen's words had been the naked, the unadulterated, truth – and I had been horribly, horribly wrong. Oh, the Harbingers of the First were no metaphors – for though I could no longer see them I felt their iron grip, and I heard them shrieking endlessly in the darkness around me. No, this was real. And if this was real, then so too were the First – and, just as I had requested, I would soon be making their acquaintance.

'It was a change in the character of their cries that told me our destination had been sighted, and yet it was some time before I too beheld the faint, red glow. It appeared more distant even than do the stars as seen from the earth, burning feebly as a cooling cinder; but alone in that cursed blackness it might as well have been a flaming beacon. Steadily that pale speck grew, and with it my dread. At last it became a crimson orb and I shuddered anew, for as its sickly rays reached me I saw once more the repellent forms of my captors rippling wet and red like transpicuous meat. I saw too the place whither those ectoplasmic sails sought to bear me: a desolate planet swung through the half-light, circling the frail sun. The things wheeled about like grotesque birds of prey, and then they screamed in unison and as one they dived towards the barren sphere. All about me ghost-flesh flailed and snapped in the rushing gale that rose up to meet us as we fell.

'What now, fool Sebastian? As the surface of the alien world rocketed towards me, the fear which had been simmering nauseously within me once more gripped my mind with icy fingers. What fresh horror awaited me here? I fought then with the idea of attempting the Transition. If I could only reverse the process and pass back through the polyhedral gates into our own dimension, then perhaps I could escape whatever terrible fate lay ahead! But there could be no going back. Even should it prove to be possible, to force my consciousness back into my lifeless remains would surely be only to condemn myself to a different hell. No, I would have to brave the unknown, hoping against hope that an opportunity for escape would present itself. But I did not feel brave.

'We alighted at last on that dead world in a chorus of exultant howling and a cloud of ochre dust. As the dust settled, I saw that but for the cavorting horrors that surrounded me, the place was as desolate as the kosmic abyss through which we had flown. A gelid wind howled incessantly across a flat and empty plain, and from horizon to black horizon I saw nothing but cinders and rubble, all bathed in the dusky glow of the failing star. It was a true waste. Returning my gaze to my captors, I saw that the things were drawing away from me, tendrils waving in their wake – and just for a glorious moment I believed that I had been released. But of course it was not so. Whatever force they had exerted upon me still held me fast, and I could only watch as they formed a circle around me, and began to dance.

'It was an abhorrent sight, at once hypnotic and repellent – together they became an undulating mass, weaving and churning and chanting in the red gloom in some travesty of tribal ecstasy. The things swept faster and faster about their circuit, and soon an unbroken ring of un-flesh surrounded me. The chill wind seemed then to gather strength, and as it whistled through the rocks I felt the ground beneath me begin to tremble. Their song, it seemed, was reverberating through that husk of a world just as my own had echoed in the void. Dust and sand swirled in a blood-red cyclone. The desert bucked and rippled. And just as the blasphemous hymn reached its maddening crescendo, it ceased. The things skittered and span away across the plain as though flung off by the force of their flight. And then the ground erupted.

'A plume exploded into the sky. With a groaning and cracking of rock, a chasm was flung open, and something immense reared out of it, trails of dirt spilling from its back. All was shaking. The huge shape continued to rise, my gaze following its ascent until it towered over me and it was all I saw. It was a colossal thing. Massive and ancient beyond mortal comprehension, its size too great for living flesh. And yet, it was so! *It was alive!* Or at least it moved. Who is to say that it had flesh, or blood? Or muscle? Or bone? I do not believe that the human mind was made to comprehend such things. Mine could not. At least, I cannot recall what happened then, in those lost moments of terror. There was a voice like thunder, like worlds colliding. Roils of red filth. Boiling torrents of amber fluid. And then there was an opening – a birth. From somewhere within that roaring, pulsating mountain, a wet, black shape was disgorged.

'It came towards me. Or perhaps I was drawn to it. My being was singing then, as though I were steel that that had been struck. I felt a searing heat radiate from the black shape, a blast to flay flesh from bone. I believe that my mind must have clutched in desperation at the one familiar thing in that tumult of horror – for absurdly I recognised then, even through the rippling haze of heat and dust and flesh, the nature of that shape. It was a perfect pentagonal dodecahedron. The light of the red star flashed dully across its planes. Rivulets of viscous fluid poured from it. For a moment it hung before me –

utterly, impossibly still in the midst of the chaos as though it were the very axis about which the Kosmos turned. Then it swallowed me.

'At first I was unaware. There was but an instant of blackness, and then everything was as it had been – except that the dodecahedron had vanished from my sight. The titanic monstrosity was sinking ponderously back into the sunless pit from which it had risen. A thought leaped into my mind – was it over? Had I survived? The eddying clouds began to settle. The black and empty sky emerged once more. But something had changed. The fresh horror was upon me.

'I could feel its shape – *my* shape. Restricting me. Confining me. I sensed its angles, and they were a cage around my being. Every edge of the thing was a prison bar, cold and utterly immutable. I had been consumed. I had become one with that black object. And, just as that sickening comprehension was growing within me, the ground dropped suddenly away. I was rising, unbidden, into the air. I hung briefly over the chasm from which the mountainous thing had reared, my flanks steaming and smeared with the slime of my rebirth, and for a few moments I glimpsed its forbidding depths. Then I was flying, and it was already behind me.

'The rock-strewn ground rushed by, a blur beneath me. I swooped down to meet it, skimming but a hand's breadth above the surface of the planet. My new form was agile and swift, but it was not under my control. I made no effort to resist my polyhedral assimilator, for I knew by now that such a struggle would be futility itself. The mind of man, I had learned, was not such a powerful force outside of the comfortable cradle of his own world. That world was one that I doubted I would ever see again. What was to become of me now? What awaited me at the end of this new, nightmare flight?

'I sped onwards, always straight ahead, never deviating from my course over the surface of the featureless planet. It truly was a barren place, that crumbling world under the dying sun. I saw not a single sign of life. Nothing but endless, arid, deserts of rock and sand all bathed in the same, ruddy glow. I dipped and weaved across countless miles of wasteland, and all the time the light of the sun grew ever more distant and feeble. Evidently my bizarre, new body was a tireless one.

'And so it was that as my unflagging flight continued, I saw the sun dip down beyond the distant horizon behind me to disappear completely. With the aid of the alien form that I now inhabited, I had outrun the sun and arrived in the blackness of the night – the dark side of the planet. No other star pricked the blackness of the sky above me, and the darkness below was absolute. Once again, I was blind.

'Ever onward I flew, crossing whole, night-locked continents of frozen tundra. Just as I was beginning to think that I might be fated to drift over this empty world for all eternity, I saw something in the darkness ahead. How I saw it I am unsure, for the thing was as black as the night itself – but then, I was not observing it with human eyes. The structure jutted from the desert like an arrow from a wounded flank. It was so slender that it seemed to waver slightly in the merciless desert wind, yet it was of such impossible height that its tip was lost in the æther above. The very existence of that black pylon seemed to violate the laws of physics as I knew them. This was no arrow; this was a cable that anchored earth to sky.

'As I sped towards the pylon and it grew ever more immense in my vision, I saw that it seemed to radiate a deeper darkness all of its own. That fearsome emission leaked into the starless sky, swirling about the incredible tower like a living, black vapour, blearing its form into the darkness of the sky. But as I struggled to focus upon it, I was struck by an unaccountable feeling. The tower before me was an utterly alien structure, erected by the industry of unknowable beings for purposes that were just as unfathomable. It was set upon the darkest, most desolate plain of a deceased world, a planet beyond the furthest edge of the Kosmos, billions of miles distant from my own home, and where for centuries unnumbered no man could possibly have ventured. Yet something within me told me that I recognised it - that I had seen its like somewhere before. It was not until the pylon stood over me, trembling like a blade of grass in the merciless wind, that my recollection finally surfaced - though it brought me no relief. The answer plunged my mind into reeling confusion. For that weird, black tower - so seemingly frail and yet unyielding- resembled nothing more than the very House in which you now stand.

'I did not have long to ponder upon this most unsettling of coincidences. My immediate situation held a far more pressing concern - for you see, the force that had dragged me to that place through the blackness of the night showed no signs of abating. I banked past ridges and swerved around rocks, invisible in the impenetrable dark, but always that looming pylon was ahead of me, filling my sight. As I shot over those final yards of frozen tundra towards the tower with undiminished speed, a panic grew within me. I was going to collide with it. From what manner of material my new body had been constructed I knew not, but my guess was that it could not be indestructible. And, as I felt with keenness the terrible cold of that planet and the relentless force of the wind buffeting across my angled planes as I flew, I feared that the appreciation of pain would *not* be beyond the capacity of this strange flesh.

'That was the first time that I tried in earnest to struggle against the alien will of my dodecahedral shell. Desperately I fought against the force that drove me. But it was no use. The shape and I were one, and strain as I might to halt my flight or even to alter its direction by a single degree, it was impossible. I might as well have leaped from a cliff-top and attempted to defy gravity, so inexorable was my charge. I cursed myself for my earlier pessimism, for not trying sooner to resist. I might at least have bought myself some time. Mere moments remained until I would slam into the pylon. I was to be obliterated.

'I strained to blot out the moment of the final impact, but cruelly I had no eyes that I might close. The black wall screamed towards me, curls of onyx mist seeping from its surface. I swallowed my terror and braced myself...'

ELEVEN
Prisoners of the Frozen Vault

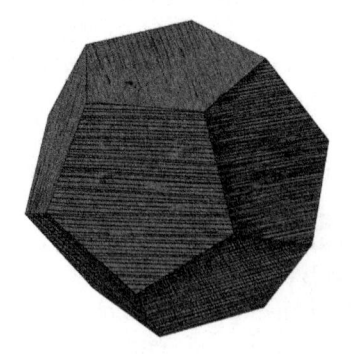

'I was still moving. Still hurtling through blackness. The pylon was gone, and I had not been destroyed. Had it been an illusion? Had the alien structure been some manner of fiendish mirage? I was still surrounded by an inky darkness – but this was not the darkness of the desert night. I cast my awareness about me and sensed rushing speed and enclosure. Then a strange thing met my sight. Behind me was a blotch of some other blackness, red-tinged and enclosed within the surrounding gloom as though by a frame of night – and looming into the edge of that frame was the seething outline of the impossible pylon.

'As my mind reeled in disorientation, the reddish patch dwindled. Then the scene came suddenly into focus and I felt very giddy indeed. I was plunging *downwards.* Somehow, at the very last moment, I had unknowingly executed a turn so sharp as to defy momentum and plunged into a chasm that had been invisible in the darkness. Relief flooded through me – I was not after all to be smashed to pieces against the walls of the monstrous, alien edifice. However, I was now plummeting with terrifying speed into the depths of some abyssal orifice at the foot of that same construction. The window onto the night sky was now a mere suggestion behind me. When, I wondered, would this appalling chain of events finally reach its conclusion?

'As though in response to my despairing thoughts, I felt myself come abruptly to a halt. The descent had ended and I was hanging in a lightless gulf. A recollection of the long-ago time when I had first arrived in the void came to me then – but this time there were no stars to fill me with awe and wonder. There was only a darkness so acute that I might have been struck blind. Straining to see above me, I could barely glimpse what I knew to be the pylon, although from the place where I hung it appeared as no more than a watery suggestion – a jet reflexion in a pool of black.

'I found with an incredible sense of liberation that I was now free to move. It had seemed like an age since I had last been the master of my own actions. Free at last, I began tentatively to move about, investigating the tunnel down which I had been flung. It was narrow – barely twice the width of body. However, as I realised then, I had no real idea of how large my body actually was. Nothing I had witnessed since my being had been melded with the form of the dodecahedron had served to demonstrate its true scale; the geographical features of the planet might well have been of any size, as might its frightful inhabitants. Up until that point I had assumed that my mass was more or less equal to that of a human frame – but really I had no good reason to believe that this was true. I put this disturbing thought aside.

'Whatever my true proportions might have been, I was soon to discover that I was utterly dwarfed by the scale of the vault beneath the pylon. The thought of the horrors that might lurk in the depths of that frozen crypt filled me with dread, but I had been free to move for some time and as yet I had remained entirely unmolested. No awful gibbering suggested the presence of the Ionuoiu or their kind, nor was there a trembling and heaving as of subterranean titans. Indeed, the only sound in that place was the distant moaning of the wind as it blew across the mouth of the pit, high above me on the surface of the planet. And so, as I had penetrated the veil between dimensions, traversed intergalactic space and crossed the whole of an alien world to arrive at that place, I decided that I should make at least a cursory exploration of it.

'I ventured as far as I dared from the mouth of the tunnel, but after travelling in one direction for what might have been several minutes with one of my planes pressed against the roof for guidance, I did not come upon the wall that I had expected to find. It was a panic-stricken journey back, fearing that I might fail to locate the tunnel mouth once more, and I struggled to keep my actions sober. But with gargantuan effort I managed not to succumb to terrified flight, and to fumble and scrape my way back to the tunnel without incident. From there I repeated the process in several other directions, each time achieving the same result. There was nothing – neither walls nor cracks nor protrusions, nor, to my great dismay, other passageways. The vast and featureless expanse of the roof was all there was.

'That was as much as I felt I needed to know about the vault. Nothing worthy of my attention had presented itself to me, and I was not prepared to venture any further into the depths of that place in case I should present myself to something that should find *me* worthy of *its* attention. I had experienced as much as I cared to of this hellish place, and I felt that I should now focus my efforts on returning home to the world that I knew – even if it was to be in this outlandish body. It seemed that my captors had abandoned me – that I was no longer their concern. I wondered, though, what the purpose of the whole, nightmarish experience might have been. I tried not to consider the events in depth, for the details sent my mind sprawling into paroxysms of fright, but it did seem to me that I had not been privy to an experience of the magnitude that the Eelen had described.

'Had I truly been in the presence of one of the First of Nhionbi? The mountainous horror that had burst from the ground back on the crimson-washed side of the planet had certainly been of godlike proportions. But had it been a god? It had certainly not communicated with me in any way that I could understand – but who was to say that I was even capable of comprehending the speech of the almighty? And why had it banished me to this cavernous dungeon? To be frank, I did not care. My only wish was to leave that place. It was by no means the hardest decision I had ever made to attempt the ascent to the surface.

'Blindly I blundered about until I located the entrance to the tunnel, and then I slipped into it and willed myself to rise up. As I ascended, the desolate howl of the wind from the surface resounded down the burrow to greet me. The climb took far longer than I had anticipated, and a good deal more effort. I had been falling at incredible speed as I entered the tunnel, but under my own volition I found that progress was unbearably slow and laborious. It was as though some great weight pressed down upon me.

'The dimensions of the tunnel seemed to be much smaller than I had imagined, too – it was barely wide enough for my form to squeeze through, and often my corners scraped unpleasantly against its sides. As the feeling grew that I might become inescapably jammed in that lightless hole, I was seized by a choking sensation of claustrophobia. I fought the panic, but without the aid of lungs with which to draw in calming breaths, it was all but intolerable. Again I pondered the strangeness of remaining so attached to such processes even when they are rendered so utterly irrelevant.

'As I continued to climb, I thought of how I should be a damn sight kinder to my chimneysweep – the poor, young rapscallion – should I ever have the miraculously good fortune to see him again. If his job was even one thousandth as detestable as my climb, then he was a brave boy indeed! At that point I would have traded all of my worldly possessions for the chance to elbow my way up the narrowest and most soot-choked chimney in creation rather than that one. But no such merciful opportunity was presented to me.

'It was only by occupying my mind with such trivia that I managed to continue that most harrowing of ascents. The patch of night and the gaseously wavering outline of the pylon grew more and more distinct with each passing moment. The effort that it took to rise through the tunnel was increasing also, so that it took all of my will to prevent myself from sliding back down again. How I wished for hands, and for a simple ladder to which I might cling! I pushed on, up through the enveloping blackness. I was becoming desperately fatigued. The only thought to keep the candle of my sanity from being snuffed entirely was the prospect of escaping that black womb to be born once more into the arctic night. The pylon swayed above me like a sapling in a gale. It looked almost alive.

'The last few feet were a torture beyond almost anything that I had endured. A crushing weight pushed down upon me. The wind shrieked and whistled dæmonically across the tunnel's entrance, and the tunnel itself seemed to clutch at me like a fist, refusing to let me pass. I struggled against it, drawing upon what meagre reserves of energy remained in me, until I arrived, shaking and hurting, at its very end. I permitted myself a small and hysterical laugh. I had done it! I did not dare wait to savour my victory, though. With supreme effort I concentrated all of my strength, and with my whole being screaming with the strain I threw myself out of the tunnel's mouth and towards the liberty of the night.

'Something slammed into me. Stars exploded across my vision. Stunned, I dropped back into the tunnel. I was giddy, bewildered. What had struck me? All that my vision reported was darkness and the steaming base of the pylon. Shuddering violently under the phenomenal weight that pressed upon me, I waited for as long as I was able to see that it was safe – and then once more I gathered my strength, and once more I hurled myself towards the surface. Again a smashing impact, and again I was sent spinning crazily away. This time the force threw me further back, spiralling down into the tunnel.

'I do not know where the energy for the next push came from. With excruciating exertion I struggled back up the tunnel and flung myself desperately into the opening. A force like a blow from an iron plate struck me. I reeled away. I think I knew then what was happening, but it was a possibility that was entirely too terrible to contemplate. A barrier, invisible and impenetrable, had been set over the mouth of the tunnel, sealing it closed. All of my hope faded. I was trapped.

'A fit of sheer rage seized me. I screamed wildly into the night, and the night returned my cry. I lost control then, and in my mindless desperation I threw myself again and again and again at the opening, battering my form relentlessly against the unseen obstacle. Pain began to lance through my body, but still I continued my frenzied onslaught. Then all was a blur of darkness and agony and despair and I was falling, falling away until the vault had swallowed me again.

'Much later I awoke from a dream in which the world was composed of nothing but screaming and blackness. It took me some time to realise that I had rejoined the conscious world. The shrill cries continued to pierce my consciousness, and the darkness was as acute as ever. After long, agonising moments of confusion I regathered my wits and recognised the sound of the arctic wind howling across the entrance to the tunnel, leagues above me on the surface of the world. With that thought came recollection, and in turn recollection brought down upon me a crushing wave of dejection. I was imprisoned and helpless. My only chance of escape had been denied me. I was trapped, perhaps forever, in that lightless, subterranean crypt.

'A miasma of pessimism enveloped my mind, tainting my every notion. I let it take me in its black and terrible embrace. For a long time I simply hung there in the vault, unable to form a constructive or even a coherent thought. I was utterly blank, and I remained that way for what seemed like forever. The one constant in my stupor was the un-light of the pylon, waving mockingly at me from the tunnel's end. I think that it may have been that sight that ignited my indignation and allowed me to melt through that paralysing veil of numbness – for slowly, I came around.

'I knew with utter certainty that I would never willingly enter that tunnel again. I felt that I had come uncomfortably close to a second death as a result of my foolhardy venture – but perhaps this time true death, eternal death. So far as I was able to discern, that left me with but one option. In my exploration I had tested every direction but one – the one that I most dreaded – the unplumbed depths that lay *beneath* me. Perhaps there I would find a means of escape. The time for procrastination had ended.

'I chose to descend in as straight a line as I could contrive, using the apex of the roof for my point of departure. I had planned to use the weird emission of the pylon as a guiding beacon, but that idea was soon forgotten as I lost sight of it after but a few minutes. I descended slowly and timorously, for I knew not with what manner of obstacles or other *things* I might collide. But just as I had found in the upper regions of the vault, there was nothing. I sensed no presences around me. No fiends lunged out of the dark to waylay me. The air – if air there was – was still and calm, and in time even the noise of the wind died away.

'The vault was immense. Larger even than my initial explorations had led me to believe. Quite what the purpose of such a vast space could be, or might once have been, I could not begin to guess. I do not think that I should have wanted to know even had I been given the opportunity to discover it. Although the speed at which I was travelling was admittedly not great, it seemed that I was descending for an eternity. But then, time had seemed to be of little consequence since I had left my body behind, and this was not the first occasion on which it had slipped away from me completely. I began to imagine myself a diver, kicking downwards through gloomy fathoms towards a distant seabed, and the humanity of that image comforted me somewhat. It was a debatably happy coincidence that the darkness of that place was so tangible that it felt almost as though I were submerged in icy waters.

'I had become so accustomed to my downwards motion that it scared the wits from me when finally my lower plane collided with something solid. It was quite a blow – I suppose I must have inadvertently picked up speed as I travelled – but the pain was momentary. As the sound of the impact rang out I was surprised to hear, instead of the dead tones of a noise swallowed by emptiness, an echo of reflected sound. Evidently the place was not so vacant as I had supposed. I slid cautiously along the surface, finding it to be flat and smooth, and apparently of the same stone or stone-like stuff as the far-off roof had been. Then I came to an edge. Perhaps this was not the floor of the vault after all. Cautiously I slipped down what proved to be the structure's side, and followed its contour to the true ground – or, at least, to the level beneath. After a few minutes of investigation of this nature, I decided that what I had come across was a structure whose dimensions approximated those of a small house.

'I suppose that the spatial sense is perhaps devolved more in me than in most, and so it was that by bumping and groping around in the pitch-blackness, I was able to paint a mental picture of my surroundings. I did not spend a great deal of time examining each separate structure, for to my mind at least they were in essence alike – seemingly featureless, irregularly-shaped things of varying size. Some were small as the first had been, whist others took long minutes to navigate, even at speed. Others had fluted spires that were taller than I felt inclined to determine; evidently I would have come into contact with one of them much sooner had I not taken a path straight down from the dead centre of the roof. But in time what I was to discover about those structures was that there was no end to them. I passed over another and another until I no longer cared to count. If these alien edifices truly were buildings, then I had arrived in the midst of a city.

'I floated quite aimlessly through the streets of the invisible city beneath the pylon. It was a sprawling place of endless pathways and passageways. Its countless rows and clusters of buildings were sometimes pressed closely together, and at others distant from one another as though ranged around a plaza. Sometimes I would come across a building perched on the edge of an abyss that plunged still deeper into the bowels of the planet. I drifted alone along strangely sloping verandas, and tarried in sunken grottoes. I glided over fluidly curving bridges that I felt sure would have been spectacular, had there been light to show them and eyes with which to see. For days I wandered sleeplessly and without direction – for my body was untiring, and I had nowhere to go. For now that I had found the city, I found also that there was precious little for me there. Of course, I had hoped to find some means of egress – perhaps another tunnel or something of the sort. But that black metropolis? It offered me no escape and no sanctuary.

'Inside that place, a tomblike quiet reigned. My own passing made no sound – unless, that is, I should collide with a building, and then the echo resounded unnervingly until it died. Otherwise, nothing so much as a whisper was to be heard. No water dripped, not a breath of air stirred. Of sounds of life there were none. As if further proof were needed, the place was evidently deserted – and in truth for that I was grateful, for I would have been loath to meet the sort of things that would have peopled that sunken city.

'As I wandered, though, I found myself wondering what manner of creatures they might have been. Somehow I could not reconcile the image of the atrocious, amorphous things that had abducted me with what were essentially houses. I did not believe that monstrosities like that would or even could dwell in any kind of domicile that I would recognise. The most perverse and unimaginable nether-places of the Kosmos were surely theirs. Not *houses*. The thought of their boiling forms filled me with revulsion in a way that these buildings – weird though they were – simply did not.

'Whose dwelling place had this been, then? And why had I been brought to it? After all, I had been banished to this frozen crypt quite against my will. I wondered if the adepts of Nhionbi had been subjected to such treatment during their own astral journeys. It seemed doubtful. Presumably they would have had some means of conversing with the First and their servant-things – they would not simply have blindly invoked them and then cowered in mortal terror as had I. But then, they would also have been able to return to their bodies, bodies that were anointed in sacred oils and spices and lashed to an altar somewhere back in Nhionbi. Thoughts such as these occupied most of the sleepless days and weeks that I roamed the deserted city under the ground.

'It was as I was sailing down a wide pathway, on what I estimated to be my forty-eighth day in the vault, that I heard it. I stopped dead. If my new body had contained such a thing as a heart, then I am sure that it would have been pumping furiously in pure alarm at that moment. As it was, I was grateful that it did not, for that way no anxious beating obscured the sound. It was a voice. *Someone was calling to me through the blackness!*

'I remained perfectly still, wondering for a time if I had truly heard anything at all, or if perhaps it was my hearing, so long accustomed to silence, creating its own cruel sport. Perhaps the darkness and loneliness had broken my mind. It was a possibility that I had pondered on.

But then it came again. A voice! A cry from out of the dark! It came floating to me as though borne on a subterranean wind – though of course there was none – and though I could not distinguish the words, I felt sure that it was calling out a greeting. The sound was distant, but still it could be followed! I set off at once.

'Excitement filled me, but it warred with trepidation. Besides those of my own clumsy actions, this was the first true sound that I had heard for many days – and for it to be a *human voice*, in *this* of all places! – well, I could hardly credit it. But I dared to hope that this might just be another who shared my plight or, better still, might be able to aid me. Still, the other possibility loomed large: that this was a trap. But I banished such fears from my mind. I was already quite comprehensively trapped – there was surely no need for further deception.

'And so I followed the sound of that voice through the blackness. It was leading me onwards, ever deeper into more distant regions than I had yet dared to venture in my wanderings of the underworld. Indeed, I had been pursuing it for what I judged to be many hours before the queerest realisation came to me. The caller was surely far, far off, and yet the voice was clear as day – for remote though it seemed to be, the cry carried no echo. Instead of a baffling, shimmering melange of cries reverberating out of the dark, I heard but one, clarion call. What this could mean, I knew not, but by then I hardly cared.

'I had become quite accustomed to traversing the city as a groping blind man, and in time I had developed a blind man's sense for that which surrounded me. Still, I reined my haste and moved with as much caution as I could muster, for the thought of becoming trapped beneath some toppled wall or minaret harried at my mind. Thus the hours of my sightless pilgrimage seemed interminable.

'As mile after unseen mile slipped away beneath me and the call grew louder, a further paradox presented itself to my mind: though that call suffused my consciousness, I could discern not a single word of it. Still, words meant little in a place such as this one, and I knew that the voice called to me, and to me alone. It was a greeting, a beckoning.

'As I crested a ridge, the sound of the voice became yet stronger. It was declaring peace and friendship, and it rang with the warmth of joy and relief, a spring thawing to my long-frozen heart. It told me that I was not far away now, that I should come without delay. I called back that I was *nearly there*...

'I came then upon a place that I fancied somehow more desolate than any I had yet traversed. For all that another was close by a dreadful pall of loneliness, of deep loss, seemed to hang over it. Worse still, my fears of becoming immovably trapped beneath fallen masonry seemed now on the point of realisation, for I found that at some point that had escaped my notice I had entered – or been drawn into – a veritable warren of tumbled stone. No longer did I possess the luxury of choice, and I proceeded only by whichsoever path through the ruins my form would permit me. Below me was a scree of rubble prone to sudden, violent slides into yet deeper abysses, and above me a mass of profound weight which I surmised had only remained in its present, precarious configuration by virtue of the stillness of millennia. A false move would surely bring the whole heap down upon me.

'Claustrophobia took me once more in its grip, but this was a fear of a different species to that which had seized me so far above. This place sought not to expel me as had the detestable tunnel, but to keep me fast in its black grasp, to pinion me in my undying shell beneath its shattered bulk for eternity. I had interred myself, I lamented, in my own barrow. I would have fled then, even with the voice calling me onwards, but it seemed to me that I had escaped each twist of the way by sheerest luck alone, and I knew with a cold certainty that I would be accorded such fortune only once. Thus the way seemed to close behind me. The only path lay ahead.

'Still the voice called me on. *Come closer*, it seemed to say, *Come to me!* And what choice had I? Once more I had sealed my own foolish fate. There was nothing for it but to edge my way through that frigid, fractured honeycomb of pitch, my being so tense that at any moment I might myself splinter into shards. But if I had once been close to my unknown goal then it seemed I had strayed from the straightest path, and in those early hours and days I had not even heard *the other sound*.

'The sound whispered out of the debris-choked passageways before me as though it was the burrow's own ragged breath. Indeed, right away I knew that sound for breathing. Gods, it was a horrid noise. A rasping. A death rattle. But whose death it augured I could not tell. The voice that called me onward had now become plaintive and desperate, weaker somehow than before though surely closer, but I had long since ceased to call in response. In truth I dared not. For as I journeyed ever deeper into the tangled strata of stone I became ever more convinced of a terrible truth: the place towards which the voice from the depths was calling me was the same as from which exhaled that deathly breath.

'I wish I could say that I had been brave. But in truth I went on only because I dared not go back. I could not but follow that call, although for all I knew it called me to my doom. And so I followed it through those final maddening yards or miles of tunnel, as all the while the gasping breath trickled down to me through the corpses of buildings until – at last – I emerged.

'Around me I sensed once more a vasty space. I had by virtue of my cowardice escaped the intolerable confinement – and for that I might have been glad – but in the instant of my emergence that oppression was replaced by a sensation of exposure so acute that I shrivelled beneath its glare. For from the very air around me, from every direction at once, seemed to emanate that rattling, bubbling breath. It was the sound of something *alive*, in this place beyond all life. But what it might have been I could not guess, and it seemed that there was no means by which to escape it. It was almost enough to send me scurrying back into that maze like a rat into his hole – almost, but not quite. For calling me onward was the voice.

'*Come to me!* it called, fragile, nectar-sweet and yearning. And so I went, drawn without hope of resistance through the fear of death towards the promise of life. Distended minutes passed as I sailed ever onward, my being singing with peril until the level ground beneath me fell away and I descended with it. Below me now, it seemed, were steps – level upon level of terraces all washed in the ghastly sound and at whose base I knew without question I should discover the source of the siren call. I fell, spinning, through honey and darkness and fear.

'And so my long descent ended, and I came then upon the deepest region of the vault. I hung there in eddying currents of black and gold, riven with doubt in the moment of my arrival. Should I go on? Might I even now escape this fate? But of course the choice had never been mine. Even in the darkness my presence was known, and a swell of something that might have been joy flowed out in a tide towards me. *Come, friend! I am here!* Silent, numb, I drifted nearer. The ragged breath was no longer all around me but issuing forth from some echoing maw ahead, and towards that darkling mouth I went.

'Dumbly I presented myself before the yawning portal, and awaited that which hauled itself across the flagstones towards me. There have been eternities since that moment when I wished I had turned away – wished that I had fled and spared myself the pain to come. But I did not. And when it touched me, I knew at once that my fate had been sealed forever.'

TWELVE
Tall Tales Told in the Dark

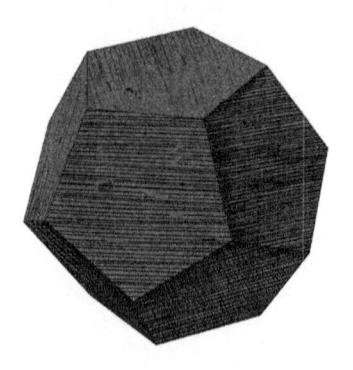

'That it was a hand I knew in an instant. A hand – a *human* hand. Five soft fingertips whose touch blazed through me as though each were a star in a constellation of white light, so that for a single beat of the heart I no longer possessed the darkness within me was no more. But for a heartbeat only – for in that same instant a scream rang out and the hand and its radiance were snatched away. In that moment of our touching our fear had been inverted, and now hers shuddered through the vault in chill waves in place of mine. Yes, I knew in the briefest graze of her fingers that she was a woman. And if the sweet light that had thrilled in my being had been the symptom of her touch, then what dread radiation might my own horrid flesh have imparted? I could but guess, but I heard her recoil, gasping and heaving, into her hiding-place.

'*Come back!* I cried, but the hand did not reach out again. Nor did the sweet voice call me closer. Instead I heard now a new voice, cracked and small and quaking, chanting words I did not know. Who was this new woman –

what was this foreign tongue? It was happening even as I struggled vainly to understand. For though that voice shook with weakness, its strange utterances seemed moment by moment to mount one upon the other with a gathering strength of their own, so that soon they reverberated through the immenseness of the space around us, ringing in its very atoms. Too late I recognised the likeness of my own long-ago incantation and the power of which it spoke – and before I could react, a furnace-blast of heat rippled into being and sent me sprawling away in blistered confusion.

'*Come no closer*, warned the first voice – once so warm, now cold and tight – *or you will burn*. Still prickling with the charring blast, I felt no urge to disobey. For a time I waited, gathering what shreds of my wits I still possessed, and listening to the sound of the breathing as it slowed from a pant to a shallow rasp. There was nothing for me to do, nowhere that I might go. And so I waited. And after a time in which centuries might have passed, she spoke again. *What are you?* she demanded.

'Then it was my turn to be silent. How could I explain, when I did not even know myself? I shall not relate to you the details of the tortuous process by which I made my account, and by which at last I gained her trust. Suffice it to say that she would ask of me a question, then I would reply – and should my answer please then I would be permitted a question of my own. More often than not my answer did not please; the Tablets, I thought at times, had given up their secrets more readily. And so it went. The performance was one from some theatre of the absurd: the dead, polyhedral man and the peculiar woman, conversing with but a glimmer of understanding in the inky darkness, an invisible waterfall of flame between them. It felt so all the more for the fact that it transpired upon a stage.

'It was one of the things that I learned first from Sün – for that was her name – in the long hours before she trusted me enough to reveal something of herself. For though I had wandered that place for days beyond reckoning, I had not beheld it for even a moment – and Sün had *seen* our prison. The sunken place of steps in which we had found ourselves was an amphitheatre. It was a not a word spoken in that queer tongue of hers, I am sure, but she described to me the place through which she had dragged herself, and to this I appended the evidence of my own wanderings. Thusly I deduced that this was an arena more colossal even than the great, tottering relics of Julais – and surely as ruinous. But for all its dilapidation it remained a miracle of architecture of a type unknown to men of Verdra. It was some cunning facet of its construction, some marvel of the acoustic Science still functional even in the extremes of æonian decay, that had projected to me the sound of Sün's dying breath as once it had done for the long-dead orators of that world.

'For yes, Sün was dying, and the breath, once so terrible in the darkness, had been hers. This fact came to me in a slow dawning that I elected not to mention, for it showed me for the fool I was. Quite how I had not discerned it before I knew not, but it was a matter of supreme obviousness now. Our calling to one another across the wastes of the vault had been no merely *physical* affair – for had I in this new anatomy of mine any such thing as a mouth, a tongue? Lungs? A throat? Of course, I had not. We had spoken not with the voices of our bodies, but with the voices of our minds. Our true voices. And when the poor wretch who had been calling out to another soul for aid had been advanced upon by this cowardly, dim-witted clod in a freakish body of alien flesh – well, it was small wonder indeed that she had sought to protect herself. The words of power that Sün had spoken, the incantation that had thrown up the burning wall of force, had been in her own tongue – entirely foreign to my ears. How fortunate it was for us, then, that our minds spoke for the main part not in words, but in concepts alone.

'In creating the wall, Sün had expended the very last of her energies. Until that moment she had been conserving what little strength remained to her, and that, it transpired, had been her ruin. When first she had found herself in this place, Sün had for a time believed herself blinded – and it was only when her words had brought forth her light that the ghastly sight of the broken arena spread out before her had met her eyes. I think perhaps she offered me a small mercy when she refused to describe just what manner of doom had befallen the place. But whether it revealed fair sight or foul, the light had imperilled her, or so she believed – for who knew what denizens of the underworld might be lured by its glow? And so she had gone on in darkness, and so she had fallen. Her leg had been smashed apart like a dry twig, and many of her ribs were fractured, but she had hauled her broken body to the shelter of a structure – this orator's box – in which she had since lain. A little of herself she had used to numb the pain and staunch the bleeding, but fool Sebastian had made her use the last. We would remain in darkness. And to own the truth, for that I was glad. For though I had not looked on a human countenance for days unnumbered, I did not think I could bear the sight of such a deathly one as I knew poor Sün's must have been.

'In time, as Sün's strength faded, so too did the burning wall. Just what it was that convinced her at last to trust me I suppose I shall never know. Perhaps it was sheer resignation like that which had allowed me to go on into darkness, knowing that I was already irrevocably damned. But in truth I think not – for from the very beginning I knew that she was far stronger than I. Whatever it was, she was surely brave. The burning force was a ward against malevolent spirits, you see, and it had had not merely repelled me as had the tunnel's barrier above but seared me as though it were my very bane. And yet, she allowed me at last to approach her, and I felt once more the ecstasy of her hand upon my flesh.

'The glow that suffused me at her touch was dimmer now, but no less ecstatic for that. She was weaker, surely. And so too must some of the horror emanating from my own body have dimmed – perhaps burned away by her flameless flame – for she was no longer repulsed as before. Apparently I was somewhat warm to the touch, and my surface was akin to that of polished stone, though it was slightly yielding, like petrified flesh. That hand of hers felt tiny against my planes. I tried not to dwell upon this fact, though, for it implied that my body was of monstrous size. My already tenuous relation to humanity was slipping ever further away. Still, in time she came to nestle against me as though I were some faithful hound, if not a man, for it was deathly cold in that place and mine was the only warmth. There can have been little real comfort in my alien half-embrace, though for my part her breath upon my panes was a kind of bliss. But in the end it was this strange intimacy, I think, that allowed us to converse together as friends. And so it was that I began to impart my story – the tale as I now recount it to you.

'The life before my death, as you know, was an unremarkable one. But it did not seem so to Sün. Indeed, there was little I spoke of that was not unfamiliar – fantastic, even – to her. What was a "university"? What was its purpose? And why ever would somebody wish to know so much about numbers to begin with? Her ignorance was bewildering. I explained as best I could, but she thought it all amusing nonsense. She would stop me to query the strangest of things, mundane things – what was a "coach", or what was the meaning of "money"?

'What's more I found that none of the places in which my tale transpired were known to her either. Iremouth I could understand, but Broadflight – Stoancastle, even – not a one of them provoked even the slightest flicker of recognition. The names of countries and continents were unknown to her. To begin with this did not perturb me greatly, for her foreign tongue and indeed her name had already led me to believe that she must have hailed from a remote land indeed. Perhaps, I thought, one of the wild regions that the civilising touch of the Empire had yet to reach. Indeed, it had occurred to me that primitive cults were still at large in the untamed hearts of savage jungles, and that perhaps some were even ancient enough to share their genealogy with the rituals of Uush'Ton. Was *that* how Sün had arrived here?

'After a moment I dismissed the idea. Her voice was endowed with an articulacy that belied such a theory – I could in no way reconcile the image of grimacing, painted savages and pounding tom-toms with such eloquence as hers. When my puzzlement led me into asking her directly whence she hailed, her answer surprised me greatly. She told me that her home was a place known as *Ghner*.

'My reaction was much the same as yours. Ghner – a nonsense word if ever I had heard one! A name fresh from a children's fable! An enchanted village, where the færies and pyskies prance! But what if I was to tell you that Sün's Ghner was no village, but a country? A vast place, wild and majestic, and home to many peoples? That I knew nothing of it was as surprising to her as it was to me. Indeed, she found my lack of knowledge somewhat absurd, more so even than I had found her ignorance of *our* world. Still I clung to the idea that in some blank corner of the globe not yet inked in Imperial purple, a settlement might yet exist whose primordial vernacular had yet to be corrected. Of course, that she referred to that globe not as *Verdra* but as *Ahd* and was but a symptom of the same circumstance.

'We needed very much to understand each other, Sün and I, for we were stranded there together, and we had come to know that our only hope of salvation lay in one another. But there was a strange calm in the sweet lull of her voice, a sense of safety and sanity that softened the terror and the enormity of our situation. I wondered how I could ever have failed to hear the femininity of that voice. At times, as her voice washed over me, I almost forgot that we were imprisoned there on that alien world. She told me so much. And with each further detail that she supplied, my conviction began slowly to crumble. For what possible reason could I have had to disbelieve her? Was my own tale not incredible enough? And how else might a society such as the one she described have entirely eluded the attention of modern civilisation – unless it was foreign to the world itself?

'There was great poetry and beauty in Sün's mind, but there was a great yearning too. It hurt her immensely to be away from the home of which she spoke – but it was a far deeper hurt than the mere longing of homesickness. Her very being was dwindling in that accursed place, and the part of herself that she had expended was not returning to her as it always had before. It seemed that it was simply not a part of the fabric of that dead world. She was fading steadily like a flower hidden away from the sun, and she bitterly cursed those who had brought her there. It was during a funeral rite that they had come for her, and I listened as she told me how they had spirited her away before the very eyes of her people.

But it was not merely listening – she *showed* me. I saw, I *felt* just as she had done.

'Üsha was dead, and there was a void in Sün's heart. There was joy there, too, for even as Üsha's grip on her student's hand had grown weak and her eyelids had fluttered closed for the final time, Sün had known that the greatmother's spirit was now rising up to walk the shining path to the spirit-place to become a part of all that was. But just as quickly as it could well up, the joy seemed to trickle into the hungry void, and Sün felt empty again. Tears welled too, coursing down her painted cheeks in rivulets so that cloudy, blue drops fell upon her robe. She wiped her face, her hand smudging a trail through the dots and whorls – no matter, the rite was done now, and besides it would not do for the others to see the new Aïy-udangana in such a way before she had even begun.

'Sün rose and lit the censer, filling the chamber with the clouds of fragrant smoke that would rise up with Aïy-udangana Üsha, greatmother of the village and adopted mother to her student. The new Aïy-udangana looked down upon her teacher-mother. In death she was smaller, somehow, withered and diminished in the absence of her spirit. But her face was still beautiful, yellow as the ivory of the censer and carved as intricately by the years as that sacred vessel had been by its ancient craftsman. She took up the bowl and bent to paint Üsha's face – first the sunbeams that radiated from her eyes, and then Sün's finger traced in jade the foggy lines of ink that decorated the greatmother's brow. She stood back and appraised the redrawn spirit-eye, that symbol which in Üsha's life had protected her mind from those who might seek to waylay her upon the spirit roads, and now in death would bar such spirits from her empty body. Sün swallowed more tears. The sickness had stolen

Üsha's voice many days before, but as she had clasped her pupil's hand in those last moments she had told Sün in her true voice that it was her time to leave, and that she was not frightened of the spirits that in life she had commanded, nor was she frightened of dying. No, the greatmother had not been afraid to die, but Sün was afraid now that she was gone. For Üsha's parting words had been strange, and she knew not what to make of them. And yet she had sworn, sworn upon all that was good in the world that when the time came she would give the last of her light for Ahd.

'Sün sang the final words of the rite as she put on the headdress, and then for the first time in many days she left the greatmother's side. Outside, the others lined the way, singing and beating the drums and gongs. For a moment she blinked in the sunlight streaming golden into the clearing, then bowed her head to the people. Despite the greatmother's passing, the village was alive with joy that summer – joy for the fruit that swelled on the trees, joy for the births of the strong babies, and joy for her. She knew that none had questioned the greatmother's choice of the new Aïy-udangana for even a moment. After all, who else but Sün might have banished the long-necked wolves from the fields? Who else wove such cunning charms as those that healed the corn-blight or knitted broken bones, or kept the scythes ever-sharp? And who else might have done these things with such skill and delight? Still, she was glad that, beneath the majestic crest of horns and feathers, the fringe of beads now hid her eyes, for that way none would see her fear. She was young, much younger than the others, and she knew that although they did not begrudge her, her udangana sisters would look to her now for guidance. And what guidance could she give when she had not yet found her words?

'The horth-pelt draped about her shoulders was weighty and thick, and in the sticky heat the heady scent of the oils and smoke that over the years had come to infuse it mingled with the cloying sweetness of the rapeseed wafting in from the fields. Under its hot, fragrant bulk Sün's sweat prickled, and her vision began to swim. Drunken flies danced before her face. As the drums pounded and the voices swelled, her last few steps were swaying ones – hurriedly she gave thanks to the sisters who had brought water and blessings to her dwelling, and staggering inside she flung off the headdress before the faintness took her.

'It was cooler inside the hut, calm and dim. She had emptied it of all but the pitcher of water, her bedding, and the woven mat. She took a cup of the sweet, cool water, sipped it gratefully until the weakness had passed. Now that she was calmer the claws of hunger began to rake at her belly once more – but the feast was days away yet, and now was a time for fasting. She settled herself on the mat, folded her legs together and straightened her spine. She took a last, longing look at her bed, then pressed her palms together before her tattooed brow and closed her eyes. There would be no rest for her now until the words had come.

'Soon the noise of the village had faded away behind the words of the mantra. All was lightness and space, and in her core Sün cradled the blue-green jewel of Ahd. It had always been Ahd that she held within her; the greatmother of all greatmothers lived in her just as she lived within her world. There could not be one without the other. Beautiful Ahd spun slowly and peacefully, her seas and rivers glittering and her great forests chattering with life, until Sün melted into the spirit-place. It was the place whence the knowing came – whence the words came. Here, beyond time, beyond thought, she floated forever, waiting for them to come.

'When Sün emerged, blinking again in the brightness of the afternoon, the udangana who had kept their vigil outside did not need to ask her if she had found them. They embraced her, and told her it had been five days since Üsha's passing. As she had sat in meditation, the preparations had been made – costumes sewn, fruits and grains and firewood gathered. Everybody had been waiting.

'Sün let them dress her in the new robe that they had made for her – for her! Its long, plaited tassels had been dyed in all of the colours of the summer, and upon it were embroidered suns and moons and leaves and branching trees. Such a lovely thing she surely did not deserve, but Aïy-udangana Üsha had spoken, and Sün, though she did not understand, would never speak against her. And so she stood and sang the songs of grateful acceptance as about her wrists they knotted cords of charms and tinkling bells, and upon her arms and face they painted the designs of the one who would speak. And by the violet, cricket-heralded midsummer's dusk, she was resplendent, and ready.

'The procession followed the path of red and swollen Father Sun as he blazed down through the purple twilight towards his night's resting place behind the far mountains. The people were garlanded all in wild flowers, and sang softly as one as the children scurried about their feet with berry-stained faces. At the fore of them walked Sün, head down and chanting quietly with their song, and behind her floated the earthly body of the greatmother, borne aloft upon the ancient, sighing craft. As they wound their way through the fields and across the babbling ford, the languorous evening smelled green and golden. Before long they were on the hill path, and Sün glanced back to see the long line of torches bobbing below her beneath the glowing sky, and as she did she felt the void in her heart begin to heal. For though they had not yet arrived at the place of healing, there before her were all of her people – the elders and the skipping children and the mothers with their swaddled infants – and she knew that in this good world that provided for them nothing had been truly lost. The Sun had set upon one of them, but he would rise again and shine again just as always on the others. And perhaps she did not know the way just yet, but at least she had found the words, and in time she would become as strong as venerable Üsha. Then she would guide the others – and when she too passed, the cycle would begin anew. There would always be another summer.

'They reached the brow of the hill as Father Sun was settling into his mountainous bed in the west, so that the standing-stones flung long shadows across the hilltop like streaks of a night that was impatient to fall. The towering stones had stood there for as long as there had been a hill upon which they might stand. They were not set in a circle or heaped in a cairn as are the monuments that people build, and yet they had a purpose about them that was somehow greater. Ahd seldom chose to reveal her mysteries to the people, but they knew within themselves that this was a special place – a powerful place where the great-greatmother's love was strong, and that was why they came there to be healed. Sün placed her palm against one of the scarred and mossy giants. It was still warm from Father Sun's kiss.

'Soon a warm and chirruping darkness had descended upon the place of the stones. A great pyre had been built there, and the old Aïy-udangana, resplendent in her robes and flowers, was laid out upon it. The pyre was not put to flame just yet though, but smaller fires around the hilltop were lit one by one, and herbs were thrown into them so that an intoxicating fug of aromatic smoke wreathed the hilltop, billowing orange in the firelight. Then, as the ceremonial fires crackled and roared, the booming of a great drum was heard and the people began their dancing. Soon the hilltop was alive with leaping, whirling figures, robed and masked in the likenesses of wild animals and spirits, dancing the steps that their ancestors had danced since time beyond mind.

'When the dancing was done, the udangana called out Sün's name. She stepped forward, her heart pounding louder than the drum and her throat tight, and she felt hands gently take her arms. Glancing around, she saw the kind eyes of her spirit-sisters smiling at her from behind the faces of crow and fox. She allowed them to lead her to her place in the centre of the throng, before a looming stone that dwarfed her utterly with its bulk. Then, with their hands clasped and swaying together, the people sang to the spirit of their departed greatmother, and they sang to Sün, their new Aïy-udangana who one day would be their greatmother too. Tears welling once more in her eyes beneath the deer-mask that she had chosen, Sün bowed deeply to them all. And then she called out her words.

'They were the words that she had found when she had wandered the spirit-place, words from that *other* language that was not the same as that in which the songs of her people were sung. And as she spoke those words, her light came. Sün's breath caught in her throat. There before her was a point of brilliant whiteness, a thing like a firefly frozen in the air. She cupped it in her hands and felt a fluttering like wings. The light grew, glowing scarlet through the flesh of her fingers, until she released it once more and it rose into the sky above them so that the place of the stones was lit up like brightest day by its radiance. A sigh rippled among the people. Then, when at last all of her words had been spoken, the people sang again, but this time the sweet sadness of the song was tinged with wonder. As the voices swelled, Sün took up a flaming brand and thrust it deep into the pyre. Bright flames blossomed across it. But even as the fire began to spread, from somewhere there came an incredible crack like sharpened thunder, and the song of the people turned to screaming. All of a sudden there were cries – cries of surprise, cries of fear, of pain...

'Sün's light went out. She span around, and saw that the circle was breaking apart and that the people were scattering into the night. And wading through the crowd, knocking her people flying like dolls, were two monstrous men. The people of Sün's race were small and slight, but these brutes would surely have towered over all but the most massive of any race of Ahd. She realised with an instantaneous certainty, and with a lurch that sent her heart leaping into her throat, that they were heading straight for her.

'She was not the only one to see it. Casting off their masks, some of her brothers and sisters had formed a ring around the monsters, knives drawn and defiance shining in their eyes. And in no more than five heartbeats every one of them had been pounded to the floor by merciless, crushing blows.

'Fear and indecision froze Sün then. She had no magick that could harm a man – some udangana of other orders did such black and forbidden things, but for Sün it was the antithesis of her craft. But her people were lying wounded, and she could help them! She tried to go to the fallen ones, but terror was pumping through her very veins and her body refused to obey her. The attackers were but yards away now, and as they bore down upon her she could see that their clothes were strange, and that in their hands they carried odd, silvery objects. Who were they? Why were they hurting her people? She had never seen men like these before, so outlandish and so brutal. As two pairs of huge feet pounded out the last few steps towards her, one of Sün's brothers stepped between them. He flashed her a brave smile but his eyes were wide with fright. Then he held up one hand in a gesture of defiance as though he meant to halt their lumbering charge – and in his other hand he gripped a slim, ceramic tube. A weapon! Sün recognised it at once as one of the ancient arms that her people had inherited – but so, it seemed, did the monsters.

'The closer of the giants stopped dead in his tracks, swatting away the men that still ran at him with careless strokes of the back of his great hand. The other, who Sün could now see was the very image of the first, came also to a standstill. Sün's protector raised his shaking hand, jabbing the tube in the nearest brute's direction as a warning. Both knew that with one touch of the stud on its side, a column of searing fire would erupt from its mouth. The fiend pulled back his lips in a wide, predatory smile framed by a tremendous moustache that of itself was like some ugly beast. Then he threw back his head and he began to laugh. It was a deep and malevolent sound, and it rang out menacingly across the hillside. Sün's defender glanced nervously around at her, tears shining in his eyes. For a moment their eyes met, but as they turned back again they saw that the giant now had his own hand raised.

'There was a click, and then with a thunderous bang the villager's head burst apart in a wet spray. His body dropped to the floor like a puppet whose strings have been cut. The moustachioed brute stood for a moment with the smoking weapon in his outstretched hand, then like some fearsome greatcat he leapt towards Sün. The ground between them disappeared in three effortless strides. Sün turned to run but the man was already upon her, and he bundled her up as though she were nothing more than a child. She kicked and struggled against him, but to no avail. His grip was iron. Then the only things she saw were snatched glimpses of the scene as he bore her away – crushed garlands of flowers strewn upon the ground, petals soaked in red, a burst of azure flame lancing past her, motionless friends all twisted in the dirt and trampled grass, the dancing sparks of the pyre leaping high into the night sky…

'The giant jogged easily down the hillside, ignoring the beating of Sün's fists upon his broad back. The heavy footfalls of another alongside them told her that her abductor's companion was close by. They ran on until the hilltop was nothing but a distant, flickering glow with the stones silhouetted against it and the cries of the villagers could no longer be heard. When at last they stopped, she was thrown roughly to the ground and the breath was knocked from her body. She struggled to her knees, gasping and spitting the vilest curses that she knew, but either the brutes did not understand her or they did but they did not care to show it. One of them held her arm as a cat holds a bird while he spoke to the other briefly in a foreign tongue. Then he put his hand inside his peculiar, brown coat and when he pulled it out there was a glinting needle in it. He stabbed it roughly into her arm, and she began to protest but soon she found that her mouth no longer worked.

'Sün collapsed back onto the wet grass. There she lay, unable to move, and then one of their faces – she could not tell which – loomed into her vision. He grinned at her, and then she knew that it was the second man, for this one seemed to have thick hair sprouting from not just his nose *but also his mouth.* Disgusted, she tried to turn her head, but nothing happened. After an unbearably long time the face slid out of view and something else replaced it, something that looked like an expanse of fabric with a dour pattern of flowers upon it. A bag. Then the bag opened wide.

'Sün would not – *could* not – show me what she saw within it. But suffice to say that the next time she dared to open her eyes, all was inky black and deathly cold and she knew at once that she was no longer in Ghner.'

THIRTEEN
Entrance & Egress (II)

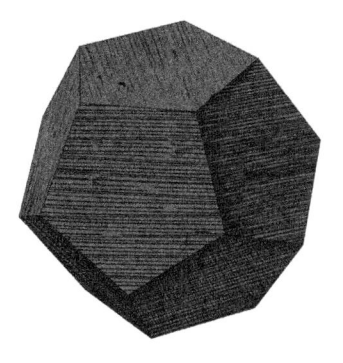

'We had both been brought to that sepulchral world – I as a result of my own reckless actions, and poor Sün by the wicked design of others. As to the reasons for this, we could hardly begin to guess – and none of our guesses, might I add, made pleasant speculation – but now that we had made one another's acquaintance, a spark of hope had been kindled in the darkness. Together, we might somehow forfend what once had seemed an inevitable damnation. And so, through the hours of a midnight unending, we plotted our escape.

'I had related to Sün the miserable experience of my attempted flight by means of the tunnel above, and we were in the firmest agreement that that particular course of action should under no circumstances be attempted again. In any case, it would have been an impossible undertaking. For even had that diabolical oesophagus not been sealed by an impenetrable barrier, then I doubted that I could ever have borne Sün's weight all the way to the surface through its stifling contractions and with the burden of its unnatural pressure bearing down upon us both.

'Exploring the city further seemed also a virtual impossibility. Had Sün been fit enough to clamber onto my back then I believe I could have carried her – I *would* have carried her, but carried her where? I had not managed to locate anything even vaguely resembling an exit to that place in many days of blind wandering, and that had been without the hindrance of an injured passenger. Besides, I doubted that she would have been able to grip onto me, as for a mount I was hardly the most accommodating of shapes, and what's more her injuries caused her great pain, even at rest. And as though these woes were not sufficient, Sün was beginning to develop a dangerous fever, and she complained of being ravenously hungry. Until that point I had quite forgotten the meaning of hunger; it was not a sensation to which my new body was prone. I had been roaming the underworld for who knows how long untroubled by lack of sustenance, but for Sün there was no such luxury. And it was from out of that very thought that our idea was born.

'It was Sün's body that was trapping us in the vault. It shackled us to that cavern, for we were restricted by it on almost every count. It was Sün's body that meant that we could not move, and aimlessly waiting there – though we were both loath to admit it – meant waiting only to die. For it seemed more than likely that her death would indeed soon come – she would die of her hunger, or of the cold, or if not of these then of her fever and her injury. My own body was dead already. Yet I was living evidence that consciousness could survive independently of a fleshly shell, and it was this fact that we hoped would be the vehicle of our deliverance. As you know, I had feared to affect the Transition a second time as I was petrified of what might occur should my soul be returned to what was no doubt by now my mouldering corpse.

Such an escapade would surely have spelled death – or else some kind of terrible living-death. But Sün was shrewd and perceptive, and she realised that returning to my body might not be the only way. Perhaps there was a way that we could leave *both* of our bodies behind.

'Although Sün's craft and my own lifework were radically different disciplines, we found that they were not at all opposed in the principles that underlay them. Indeed, in matters of astral projection I was but a mewling infant in her presence. She and the other udangana learned to walk the spirit-roads with little more than a nurturing of their intuition, for their ability was innate. What a clumsy, lumbering thing felt I with my drugs and my rote-learned rituals! But then we had come further than even the Aiy-udangana were wont to wander and what's more, it seemed, to a place wherein even such powers as theirs were rendered all but null. Still, as I explained to her ways of the Transition, I found that her awareness of the workings of Space, too, was developed to a delightfully advanced degree, for the bringing near of distant things was also a charge of the sisters. It was in this way that her people called stray animals back to the fold. And this was to be our deliverance – for especially keen in Sün was the awareness of the whereabouts of her homeland, which she felt like a beacon to her heart, a beacon shining forlornly out to her lost soul across unguessable gulfs of Space.

'So it was decided that I would affect the Transition of Uush'Ton once more. This journey, though, would not convey me back to my physical remains, but to another location entirely – and what's more, this time I would not be alone on my travels. With Sün's guidance, I would attempt to journey to her world, Ahd. And she would accompany me, as my passenger and my navigator.

'For the essence of our interaction was, in simple terms, a bonding of minds – a bond that we planned to strengthen in a way that would transcend all previous bonds. Sün believed that she could fuse her mind with my own, and in that way, as one assimilated consciousness, we could pass through those polyhedral gates and find our liberation. The thought of dear Sün's body slumped as a mindless husk in that black cavern chilled my soul. But ghastly though that image may have been, still it was infinitely preferable to the alternative. We began our preparations at once.

'Now, I will admit that never in my life had I much to do with the fairer sex. It was something that I had attributed to various factors – not the least of which I suppose were my lack of means and my obsession with my work. It really did leave me with so little time to spend upon courting and such. Always one more conundrum to solve, one more equation to balance. Not that ladies often paid me a great deal of attention – or really even gave me the time of day, for that matter. I don't suppose that I was truly ugly in life, but perhaps my face was just that much shy of handsome for it to handicap me in matters of the romantic sort. Still, I must confess that it was not something that concerned me greatly. I looked upon the amorous interactions of others with the same kind of mystification with which they would have viewed my own pursuits. All that loneliness, all that longing – whatever was its purpose? It seemed at best counter-productive to me. The baffling complexities of courtship, the love songs, the flowers, the heartache – why bother to expend one's energy on it all? But when, in that dark and alien place, we came together for the first time – well, *then* I conceived of the goal of it all.

'For are giddy, young lovers not forever and always entranced by the notion of finding the mate of their soul?

Are they not consumed by the desire to discover another who might feel the passions of their heart and mind as dearly and keenly as they do their own? But their quest is flawed – it is impossible, I say! For they can only truly know that most superficial of constructs: the *facade* of their sweetheart's being, that thing that is nothing more than a surface ripple upon the vasty deeps of thought and feeling that lie within! That is unless they, like Sün and I, flow and merge together to experience oneness in its purest, its most blissful form! Oh, if one single pair of lovers ever has the impossibly good fortune to experience joy even a fraction so intense as did we – why, then they should justify every tedious, lovelorn ballad that ever was penned!

'*And yet we were not lovers.* Sweet and sweeter though it was, our union was one of utility, and it had a greater purpose. But that did not in any way serve to lessen the euphoria that we felt, a euphoria to which the horror of our situation lent a bittersweet tang.

'And so, thus entangled in the mind of Sün, I began to work my own variety of magick. Thank Gods that the tether to my body had already been cut, for there was no *dote* to do it for me. But still it was not easy – indeed, the fact that Sün was swimming within me made the visualisation of the Polyhedra more challenging than ever it had been before. Her pain could not be left behind her and so, hurting with her, I too suffered. As I willed it, the Shapes would begin to form, their myriad luminescent planes drawing together in the glowing expanse of my mental gulf – and just as I would feel her sigh of awe they would fly apart again as though repulsed by some mighty force, shattering with a glittering din that raked agonizingly through our being.

'I would draw my intellect together again and begin afresh.

'The Shapes would come, melding themselves fleetingly into their magnificent totalities, only to melt away to nothingness once more. At times they would attain true form, and we would race gleefully towards them – only to find as we drew near that they were misshapen and warped and useless, and then our heart would sink. How many ways were there for me to fail? But soon enough my will would rise again – and soon enough those ghostly Shapes were made, spinning in their glorious geometrical perfection through the consciousness that we shared!

'We rested awhile then, for although we knew that our goal was within our grasp, we knew also that if we were to stand any chance of success then we needed to be strong. Sün, fevered and shaking, drew out of me and fell at once into a deep sleep, and at once I felt empty and hollow. It was a hollowness that had not existed in me before. I sat quietly by her and listened to the sound of her breathing. Each one of those breaths set the whole of her tiny frame to shuddering. And as that sound carried to me through the darkness, more disquieting now than even it had been in the days before I had known it for hers, I became more aware than ever that our time was short.

'With Sün sleeping fitfully beside me, I found myself alone and idle once more. And that was when I saw it. It was a miniscule thing, a speck so small as to be all but imperceptible. High, high above me, shining down through miles of stygian blackness, was an infinitesimal mote of glowing red. So far as I could discern, it could mean but two things. First, that my aimless wanderings had somehow brought me full-circle, and that the great amphitheatre in which we abode was directly beneath the dreaded tunnel. Second was a thing more significant than the fact of how easily and how thoroughly disoriented I had evidently become.

'Daylight had come at last to the world above.

'When Sün awoke, I showed her the light. With eyes of flesh she could not see it so well as I, but she cursed it nonetheless. For all she cared, she spat, this vile hole could remain in darkness for all eternity – she had no wish to behold it again. Neither had the coming of the light brought me any comfort. Having nothing else to focus upon whilst Sün had slumbered, I had spent a good deal of time in contemplation of it, and as that time had progressed its presence had instilled in me a growing sense of unease. And what's more it seemed that I was not the only one to be so affected – for that was when I heard the *other* voices.

'This time I knew that what I heard had not been concocted by my imagination. But this time I also knew that those voices were not calling to me as Sün had been. Neither were they the true voices with which Sün and I conversed – no, there was nothing of the coherence that marks a true utterance in those desolate shades. Most were little more than emanations of dread and melancholy that drifted through my consciousness. Others were more difficult to identify. It was, I thought, as though their owners were used to feeling in *other* ways. Still, I think that even had they embodied the very essence of articulacy itself I should still have had a job to distinguish their implications – for there were so very *many* of them.

'At first there was but a fleeting impression – a brief, mournful sigh from somewhere off in the depths of the vault. Then, just as I was wondering if I had truly heard anything at all, another joined it. Then another. And another. Soon there was a maddening host of them all babbling together. What did they want, I wondered? Help? No, I was sure that the owners of those half-voices were quite unaware our presence. But from where had they come? Had they silently shared our prison all along? And if so, then why had they chosen this of all moments to become animated? It seemed to me that the appearance of the red light had awoken them, bringing them to life as though they were tendrils of some ghostly plant unfurling in the rays of that dread sun. Whoever, *what*ever those voices might have been, they all had one thing in common: they were afraid. And that fear in turn infected my mind – for it implied that the sun's ascent heralded something far more than dreadful than merely the coming of the dawn.

'It did not surprise me to learn that the plaintive voices had reached Sün in her sleep, so that her already troubled dreams had been haunted with eerie, desperate cries. She too felt that they were not calling for our aid – and it was just as well, for we knew with a strange certainty that those things were already quite beyond any hope of rescue. What was reaching us was surely nothing more than an ancient and eroded echo of a mechanical impulse, a palpable emission of primal terror somehow branded into the fabric of that place. Despite the unwelcome intrusion, the rest seemed to have done Sün the power of good, and she felt much stronger. Once she had finished venting her loathing of the alien sun, the voices, and our situation in general, she declared that it was time – and for my part I was quite heartily inclined to agree. Of course, I had not the slightest flicker of regret to be leaving that hellish cavern, but I could not help but be touched by sorrow at poor Sün's plight – she would be leaving her body to rot. I hoped that it would not prove to be a rash decision. I had not yet even seen her face.

'Sün bid her body a long and elaborate farewell according to the custom of her people upon parting with a cherished friend whom they know they will not see again.

Then she laid herself down as though to sleep once more, composing herself in a manner that she considered fitting for the last pose of her mortal body - dignified and defiant - and she reached out her mind to mine. I opened myself, welcoming her in, and she flowed into me, filling the lonely void that had been left by her departure. I sensed that she too felt the relief of our joining and the strength that it gave us. Bolstered by this oneness, and with the dread of unknown danger snapping at my heels, I needed no further incentive to throw myself into the task ahead.

'The Polyhedra came with surprisingly scant effort, erupting into being at my merest suggestion. What elation! I felt our spirits laugh together with delight as the dazzling Tek'lon Polyhedron shimmered into existence there in front of us. Ha! We had all but won already! We knew at that moment that even the gods of that black crypt had no power to hold us! They had sorely underestimated the ingenuity of their two human captives, and now those captives - each of us so feeble in our affrighted seclusion - had together fashioned a force that would rend their prison asunder!

'We stayed for a moment merely to revel in our triumph and watch the first Shape hanging there, glinting and twisting in our mind, and then we plunged. As we dived into the crystal angles of the Polyhedron, it at once retracted and bloomed again, bubbling into the form of the next portal. Then Polyhedra burst into existence all around us. I felt Sün trembling inside me, and I willed her to hold tight as we somersaulted into the melee of facets and faces. We swooped into another Shape and another, plunging through gate after gate, each time emerging into a further realm of infinity.

'Suddenly we were in the midst of stars - and although those stars were dim and shrouded, I knew that we must at last be drawing near to our destination. Just as they had during my first Transition, the Polyhedra began to form independently of my thought, and a relentless barrage of Shapes assailed us. I felt Sün's fear as the bombardment intensified, felt her shrivel in terror as kosmic forces pushed and plucked at us, but I had been there before and I was *not* afraid, and I held onto her being tightly as we veered crazily through each successive gate. Then, with a mighty lurch, Space seemed to invert itself and the final Shape was at last disgorged. We screamed through the pulsing abyss towards the thing, and for a second we saw its angled expanse spread out before us...

'Everything was still. But we were not in the kosmic void. No stars surrounded us, no far-off galaxies wheeled. I cast about, looking this way and that, and I soon discovered our location – it seemed we were *within* the gate! On every side of us the interior of its immense, translucent planes could be seen, drifting slowly first one way and then another as though the vast Polyhedron were rotating upon a series of unfathomable axes. We remained that way for a while, watching the thing spin around us. In the calm of that place, I felt Sün's fearful quivering cease, but I also felt a question growing within her. I knew already what that question was, but in my shame I knew not how to answer it. For we were where we should not have been – we had entered the portal but not passed through it. We were still within the netherplace of my mind. The Transition had failed!

'I had failed Sün. I had failed her, and that meant that we would have to return. We would have to go back to the black cavern and the voices and whatever had stirred them up and then we would die. First Sün, then no doubt myself. But *why* had it happened? The Transition had been occurring exactly according to plan – better, even, than I could ever have anticipated! What was this final obstruction?

'I wracked my mind for the answer, but none came – not from me, at least. It was Sün who noticed it first. She may not have known much of the Formulæ, but she at once recognised that which had thwarted us. She turned our gaze out towards the revolving planes of the polyhedral gate within which we hung, and for a while that gate was all that I could see, but at her insistence I focused *beyond* it – and *then* I saw what she had seen.

'At first there was just a suggestion of movement, slow and incredibly distant, but then, as it continued, I realised that the movement itself had form, a form that had been invisible as its colour mirrored the blackness of the void. I traced that form across the sky, followed the lines, observed the intersection of the five-sided planes that they delineated – all the time growing sicker and sicker inside, for I knew then what it all meant. For surrounding our gate, *sealing* our gate within its own wicked angles was yet another Polyhedron, a looming thing of such incredible size that it seemed that in beholding it we beheld the form of the very Kosmos itself. That twelve-planed shape was sickeningly familiar in its geometrical perfection – *for it was the shape of my own body* – a perfect, black dodecahedron.'

∽

Flintwick drummed his fingers upon the windowsill as the maid hurried along the corridor towards him. Almost everything about her irritated him quite intensely, from her skittering gait to her perpetual unpresentableness to that twee Scornländian accent made yet more unbearable by the taint of the worst parts of Ghastian slumtongue that hung about her every utterance like the stains on her pinafore. She even looked, in a malnourished kind of a way, like one of those aggravating little troll creatures that the færie stories always had roaming those northern valleys – had one been captured and stuffed into a serving-girl's dress, that is. This is what one let oneself in for when one invited foreigners to labour on the estates – but then, the Scornländians were unerringly efficient lumberjacks, and the forest would hardly fell itself. Still, he would have sacked her on first sight had Lord Naught not been so inexplicably fond of her. At least her runtish size made her quite suited to the surreptitiousness of her most recent assignment.

'Well?' he demanded as at last she scampered up to where he stood.

'Sorry, Master Flintwick,' puffed the girl, curtseying ineptly. As usual, she was somewhat bedraggled and her pinafore was creased as though she had slept in it.

'For what, girl?'

'Well, for being late, Master Flintwick. You see, I thought I should get a broom – '

Flintwick blinked repeatedly. '*A broom*, Agetta? And why ever should you require *a broom* for the task of listening on the outside of a door?'

The girl seemed to be examining the somewhat scuffed toes of her shoes. 'In case they should see me, Master Flintwick,' she mumbled. 'I thought I had best look as though I were sweeping, in case I should be caught, like, for else I should have had my ears boxed.'

'Pah! I shall be the one who decides upon whether or not it is appropriate for you to avoid your beatings, girl.' He glanced at the un-boxed ears beneath her lopsided cap. 'So, they did not, then?'

'Did not what, Master Flintwick?'

'Well, catch you of course, girl!'

'No, Master Flintwick. They locked the door again and they stayed inside, you see.'

THE SHAPES

'Very good. And what did you hear, Agetta?'

Agetta twisted one toe on the carpet. 'It sounded like Church, Master Flintwick.'

Flintwick closed his eyes and blew out an exasperated sigh. '*Church?*'

'Oh, what I mean is like an old man who was unhappy, like, shouting a lot about the Gods and suchlike, Master Flintwick.'

'Hmm.' It was just as he had suspected – the "Bellhouse" ploy was continuing. 'And I take it they are still inside?'

'He din't sound very much like he would be stopping soon, Master Flintwick.'

Flintwick nodded. 'Very good.' He slapped the windowsill, and the maid flinched. 'Well, be off with you, then!'

She curtsied again, and fled.

'And if I ever catch you eavesdropping in this House again I shall deal with you very severely, d'you hear?' Flintwick called after her. 'And for Gods' sake tidy yourself up!'

So, to the task in hand. Alone in the corridor, he reached into his pocket and produced a sizeable bunch of numbered keys. He quickly identified the correct one (secretly congratulating himself on the efficiency of his system) and, after checking over his shoulder to ensure that he remained unobserved, slipped it into the lock.

Carnaby's room, or the room in which Carnaby had been quartered, looked very much as it had done the last time that Flintwick had seen it. Admittedly this had been some time ago – there were so very many rooms in the House that to maintain a strict rota of personal inspections as he would have liked would have constituted a full-time occupation in itself. Dunsany, the head butler, and his legion of underlings were entrusted with this task and, at first glance at least, it seemed as though they had done a job worthy of only minor reproach. There were fewer blankets upon the bed than Flintwick would have liked to have seen for this time of year, but then, he reminded himself, this was not in fact an inspection of that manner – and in any case it would not do for Carnaby to be made any more comfortable than was strictly necessary. He checked the sheets for evidence of seminal emissions – not incriminating, admittedly, but a useful gauge of character nonetheless. None were apparent, yet.

Next, the dresser. It was sparsely populated: tins of hair lacquer and moustache wax and the requisite combs for each, a sizeable bottle of cologne whose muscular odour refused to be confined by its stopper, and little else. These served only to inculpate the man as a popinjay and a preener. Surely there had to be more.

The greater part of the "Doctor"'s possessions had been conveyed into the basement room where at that moment he was holding his court of deception, but several crates of books had found their way to the chamber. Flintwick bent to examine their spines. *Experimental Researches into Elyctricity. A Collection of Observations on Elyctrodynamics.* The remainder appeared also to concern that fad of the moment. Well, Carnaby was perhaps not entirely brainless but nonetheless a fool if he believed there was a future in such nonsense – presuming, indeed, that these were genuine objects of study and not the props of a charlatan. The next crate contained volumes on geometry, calculus and suchlike. They certainly *appeared* scholarly enough, judging by their covers, at least – but then, one should never form an opinion of a book on that merit alone, Flintwick reminded himself. He began to leaf through *The Practical Application of Semantics and the Art of Summoning,* but quickly reinstated it in its place in the pile after discovering that its contents were both decidedly unwholesome of character and also quite beyond his understanding.

So, nothing of use here – and it seemed as though there was little else in the room that was not native to the House. Flintwick's chances for the exposure of dupery and ill-intent were dwindling. After a brief rummage through the empty chest of drawers and the similarly empty though spider-haunted nightstand, only the wardrobe remained.

He flung open its carven doors and peered inside. Several identical shirts hung next to one another, along with some trousers and a waistcoat. A search of the pockets revealed little more than fluff and a mentholated boiled sweet. Flintwick closed the door and stood for a moment. But what was this? There, half-hidden by the elaborately-scrolled pediment that crowned the wardrobe was a case. Mounting a nearby stool, he steered the case out past the fragile wooden curls.

It was not even Carnaby's property. Folded neatly inside the case was a dress, and on top of it a little bonnet that appeared to consist almost solely of lace and ribbons. He sighed. Who had the last occupant of the room been? Admiral and Lady Grice, as he seemed to recall. He lifted the dress out, in case some further clue to its owner might present itself – a label or suchlike. No such thing was apparent, but Flintwick at once crossed Lady Grice from his mental list. A creature of such slight build could have no need for a garment of such preposterous size as this one. Neither was the wig hidden beneath it likely to be hers – whether the wife of Admiral Grice had grown her tumbling, auburn hair from her own follicles was unknown to Flintwick, but in any event she would hardly have worn the bushy, raven-hued thing in the case.

Flintwick sighed, and returned the case to its perch. He had learned nothing whatsoever of the man or his motivations. Still, there was always the assistant's room.

⁓

'I suppose that I should have known. I should have realised that I was out of my depth. I should have realised that we were in the thrall of powers quite beyond the ken of a cosseted fool like myself. What did I, Sebastian Bellhouse, the shit-scrubber of Broadflight, know of this place, this Uush'Ton, this Beyond into which I had so unknowingly flung myself? What had I hoped to achieve?

'Our ill-fated flight had been a pointless endeavour – a useless waste of ill-afforded energy. And now that Sün had been forced to return to that body which she had mere minutes ago had bid farewell, weaker than ever before from our exertions, I felt deeply ashamed. I cursed myself then as the blood-red glint of the alien sun shone down through fathoms of darkness that still rang with terrified cries to where dear Sün and I languished once more in our frigid prison. I cursed my confounded naïveté.

'Should it not have been obvious that they – whoever *they* were – would know of the Transition? *They* knew perfectly well that it was by means of that kosmic portal that the people of Nhionbi had found their way to that place – and *they* would know just as well that those people had left through it. And evidently *they* did not want *us* to leave.

'Now it was my body and not Sün's that anchored us to our prison. But it was not my body, not *truly*. It was the container in which my consciousness had been confined – but it was not truly that, either. It was more as though my very soul had been suffused with the stuff of that alien object, and as though that suffusion was so inextricable that its physical form now determined my psychic capabilities. I was sure that it was no coincidence that the dodecahedron was the shape to nullify the effects of the Transition; it seemed that something within its particular combination of angles served to negate the process completely, as surely as briny water refuses to freeze. *Why* had I not noticed its conspicuous absence from the ritual beforehand? I felt like a man who had discovered the key to his prison – only to find once he had opened the door and tasted free air that the same key had somehow clamped the manacles tighter than ever about his legs.

'Even as I was thinking these things, I think that I already knew. I felt, with a cold and dreadful certainty, what it was that we had to do. We had to destroy the angles. There was no other way. We would have to break apart the prison that constrained us, and this time it would have to be done by a much less subtle means than the intricate ritual of Uush"Ton.

'When I asked Sün to find an implement with which to perform the operation, she did not at first grasp my meaning. And when at last she did discern it, she implored me to reconsider. She said that she would not do it, not to me. I could not make her do it. She was not that important, she said, it would be better for me to find some other way out, to leave her here. I would have a better chance on my own. There *had* to be another way! But for all her protestations, she knew as well as I that in truth there was none.

'So Sün sat propped against the podium with one hand laid tenderly upon my flank, and in her other hand was a rock – large and wickedly jagged – that she had pulled from a pile of rubble that littered the stage.

She stroked me gently, her fingers tracing the edges of the shape that imprisoned us. I told her not to worry. Not to stop. That it would be hard, but that she must not falter. And above all that she *must not* think about me. She sighed, and I felt her breath warm against me, then she pressed her soft lips to one of my planes. She did not pull away from that kiss for a long time. We had shared a mind, but it was that one, long moment, so ordinary and yet so profound, that I shall remember for the rest of my days. Then it was time. Now, I told her. I heard her swallow nervously, heard her anxious breath. *Now,* I said! She raised her arm. *Now!*

'The first blow landed like a burst of white fire that seared through my being. The pain was worse than I could ever have imagined. But I steeled myself and I did not cry out, and before the pain had even begun to ebb the next blow had landed, smashing agonisingly into my flank. I was knocked sideways by the impact, my body singing with hurt. I braced myself. *Again,* I cried! *Do not stop!* Again Sün hefted the rock above her head, slamming it with a two-handed grip into one of my corners. This time I could not contain it and I cried out – her blow had torn off a piece of my flesh. I was ablaze with pain, but it was working! I felt Sün hesitate, heard a small whimper break from her lips. *Again!* I cried, *Again!*

'The rock smashed into me once more, ripping another chunk from my side. Then I did not even try to hold back the scream of sheer agony that burst out of me, and through my scream I heard Sün begin to weep. But she swung again, and again the rock tore into me, and again I screamed, and after that I did not have to tell her any more. She had become a sobbing automaton, retching and crying out my name as she mindlessly pounded the rock into my body until her hands and arms were slicked with her own blood and her blows had become a relentless rain of searing agony. Then the pain drove all thought from me and then it was as though nothing had ever existed but the endless pounding and raking and the agony and the blackness and I was shrieking and Sün was shrieking with me in such horror and revulsion that we humbled the thousand cries around us and the vault resounded with the cacophonous din of our torment.

'When my mutilation was complete, Sün collapsed to the floor, all but unconscious. There was no energy left within her to weep any more, and her throat was ragged with screaming. I simply hung there, numb and empty and without thought, surrounded by the moaning voices that still carried through the vault like the echoes of our own grief. My disfigured body had been reduced to little more than a ball of scarred matter. At that time I had not the capacity to feel triumph – but triumph is exactly what I ought to have felt – for the mounds of weird flesh that littered the ground all about me were testament to the fact that each and every line and angle of my form had been erased.'

∼

Flintwick closed the door quietly behind him. The first thing he noticed was that, in contrast to Carnaby's austerity, the assistant's room was far from a picture of neatness. A heap of crumpled clothes lay upon the bed, books (including *ugh!* a *novel!*) were piled everywhere and an incredible number of spent candles littered the floor and furniture. To cap it all, there were also muddy marks soiling the fine carpet. And this the result of a single night and day! It was an exceedingly discourteous in which way to conduct oneself. Flintwick resisted a powerful urge to tidy the things away – to do so might well alert the servants on their evening rounds to his intrusion of the room. Could one be an intruder in one's own home? It was certainly beginning to feel as though that were the case. Still, if he could locate some *evidence* of some kind, well, then things might take a decidedly different turn.

Flintwick occupied himself with rummaging through Stoathill-Warmly's pockets. His search yielded nothing more intriguing than an enamelled pillbox containing three disintegrating tablets of what looked to be coca, a case of Urish cigarettes, and a matchbox decorated with a scene of Hingham Cathedral. This was becoming increasingly displeasing. He would not have been in the least bit surprised to discover that a stash of Lord Naught's silverware had indeed been secreted within the boy's waistcoat, but it seemed that he had been misled. He made a mental note to have young Steven flogged for tittle-tattling, as it was in all probability him who had made off with the forks anyway.

After as lengthy a search as he deemed judicious, Flintwick found that, despite its disarray, there was as little of use to be found here as had been yielded by Carnaby's quarters. Just as he was turning to leave, however, a movement caught Flintwick's eye. He turned to see the curtain swaying. For goodness' sake, the boy had left the window open! It was still raining and, although Flintwick knew full well that rain never seemed to enter the House no matter how violent the downpour happened to be, the principle still stood. Besides, Stoathill-Warmly was unlikely to know of this peculiarity, so that hardly excused him. He walked back into the room and yanked the curtains apart. The window was indeed open to its fullest extent. Flintwick clicked his tongue in disapproval. As he made to close the casement, however, he noticed something very odd – something so odd, in fact, that he was forced to lean out into the night air in order to investigate further.

Just as he had thought – no, *known* – the window had the good fortune to look out upon a rather pleasing view of Iremouth. The lights of the city twinkled merrily below, and Flintwick for a moment imagined that he saw another of the shooting stars descending. Back to the matter in hand, Nicholas, he reminded himself, wiping the rain from his face. The fact was that there was a drop of fifty or more feet from the level of the window to the ground where a tangle of unruly bushes grew. He shook his head in puzzlement. This, if nothing else, would warrant further observation of the boy.

For there, upon the windowsill, was a pair of things that bore more than a passing resemblance to such marks as might be left by a pair of heavily muddied boots. The strangest thing about them, though, was that the wet soil and grass that comprised those footprints was not on the *inside* of the sill where they might be left by a person exiting the room by such unconventional means, but on the *outside* – as though someone had used the window to come *in*.

∽

'As Sün lay by my side, she sang to me softly in the tongue of her people. Though her voice was cracked, her song was more lilting and beautiful than any I had heard, and it comforted us both.

'The sunlight was growing ever stronger. The point of radiance overhead now resembled nothing more than the tired star that was its source. It must have been broad daylight in the world above – or as close to it as that loathsome place could get. I imagined the wasteland all washed in the red glow of the star, and the writhing pylon that jutted from it casting its slender shadow across the tundra. The voices that haunted us waking and sleeping still sounded their distress like some awful parody of the dawn chorus where the song of birds had been replaced by inhuman moans. But what exactly did they fear? What new terror would the sunrise bring? What did they know that we did not? Now that we had managed to destroy my dodecahedral form, we hoped that we would not be obliged to find out.

'But it seemed that for every step forward that we took, we were forced to take another two long strides in the opposite direction. The exertion involved in my maiming had drawn upon reserves of energy that Sün could ill afford, and she had become very weak. As for myself, I felt as though I were made all of teeth that had been hammered down to the pulp. It would be some time before either of us were strong enough to attempt the Transition again.

'While we rested, we talked of the things we would do when at last we reached Ghner. Sün was radiant with hope – she felt sure that if we could find her people then we would be able to communicate with the other udangana, and that they would know her and they would be able to help us. She was not yet sure exactly what it was that they would do, but she had an idea that perhaps they would fashion us new bodies somehow, for though such things were unusual and undoubtedly challenging, they were not at all beyond the means of their arts. Then, she said, when we were together and whole and safe, she would show me all of the simple wonders of the land that she loved, so that I could see with my own eyes the things which I had only ever beheld in stolen glimpses. We would walk together under mossy boughs through pleasant, shady forests, and wander in sunlit fields, and we would follow the babbling river up into the hills where she would take me to the place of the stones. And we would live together in her village, a simple place that had never been sullied by the shadow of a manufactory or a workhouse, and we would watch the people dance and sing as the seasons changed. I felt very glad that we would not be returning to my world - *this* world - for the little that I had seen of Ghner had convinced me that it was a better kind of place, and I believed that with Sün I could find the true happiness that I had ever been denied in my old life.

'It was at that very moment - as my mind was filled with pleasant visions of leafy woods and golden fields, all balmy in the summer's dusk - that it happened. All at once the air grew heavy, as though suddenly it had become saturated with dark portent. I heard Sün catch her breath, felt her tiny hand reach out and anxiously touch my furrowed hide. But we were not the only ones to sense it. The chorus of voices seemed to grow more urgent in its gibbering refrain, as though something had stirred them to a further pitch of terror. Something was happening. Instinctively I looked up and I saw the speck of sunlight shining high above. Then, in a heartbeat, it flared wildly like a spark igniting a flame, and where the speck had been a vast, red maw gaped. But then there was a sweeping movement, a great, undulating shadow, and the light was gone. Something had entered the tunnel. *Something was coming.*

'Then a new sound drowned out the clamour. I thought at first that the feral howling of the surface wind had somehow reached the vault, but in my heart I knew that such a thing could never truly be. No mere wind could ever have engendered a sound so horrid as that one - nor could the throat of any living thing. And yet it was a cry. It was a cry that tore through all sense and reason and plunged my mind into a bottomless abyss of despair.

'In an instant the vault was gone, and in its place I saw stark and dreadful truth. All meaning and order shrivelled away then, like skin in searing flame. Language evaporated. Number melted, meaningless. I knew then the utter futility of the existence of humankind. I was infinitesimal, amoebic, a powerless mote of nothingness in a frigid Kosmos of unbroken midnight gloom, across which ancient gods screamed hideous, black whalesong. Their maddening cries resounded endlessly in the chasms that stretched between the husks of dead stars at the end of all life – mocking, exultant, terrible.

'It was as though a pit of suffocating tar engulfed me then, and I floundered in it, gasping for breath as fearsome godscreams rang through my mind. But even in that bleakest of all places, I heard someone call out to me, a brave voice raised above a raging gale. It was tiny and distant, but it was filled with strength. It was my Sün! And when I heard her voice, I knew that I must fight. Although I had glimpsed the naked reality of existence and seen the terrible truth of the Kosmos stripped bare of human illusion, I found that I could not surrender myself to despair. *Not yet.* I held fast to that one thought; even if my own existence was purposeless, well, then as long as I had Sün then at least I should not be forced to endure that existence alone! She was depending upon me, and I could not abandon her.

'With that thought, I broke the surface. I burst, gasping, from the darkness of my mind into the darkness of the vault, the real darkness where poor Sün lay shaking feverishly beside me, shouting my name again and again. While I had been gone, the place had become filled with a tempest of noise and wind. Vicious, frozen gusts buffeted at me. Poor Sün cried out deliriously in her distress. All the while I could feel the god-thing above us, surging downwards through leagues of darkness, a seething storm cloud of black and alien malice. I called urgently to Sün, told her that she must come to me now. There was no time, no choice for us to make – *it must be now!*

'This was the moment for which we had been preparing, but now that it had arrived we had been caught off-guard. My mind was reeling wildly with shock, and I knew that Sün was terribly weak. She was fading, her life now all but expended. Even her mind-voice had become frail. With what little strength she had, she stretched herself out to me and her body fell limp. And at that same instant, the god-thing spilled into the ampitheatre, baying and threshing like some amorphous wraith of nightmare. The fierce wind rose up to meet it, driving before it frozen debris that glanced off my body and lashed at Sün in a furious hail. She faltered as the wind pummelled at her, her pain almost overcoming her for a moment, but I reached out to her and pulled her consciousness to me, dragging her into the scarred and damaged place in my mind.

'I struggled to hold onto her, absorbing her pain, siphoning it into myself. Even as her agony tainted me, I felt the warming wholeness that came from our joining – but it was not enough. I had to open the gates. I *had* to make the Polyhedra. I strained to focus my mind. *See the lines,* I willed myself, *see the angles!* I tried to leave the vault behind, to retract into my mind-space, but the subterranean storm was battering at my mutilated body and a thousand voices were wailing and the invisible thing was coursing, expanding through the blackness towards us... it could smell our souls, and it knew that we were there... Sün was panicking, struggling, and the first Shape was forming... *the first Shape was there...*

'We dived...

'I knew in an instant that it had her. Sün's cry of terror would have frozen my heart in my chest. I felt it penetrate us, a thing that was like a writhing tentacle of malignant shadow, and I felt it catch her in a crushing grip like jelly and acid and iron. She called out my name, but I was paralysed. Pathetic. I could not hold onto her. I could not so much as summon the strength to call back. All I could do was gape in horror as it pulled her slowly out of me. She was screaming wildly for help. As it dragged her being into itself, I felt her clawing frantically at me, scrabbling to hold on. Felt her draining out of me. Felt her begin to dissolve. Then the member withdrew and I fell slack.

'The reality of the vault faded back into my consciousness, with the din of voices and the chaotic wind swirling all around me. I could still hear Sün's desperate cries. I knew that I could not help her now. Shaking with grief and shame, I began to focus upon the Shapes. A dreadful calm descended upon me then, and everything became very slow and quiet. I was overcome by a sensation of swimming in warm milk. The screaming stopped, and the Tek'lon Polyhedron appeared, a luminous outline imposed upon the silently seething blackness. I drifted almost sleepily towards it. Then, just as the Shape yawned wide to swallow me up, a light flared ahead of me. It was a light so pure and so breathtakingly beautiful that at first I thought it to be in my mind. But as the light burned on, I realised that it was *not* in my mind, that it was real, and that it illuminated the vault with its white radiance. So transfixed was I with the unearthly beauty of that light that I barely registered the vision of boiling hell that consumed it.

'And then Sün's light burned out and the hell-thing was gone, and the vault was gone, and she was gone.'

FOURTEEN
Lost & Found

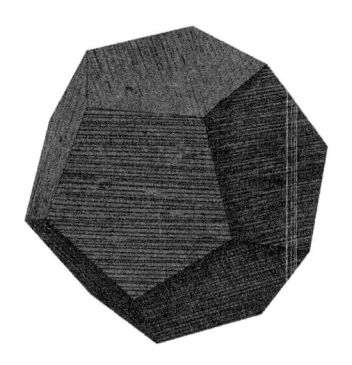

'Utter solitude is a maddening state – and when experienced by a man bereaved, it is transformed into an unendurable torture. I felt almost as though I had been happier trapped inside that lightless crypt. There – for a few, brief hours at least – I had been *whole*. Sün had lived within me, and now she was gone. Now the only companion that I had to accompany me on my journey was grief. It pressed down upon me as though it were a great sheet of lead that smothered all thought beneath its crushing mass. Not that I had any need of thought; I traversed the void as no more than an empty shell.

'I harboured only the vaguest recollection of my escape. It seemed that one moment I was not in the kosmic void, and the next I was. I cannot recall where I emerged, except that I am sure I was no longer in that hateful region where the dying, red sun burned. Perhaps I was once more at the very furthest shore of the Kosmos, but I did not care to look around me – nor, I think, was I truly able to do so. I simply moved. I moved just as a migrating bird does, or as a fish might as it thrashes its way upriver to spawn: that is, without conscious thought, without will or true knowledge of my actions. Are such beasts aware of their goals, the purpose of their journeys? I think not. What drives them is a non-thought. It emanates from an ancient place, somewhere deep within the most primal recesses of being. And I felt it just as they must: a mindless compulsion.

'But I was different, for I knew the source that impulse – and it was synonymous with the source of my misery. It came from Sün. For although I felt that a part of my self had been torn away with her, she had also left a trace of herself within me. That trace was indelible, for it was not a thing but a nothing. She was an after-image of the sun burned into my eyes, the print of a hand upon the cold, dead clay of my soul. There was an empty void within me that was the exact same shape as her. And, just as in a time so impossibly long ago an absence had compelled me, so too now was it the absence of Sün that drove me on. And though I had never set foot there, nor even beheld the place except within our mind, I knew that at the end of my journey lay Ghner.

'I did not know if I would ever reach Ghner at all; indeed I no longer cared. I simply drifted among the stars, numb and indifferent, with nothing within me but the sick churning of grief. I had once viewed the countless suns of the Kosmos with awe. Now I saw nothing but slowly dying fires. Who cared for their light? Pah! It would not last. Soon enough they would be as cold and dead as my own soul. And besides, what could that light ever hope to illuminate but the brief and paltry lives of those unhappy mortals whose only future was to perish upon the frozen corpses of their worlds? The ashes of their loved ones? And when that light failed, as inevitably it would, and all existence was locked in perpetual midnight – well, then the Kosmos would end its days as the playground of the god-things. No, I did not deign to give the stars so much as a second glance. Even the purplish thrumming of the grid, that all-pervading ætherial fabric that once had glowed with such profound and mysterious meaning, meant nothing to me now. Indeed, if I was even so much as cognisant of it then it seemed no more to me at that time than the pathetic tatters of a malformed web spun by an ailing spider.

'I drifted through clouds of ice and rock. I passed world after world. From time to time, ponderous, alien things would molest me. They would come flitting or worming out of the depths of the void, and for the main part I was scarcely aware of them. I felt nothing but pity for those things as they drew alongside me, and so I let them examine me until they grew bored or travelled beyond their limits and went away. I doubt that they saw much of interest in me. Once I glimpsed a ravenous, dark gash in the fabric of the Kosmos – it seemed to be devouring itself and everything around it. I wished that it would grow so that the job might be completed more swiftly, that it might swallow the Kosmos and have done with it. What good could there be in prolonging the agony?

'I existed in that way for an age. I drifted along my swallow's course through the Kosmos until I had forgotten myself and everything that I had ever been. Now that I look back, I realise that at that moment every last ounce of my humanity had gone. I had shed my flesh. I had been stripped of thought. I had refuted free will, forgotten speech, lost hope. I was a shadow of a being.

'Through the swirling gloom that I had become, I barely registered the world that loomed out of the void.

After all, I had paid no heed to the others. I think that perhaps I *felt* it, somehow. Something fell into place within me, like a tumbler falling in a lock - and it was there, a great wide disc of iridescent blues and greys, all marbled with seams of white. A sun was ascending on the far side of that disc, its light breaking on the graceful curve of the horizon and spilling out across the ocean in a shining flood. At that moment I *knew* without thinking that I had arrived - the space that Sün's passing had carved from my being told me so as surely as, in life, I had known that the sky was above me or that the ground was beneath my feet. It was Ahd.

'Though I knew then that my journey had ended at last, I had not the capacity to feel a thing. There was no sense of triumph or of relief; I had quite forgotten the meaning of such emotions. It was simply a fact. But as I drew ever closer to that world something did begin to stir within me, a sensation that, having felt nothing for so very long, I at first found hard to interpret. And as I grew closer still, and I beheld the magnificent sweep of the islands splayed out before me, the sensation grew stronger and stronger until at last I realised - it was simple familiarity. It could only be Sün's recognition of her home.

'But the feeling was imbued with an immediacy that the notions I had received from Sün had until that moment lacked. Perhaps the connexion that she had held with her Ahd was stronger even than I had imagined. It certainly was a world of singular beauty - with mighty continents poised in sublime equilibrium, and a thousand archipelagos scattered across its glittering oceans. Somewhere among those myriad lands, I thought with sadness, was the place that Sün had once called home. Might Ghner be located in that place with the rugged, fractured coastline and the mass of grey peaks frosting its northern reaches? It looked a proud land; a fitting location indeed. Or, I wondered, coming more alive by the moment as I scanned the terrain, could it be somewhere in the neighbouring island with the wide bay? The bay that struck the eye with its dramatic curve, just as the Bay of Fools on the coast of Erath does? Or perhaps her village lay in the folds of the hills that spread over the island to the west of it – the island whose profile so closely mirrored that of Scornländia...

'Everywhere I looked I began to see more outlines that I seemed to know: here in the east was the wide, untamed expanse of Arung, there the mighty Cape of Gorm... It was as though I beheld a perfect map of the world – not some alien world whose image was foreign to my eyes, but a familiar world, a world whose geography I would recognise for as long as I continued to exist – for it was *our* world! It was Verdra! I was sure of it! Wind and tide and heaving earth could never hope to hew *two* worlds of such surpassing similarity!

'Then, just as that host of voices had awoken in the depths of the vault, a host of sensations began to reawaken in me, feelings that had lain dormant for years beyond recall. At first my old friend bewilderment came upon me. In all the time that I had wandered the Kosmos alone I had never once thought to interrogate the questing impulse within me – why should I, when I had known emphatically that it had come from dear Sün? But faced with the evidence of the world that I saw before me, all that I thought I had known was thrown into doubt. That world was not mystical Ahd – it was *my* world. Had I somehow mistaken an impulse of my own for Sün's? And even had I done so, then how could I possibly have discerned the location of one single planet in a whole Kosmos, especially without intention? Despite this misgiving, I dared also to entertain a somewhat pleasanter feeling: *a surge of hope.* For if what I saw before me truly was dear Verdra, then there would be people – people that could help me! I could find somebody who would understand, a Scientist or a physician or some other wise person, and I could tell them my story! They would know – *somebody* would know how to help me! With every passing second my reckless optimism grew. Soon I might be once more among the streets of Broadflight. Why, with any luck I could soon be home!

'And so my skies changed from deepest black to dusky blue. I did not regret that I was leaving the emptiness of the void behind me, for I knew then that – human or not – it had never been a place for a being like me to dwell. I came down over the foamy, grey expanse of the Urish Ocean. Ah, the sea! I should never have imagined I would feel so very glad to see the sea. I had never much cared for it in life. But then I thrilled to see the swell of the waves upon its wild, shifting surface; the fact that I had passed worlds upon which that ocean would have been no more than a doll's house ornamental pond had robbed it of none of its mystery and magnificence.

'Of course I – like every schoolboy – owe my knowledge of fair Verdra's visage to those admirable fellows of the Imperial Cartographic Faction. And as I had earlier viewed the world from out in the void, I must admit that I was very much struck by the skill and accuracy of those mapmaking gentlemen – but also by the impression that their estimation of Verdra's proportion of land to sea had been, if anything, rather too generous. The oceans, you see, seemed verily to rule the globe as I had seen it below me – laying claim to a much greater proportion of its surface than my classmates and I had been led to believe. I was unable to cast off this thought as I made my way across the sea to

Grand Uria, and home, and when at last the coastline hove into view it was compounded.

'For you see, the shoreline of Wheatshield seemed rather craggier than I had imagined it to be, and it was all but bereft of the pleasant, sandy beaches of my memory. There were no fishing-boats, no little whitewashed beach-huts, no pleasure-seekers abroad – but then, I told myself, night was falling after all, and the weather was nothing if not inclement. Still, it was as though an uncommonly high tide had come in and swallowed up a large portion of that place. I did not give much thought to it, though, for I was far too preoccupied with thoughts of my own predicament. I was all but home – but how might I locate one who could converse with this sailor of the void?

'I crested the cliff, and then I was gliding over the twilit moors of Wheatshield. I felt myself a swallow returning now that a long and bitter winter had passed. I wished that I had lungs once more so that I might breathe the fresh, Urish air that whispered in the gorse and the long grasses of the moors. But even as this wish was forming, I saw it for the first time. There *was* no grass upon that moor. Indeed, there was nothing at all. Nothing but grey dust and ash.

'Something inside me lurched in alarm. It was impossible – unthinkable! Where once had been the pleasant green of Urish land there now was desert. Featureless desert. Endless mounds and dunes of grey, monotonous nothing. Not a single tree broke the undulating expanse, not a building nor even so much as a fence. Nothing moved, besides a swirling of ash-coloured dust, strangely scintillant in the leprous light of the rising moon. My mind reeled. What had become of this place? What strange doom had befallen Wheatshield?

'I did not linger in contemplation. A panic was rising within my being, and I needed to be away from that place as swiftly as possible, for it spoke of a catastrophe that I did not care to know. Images of the noxious bombs of the War flashed in my mind, but I pushed them away. Surely no force on Verdra could ever have sought to oppose the Empire since those days of slaughter - and besides, I craved *life*, not this vision of nothingness. I needed *people*. Even should no soul exist who might put an end to my plight, I needed once more to look upon the face of human being. And so I left that blasted place, and moved inland towards where, if my memory served me correctly, I would find a town named Westone - a place where I had holidayed as a youth.

'I found that the road to Westone too had been subsumed by that featureless desert of dust - nor was there even so much as a track through the shifting dunes. Nor indeed was there a soul to leave one, neither a man nor a beast. And so I went on, in what I believed to be the town's direction, skimming bodiless over the crumpled sheet of grey. The moon had risen now behind me and in its light, where once had been gay little guesthouses and cottages, I saw nothing but greyly glinting nothingness. Not a trace of the town was to be seen. Only rippling auroræ of queasily shifting hue chased themselves ceaselessly over the blankness like mindless ghosts in endless pursuit of their own tails. I shuddered as dread settled upon me as those lifeless particles had settled upon the land of my birth.

'I soon came to know the extent of that desert. It seemed that it had not been content with its conquest of the insignificant town of Westone and that it had therefore proceeded to consume the entirety of Grand Uria. The ocean of glimmering, ashy powder stretched off as far as my sight could reveal in every direction but behind me, where the real ocean pounded and roared. Nowhere in the world that I had known did a desert like *this* one exist, except perhaps for the Lithian Desert, and even that wasteland was surely never so vast. No, this was not the Verdra of my memory. Perhaps I had come upon Ahd after all. It was a selfish thought, I knew, to wish this fate upon another world - upon dear Sün's world, no less. Indeed, it was a vain and stupid attempt at self-deception - but somehow for a short while that absurd denial was better than accepting the truth. Still, I was not surprised at all when at last I came upon what once had been the region of Stoancastle and found that our capital, the greatest city in all the Empire - nay, in all the *world* - had succumbed entirely to the reign of the dust.

'It was as though Stoancastle had never existed at all. The desert was all but unbroken. Once it had been a place of great halls and opulent hotels whose architecture was the envy of the world. Now, but the merest suggestions of ruins jutted from the dust here and there, crumbling fragments picked out by the moonlight and casting long shadows over those sickly phosphorescent dunes. There was nothing more. Once it had been a place that had thronged with lords and ladies and crawled with beggars. It had been a place of shops and cafés and gin palaces and parks and squares and brothels and manufactories and museums stuffed with treasures from every corner of the globe. But no longer. That desert had devoured it all. It was all gone.

'The extent of my idiocy hit me then, and I found that I was obliged to curse myself once again. Of course it was *gone*. Oh, it is a queer thing just how myopic man can be. Ask any educated fellow and he will be able to tell you - at great length, no doubt - of half-a-dozen mighty civilisations of the past. Yet ask the very same fellow about the end of *his own* epoch – and he will scarcely be able to conceive of it. But that time *will* come. It is inevitable. But amidst the blind joy of coming upon Verdra, I had not for a moment allowed logic to inform my thoughts. In my mindless state I had traversed a stretch of Space so vast that Time itself had been rendered irrelevant. Who knows how many galaxies I had crossed in my return from that nightmare world? Until that point I had scarcely considered the scale of my journey, but now that I did I became certain of one fact: it had been a journey of lifetimes. Centuries. Æons, even! In the time that I had wandered the void, a thousand empires might have risen and then fallen again. Evidently it had been so. Most will never have the opportunity to witness such things as they come to pass, and I had never once in my life or even my un-life imagined that I would do so. And I tell you, it was a cold thing indeed.

'I did then the only thing that I could do, the thing that so many of my posthumous experiences had conditioned me to do – I kept on going. Once more benumbed, barely daring to hope, I kept moving, kept drifting over that never-ending moonlit desert. I tried in vain not to imagine what manner of dreadful fate might have erased a civilisation that had ruled the globe. Again the madness of war flitted through my mind. Ghastly visions of flesh-eating plagues. But now that I had tasted the blackness of the nether-places of the Kosmos, atrocities of human magnitude seemed only the most prosaic of horrors. No, I could not help but imagine that *something else* entirely had befallen my country. Indeed, I began to imagine that the human race – *life*, even – might well be extinct from this awful parody of my home. The black tomb on that that dead, red world, it seemed, had by comparison been a veritable cradle of life and here I, a dead man, was the only living soul.

'By the time the moon was setting once more I had crossed the whole of the country and observed not a shred of evidence that civilisation had ever existed in Uria, let alone survived. The sun had not yet risen by the time I reached the sea, and so as I began my crossing there was nothing to see below me but a suggestion of surging grey – hardly different from the land I had left behind. Perhaps Time might have treated Julais with greater sympathy, I thought as I passed over the waves. The sickness I felt at the vanishing of my own people did not leave me, but Julais had always been a strong nation – if in any other place there might remain living people then it would be there. I came upon the shores of that land just as dawn was breaking. The sun had not yet shown itself, but a rosy glow coloured the eastern sky ahead. A half-remembered proverb came to me then, but I could not quite recall whether the redness of the heavens was supposed to signal joy or despondency.

'It was the latter, it seemed – for Julais had fared no better than our own nation. The nearest I had come to the island in life was skirting its coastline during a pleasure-cruise that I had once taken with a wealthy aunt of mine. I recalled how we had passed colourful little fishing ports with tiny, waving figures perched upon their sea walls. No such sights greeted me then. Instead only jagged, fractured cliffs jutted from the foam, grey waves booming mightily against them. I passed over them without so much as pausing to glance down. Those waves had dragged all trace of the pretty villages down to the bottom of the sea many lifetimes ago.

'I made my way inland. Desert all. Where once would have been gently rolling hills clothed in green pastures and plenteous vineyards as far as the eye could see, now was a silent, ashen, wind-carved expanse of nothing under a burning, empty sky. To see such desolation lit by the rays of the sun was somehow more terrible yet than it had been by the wan light of the moon, and I found myself wondering once more what could possibly have wrought this devastation. Was this the work of man – these, the ashes of his own self-cremation? Or might Nature Herself have turned upon her ungrateful children, and blasted them to atoms in revenge for their all-consuming greed? But as the sun approached its fullest height and the smothering stuff, at once utterly dead and yet somehow simmering venomously with malevolence, returned a perverted, glowing shadow of our fair star's radiance I knew with unshakeable certainty that such a thing could never have been of Verdra's making. The cataclysm that had laid our planet low had surely come from Beyond.

'The garden city of Malber had lain – or at present, I suppose, lies – well inland, and it was in this direction in which I headed, hoping against my dying hope that there I might find people. As I entered the Mese Valley, intending to follow the dust-choked river all the way to the capital, I saw that something broke the line of the flattened horizon of slag, silhouetted black against the rising sun. I knew in an instant what it was. Indeed, I knew it almost without conscious thought. There was something about that colossal structure that reeked of man's ardour for that which he cannot see – an air of the unwholesome passion that drives him to raise such displays of vile and abhorrent grandeur in the vain hope that it will ingratiate him to those he venerates. The thing on the horizon was a temple.

'And as I followed the path of the lifeless river of slurry towards it, a sound came to me. It was muffled strangely by the dust, but still it was there. Pounding, rhythmic, menacing – the beat of a drum! Could it be? Was this the work of human hands? Or was it some great machine within the mountain of carven stone, still labouring neverendingly in mindless obedience to its long-dead masters? In truth it mattered not, for there was no alternative. I had to know. And besides, what danger could exist here for me, a bodiless, immortal ghost? At last, my centuries of isolation might be at an end!

'As I came into the temple's shadow, I was able to observe the true nature of that place. There was something of the Lithian zikkurat in it, yet also something of those vulgar monoliths that brood upon our hills and moors. It was built of massive blocks of stone, mighty slabs whose quarrying and hauling must have broken the backs of generations of men. Only faith can bend the will of men to such sacrifice – and only a faith of an utterly deviant nature could inspire the design of such a ghastly edifice as that one. It was then that I began to doubt the wisdom of my approach, for this was not a church such as civilised men might build, but rather some blasphemous shrine at which heathen savages might bay and gibber beneath the moon.

'As if in confirmation of that thought, a wild shriek pierced the air. I blanched – for that cry stirred within me memories of the most unwelcome kind. But this was not the cry of any man, savage or otherwise. I cast wildly about to find its source, seeing nothing. The valley remained as dead as before – nothing there moved but the cloying river, and the towering slopes of dust collapsing slowly into it. Beyond them, nothing but distant, nimbus-haunted hills. Again the cry rang out, and again I blanched, cowering though there was nowhere to hide. And it was at that moment that they dropped out of the sky.

'It was as though a roiling storm cloud had descended upon the mountainside, and at once the morning sky was darkened with the rank mess of their bodies. Oh, pray that you may never know the hateful form of those *things*! Those things, those *abominations*... Oh, they had seemed so grotesque in the depths of the kosmic void... but to see them *here*... to see their foulness polluting the skies of even this travesty of our world, their darkness drinking up our morning sunshine... I shrank back, as if to flee, but it was too late and they were everywhere. Nowhere to turn.

'I knew full well that they could see me. They *knew* me. I could sense their recognition – an inhuman, undying memory of me that they had borne down through the long millennia since first I had called them out of the void. And as they moved towards me, as I had known all along that they would, a great bitterness washed over me. All that I had done – all of my struggles, all of my anguish – all of it had been in vain. I could not save Sün and now I could not even save myself. But then, I thought, if I was truly honest then I had known that too. Coming upon our world had fooled me into thinking that I might have had a chance of survival – of *life*. It had fooled me into thinking that perhaps there was light in the Kosmos after all. And I, like the fool I had always been, had chosen to believe my own pleasant fictions. Ha! Such unfounded hope will always be the great folly of our race.

'There was no urgency in their approach. Perhaps they sensed my resignation. For I knew then that even should I contrive to escape again, then they would simply wait another million years. And another. And another. Let them come, I thought. Just let it be over. Tentacles like fronds of spiny seaweed wrapped languidly around me, and with an odd kind of serenity I felt myself becoming paralysed. A quietness came then, and once again I heard the beating of that drum. It was growing steadily weaker, like the failing of a heart. Through fading sight I caught a last glimpse of the shimmering disc of the sun rising beyond the hills of Julais – that sun seemed so much *larger* than I had remembered – before squealing, gelatinous non-flesh enclosed me once and for all, and I saw no more.

'It was dark then. But it was not the darkness I had expected. It was not the surging, organic gloom of the abominations' innards, nor the velvety dark of the kosmic void, nor even was it darkness of the impenetrable kind that I had endured in the vault – no, I knew somehow that the place in which I found myself then could never be penetrated by anything as simple as mere light. This, I knew with a sensation of relief so profound that even in the midst of my annihilation I swelled with joy, was a darkness that until that moment I had yet to experience. Here, at long last, was the darkness of death.

'Suddenly a burst of bluish lightning crackled through the nether-space. A brilliant spiderweb glowed then faded. In that same instant something began to pull viciously at my being – a blood-red, sinewy force that wrenched at the strands of my self so intolerably that I believe I must have cried out. Yet there was something familiar in that rending. It was a sensation such as a man might feel as he stretched out atrophied limbs after long years of constraint – though they sang with pain, it was the pain of their reawakening. Then the lightning crackled again, stronger this time. My being screamed. Visions of squirming veins thrashed before me, veins lit from within by cobalt fire and spewing gouts of hissing sparks. I was torn, reformed. An intricate latticework of elyctrical agony imprinted itself upon me.

'There then came a sound like a thunderous gale drowning out all of the voices that I have ever known. It was every voice and yet no voice at all, a voice that screamed deafening whispers whilst in an echoing cavern great engines ground and clashed and boomed. As the tumultuous noise roared through the black space, I spun crazily upon eddies of meaningless sound, a dead leaf that might at any moment be sucked away to some deeper chasm of nowhere.

'But if the sound was a gale, then the colour was a flood. It crashed down upon me, a scalding ocean unleashed in my senses. Every hue and shade that could ever be conceived rushed over me and through me, burningly vivid and maddeningly intense. A chaos of inchoate forms danced and lunged in my vision. For an endless time I was battered and buffeted by the merciless torrent of sensation and I could do nothing but let it tear through me.

'But at last the torrent began to ebb, draining away until all that remained was a single, shadowy image whose edges streamed and fluttered like wind-blown flame. Gradually it swam into focus, and I realised that the vision I beheld contained three figures. One was tall and dark, one slight and pale as a ghost, and the other thin and twisted like an old tree. And that, gentlemen, was how I came to make your acquaintances.

'So can you now understand why it is that I am forced to seek peace in the only place that it can ever be assured? Why it is that merciful oblivion can be the only sanctuary from the shrieking hell that is the Kosmos? *Why it is that I must have death?* All that I have known will die! The only soul that I have ever loved is long, long dead already. And here am I, a bodiless, hopeless ruin of a being, left to wander the Kosmos, alone and in limbo, until I am at last consumed by the fiends that pursue me! And all the while I am haunted by the things that I have lost and the things that I have seen. Oh Gods, the *things that I have seen!*

'And yet there is one thing I have *not* told you yet.

'It is a thing that I have striven to forget, a thing that I have struggled in vain to delete from my tainted memory, a thing of which until this very moment I have not permitted myself to think, for there are some things that the minds of men should not be able – were never *meant* – to comprehend.

'It is the reason that I am still haunted by the voices from the vault – the reason that until the ultimate joy of my final disintegration those terrified cries shall prey upon my soul as the horror beyond all horrors. For in the brief blossoming of luminescence that lit up the unspeakable god-thing of Nhionbi and marked the end of sweet Sün's existence, I saw *something else*. There, towering in the midnight depths of that place, stretching further in every direction than even Sün's blinding radiance could reveal, was a great wall of incalculable height and breadth – and every countless, deathless, screaming block within it was fashioned in a shape that I have come to know and dread: *a perfect, black dodecahedron.*'

As the final words of Bellhouse's tale crackled from the tortoiseshell horn, an uneasy silence descended once more upon the darkened basement chamber. The perpetual rain still lashed fiercely against the walls of the House. Edward squinted at his pocket watch, whose tick seemed suddenly to have grown uncommonly loud. It was a little after three. Naught shifted in his chair.

Then Bellhouse spoke again. 'You would be wise to heed the caution that I have given you – yet somehow I know that you will not. Still, for my part I shall consider myself exonerated of any blame for what might befall you. And if you, like me, choose to fling wide those dreadful polyhedral gates of the mind and step through them to tread the same dark paths between the stars that I have travelled, then at least you will do so in full knowledge of the consequences of your foolish actions. Now I ask but one thing of you: that you keep your word and put an end to my miserable existence!'

Obadiah stood and placed his hand upon his broad chest, covering his heart in what might have been construed a gesture of sincerity. Somewhat incongruously, a broad smile adorned his face.

'I thank you kindly for your concern, Bellhouse,' he boomed. 'But I think it only fair that you should know I have absolutely no intention whatsoever of doing *any* of those things - with the exception of destroying your brain, that is - and I shall do *that* with no reservations at all! No, no - I think that your, ah... *unfortunate* tale has served to demonstrate quite well that to repeat your mistakes would be quite the most extraordinarily foolish endeavour that one could ever hope to undertake!'

'I am sorry, Carnaby,' sputtered Bellhouse, 'but I am not sure that I follow your meaning... if you do not intend to affect the Transition, then what was the purpose of all this? What exactly is it that you intend to do?'

Obadiah threw back his head and laughed loudly and long.

'Why, haven't you guessed it by now, Bellhouse?' he said at last. 'Neither myself nor Mr Stoathill-Warmly has even the *slightest* desire to go gallivanting off around the Kosmos in search of super-natural beings! Oh, heavens no! No, why ever should we wish to do such a silly thing as that - when it would be so much more convenient to simply bring them here?'

EPILOGUE
Two Trysts (& an Interview)

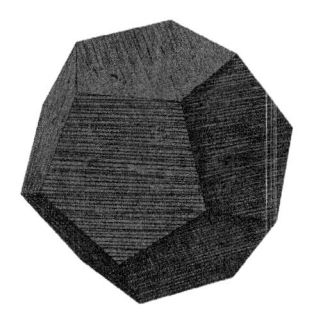

'Oh! How very *interesting!* You *must* tell me all about it!' Caviglia had said as she accepted the glass of boysenberry liqueur, and Naught had been inclined to agree. It *was* quite the most remarkable story he had ever heard, not least because it happened to involve him at various points, and so he had derived great pleasure from relating it to the Viscountess.

On the morning that followed that most unusual of audiences, he had been pleasantly surprised to find Caviglia and her strapping aide reclining by the picture window in his second-favourite parlour and looking over the morning's papers. The servant had left almost immediately, and without a word. Caviglia had complained of a sudden tightness of the throat brought on by the thin air in the parlour (Naught had not been aware of the poor air quality himself) and had therefore suggested they relocate to the comfort of his personal apartments. At this point Naught, who had suffered greatly following the last occasion on which he had applied himself to the labour of wheeling the chair, had begun to lament the departure of the servant.

They had sat together surrounded by Naught's crumbling tapestries and the muted bubbling of his tank and Caviglia had listened devotedly to her host's version of the tale, her pale fingers tightly gripping the handles of her iron chair. Every now and then she had made polite noises of wonder or dismay at the appropriate points as the particulars of the story dictated. Thankfully Caviglia's exclamations generally seemed to coincide with the instances which prompted him to say his special words, thus diverting attention from the latter. It was a very *exciting* story, after all.

Naught could not help but notice that Caviglia's eyes had a habit of wandering in the direction of an oversized crocodile-skin hatbox that she brought along with her and which sat in a rather prominent position by the hearth. All of his attempts to enquire as to its contents had been coyly but subtly deflected by a range of questions. She seemed to be possessed of a surprising appetite for the subject of Arcanology, and was never short of queries, especially when matters concerned Doctor Carnaby and his assistant.

'And so you say this Carnaby chap intends to... *do away* with Mr Bellhouse once and for all now?' she asked lightly, toying with the bauble at the end of one of her hatpins.

'Oh, certainly! Yes, I believe he intends to *do the deed* later on this evening, in fact!'

'Why?' murmured the Viscountess.

'Eh?' said Naught, unsure if he had heard her correctly. For some reason his hearing often became somewhat impaired when he took more than a measure or two of liqueur, and by that time in the afternoon he had already taken several.

'Why, how perfectly ghastly, I said! But then, I suppose, the poor fellow seems to have suffered a great deal already, what with those nasty great birds chasing him all about the place and whatnot!'

Naught sighed. 'Well, I wouldn't say they were *birds* exactly, Caviglia...'

'Oh, octopuses then!' the Viscountess continued, flapping her hand to indicate that she was unconcerned with such trivialities. 'And if it is his wish to die, then who are we to stand in his way? Let him end it if he chooses, I say!'

'I had rather hoped we could keep him,' Naught shrugged. 'He's a damn sight more interesting than most of the dreary types around here. And just think, what a talking point he would be at parties! *Would you care to meet my friend Mr Bellhouse? Certainly, who is he? Well, if you would like to flick this switch...*'

'No, no,' said the Viscountess hurriedly. 'I'm sure the Doctor knows what he's about. He is, after all, a Doctor, is he not?'

'Well yes, I suppose he is – although you might have a job to convince old Flintwick of that! Oh, he's been saying some things, I can tell you! Hoo! He really can be such an old grump. I didn't dare tell him how they all seemed to think it was *me* who did for poor old Belly! Even Belly! Can you imagine it!'

The Viscountess placed a splayed hand upon her chest and gave a sharp intake of breath. 'Ah! Beastly!'

'Isn't it just! I do rather think it says a lot about a man if he sincerely thinks you *killed* a chap in cold blood and yet he still wants to sit down with you for a chat about him. I can't think for a moment where they all got the idea but – well, I haven't had half so much fun for as long as I care to remember! I've even asked him to stay, you know, seeing as he and his young assistant appear to find the circumstances so agreeable here. And he, of course, has accepted!'

'Indeed? He will be *staying?*' asked the Viscountess, sitting forward in her chair.

'Oh, yes, yes!'

'To what end?'

'I must confess, I'm not entirely certain, Caviglia! Who knows what it is these academic types *do*, exactly? Not a particularly great deal most of the time, I'm inclined to think.'

'Too true,' said Caviglia, but she now appeared to have become somewhat distant, her eyes scanning a point on the ceiling just above Naught's head. A moment later, though, her eyes once again met his and a thin but suggestive smile appeared on her sallow face. A finger twirled her rooks' feather boa. Then one of her pale hands snaked out to entwine its fingers with Naught's as she looked up at him through her lashes and asked: 'And how is it exactly that Doctor Carnaby will be killing Mr Bellhouse, do you think?'

∽

'Come along, Edward my boy!' said Obadiah. 'Let's get this over and done with!'

He took a last glance down the corridor and, on finding it satisfactorily empty of observers, closed the door firmly behind them. Edward cleared a jumble of wires and other components from the trolley and placed his satchel in the space. There was a clink of glass as he opened the satchel, and then with a thickly-gloved hand he retrieved a small phial of white crystals from inside it.

'Ah, good,' said Obadiah, nodding. 'I see you have the stuff. Now, we'd best just give old Bellhouse one last chance to change his mind before he gets a taste of that little concoction and it's too late for him, eh?'

'I suppose it would be the polite thing to do,' replied Edward. He eyed the canister somewhat apprehensively, holding the phial out before him in two gloved fingers as though it were threatening to burn the flesh from his bones. Indeed, with one slip it might well have done just that.

'Well, let's get to it then!' barked Obadiah. 'We don't have all night, you know!'

The components of the array were still connected from their previous application, and so it was a work of moments to activate it once more. A familiar droning filled the chamber.

'Bellhouse!' yelled the Doctor into the ear-horn. 'Last chance, Bellhouse!'

He waited expectantly for a moment or two, but no reply came. He looked at Edward.

Edward shrugged.

'Have you – ' the Doctor began to ask, but Edward pre-empted his question and nodded in the direction of the vocaliser by way of an answer. It was plainly activated, and was emitting its steady, ambient hiss.

Edward shrugged his slight shoulders again and made a wordless gesture of puzzlement.

Obadiah shook his head and let out an exasperated breath. 'Bellhouse!' he shouted, colouring slightly. 'Answer me, man!'

Again there was no reply, save for the fizz of static.

Obadiah spent the next quarter of an hour or so bellowing into the ear-horn, instructing Edward to recalibrate it, then, with visibly rising irritation at the lack of results this produced, bellowing into it once again. At one point he even resorted to unscrewing the lid of the canister in order to ensure that the geometrician's brain was still inside – which, of course, it was.

Eventually the arcanologists were to leave the basement in a state of thorough perplexity, but with hands unsullied by the unsavoury act of euthanasia that they had been prepared to perform. For the conclusion that had suggested itself had at last become inescapable: although the brain of Sebastian Bellhouse was undeniably present, the mind of that most unfortunate of gentlemen was not.

~

'Good Gods!' exclaimed the Dean of the Hingham Medical Institute, his white eyebrows shooting suddenly upwards like two alarmed birds darting for safety in the thicket of his hair. 'Certainly *not!* Human organs are not just... *handed out* willy-nilly to anyone, you know! Yes, it is necessary for us to study anatomy in order to advance our Science, but believe it or not, Inspector, even we pioneers of medicine manage to retain a modicum of respect for the sanctity of human remains!'

Inspector Ladygloves purposefully crossed his legs and continued to pack tobacco into the bowl of his pipe, all the while peering intently at the Dean over the gold rims of his spectacles. Once he had completed this task he carefully screwed the lid back onto his enamelled tobacco tin (three precise turns) then patted down each pocket of his coat before he located his matches. His eyes never left the Dean's. He then struck a match, the flare momentarily illuminating his lined face, and lit the pipe in four measured puffs. The Dean, who like so many of the Inspector's interviewees felt that the man's steel-grey gaze had pinned him bodily to his chair, was quite unable to do anything other than watch the ritual. It was not until the office had been filled with an aromatic haze like some æthereal augmentation of his cloudy, grey beard that the Inspector chose to continue.

'So to your knowledge you have not given permission for any scholar or other person to remove body parts such as *these*,' - he leaned forward through the veil of smoke and tapped a photogram upon the Dean's desk - 'from the university's medical facilities?'

The Dean glanced at the picture again. It showed a room in a state of considerable disarray, jumbles of unidentifiable rubbish cluttering its floor. Shelves rising from behind this bizarre detritus carried the intended subject of the photogram: an assortment of jars, their contents masked by the glare of the flash on the glass. Further photograms spread out upon the desk illustrated the nature of the grisly collection in greater detail.

He shook his head. 'I am sorry, Inspector Ladygloves, but as I have told you already, I have done no such thing. The study of anatomy is limited to those who we choose to licence. Where did you say you had found this little lot?'

'The offices of one Doctor Obadiah Carnaby,' replied the Inspector.

For a moment the Dean faltered, unable to sift a name that he recognised from the Inspector's pleasant but propulsively rolling burr. The Dean had never ventured over the border to the Wild Auld Lands himself, and consequently found himself unable to recall whether the intonation marked the Inspector as a Highlander or a Glensman. 'Ah, *Carnaby!*' he exclaimed at last. 'Yes, Carnaby, Carnaby...'

'The founder of the Institute of Arcanology?' offered the Inspector.

'Ah! Yes, I know him. Big fellow. Angry. Fine moustache, though. Always with that pale young assistant of his.'

The Inspector nodded his grey head. 'I believe that we are speaking of the same man. My men were called to attend an incident of burglary at the Doctor's building, and during their investigations they happened across this horde.'

'Well, what does *he* have to say about it all? Would it not make more sense to simply ask him?'

'He is not here. It seems that he has not been here for some time.'

'Well where is he, then?'

'That particular detail is yet to be established. But for the moment you must assure me: are you *absolutely* certain that you have not given this man permission to use your facilities or their contents?'

The Dean opened a drawer and pulled out a thick ledger. 'This,' he said, 'is a record of our transactions. I think you will find that it is all in order – that is *without* the inclusion of the name *Carnaby*.'

Inspector Ladygloves accepted the ledger and briefly leafed through it. 'Just as I thought,' he nodded. 'I will have to retain this for a while,' he said, sliding the book into his case.

'Be my guest,' nodded the Dean.

'And you are not aware of any thefts from your own facilities of late?'

'Do you mean, has anyone been to wrack my brains?' chuckled the Dean, but the look upon the Inspector's face silenced him immediately.

'This is a matter of utmost seriousness, Professor Boswith,' said the Inspector, taking another long pull on his pipe. 'I would hope that you are not mocking me.'

'Yes, of course. I apologise. That is to say, I believe that Doctor Carnaby is the only victim of theft that I am aware of. Was much taken?'

'I am not able to divulge that information. But I should warn you that whilst Carnaby has been the victim of one crime, we have strong suspicions that he may well have been the perpetrator of others.'

'Oh!' said the Dean. 'You do not mean – '

'If what you tell me is true then at the very least the Doctor has probably been involved in the appropriation of your facility's resources. My men will verify this soon enough,' he patted the case which contained the ledger. 'But if, as you say, no... *items* have been stolen – or purchased – from scholars of your establishment, then we may be looking at another charge altogether.'

The Dean gaped. 'Surely...'

'There have been *disappearances* lately, Dean. Working girls, in the main. Until now not much time has been devoted to the issue – I'm sure you can appreciate how hard it is to deal with these people.'

'I don't,' said the Dean hurriedly. 'Deal with them, that is.'

'Well, it may not surprise you to learn that they are rarely pleased to speak to me or my men. But this discovery may well throw new light upon the case. I trust that you are able to appreciate the necessity of keeping this information to yourself, and that you will inform me of anything you may find to be relevant?'

'Oh, certainly!' agreed the Dean'

'Excellent. Well, there is only one more thing, then.' Inspector Ladygloves rose and fished in an inside pocket of his coat. He produced a small frame containing another photogram. He held it up so that the Dean could see it. 'Do you recognise this lady?' he asked.

The Dean peered at the picture. 'No,' he replied. 'I cannot say that I do.'

∽

With fumbling hands, Naught grasped one of Caviglia's hatpins and pulled on it. The pin slid out with a protesting shriek of metal upon metal.

The hat struck the floor, tolling like a votive bell.

Caviglia tossed her head, and her iron-grey hair dropped lankly to her shoulders. Her eyes, mottled yellow like old milk, met his, glistening like caviar. Her lusty gaze fell meaningfully upon the oversized, crocodile-skin hatbox.

'Open it!' she urged in a throaty whisper.

Naught bent, popped the catches, and swung open the lid.

Within the box, nestled in a protective cleft of purplish satin, was a mask. Naught's eyes once again met Caviglia's, and she nodded fervently. He lifted the mask with both hands. It was heavy and cold, and as he hoisted it into the air, a tangle of rattling pipes of jointed resin trailed behind it. It was a helmet of burnished copper and rubber flanges, featureless but for two flat discs of glass ringed by rivets. Naught turned the mask in his hands, examining it. From its rear sprouted an irregular cluster of straps and tubes.

He suddenly became very aware that the only sound in the chamber besides the soft, insistent bubbling of the tank in the background was the rattling of the pipes in his shaking hands.

Caviglia watched Naught as he stood face to face with the mask, staring into its wide, empty eyes. She licked her lips.

'Will you put it on?' she cooed, craning her wrinkled neck towards him.

'Ah, yes,' said Naught, feeling slightly foolish. He hefted the mask. Caviglia proffered her head once more and he clumsily jammed the mask onto it. It sat in a slightly lopsided manner on her square shoulders.

Naught bit the inside of his lip in embarrassment and adjusted it. Caviglia's eyes slid into view behind the glass plates.

'*Disrobe!*' came her muffled command from within the helmet.

Naught hesitated, then turned away from her and began to unbutton his velvet coat. The Viscountess's hand, vice-like, grasped his arm from behind and spun him around to face her. His pulse raced, and he was sure that his fear could be seen – but his arousal was stronger. As he continued to undress, taking what he hoped was nonchalant care not to crease his fine things, Caviglia reached behind her head and purposefully tightened the straps.

Together they plunged into the dark soup, and all was rushing and roaring in a torrent of bubbles and limbs and passion. Naught lost his grip on her, and then he was floundering, unable to distinguish his lover through the tepid, vinegary fluid. Just as he began to think that the tank had sucked her away into its depths and consumed her, she returned. With her twisted body dappled by a shaft of amber light from above, she loomed out of the murky depths towards him. Naught baulked for a second, churning his arms in panic, and then she was upon him, surging forwards through the liquid with the power and grace of an undersea predator. Around her head the serpentine coils thrashed and snapped crazily, spewing jets of bubbles that wreathed about them. She drew him to her with a grip of iron desire, and so they made their union there, tumbling and writhing together through the awful gloom.

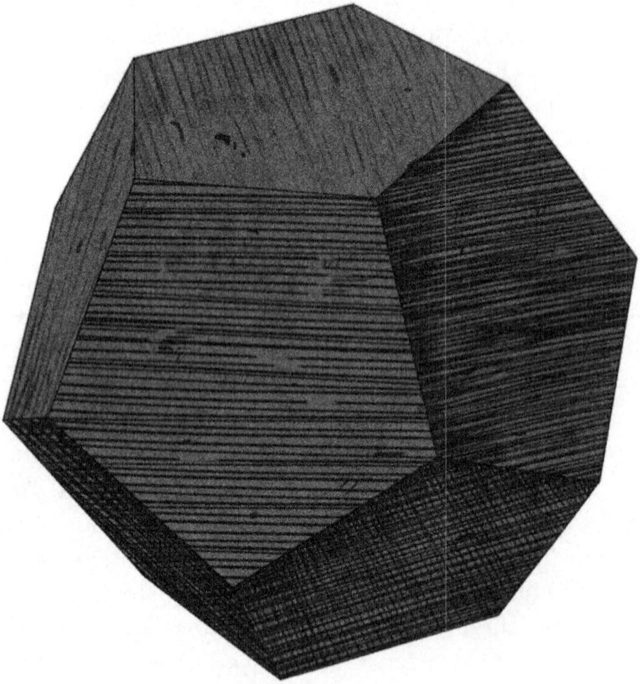

NEXT

The story continues in
*The Transfiguration of No
Book Two: The Machine*

Available now in paperback
and for Amazon Kindle

For more information please visit:

www.iamstegosaurus.com/no

To get in touch please contact:

the.transfiguration.of.no@gmail.com

OLIVER ROGERS

Oliver Rogers is a writer and artist from the UK. He creates fiction and poetry for adults and for children, and has written extensively on unorthodox contemporary art for leading websites and galleries. His own artwork, like his writing, is strongly influenced by esoterica, psychedelia and the occult.

He holds undergraduate degrees in Illustration and Literary & Cultural Studies, and a Master's degree with Distinction in Modern English Studies. His knowledge of the esoterica that inform *The Transfiguration of No* was drawn initially from intuition, and was deepened by several subsequent years of research, study and practice.

He lives with his wife and son in the seaside town of Hastings, England, where pagan festivals still mark the turning of the seasons.

Printed in Great Britain
by Amazon